SHORT STORY WRITER AND NOVELIST OWEN MARSHALL has written, or edited, twenty books to date. Awards for his fiction include the PEN Lillian Ida Smith Award twice, the *Evening Standard* Short Story Prize, the American Express Short Story Award, the New Zealand Literary Fund Scholarship in Letters, Fellowships at the universities of Canterbury and Otago, and the Katherine Mansfield Memorial Fellowship in Menton, France. He received the ONZM for services to Literature in the New Zealand New Year Honours, 2000, and his novel *Harlequin Rex* won the Montana New Zealand Book Awards Deutz Medal for Fiction in the same year. In 2002 the University of Canterbury awarded him the honorary degree of Doctor of Letters.

Owen Marshall was born in 1941, has spent almost all his life in South Island towns, and has an affinity with provincial New Zealand.

The author gratefully acknowledges the inaugural award of the Creative New Zealand Writers' Fellowship in 2003.

National Library of New Zealand Cataloguing-in-Publication Data
Marshall, Owen, 1941-
Watch of gryphons / by Owen Marshall.
ISBN 1-86941-706-2
I. Title.
NZ823.2-dc 22

A VINTAGE BOOK
published by
Random House New Zealand
18 Poland Road, Glenfield, Auckland, New Zealand
www.randomhouse.co.nz

First published 2005

© 2005 Owen Marshall

The moral rights of the author have been asserted

ISBN 1 86941 706 2

Design: Katy Yiakmis
Cover design: Matthew Trbuhovic
Cover photograph: Elizabeth Trubuhovic
Author photograph: Rosslyn Hood
Printed in Australia by Griffin Press

watch of gryphons
and other stories

owen marshall

ALSO BY OWEN MARSHALL

Supper Waltz Wilson and other New Zealand stories
The Master of Big Jingles and other stories
The Day Hemingway Died and other stories
The Lynx Hunter and other stories
The Divided World: Selected Stories
Tomorrow We Save the Orphans
The Ace of Diamonds Gang and other stories
Burning Boats (ed.)
A Many Coated Man
Letter From Heaven (ed.)
Coming Home in the Dark
Beethoven's Ears (ed.)
The Best of Owen Marshall
Harlequin Rex
Spinning a Line (ed.)
Authors' Choice (ed.)
Essential New Zealand Short Stories (ed.)
When Gravity Snaps
Occasional (poems)

contents

Buried Lives   9

Passing Triptych   35

Facing Jack Palance   45

The Fan   49

A Kind of Living   59

Poetic Licence   85

A Modern Story   101

Family Circle   117

Images   141

Fellow Citizens   147

Buster   161

Minding Lear   171

Margaret's View   213

Arnal Retent and a Place in History   225

Journey's End   231

Voices with a Common Theme   261

Celeine and the Pygmalion Theatre   271

Hodge   283

Watch of Gryphons   289

buried lives

MY MOTHER'S BROTHER HAD A FARM on the pale loess clay and limestone of North Otago. It was an average farm concentrating on early lambs for the works, and even during his last years my uncle never received any startling offers for it. Its dry hills weren't suitable for dairy conversion, and its soils didn't favour the grapevines that became all the rage in the nearby Waitaki Valley. Yet it was sweet country when it did get rain, and quite free of gorse. The short-grassed paddocks in the downs were rilled with sheep tracks: occasional outcrops of limestone were the grey of cigar ash. Almost always there was above it an unclouded egg-blue sky and, although only landscape was visible, in the evenings skeins of seagulls beat their way towards the sea.

I visited a few times as a boy, but I lived there only once for fourteen months after I had a breakdown in my third year at university. My mother preferred to call it a crisis, my father told people I'd hit a rough patch, my mates probably reckoned I'd flunked out as a pothead. I had a breakdown, no matter what you chose to call it. It happened because of a relationship I had with a flatmate and his twin sister. I was getting stoned on prime West Coast shit a lot too. It sounds like a soap opera, I know, but the pain, guilt and confusion of it all finally brought me to an emotional standstill, and I could barely remember to eat, to close the door when I went to the lavatory, or attend the lectures for which I'd enrolled. I felt I lived my life on the bottom of one of those great sea aquariums with species foreign to me passing as dim shapes soundlessly, and with their own fixed purpose, overhead.

Uncle Cliff and Aunt Sonia were contented people in whose home depression was an unfamiliar visitor. Sonia was the bright and vocal partner, Cliff a stubby, sunburnt man who thought the best of people. They had two daughters of effortless achievement. Evie had already qualified as a doctor when I went to live at the farm; Samantha was completing her architectural degree, and came home a few times while I was there, making me feel even more a failure in comparison, but through no intention of hers.

I was welcomed in the wooden, red-roofed farmhouse and given Evie's room, which was a chrysalis she had discarded, but still exact to the life she had led at home. Blue and yellow banded curtains, a tray of dwarf bottles of perfumes, lotions and nail polishes on the dressing table, sellotape marks on the painted walls where her posters had been, and on the kitset bookcase her gymnastic and debating trophies — including a small greenstone plinth for best summing up at the South Island inter-secondary school championships. Most of the books were from Evie's childhood, which wasn't all that long ago, but some, less read and more dignified, were prizes she had won at high school: *The Works of Jane Austen* published by Spring Books, *History of Rome* by M. Cary, and a hardcover *Moby Dick*. Clothing she no longer needed remained folded in the drawers and hanging in the wardrobe, all with a faint, girlish fragrance. At various times and in flagrant abuse of her privacy I examined all of Evie's life left behind: even the seven letters from Shane Tomlinson which were tied in a small bundle with dental floss, and hidden under a pile of notes for scholarship biology. In the sixth form she had the best legs in the world according to Shane.

Dr Evie's room spoke of normality, cleanliness and achievement. It had no sign of the trivial sordidness of my own life, and in the months I inhabited it I felt like a Visigoth camped in a Roman villa. Even my male clothes and large footwear seemed uncouth and out of place. I masturbated seldom and with great furtiveness, aware of the disgust in the expressions of Evie's dolls ranged behind the trophies. In a strange but powerful way I associated Samantha and Evie and their white, girlish rooms, with Rebecca, twin sister of Richard, and a good part of the reason that I was in my uncle's house at all surrounded by a specific family folklore to which I did not belong. 'What shall we do that's terrible?' Rebecca would say when we'd been drinking, or smoking shit, or just because lectures were over for the week, and by terrible she meant some excess she could laugh at. How different she was from my cousins, yet similar in the ease with which she achieved those things she wanted.

Outside the house was completely different: I belonged there from the first. The yards lay down the slope from the farmhouse, and on the south and west sides were windbreaks of pine and macrocarpa which reached over the implement sheds, the dog cages and the disused concrete dip. The downs rose and fell beyond with paddocks worn to bare dirt at each gateway, and the sheep tracks straggling away over the short, brown pasture. Some of lower land would be green with lucerne, or in season the low, paler foliage of turnips and chou. From the top hill paddocks you couldn't see the red roof of the farmhouse, or any neighbouring houses, just the grassed hills tumbling towards the Waitaki and back towards the mountains. When I got the shakes, or felt the foreign shapes of the aquarium too oppressive, or Aunt Sonia's cheerful solicitude became too contrary to my own apathy, then I would have a long run, or let out one of the dogs and walk up to the back of the farm. The dogs enjoyed the release, but they never obeyed me. It was only occasionally that I did something useful there — rescued a cast sheep perhaps, or secured a bit of fence washed out in the gully, but Uncle Cliff always thanked me, as if he had sent me there expressly himself. It was a landscape of masculine reticence, which was something of a comfort: perhaps it was the extension of my uncle's temperament beyond himself.

During my time on the farm, Cliff never once mentioned the reason for my presence, and insisted on paying me a small wage. He told the neighbours and friends we met that I'd been kind enough to come and give him a hand for a while. We could work for hours together without words, or awkwardness; at other times he would talk of parts of his life spent crayfishing in the Chathams, and in North Island shearing gangs, before he'd bought the farm. In the winter, bulked up even more with jersey and a frayed parka, he looked almost square: as if he would reach the same height on his side as standing up. Out of the house he allowed himself a few roll-your-owns each day, and there'd be a brief flame at the cigarette's tip as he lit it. His other indulgence was mints, like great white pills, and he always had some in his pocket to share. Whenever we were close, putting in a strainer post perhaps, or bent over a recalcitrant engine, I would have the hybrid tobacco and mint smell of his breath. If I come across those scents now I'm reminded of his straight-grained goodness.

I was able to relieve Cliff of most of the tractor work while I was there. Years of hard slog were catching up on him, and his back played up on the jolting tractor. Harrowing and discing especially are repetitious, undemanding tasks, and I spent hours outwardly circling in the worked paddocks, while inwardly still circling Richard and Rebecca.

Our flat was in the North East Valley, not far from Castle Street, and an easy walk in to the university. It was in fact an old cottage, low in the valley so that in winter the sun came only for late lunch and then went away again. Colin, Eric and I lived there in our second year, and when Colin went overseas after the holidays, we put a note on the Stud Ass notice board, and Richard came in. He was doing economics, marketing, stuff like that; his twin sister, Rebecca, was easily passing science subjects, and was at Knox College not far from us.

Your flatmates aren't necessarily your best friends. Sometimes in fact you lose your friends by having them as flatmates and finding they're a pain in the arse to live with. Sometimes they're just people who pay their share of the rent and do their own thing. Richard had his own friends, with whom he spent a lot of time in his room. His attitude to his room, and to clothes, should have been a signal to me quite early on, but I was slow to pick up on it. In our rooms Eric and I had a heap of assorted blankets on our beds, and one covering the bare floorboards to stand on in winter. Richard, though, went to the op shop and bought an enveloping green and yellow cover, and later to some other second-hand place and bought curtains which he said had the same yellow in them. Once, when he'd been walking up the path behind me, he said that I should let my hair grow longer: that it would suit me that way. He had a sharp wit that I enjoyed, and was a very generous guy. He had a particular dislike of overweight people, and those who couldn't express themselves cogently.

Rebecca first came round to the flat to help with the curtains. Eric and I decided right away that Richard's room was justifiably the focus of the flat for as long as she wanted it that way. She was short, lithe and dark haired: her skin was very smooth and she had a half, I-know-what-you're-thinking, smile. 'You guys don't really want to help with curtains, do you?' she said.

'I don't mind giving a hand,' I said. She came round more

and more after Richard and I clicked. She said she got sick of the routines and restrictions at Knox. Sometimes she cooked a meal; sometimes she got on to Eric and me about doing chores about the place. She and Richard didn't like too much of a mess. Sometimes she'd come very late after a party, or dance, and sleep over in Richard's room, and be wearing some of his pyjamas when she came out bleary in the morning. 'You think they bunk in the bed together,' said Eric, 'or Richard puts pillows and stuff on the floor?'

'I'd invite her in myself,' I said.

'Jesus, so would I,' Eric said.

But then neither of us was Rebecca's brother, which was all the difference surely. I noticed on one of those mornings that she had painted toenails — her small, sallow foot on the cracked lino of the kitchen floor and the pearl-purple hue of her toenails.

There were two nail polishes on the tray on Evie's dressing table in the room on the farm. The plastic tops were the same colour as the thick liquid inside: one was pink and one was red. Both simple, unambiguous colours. Evie's window looked out onto the side lawn of the farmhouse and a large walnut tree with spatulate leaves and the blackening nut cases scattered like sheep shit in the grass underneath. That was one of the jobs I did for my uncle and aunt: I collected up the nuts, shucked them of the tattered, rotting cases, and spread them to dry on the wire of an old bed frame on the verandah. My hands were stained tobacco brown for days, and Aunt Sonia said I shouldn't have bothered, shouldn't have made a mess of myself like that. She knew, though, that it was an attempt to thank them.

Aunt Sonia was one of those central people around whom family and friends revolve. She laughed and talked a lot, and stimulated others to talk while she nodded and smiled as an encouragement to go on. Some women have natural warmth, and she was one. She must have had times of pain and despair, of glum despondency and self-doubt, but I never saw any sign of them. Maybe Cliff was the only witness, maybe she had her black times standing solitary in a closet, the back of the door touching her nose, her face relieved of any need to register optimistic expression.

In the first few weeks I found her kindness and resolute joy in life crushingly unbearable. I would expend all the smiles I had in response to her, until just a rictus remained, and I would excuse myself, and go and sit on Dr Evie's bed, or, more often, go off into the passive indifference of the landscape. Aunt Sonia's emotional energy and eagerness for reciprocation only made me more aware of a chronic malaise within myself. The more outgoing she was, the more difficult any matching emotion on my part.

Like the rainy day when I'd been there only two or three weeks, and Cliff had gone to town to see the bank manager and do other wet weather business. I spent the morning stencilling some of the wool bales, and then came back to the house for lunch. Aunt Sonia had been baking, and the misfits from the batches were my appetising follow-up to an asparagus quiche: misshapen apricot muffins still warm at their fruitful heart, the end slice of ginger crunch, the Afghan made from the last of the mix which had become the runt of the litter. She was packing all that had passed muster into round tins as I ate. She was taller than Cliff, graceful despite the years of physical work, and she vibrated slightly with energy, whereas he toiled with an easy rhythm, or sat quite still with conscious relaxation.

'You know we'll help if we can,' she said. 'You know that.'

I said I did and was thankful for it. 'Sometimes it helps to work through things if you talk them out, use other people as a sounding board,' she said. 'I don't want to pry, or make any judgements,' she said, 'not at all, but if you do want to talk about things then I'm always here.' I said I knew that and appreciated it. I said maybe later I'd feel like doing so, and that there wasn't any big thing to talk about anyway, really. Just sort of getting too tied up with personal relationships at the university. 'Evie and Samantha were just the same,' said Aunt Sonia, putting the

Afghans deftly into the blue tin as if they were eggs going back into a nest. 'They had all these problems with boys and body image at the same time as coping with exams. Things get blown up out of perspective when you're under pressure, I think.' I told her they did. I didn't tell her that part of my own problem was a boy, but I told her that I appreciated her offer to talk about things very much, and that having time out on the farm was just the thing I needed right then. Much later I thought it immensely to her credit that, despite her natural disposition to be involved in the lives of all those around her, she never brought up heart-to-heart talks again.

Richard was keen on a candid talks too, not believing that anything should be held back in a friendship. He had his own television in his room, and he started inviting me in to watch stuff. We'd sit on the bed, with some of his matched green pillows against the head board to prop us up. He had a real knack for predicting the story lines. I thought maybe he'd seen them all before, but when we went out to films he was just as accurate. 'I bet she kills herself with an overdose, and leaves a note incriminating him,' Richard would say, or, 'It's just soooo obvious, isn't it, that Mr Gendarme is in on it.'

He had this interest in families. He asked me quite a lot about the relationships in mine, and told me a good deal concerning his. His father was the CEO of one of the big power companies, and a wheeler and dealer of shares in a big way as well, Richard said. He supported the family abundantly, but lived three blocks away from them in Thorndon with a younger woman who taught French at the university. 'My mother never talks about it,' Richard said. 'She either believes, or pretends, that it's nothing untoward. They have dinner parties at our house, and Dad stays overnight, and then the next day he goes back to his own place. At Christmas time his partner goes to her family in Marseilles, and Dad comes to us for a family week of presents and reminiscence. Rebecca and I go between the two houses as we like. She says it all comes down to money, and perhaps she's right. Money allows you to escape convention and yet maintain appearances in a way.'

'Does your father ever talk about it?' I asked.

'Not much. He says take what you want: take what you want, and pay for it.'

Eric never got invited into Richard's room, and I felt a bit guilty. The two of them didn't hit it off somehow. And fewer of Richard's friends came once he was well settled in. Rebecca, though, came more frequently and I was all for that. She'd bang on my door. 'You want coffee?' she'd call. 'Come in and have it with us.' Sometimes the three of us would sit propped on the green and yellow bedcover together; sometimes if it was cold Rebecca would sit on a cushion by the heater and look up at us to talk. I was always aware of her. Even when she wasn't in my field of vision I would know just how she was sitting, or leaning back on the pillows: how relaxed her slim body was, how her dark hair would sway at the side of her face as she talked, how when she was amused a small double crease at the corners of her mouth gave a sudden parenthesis to her smile. She would flip off her blue sneakers and her feet were almost absurdly small, the painted nails winking like gems.

I've got sisters, but I never talked to them the way Richard and Rebecca talked to each other. And I've never heard brothers and sisters talk so unreservedly to each other. Maybe it was because they were twins; maybe it was because they came to treat me almost like themselves. 'You randy little bitch,' Richard might say lightly when she talked of a night out with one of the Knox College guys. 'You make sure you keep those rugby boys out of your pants.'

'What is the smell in this bed?' she might say. 'I hate to think who you've had in here. It should be fumigated before I come round here again. You been shagging an orang-utan or something?'

I never found that smoking shit gave me all that much of a high, and Richard could soak it up and just be mellow, but

Rebecca could get really up on it. Maybe it was her lesser body weight or something. After a few foils, or time with the spottle, she was most likely to grab me, and ask what we could do that was terrible. At Queen's Birthday weekend the three of us had a session in Richard's room. Eric had gone home. We went out late for takeaways into a pale, cold drizzle, and Rebecca walked between the two of us with one hand in her brother's coat pocket and one in mine. 'Shit, it's cold, isn't it,' she said loudly. Maybe it was wishful thinking, but I reckon that, as we walked, her hand in the pocket lining pushed down towards my cock several times. 'Jesus, we all need to get warmed up,' she said. The whites of her eyes caught the street lights as she looked up at me.

On the way home we passed one of those wooden houses crammed up to the footpath. We could see a party going on. A group of old people, in their fifties and sixties, all animated and on the go, their faces crowded with gaudy, exaggerated noses, chins and eyebrows like papier mâché heads. To us, pausing in the wet night outside, their gaiety seemed absurd, and they themselves ridiculous in abandonment. 'What a load of wankers,' said Richard, and we stood laughing and unseen in the darkness to watch them.

'Time for a wake-up call,' said Rebecca, and in one motion took her hand from my pocket, seized an empty milk bottle from the letter box, and flung it at the window.

The party people shrank back with appalled, vaudeville faces for a moment as the window glass shattered; one or two of them cried out with the shock of it. Half pissed and half high as we were, it seemed both catastrophic and enormously funny. We fled, whooping with laughter, Richard and I dragging Rebecca, who said she wanted to see what the old farts would do.

It wasn't just drink and shit, of course, but the derisive power of being young, and being good-looking, and being sure in your own mind that you would end up doing so much better in life than the adult people around you. We left our coats on kitchen chairs and went into Richard's room, kicking off our shoes before climbing under the cover and setting out the containers of Chinese food to share. Rebecca was in the middle again and her soft breast pressed against me whenever she leaned my way for sweet and sour pork. 'We shouldn't have done it, I know,' she said, 'but they were so gob-smacked, weren't they. People who dress like that, cardigans and all, deserve everything they get anyway. We should send them a fucking note saying that the style police took action against them.' Her jersey was dry, but her black hair was damp, shiny, and the wetness released a strong scent of some shampoo, which mixed with the smell of wine and marijuana on her breath when she laughed, and the Chinese food, to make a potion I found strongly erotic.

'Those poor pricks when you smashed the window, though,' I said. 'What the hell got into you all of a sudden?'

'I told you that the world needed something terrible.'

'I hate to think what, or who, gets into her at times. It doesn't pay to ask,' said Richard. He was pushing his shoulder against her playfully so that she pressed more against me.

'Shut up. You can talk.' She was excited rather than offended.

Her words and laughter were quicker, higher. 'But even if you're a criminal we still love you,' and Richard gave her an exaggerated kiss on one side of her face, which was the opportunity for me to kiss her on the other. I wanted to roll right over on her, despite the pottles of food, and kiss her on her lips, feel the length of our bodies together. I wanted to tell Richard to get out of his own room and leave us alone together. Instead he put his arms around both Rebecca and me and started some mock, half-arsed talk about us being three musketeers and facing the world together. I slipped one hand under Rebecca's jersey, but even in the tactile satisfaction of that I had the uneasy awareness that Richard was stroking the back of my neck with two fingers. 'Don't anybody chunder on my bed,' he said, and puffed his cheeks to show he'd overeaten as well as earlier indulgence.

We spent even more time together after that. I often asked Rebecca to come out with just me, and she did sometimes. We went to a few pub band nights and some art films, but she liked best to do things as a threesome, and Richard took offence if he wasn't invited. It was a situation new to me, and I told myself that it arose because of the natural closeness of twins, and that Richard wasn't my competitor for Rebecca in any way that worried me. After all, if it hadn't been for Richard, I'd never have met her at all. Maybe if Rebecca wasn't there, the friendship I had with him may have developed in a quite different way. But that was an uneasy speculation I never dwelt on.

Life turns on such apparently fortuitous things. For if I'd never known Richard and Rebecca, then I wouldn't have spent those months on my uncle's farm, and Cliff and Sonia would have been just one-dimensional relations I'd met occasionally as a kid. The most obvious feature of a person's character may be the salient one, but equally as often you find it quite insignificant when familiarity has been gained. My aunt's warm engagement was the true representation; Uncle Cliff's quiet distance disguised an equal benevolence.

He was aware the old country ways were changing as farming became more technical, new land use replaced pastoralism, and the city populations, growing in both numbers and affluence, pushed their vacationing and holiday homes even into such areas as the Mackenzie Country and the Maniototo. 'We've been the Celtic fringe,' he said, 'and of course we'll be overrun.' He had an unspoken belief that the satisfaction gained from living in the country diminished in proportion to the increased number with which it was shared. Family was different, of course, and I think he liked having me around. Although he never asked about my state of health, he would suggest tasks we could do together if I'd been quiet and by myself for a long time. 'Would you like to give me a hand dagging and drenching a mob?' he might say, or 'I thought maybe we could do a lambing round together before it gets dark'.

One day in the autumn drought we went out with Caspar Waldren to see if we could find water. Waldren was a retired farmer and water diviner who lived in Oamaru, but still spent a lot of time pottering on the farm he'd relinquished to his son, and on other properties which he'd come to know well during a long life. He had a big reputation for being able to find underground water, sometimes by using a fresh willow wand, sometimes number eight wire bent like a clothes hanger. He had boots worn grey at the toes and an excess of brown, weathered skin on his very thin frame. He was sprouting a lot of hair from nooks and crannies such as his ears and eyebrows, and when I was introduced to him he looked thoughtfully into my face, and said he'd met my mother a couple of times. Despite the heat he wore a tattered pinstriped suit coat. He was an absurd old git really, but my uncle treated him with respect, almost deference.

We took the ute along the lower part of the farm, and when we stopped, Waldren went to one of the willows along the dry creek line, broke off a thin branch and stripped it of bark. As we walked over the short grass in the glare of the sun, the two of them talked mainly about neighbours and local stuff from years before, which meant nothing to me. Caspar Waldren held the willow branch with cocked wrists so it was bent in an arc on his lower chest. Every now and again he would stop, or do a small circle while the willow trembled with a life of its own in his hand, but no mention was made of water and their conversation continued just the same.

We reached a place in the little valley from which the gravel road could just be seen, and close to a fence and gateway where Cliff and I had set up a temporary tailing enclosure some months before. A few tails, shrivelled and dark, were still lying in the grass of the paddock. Waldren was talking of a rare snowstorm that had hit years before. His voice was surprisingly strong for such a slight man, but had the hoarseness of age. The willow in his hand began to buck, and then flipped over and pointed to the ground. 'Whoa, me old beauty,' said Caspar Waldren calmly, and he walked over and around the spot until he stood where the willow branch gave the strongest reaction. 'This'll be it right here, Cliff,' he said.

'Great,' said Cliff. He had a waratah with him, daubed at the top with white paint, and with body weight alone he pushed it as far into the dry ground as he could. 'Thanks for that. Let's go back and have a few beers.' That was the old guy's payment for his divining, that and Cliff's unquestioning acceptance that there was indeed water down there.

We wandered back to the truck, and as I listened to Waldren going on about the things that interested him, I thought how much a world apart he was from my life at the university. As we bumped back along the farm track to have beer on the verandah, Richard and Rebecca might well have been together on the bed in the flat, driving the smoke of some really good shit into the spottle and getting stoned right out of it. 'That's it. Jesus, that's the stuff all right,' Richard would say, and flop back on the pillows and rake his fingers lazily through the rising haze of exhaled marijuana. 'Jesus, that's a lift.' And Rebecca would take just as much and lie back too, and make a noise as if even breathing was a pleasure, and have a smile that was almost post-coital on her small, pale face. How clear her face is still in memory — the thin wings of dark eyebrow, the smooth curve of her cheek, the creases of parenthesis at the ends of her smile. For a slight, non-athletic woman she was strong, the muscles of her neck and shoulders well defined and her breasts high.

The drought that year didn't get quite bad enough for Cliff to spend money drilling at old Caspar's spot, but he had no doubt there was water there all right, and he kept the place marked. Some of the best wells in the district had been found by Caspar Waldren, he told me, and he said that skill was dying out, just like so many country skills before it. I wondered if Rebecca and Richard ever thought of me, and how they'd piss themselves if they could see the life I led on my uncle's farm. I found it hard myself to understand how many ways of life, how many disparate attitudes, can be operating at the same time with no connection at all. During those months I seemed to be in several places at once, unable to get my life together.

Eric left the flat soon after Queen's Birthday weekend. He didn't give much of a reason, but part of it was the threesome thing that had developed with Richard, Rebecca and me. Eric and I had been friends for years and I felt guilty and defensive. When I met him at the pub a couple of weeks afterwards we talked briefly about it. 'Oh, man, you should move on out of there,' said Eric. 'Those two. There's not enough air between them — I don't care if they are twins. And they're always so down on everybody else. Everybody else except them is fucking stupid as far as they're concerned. Let's do something terrible, let's do something terrible: I mean, you have to say there's something pretty weird about her, and they're getting really heavy into smoking shit, aren't they.'

Neither of the twins had taken to Eric, and that was one reason for how he felt, but he was right in much of what he said. If he'd been right in absolutely everything it wouldn't have made any difference to me. It doesn't matter how long a friendship is when you love someone else. There was no person I wanted to be with more than Rebecca; no place more special than Richard's room with his chosen furnishings, the close body scents mixed always with that of marijuana in a slow convection around the two-bar heater, her hand on my chest beneath the shirt, or over my own hand on her inner thigh. The disconcerting thing was Richard, usually lying on the other side of her — or worse, lying on the other side of me: talking with us, laughing with us, ridiculing the rest of the world, when I didn't want him there.

I wanted just Rebecca and me, the natural thing, but how difficult that seemed to be. She liked to be massaged. It would start with her back, and especially she enjoyed her shoulder muscles kneaded and the very top of her vertebrae where I could feel the thick skin gliding on the bone. Richard would join in, and eventually one of us would undo her bra strap so that we could massage down the sides of her chest. It was usually me, even though I tried to conceal my eagerness, and she would ask who was being naughty, without turning her head, and after a bit say 'all right, all right,' and turn over and let us push the bra aside. She would let us draw our hands firmly over her breasts in a pretence of massage, swirl our fingers over the rougher, darker skin circling her nipples. I loved to do it, loved to do it. I have a hundred merging images of it still: the three of us in the dim afternoon light from the flat window, or the buttery glow of the table lamp at night. And the long breathing of the three of us, and her shoulders stretching back, her breasts trembling to our touch, her smile and glances both relaxed and knowing. And Richard would soon transfer his massage from Rebecca to me. 'You shouldn't tighten up so much. Just relax — all of us should just relax and go with the flow.' And in the pleasure of having his hands no longer on her, I could almost ignore that they were on me. 'Just round and round and round,' he'd say. 'It's such a lovely, natural thing to have skin on skin,' as all three of us would move in the ways that pleased us most.

'You naughty boys. You're terrible, that's what you are,' she'd say.

I knew it was some sort of thrall, as well as pleasure I couldn't deny myself. I hadn't had many girlfriends, but I deliberately got in touch with Melanie Faraday again and asked her to come to a Students' Association fancy dress party with me. Hospital was the theme and there were a lot of people in white coats, or bandages; a lot of crutches and stethoscopes. Melanie's giggle as a response to almost all contact, physical or verbal, was just as I remembered it. She had so little subterfuge, so much assumption of goodwill, and I missed the sharp, stimulating awareness Rebecca always had, which was part sexual promise, part gender hostility. Melanie was attractive enough, but despite that she seemed somehow to have a unisex psyche which stressed things in common rather than exciting differences. She danced with cheerful abandon, and giggled at the interruptions that came from friends who cut in to partner her. She drank a lot, but wouldn't have anything to do with weed, or pills. 'I'm behind in my assignments as it is,' she said, as if smoking shit would suddenly take a couple of weeks out of her life. 'I got extensions because I said my father was sick,' and she giggled.

Melanie lived with her parents, and she had her mother's car for the night, so we left the party soon after midnight and I drove down to park overlooking St Kilda Beach. 'So it's watching the submarine races again, is it?' she said. She took off her earrings and put them in the glove box. She was bigger and softer than I'd remembered, and that impression must have been a comparison with Rebecca whom I'd been with more recently. I didn't want to think of the twins: I was glad it was just the two of us in the car at St Kilda, just as our headlights on arrival had shown only couples in the other cars. It was the natural thing, wasn't it. Melanie wore a white nurse's uniform with large buttons and she gave a sighing giggle as I undid them. 'You know the rules,' she said softly. Yes, I knew she didn't actually fuck, but that night I didn't much care. It was some time before I got a hard-on, and most of the time I thought of Rebecca in Richard's room: her taut body and uninhibited talk, both of which stoked me to hell. That night with Melanie was a lesson to me that love hasn't much to do with what's comfortable, or natural, or even right. It's about some gut-wrenching imperative that drives you towards a person whatever, or whoever, might be in the way. For me it was Richard who was so often in the way.

As Melanie giggled, or kissed almost as noisily, and we fogged up the windows of her mum's car, and each of us felt the sweat on the body of the other, I knew she wasn't the woman I wanted to be touching, to be listening to, to be smelling.

One of the ways I tried to forget all that on the farm was by running. I'd been into sport at school, but didn't bother at university: all that team ethos and character-building shit, and having to turn out for practices no matter how you felt, or how many of the others there you disliked. Running by myself on the farm was different. At first it gave me an excuse to be out of the house when I couldn't face the company even of my uncle and aunt, and then I found that the effort also had a distracting, almost punishing, effect that helped me at the time. My favourite circuit took me up the main gully into the downs, around the limestone bluff which had Maori charcoal drawings in the overhang, and back down the boundary ridge and along the north side of the long pine windbreak. In the winter mornings the grass was white with frost in the shadows and bowed down with droplets in the sun: in the summer evenings the sheep shit rattled like shotgun pellets on the dry ground beneath my feet, and the sheep drowsed in what shade they could find. The bluff had a steep straggle of matagouri and briar. Sometimes I'd take a spell at the top and look over the low hills of the farm, or back to higher ones behind me. I could see part of the snaking gravel road in the valley, and the place where Caspar Waldren had found artesian water.

My uncle had become very economical of physical effort himself since his back had packed up, but he didn't deride my runs. He thought I was getting fit to play rugby and he approved of that. 'No, good on you. Go for it,' he said, and told me that he knew the coach of the local club. He'd played a bit himself years before, and liked to watch the game on television, leaning forward and contorting his worn face with vicarious effort at moments of dramatic achievement.

I was not running to anything, however. I was running from the threesome of Richard, Rebecca and myself, running until the physical effort diminished all else apart from that effort and the strange dazed elation that the metronomic action brought. Sleeping was another thing I did a lot. Sleeping and running were both releases from morbid introspection, and the need to decide a future. How easily I could fall into a deathlike sleep in Dr Evie's innocently fragrant room: sleep that was a dark grave even within the night, and made blank the concerns of life. Running and sleeping were both means of avoidance at different ends of some scale I didn't understand. One involved forcing physical effort to obliterate anxiety and guilt, the other was escape from any consciousness at all. 'Well, at least he sleeps well,' I overheard Sonia telling my mother on the phone. 'And the air is different here on the farm, of course. Yes, he seems to need his sleep.'

I hadn't slept that well at the flat after getting close with Richard. Smoking shit mellows you out, but doesn't give you good sleep. Not me anyway. I looked up the effects of marijuana on the net one time, and it said sleepiness was one of them. Some of the other things, though, I recognised in myself: anxiety, apathy after highs, altered perception of time. And it's supposed to stuff your memory too, and there's a lot about that time which is sort of drifting in my mind. Yet nothing could be clearer to me, less subject to loss, than the times with Richard and Rebecca. I could see it all with a sharpness that was almost an agony.

That was the big thing I tried to work out during my time on the farm: had I gone haywire because of smoking so much shit, or was it because of the twins? I decided maybe it was both, and that I had to make a clean break from both. It was a rational decision that I hadn't been able to make as long as I thought Rebecca would choose me. If she'd rung up, though, when I was on the farm, and asked me to come back, I know I'd have gone, as long as Richard wasn't there. There are things in your life that common sense is helpless against.

In late summer Cliff went up to Wellington for a few days to help Evie move into a house she had bought in Petone. Her big earning years hadn't begun, but as a qualified doctor she had no difficulty getting bank money for a first home purchase, and in addition to her other attributes she was shrewd in business.

A wooden house in Petone wasn't where Evie would end up, but it would be do as a starting point. Cliff had made an inspection of it, and wanted to replace some rotten weatherboards on the laundry side, and fit a much bigger, aluminum frame window in the lounge. He was appalled at the quotes Evie had received from Wellington tradesmen for the job, and quite capable of doing it himself. I knew the quiet satisfaction he would get from ferreting out sound material at rock bottom prices, and the quality of workmanship his daughter would receive. Uncle Cliff had no formal training in carpentry, motor mechanics, plumbing, or even farming, but like so many practical men of his generation he had picked up these skills of necessity from experience and from his various workmates and neighbours, each of whom had some special expertise.

He wouldn't have been able to go up, he said, if I hadn't been staying on the farm. He said that to make me feel welcome and useful, but it was true as well. It meant Aunt Sonia wasn't alone on the property, and I was there to attend to the outside tasks. It was an opportunity also for her to see what she could do for me. She knew my nature made any cathartic disclosure unlikely, and she didn't press me any longer to talk about my problems. Instead she revealed something from her own past as a sign of trust, and evidence, too, that most of us have false starts in life.

On the third hot evening of Cliff's absence we had an evening meal of cold mutton and salad, and then went out to the verandah and sat on the cane chairs which had weathered grey over years. If my uncle had been at home I may have gone to Dr Evie's room, or had an evening run up to the bluff, but it seemed impolite to leave my aunt without company. The sun hadn't quite gone down, but made reaching shadows from the sheds and trees around the yards, gave a tawny glow to westward slopes of pasture.

'Have I ever told you I studied in Sydney years ago?' Sonia said. I knew very little about her, and felt minimum curiosity because my own tribulations were crushing. 'Yes, I played the viola and studied at Otago's music department. I won a scholarship for strings offered by the Perry Academy, and went over there when I was twenty-one.'

'I never knew you were a musician,' I said.

'I practised several hours a day for years. I was in the junior sinfonia in Sydney, and a member of a chamber group which gave recitals and recorded for radio. I thought music was going to be my life then.'

'So do you ever play now?'

'Never. Haven't for thirty years. I don't even have a musical instrument in the house any more. When you've been able to do something really well, there's no satisfaction in doing it at any lesser level at all. None at all.'

A plausible conclusion, and I didn't question it, although I thought of stories of former sports champions who kept playing on in their sunset decline. 'Not easy, though, to give it all away after that?'

'I didn't even see the two years out. I was so homesick that I used to burst into tears when my folks rang, and I had a boyfriend there which didn't work out.'

We sat there on the grey, cane chairs of the verandah, in the last of the day's sun, and looked down to the yards and the still trees. I remembered I hadn't yet fed the dogs. It was a quiet, ordinary place in which to be talking of concert halls and an artistic career. Sonia's hands were hardened with work, and the knuckles swollen a little. They were not a musician's hands. 'I don't even listen to music much any more,' she said, 'and that does surprise me. But your life takes many turns, doesn't it, and there's always so much to do.'

She didn't seem to be sad about the loss of music in her life, just interested, perhaps slightly puzzled, at the way things turn out. I didn't realise it at the time, but I think she chose to tell me because she hoped in a roundabout way it might suggest to me that things which dominate your life at one point will often loosen their grip with time. However, I was preoccupied with my own concerns: having a bad patch, as my father would say. The glass was thick between me and the rest of the world, and the shapes swimming above me still threatening. I hadn't much curiosity about what had happened to Sonia's aspirations; why she had gone to Sydney to be a professional musician, and come home again to marry Cliff.

I remembered that conversation, and regretted my selfishness, less than three years later when she died suddenly of a stroke. She had been collecting eggs, Cliff said, on a rare rainy day, and when he went looking for her he found her body slumped in the tractor shed with her legs and shoes outside the overhang, sopping wet. Her arm was around the bucket, he said, and not one egg broken. By that time I'd completed my degree, in Christchurch, had a job with the council there, was breathing air again rather than aquarium water and was directly in touch with the world.

The funeral service was held in the small Anglican church of Oamaru stone, which wasn't big enough to seat all the mourners who came. People stood around the christening font, at the back of the church, and spilled out into the bright sunshine. It didn't surprise me that Sonia was so well loved. Old Caspar Waldren was there in his number one suit. He shook his tufted face sorrowfully when I spoke to him, as if he divined my failure to have sufficiently appreciated my aunt. And his surprise was evident when Evie and Samantha went against rural tradition and assisted as pallbearers. As we slid the coffin in the back, the polished top of the hearse gave off heat-waves which pulsated through my vision of the paddocks around the church, and Cliff's face was beaded with sweat and tears.

A week later I went down to the farm with my mother to give Cliff a hand with farm jobs, while she helped Evie and Samantha to sort through Sonia's clothes and personal belongings. Without Aunt Sonia the house was like a clock with the spring broken. All at once the place seemed smaller and shabbier, transformed no longer by her energy and warmth. Evie was temporarily in her own room again, and the glimpses of it while passing strengthened the disconcerting mix of feelings I had on my return: gratitude for the acceptance and support I'd received, but also the stirrings of an agony which had been caused elsewhere, but suffered largely there.

Cliff said I could sleep in the little side room, which had filled up over the years with household items no longer needed, but too good to be thrown out. But I took blankets onto the side porch, and slept on the bed-wire propped up on beer crates which each year was used to dry the walnuts. The nights were warm and I slept okay there, despite the foraging noises of hedgehogs and of possums, the sudden lighthouse beams of the moon among the passing clouds, and flashes of memory that came as dreams.

Maybe clearing away the personal remnants of someone's life is even sadder than the farewell of the body. My uncle found it impossible to face so the three women combined their fortitude to tackle it. The clothes and shoes with fragrance and signs of wear, and nothing to enclose; the jewellery, trinkets, and mementos of travel; cards and photos which have gained an inexpressible sadness. And those inexplicable possessions of esoteric significance to people we thought we knew. The closest, dearest litter of a person's life open for selection. My mother accepted a silver bracelet, wept over it briefly, then was a comfort to others again. She found a diary Sonia had kept of her time in Sydney on the scholarship, and some letters from an older, married man. 'It all ended most unfortunately,' my mother said. 'A very painful period in her life, I'd say.' She and my cousins had known nothing of Sonia's brief musical career, and I realised too late that I'd been privileged to have her talk of it.

My mother and Evie and Samantha decided not to say anything of it to Cliff, not to show him the diary, or the letters. It didn't matter how much, or how little, he knew. It was better left in the past. It was a buried life, as Sonia herself had suggested to me that evening on the verandah when Cliff was replacing

Evie's weatherboards in Petone. It was one of those dead-end roads from which you have to retrace your steps, and find another way, though the journey remains with you always. So memory works on association, not logic. 'The music became part of the pain,' my mother said.

But Sonia had kept the diary, the letters, the scholarship scroll — hidden evidence of the buried life. And she would have had her memories too, which would come unbidden as a visitation to shake her in later life, just as I had my own. Things seep into each other. Back in the farmhouse after Sonia's death I felt her loss, but also the presence of my disturbed, earlier self. While lying on the porch walnut-dryer in the warm night, I saw again Richard, Rebecca and myself on another bed that last time.

It was the Monday dusk of a reluctant spring. We'd talked, laughed, smoked shit and ended up, as so often, in that intimate almost naked huddle which was Rebecca's massage. Everything that was the world seemed to move and slide with her; everything that I wanted was there. 'You guys are terrible,' she said, and she arched her back slightly so that her breasts rose further, and she smiled at the ceiling. 'You're always after it, aren't you?'

Richard laughed and put his arms firmly around me, and I felt an intense anger that he was there, that he was touching me, that he was any part of what Rebecca and I did. It was anger and confusion I could no longer repress. 'Will you just fuck off,' I said and pushed at his face with the flat of my hand. He said something; I don't remember what. I do remember Rebecca sitting up abruptly, so that her breasts formed contours of new allure.

'You're always mad keen to be fucking me, but not so keen to be fucked yourself,' she said. 'Ever thought about that? You piss off. You're the one to piss off, right now.'

'Yeah, get the fuck out of it. We've had a gutsful of you,' said Richard.

His voice was suddenly intense, and I picked up my clothes

awkwardly while they watched shoulder to shoulder, and I left that room for the last time. As I went through the shabby kitchen, I heard them start talking to each other, quietly, intimately, as if I had never been there. I was shaking so much I had trouble breathing, and I was rendered excessively clumsy and skinned my big toe on a door frame. It came to me that all along there had been no chance of it being just Rebecca and me.

Even after just the four days that I was on the farm after Aunt Sonia's death, I could tell how Cliff was going to live thereafter. He didn't spend more time inside the house than he had to, for it reminded him of a family now all departed, and a life quite changed. He talked briefly of his future on the morning my mother and I were leaving. He and I stood in the sun by the sheds, and in a breeze which had the ends of the branches nodding. 'Work's the best thing, I reckon,' he said. 'I'm glad I've still got the farm. You never know — one of the girls might marry a farmer yet,' and he lit one of his roll-your-owns, which flamed briefly. He knew the chances of that were pretty slim, but he didn't have any hang-up about keeping the property in the family. It would see him out and that was all that mattered. Those quiet, dry hills, the stock he managed, the store of water Caspar Waldren had promised him waiting beneath his land. And when his life was finished there, another, final, dispersal would take place, sweeping away the evidence of Sonia, Evie, Samantha and of himself, except for the physical imprint he made on the land, and except for the different recollections of those who knew him.

The smell of tobacco and peppermints, or prime West Coast shit; the folded North Otago hills, or the narrow North East Valley of Dunedin; Sonia's laughter through the farmhouse, or Rebecca's knowing smile and the flash of the whites of her eyes; the texture of freshly shucked walnut shells, or cold, crumbed lino beneath my feet. All an uneasy mix in which I catch, just rarely now, a glimpse of a former and fugitive self.

passing triptych

I ONCE HAD A JOB IN a factory that made wallboard from multicoloured shredded paper. The finished product didn't look at all as if the wolf could blow the little pig's house down, but the problem was to get the vast, linear machine to compress the paper and additives to just the right rigidity within the cardboard sides. My part in the process was both unskilled and preliminary: I teased out paper from a stack of bales, and fed it into the tine-clacking maw of the machine. It was high summer, and hot in the old building, which had once been a woolstore. The dust clung to my sweating body and caused an itch.

My recollection is that often the manufacturing would be stopped, because the board coming from the far end of the factory wasn't up to standard. At these times I had nothing to do, having been rightly hired as a technically ignorant manual labourer. I would sit on the bales while others clambered around the machine, and argued about what remedies were required.

Sometimes, when there had been more stoppages than usual, two men in suits came from Christchurch, and the activity was even more tense and energetic. As a menial, I was never told who these men were, never introduced to them, but I assumed they were the backers who had money at risk.

On one occasion, after persistent malfunction for several days which pushed out board that buckled and tore, one of the Christchurch men was so agitated that he took it out on me as I waited on the bales. 'You there,' he said. 'Get off your fucking arse and sweep around the machine. Make yourself busy, for God's sake. You think we pay you to sit around like a useless tit?'

When there was a bad run we had to load the failed board onto the back of a Commer truck, and throw the stuff off in an empty paddock not far from the factory. All over the paddock were earlier loads, some broken down by the weather to just yellow, mouldering heaps. Usually Danny drove the Commer and complained that it was gutless, that they should have a tip-truck, that he was on the lookout for a decent job. For me it was just vacation work before I went back to varsity, but Danny needed something that provided a career. He and I were the navvies, and then there were two older guys with some mechanical knowledge, but rarely quite enough for our machinery. One was called Vic, and he was the foreman. I don't remember the other guy's name.

I admired Vic's placid nature and adherence to routines. He was heavily built, balding and wore clothing seconds from the working-man's shop: thick grey trousers, grey shirts and a grey jersey with a zip at the neck if the weather was cold. He was just the same if the plant was working well, or if everything screwed up and the Christchurch bosses were running about. We started work at 8.30 and stopped exactly at 10.30 for a twenty-minute break. Vic was punctilious about taking the break when it was due, and equally exact in starting work again when time was up. He was obedient to his Christchurch bosses, but not at all obsequious. He took responsibility for his own work, but not the vagaries of the plant. I heard him tell one of the Christchurch men that the board machine wasn't developed enough to be used in production.

Vic had a long history of manual employment and wasn't defensive about that. He'd been a shearer, wharfie, dozer driver, deck hand, forklift operator and maintenance man. He had a whole range of useful, but unglamorous, practical skills, and was good with working people in his own straightforward way. A successful foreman is rather like an effective army NCO, accepted not because of some superior qualification, or background, but because he can, if necessary, do your job better than you can yourself.

At morning tea and lunchtime we sat outside if it was fine, on some great wharf piles which lay on their sides and marked the gravel turning circle in front of the building. The four of us with mugs of tea and our wrapped sandwiches on the dark, finely grained hardwood. Almost all the topics of conversation were foreign to me, but then I came from a bookish family and was studying philosophy, French and classics at university. Vic, Danny and the other guy, who had the ponytail of an ageing, lapsed hippie, could talk for half an hour of the respective merits of two- and four-stroke engines, and then pick up the subject next break and talk more specifically of the superiority of Briggs and Stratton to various competitors. Or they might argue the merits of protection for external woodwork, mentioning from memory and experience a dozen or more stains, oils and paints. It was a lesson to me in the areas of rich knowledge which every occupation has. I was as tongue-tied in that company as they would have been at a conference on the philosophy of Bishop Berkeley.

At the end of the summer vacation I asked Vic for a reference, which I thought might help me to get similar jobs in the future. Vic wrote it out in longhand on a sheet of paper with the company letterhead. There were several grammatical errors, but the comments were supportive, and he made special mention of my punctuality. He told me he himself was leaving, not because the company didn't have a future, though that was his opinion, but because of sickness. 'Some bloody thing's crook inside,' he said.

On my last day I had a beer with Danny at the nearest pub before going home, and he said Vic's illness was bad, and that he wanted to have a trip around the South Island in a hired campervan before he got too sick to travel. I was nineteen years old and had no conception of an illness which wasn't temporary.

Three months later I happened to meet Danny at a rugby game, and he told me that he'd left his job at the board factory and become a grader driver. He said Vic was dead without ever having the chance to have his campervan holiday. He went down hill very quickly at the end, and it was a damned shame, Danny said. I remembered the reference Vic had done for me, which made no mention of my lack of mechanical aptitude, but said that I had always turned up on time. Vic's writing was cramped and inconsistent, and his name, Victor Gallian, seemed slightly over-blown when written in full at the end of the page. I never submitted the reference to anyone — it became increasingly irrelevant to the positions I was qualified for — but I kept it nevertheless.

Another occupation I sampled at an entry level was journalism. A hot press operator, who played in the same hockey team as me, got me a night job at the newspaper on which he worked. I was a reader, which meant three hours three nights a week reading aloud from original copy while a staff member checked rolls of galley proofs. Occasionally we swapped, but not often because checking the galleys was the more skilled job. I don't think papers have readers today, and my eyes are naturally drawn to the numerous errors they show as a consequence. Mostly I worked with Rodney Liffel, who had been chief reporter on a metropolitan paper in his time but then declined into alcoholism. By the time I arrived in the evenings he was usually already smelling of booze. If he'd managed a story in the afternoon he'd be in a reasonable humour, if not then his view of the world was caustic.

'The world is in ambush, Kevin,' he would say, 'and it gets you sooner or later.' He had a tendency to declaim, and looked a little like an actor as well: he wore a green corduroy jacket and his longish hair flopped over his pale face in a way reminiscent of Dirk Bogarde. 'Women have been dealt all the cards between their legs,' he'd say. 'Never trust a Presbyterian in business, or a Catholic in your home,' and, in regard to poetry, 'Every doggerel has its day.' Rodney seemed quite old to me then, but I suppose he was mid-forties. His disappointment in himself had magnified into a derisive disgust with his profession and his colleagues. When we were checking the galleys he would often burst out swearing at particularly trite journalese, or shriek with laughter at some unintended double entendre. He told me that the fourth estate is very close to the lands of hell, and that the best evidence of a god is that a sense of humour exists in the world.

Rodney kept a bottle of Artillery Port in his satchel and would have a gargle every now and again, usually with a perfunctory effort to disguise it early in the night, but then quite openly. He never once referred to it, or offered me a drink. Parsimony was the reason for that, I think, rather than a noble regard for my possible corruption. Journalists are notoriously mean.

If the editor was in during the night, it was my job to take him in a cup of tea at eight o'clock. 'Go on, go on, take the old arsehole his tea, Kevin,' Rodney would exhort me, reaching for his bottle before I was out of the door. The editor was a large, soft man with the mournful face of a St Bernard, and loose flakes of skin in the portals of his ears. He was the only staff member to have a cup and saucer, the others choosing from an unmatched heap of giveaway mugs on the draining board. Every time I came into his office with his drink, he looked over his glasses at me with the same bemused surmise of non-recognition, said, 'Ah, ah,' and cleared a space on his desk. Rodney said the editor once stood for Parliament, and at a full public candidates' meeting was accused of adultery by a woman in a see-through blouse. Such recollections of the trials of others seemed to lighten Rodney's own burdens for a time, but most nights ended in the same way: a morose Rodney telling me that the bloody paper had gone to the dogs, and that he should have stuck to his original ambition to be a travel writer.

'The thing is, Kevin,' he'd say, 'one has to discipline one's talent. Journalism is the grave of the writer who finds the job easy.' Sometimes towards the end of my night stint, a sub-editor would pass the glassed cubicle of the readers' room, and make a face to me of wry recognition of the situation, and sometimes sympathy for their colleague too. Rodney was by then oblivious to such signals, of course, the drink having made him almost completely self-absorbed. Once a top man in his profession, he was reduced to reader duties in the night with only me, the most junior and casual of employees, as an audience for his philosophy. So he'd sit with a wad of unfinished, yellow galley proofs in his hand, his head nodding in self-affirmation and his lank, dark hair falling over his face. 'Much is won if we succeed in transforming hysterical misery into common unhappiness,' he'd say, on each occasion thinking it was wisdom revealed to me for the first time. It came from Freud, he said, and it was the only observation he rated higher than his own. Beneath his green corduroy jacket he usually wore those coloured shirts with white collars, then quite out of fashion.

When my three hours were up, I'd make my rather apologetic escape. Though drunk, Rodney could see that even this least significant of companions no longer wanted to listen, and he was further embittered. 'Yes, piss off then, Kevin, before your ignorance is revealed as total. And don't expect me to be here next time. I've other plans than Grub Street, thank God.' He was there, however, unless he'd been on a real jag and dropped out of sight for a few days. My last night on the job he solemnly told me he'd meant to get a farewell card, but it was the thought that mattered.

I expected the worst for Rodney Liffel: kidney failure, sordid penury in a railside boarding house, clubbed to death in the carpark of the Disraeli Hotel by late-night marauders. But a couple of years later he surfaced in a full-page profile in the local paper. He had beaten his alcoholism by a process of theatrical personality projection developed by Professor Jacqueline Annade of Montpellier. Not only that, he had joined Professor Annade in promoting the movement worldwide. A photograph showed the two of them together, and Rodney was wearing a linen jacket instead of corduroy. His honours degree and impressive journalistic credentials were listed: there was no mention of night work checking galley proofs with me. I felt a lightness of spirit that he had regained a life in spite of the odds, found a willing audience and also the maturely attractive Professor Annade. It was the Hollywood ending that occurs just often enough in life to confound us as realists.

Easily the best-paid job I had as a student was working on the grading belt at Iceveg. Peas were the main crop at the time I was there, and were harvested and fed into viners out in the paddocks and trucked to town suspended in an ice slurry. I stood on the belt with several others for ten or twelve hours at a stretch and picked out reject peas, or the seedheads of other plants. Usually the factory would run shift after shift without stopping for days at a time; occasionally things were slack as the outdoor crews waited for crops to be ready. Peas were everywhere in the factory at various stages of preparation, and the smell of peas was everywhere too. After a few weeks I stopped thinking of peas as food: in the end the smell would almost make me puke. It was very boring on the belt and I looked forward to the odd stint in the coolstores, which were in fact freezers — stacking in, or loading out into refrigerated trucks. In the freezer rooms you wore an insulated coat and heavy gloves, and could work up a sweat when really going at it.

The one advantage of standing on the belt was that most of the others there were women. Some were university students like myself, but there was a core of full-timers who regarded the rest of us as temporary sources of diversion. Romance and conditions of service were the only predictable themes when working on the belt. When in a secure majority of their sex, women tend to be surprisingly open in their comments, and at Iceveg sexual banter and titillation were the main ways to combat boredom. The promise, however, was usually more apparent than real.

A shy boy seemed to bring out in the women a sort of gang effrontery, as if they felt the need to compensate for the customary male dominance of sexual innuendo. Lloyd, the boss's son, was a slim sixth former who became the focus of such attention, but it was all in good humour, and Lloyd was immensely flattered even in his confusion. The women would pinch his bum and ask him if he'd chosen a girlfriend from among them yet, or stroke his smooth face and say they'd had a dream about him, but weren't going to tell. On the other hand when Ashley, alpha male of the field crew, walked through bristling with body hair and testosterone, they kept their eyes down.

Sharon McGillivray was a born-again Christian with very thick glasses, but attractive in a slightly overweight way. She wasn't an inhibiting influence on the Iceveg belt, and was unfailingly kind and cheerful. She didn't push her religion, but shared her beliefs when she thought there was interest. Sometimes I would stand beside her on the line and ask questions to pass time during the shift. Sharon had found God because of an appalling marriage, it seemed, and the death of her small daughter in circumstances involving domestic violence, though she never spoke of that.

She told me that one night at the Women's Refuge a voice woke her and told her to go onto the porch. When she did so she noticed first that the cars passing on the main road made no noise whatsoever, and then that all the vegetation had a glow of purple light. And the voice, which was rather like that of her dead mother, told her that the world would end on the fourteenth of February and everything would have a new start.

I asked her how the world would end, and what it would be like afterwards. Sharon said she didn't know, but that she'd been completely at peace since she'd found out that everything would have a new start. Why wasn't she scared at the prospect of the world's end: the greatest of catastrophes surely? Sharon said she would have been terrified if it had been revealed just about the end of the world, but that knowing there'd be a new start was an entirely different matter. So what would this new start be, I asked her. An abundance of joyous and righteous opportunity, Sharon reckoned. That sounded to me like something she must have read, rather than her spontaneous opinion, but I was curious, rather than sceptical. Sharon and I could stand side by side in the Iceveg factory, watching the peas coming past on the conveyor belt, and talk of the end of the world. Sometimes it would be daylight and some of the women might be skylarking with Lloyd, the young bull virgin, or wondering if there'd be a New Year shout. Sometimes it would be the yellow, artificial light of the night shift when everything slowed down because of tiredness. Sharon said she found great comfort in knowing that the old world, the present one, wasn't going to be perpetuated: that violence and cruelty and selfishness were going to be replaced, and that children would have no recollection of them.

Such a conversation was incongruous, and it interested me that there on the belt, engaged in the most menial of jobs and with everything seemingly stained green and with the smell of blanched peas, Sharon and I talked of God, of an apocalypse and of a new order in the world.

Nothing happened on the fourteenth of February; not as far as I was concerned. I forgot all about Sharon's forecast until quite late in the day shift when I was coming out of a staggered tea break and the supervisor asked Sharon and me to take some trolleys of packs into number two coolstore. We put on the heavy jackets and gloves and took the first load in. Around the entrance was a build-up of baffles of white ice, but further in was just the bare metal that would take the skin from your hands if you didn't have gloves. 'Isn't today the end of the world?' I asked Sharon as we unloaded. I meant no derision, or malice.

She seemed pleased that I'd remembered and gave me a full smile. A drift of condensation came from her breath. 'Yes,' she said.

'And? So?' I said, not wanting to get too heavy.

'The whole world's gone purple,' Sharon said, 'and I feel absolutely wonderful. There's a new order and everything will be all right from now on.'

'Have even the peas gone purple?'

'Oh yes. Even the ice has gone purple, and your face is purple, but it's not the colour that's important, but the new start for the world.'

Everything was just the same for me, but I realised that was no reason to discount the end of the world for Sharon, and the advent of a new one. If there is a God then a world according to our individual needs is surely possible for each of us. After what Sharon had been through, she deserved a new world.

I was at Iceveg for almost two more weeks, and Sharon remained happy. She'd been offered a full-time job at the plant, and was saving for place of her own. She hoped later to adopt a baby girl. I don't recall if I asked her before I left if the transformed world was still purple, but I like to think for her it is, and that the new start never ends.

I'm generally content now in my own profession, but sometimes my eye is caught by the Situations Vacant section of the newspaper, or my ear by the job talk of my family, and I wonder at the possibilities of character, the wonderful variety of companionship. Seasonal fruit packer perhaps, or rolling shift night caregiver at the Lavender Rest Home; contract up-country fencing, or cruise ship employment — work and travel worldwide it says; part-time telephone pollster for Apollo Survey, window dresser for Mature Figure Fashions, or brisket puncher at the Meetex abattoir. All of us labour together in one way or another, and deepen our sympathy as a consequence.

facing jack palance

AFTER AN ORDINARY DAY OF SELLING bathroom fittings, you have a dream in which you must stand against Jack Palance. It wells up through the subconscious, perhaps as a psychic relic of all those matinée films seen in childhood, but its experience now is sober and adult; its issues fundamental and inescapable.

You know without specific recollection that you haven't long been in this small, dusty town, that behind you stretch lonely saddle days in gulches, or high plains drifting, and nights level pegging with a coyote moon. Your lips are chapped, your eyes narrowed to the sun and the horizon, but you walk with the slow ease of a tall, lean man.

The heat rises from the dusty main street, and also presses down from a burnished, implacable sky. So high is the sun that shadows don't lean out from their origins, but crouch close in. Jack Palance is in black, so he and his shadow are as one.

As you walk towards each other, all else seems to draw back to form a dramatic amphitheatre. Townspeople scuttle into doorways and down alleys; the women overawed and tremulous in the face of decisive action beyond the comprehension of their gender, the men furtive, craven, as they slip away. There is the piping, emasculated voice of the fat sheriff as he finds his false duty elsewhere, but no one is listening. The most beautiful of the women bites her lip, and her eyes widen beneath her bonnet.

Black Jack Palance gives a bitter smile, and teeth glint in his wolfish jaw. 'Well lookee here, now,' he says softly. His hands butterfly over the ivory handles of his six shooters which are in sloping holsters for speed of draw, and the belt buckle of Mexican silver glints in the harsh, western sun. Many a man has fallen to the guns of Jack Palance, but you don't let that deter you from what must be done. You remember the advice you had from old Wyatt during a poker night at the Lazy Z, about one gun being enough for any man, and usually one bullet too.

Past the old corral you walk, and the Silver Dollar Saloon with the batwing doors quivering from the mass of cowering people within, who know they see the Titans clash, and will afterwards silence conversations to say — I was there, I was there that day. But the only person you care about is Jack Palance, and you walk real easy with the balance on the balls of your feet, and your gun hand real easy at your side, and you think of the brother and friend you no longer have because of Jack Palance in El Paso, and the lover lost because of Jack Palance in Wichita, and all those sturdy Johnny Reb homesteaders and ranchers' daughters in check shirts, who look to you for justice. And your voice is an even drawl when you say, 'Howdee, Jack. I've been hoping we'd catch up maybe.'

The two of you hold up walking, and stand in the dusty main street beneath the witness of that pitiless sun. Jack Palance, who knows about these things, has you set against the wall of the bank, while his backdrop is the more difficult shimmer of the side street where the barber and coffin maker has a shop. But you don't care about that. There's a faint smell of whisky and saddle leather in the air, and an even fainter one of juniper berries.

'Are you pushing me?' Jack Palance says, and he gives his executioner's chuckle, like the sound of a small scree slide on the mesa's edge.

'I'm pushing, Jack. Why don't you make something of it?' You know your face is saturnine, inscrutable, with a faint, fleeting Mitty smile. All your life has been leading to this point and destiny is writ large in this small town.

There's a long history between the two of you, of course, and although there's no fear in the eyes of Jack Palance, there is acknowledgement that perhaps you are the one: the one sent on this blistering, wind whispering western afternoon to deliver the gift of death. Jack Palance has so often been that emissary, but today for the first time he considers another conclusion. As you face each other there is a sense that despite all that lies as difference between you, there is also an equality in courage and resolve. You and he share something which the ruck of men don't know, but in black Jack Palance it's been traduced and selfishly used.

'Make your play, Jack,' you say evenly, and the only sound is the wind blowing in from the sage brush and tumbleweed country, or is it the indrawn breath of all those invisible watchers, and behind that a faint cosmic music like guitars at the end of a sad, cowboy song. That's how it is all right, and you have a feeling at the inner core of yourself of something both calm and exultant, the serene knowledge that this is the time to do what you have to do, and this is the end of the line for one, or both, of you, clean-cut destiny played out for all to see. Good and evil under the noonday sun. And Jack Palance makes his play with defiance and malice in his dark eyes. His hands are sinuous and devilish quick to the ivory butts of his Colts; your own gun comes up as naturally and smoothly as a deer's head from a mountain pool.

The sound of those guns blows you right out of your dream, and you sit up abruptly, waking your wife. Almost at once that clean, manly and magnificent resolve begins to fade, though you explain all to her eagerly in an attempt to hold it. 'Weird,' she says agreeably, but then she never was one to wear a bonnet.

She needs your help today, she says, to move the Peace rose from one side of the garden to the other. And you just give your faint, inscrutable, ironic, sardonic, fleeting smile, knowing that although logic and incident in dreams may be bizarre, the emotion is always true. 'I think we can manage that, pilgrim,' you tell her.

the fan

ALDEN GRUNNELL WAS SUCCESSFUL WITHIN THE art world for two decades before he won both the Bigalow Modern Art Award and the Fomison Memorial Prize in the same year, but those two achievements spilled his reputation over into the general domain. He registered in the national consciousness as a major artist, and his opinions were sought not just on matters of culture, but on women's netball, party politics, naturopathy, marine reserves within the Hokianga and trends in the development of the New Zealand psyche.

With this greatly increased exposure came many more approaches from the public. One or two were vindictive, more sought assistance of one sort or another, most just wished to express appreciation of his talent. Alden was not carried away by this: he was secure in his sense of vocation, having worked for many years within the accreditation provided by his peers. He realised that the occasional savage attack reflected personal issues of the reviewer, or correspondent, rather than deficiencies of his own, and he knew, too, that the most fatuous and exaggerated flattery was also to be discounted. His reply to most approaches by admirers was standard politeness, without it appearing that way to the recipients, and he normally avoided volunteering personal access.

The letter that Alden received from Peter Pehters, however, was out of the ordinary, and he was interested from the first page, in which Peter said he loved the work of Charles Menou, and wondered if there were influences of that artist in Alden's own painting. 'Maybe the similarities I've become aware of are the response of similar personalities to a common environment, for I know that you spent some time in Mediterranean France, but they strengthen the admiration I have for the work of you both. In particular it seems to me that Menou's use of modified pointillism in his landscapes has echoes in your own larger works of the eighties.' Alden Grunnell was one of those artists who intrigued his public by silence concerning his work, rather than explanation, and he had never trumpeted any significant debt to Menou, although not denying the influence was there. He recognised Peter Pehters' insight in making the connection, and agreed with the passage in his letter which characterised Menou's last works as 'having a palette of subdued, autumnal colours absolutely in keeping with the elegiac quality of his intention'. Charles Menou was a neglected artist, and Alden was agreeably surprised that Peter Pehters was aware of his work, and valued it.

Peter's letter made no requests, solicited no reply, and simply ended with best wishes and gratitude for the pleasure he found in Alden's work. Yet it was one of the few approaches which stayed in the painter's mind, and to which he eventually replied. He did so not because he was flattered — the great bulk of letters, faxes and emails were more obviously intended to do so — but because he was attracted to the sensibility he detected behind Peter Pehters' comments. In his reply he acknowledged the influence of Menou, praised the special qualities he saw in his work and agreed with Peter about the special ambience of that part of the Alpes Maritime. 'I was last there more than a decade ago. I spent eleven days in rooms in a stone barn at the top end of the valley. The Gulf War was on, and the debate concerning it raging more widely, and each day I left all that behind and walked through the chestnut trees and smoke bushes at the top of the valley to the abandoned terraces of the mountainsides. The light, the light! and the lavender clumps and the small birds whirling in groups, and the slight haze in the south obscuring the distant Mediterranean.'

Three weeks later Peter replied from his London home, thanking Alden for his letter and giving a moving account of a recent trip to Europe, during which he had visited various galleries and private collections, hoping to secure permissions for an exhibition of Menou's work. 'And I made contact with the relatives of his younger sister. She married a baker from Genoa, and the grandchildren seem now completely Italian. They haven't any of Menou's paintings, and know little of his life, but they cheerfully showed me several letters which he'd sent to his sister when he was living in despair and poverty in Castellar.

'"Nothing happens for me here," he said. "No one would give me even the price of a paella for one of my paintings. I languish here and hear nothing from my friends in Paris. Others go from success to success, while I persist in living and painting where there are no people to advance my career. There are no influential folk, and the few rich ones have no more sense of art than a donkey's fart."'

Alden was interested in Peter's findings, and in the increased disclosure of his life and personality. He replied with unusual frankness concerning his own art and his view of others. He asked for copies of the Menou letters and said that the quotes Peter had already sent reminded him of the feelings Van Gogh expressed to his brother, Theo, half a century before. 'We don't feel that we are dying, but we do feel the truth that we are of small account and that in order to be a link in the chain of artists, we are paying a high price, in health, in youth, in liberty, none of which we have any joy of, any more than the cab horse that hauls along a coachful of people out to enjoy the spring.' Alden confessed that he himself had suffered bouts of intense depression and uncertainty early in his career, even to the point of requiring medication and brief hospitalisation. In a supportive reply, Peter said his reading led him to suppose that such was to be expected when the artistic temperament met the everyday world, and he quoted Proust: 'Without nervous disorder there can be no great artist'.

So developed a considerable friendship through correspondence, and every month or so the two of them had an exchange. As they had begun with letters, so they decided whimsically to continue, despite their use of fax, email and phone text for almost all other contacts. The time both took from their busy lives to write was a sign of the value they attached to their friendship. Peter was employed by a leading British art auction house and spent much of his time travelling to Europe and America, seeking out works and clients and establishing provenance. He was also a successful freelance curator.

The exchange of their views on art, and increasingly more personal matters, brought Alden and Peter as close together as they thought it possible to be without meeting, then after more than three years Peter had an opportunity to visit New Zealand. 'I will be going to Sydney and Melbourne in early March,' he wrote, 'and to Auckland and Wellington from the 20th of the same month. My main concern is in various private collections of early twentieth-century Australian painting, though I shall cast an appraising and avaricious eye on all sorts of antipodean treasures. My real hope in accepting the New Zealand leg of the journey was that it might enable us to meet and spend some time together at last. I could perhaps stretch my time in Wellington to another couple of days at the end, and we could get together at my hotel.'

Alden lived alone, and with rigid disciplines to maintain his emotional health as well as his professional focus. It was seven years since his last girlfriend moved out, and although they still saw each other, he knew the relief of having his home to himself. What was a day or so, one night, however, when he and Peter had proved so compatible through their letters. Alden wrote and invited his friend. He surprised himself by the anticipation he felt for the visit.

When the time came, Alden spent the morning making sure the loft room was ready for his guest. From the window which reached from ceiling to floor there was a view of that uncompromising coast. Behind the bed head was a Clairmont painting, which Alden had bought directly from the artist many years ago for the price of a week's groceries.

After lunch he went to his garage and decided to drive into Wellington in his classic green 2.5 V8 Daimler, rather than the four-wheel drive. It was something of an occasion, after all. On the trip he thought of things he wished to talk about. All those topics and opinions touched on in their letters could be discussed at length over a day or two together. At the hotel he asked the receptionist to ring his friend, and settled in a foyer chair to wait. He'd never consciously thought of Peter's appearance, and they'd not exchanged photos, so he watched the lifts with some interest. A family came down, then an attractive lone Chinese woman, then a tall, powerfully built man with a crew-cut who obviously was not expecting to be met and headed for the street. Then came Peter Pehters, a rather overweight, flowing sort of a man in a quality, dark suit, the coat of which wasn't buttoned. His hair was thick and limp, hanging over the pale globe of his face, and he put down his suitcase close to Alden to shake hands. He also had a large shopping bag which caught in his fingers and spilled parcels on to the floor. Physical awkwardness tended to irritate Alden, though he knew the reaction was unfair. 'It's so good of you to make a bed available,' Peter said. The English accent wasn't marked, but Alden found the comment odd.

Peter was ungainly getting into the Daimler, and slammed the door on the metal catch of the seat belt. Alden, speculating on the damage, found it hard to concentrate on his friend's account of an Auckland sale of early lithographs. Peter's perceptiveness and goodwill were as evident as ever, but his physical presence was an intrusion. 'How clear the horizons are here and in Australia,' he said. 'Almost all the time in Europe there is a residual pollution of the atmosphere, so that when you look into the distance it just hazes out. Down here you can see the edge of the world.' But Alden couldn't help noticing how spittle gathered at the corners of Peter's mouth as he talked.

When they reached Makara, Alden helped his friend inside with his luggage, and in the guest bedroom Peter immediately noticed the Clairmont, and perceptively discovered in it the very virtues which had led to its purchase. Even in the warmth of that discussion, though, Alden was distracted by the way that, within minutes, Peter had the contents of his case and shopping bag strewn about the room, and spilling almost of their own volition into other parts of the house. With just a murmur about his need to keep in touch with London, Peter set his laptop up on Alden's desk, and some apples that he had kindly brought as a gift rolled unconfined on the tidy kitchen bench. Halfway through a conversation about a forthcoming exhibition of Alden's work, Peter remembered he had left his electric razor at the hotel, and rang to ask that it be held for him at reception. 'I'll have to use yours in the morning if you don't mind. Sorry about that,' he said. Alden had an aversion to exactly that sort of indirect, yet familiar, personal contact.

Alden recognised in himself a tendency to be overly fastidious. He endeavoured to ignore the physical trivialities of Peter's presence, and concentrate on his friend's intelligence, his humour, and all they had in common. To no avail: Peter broke the coffee grinder from Verona, he left toothpaste blobs in the handbasin, he cracked his knuckles even as he talked wonderfully of the landscape of the Midi. He had a high-pitched laugh, almost a yelp, against which Alden had to steel himself not to wince as the night wore on. There was an oppressive corporeal quality about Peter Pehters which finally obscured for Alden those wonderful attributes of mind and spirit that had originally attracted him. Peter created a good deal of detritus on his plate during a meal, and his breath held the scorch of tobacco, although he was too polite to smoke indoors.

They didn't stay up late. Peter was to begin the long flight home the next day, and so went to bed before eleven, and kept his host awake for several hours longer with a reverberating and primeval snore. Nor was there much time in the morning, and it was taken by Peter's rather disorganised packing, and attempts to deal with email correspondence from London. 'One's business pursues one to the ends of the rainbow — here at Makara,' he said graciously, while accidentally damaging Alden's telephone socket.

As the time for departure approached, Alden wrestled with himself as to whether he should take Peter into his studio before the visit was over. It was the most personal place in the house, the place he knew Peter would most like to see, although he hadn't asked to do so. It was also the space in which his shambling clumsiness and his yelping laugh would be almost unbearable.

'Come and have a look in the studio before you go,' Alden said, when Peter had gathered his possessions at the front door ready for the trip back to the city, and the two of them went into that long, simple room which overlooked the sea and was built for natural light. There was an almost completed picture on the easel. Peter looked at it keenly, but was also fascinated by the evidence of the artist's working habits around him. The large preserving jars with bouquets of pale, clean brushes, the tin trays heaped with crushed paint tubes, the cloths, the wand which Alden used to steady his hand across a painting, the photographs and working sketches pinned on the wall nearby. Some bunches of dried flowers were strung on the wall opposite the huge window: the only sign of the occasional feminine presence. There was the natural disarray of a craft workplace, but not the accumulated debris and reckless disorder of many studios. 'So here it happens,' said Peter, 'and always with the sound of the sea.' He looked wistfully at unframed paintings stacked with their backs towards him, and one of his large feet caught a rug edge and he stumbled a little.

'We'd better be on our way, I suppose,' said Alden.

During the drive they talked of Pisarro, whose works were appreciating at auction. Peter slammed the Daimler's seat belt buckle with the door again when they stopped at the hotel to claim his electric shaver, and, from a cream and jelly bun, bought en route to the airport, scattered crumbs throughout the car, and soiled the grey leather. 'Kindness and patience are characteristics not typical of the artistic temperament,' said Peter, 'yet Pisarro was to forgo the full expression of his own gift, because he generously supported the talents of others.'

'That's so,' said Alden, and he felt guilt that he couldn't more openly appreciate Peter's own virtues.

They talked of travel in the comfort of the Koru Lounge — Avignon, Perugia, Capri — and Peter several times gave his yelping laugh while Alden glanced away. When the boarding call came they shook hands, and waved as they had a last view of each other. Alden felt a sense of relief to be going home alone, to be free of the ungainly bulk of Peter, his damp handshake, his loose, slightly regurgitive mouth, his spreading, haphazard possessions, the minor but repeated damage he inflicted on things around him. He felt relief, yet guilt for that response, and as Peter's physical presence faded, growing stronger once more was the sense of the essential man whom he had come to know so well.

Two weeks later a letter came from Peter. 'What intrusion the unaccustomed company of another can be in the house. The

French protect their homes from visitors, even friends, by meeting elsewhere, and it is a practice which has much to commend it. How generous of you to invite me to stay, and especially to allow me to see your studio, that central chamber of your outward life. Forgive me if I seemed to blunder briefly into your world, and that the trivial occupations of day-to-day living seemed to obscure at times the fundamental things we have in common. Anyway, I write now from Castellar, where the heat quivers from the stone houses and those old-fashioned half-gutter tiles, and the lemon trees all seem to have goitres on their trunks. Over seventy years ago Menou was here, at the end of the next street. Towards the end he was hardly painting at all, and was arrested for debt. Soon after he returned to Cagnes-sur-Mer where he died, as you know. The descendants of his landlady here have four sketches with which he attempted to pay his rent. They're in wretched condition, but there is one of an onion field which has something at least of his old brilliance. If you are keen I could perhaps make an offer for it, in a private capacity and on your behalf. I see it perhaps in the loft bedroom with that long view of the New Zealand coast.'

Alden was very interested in the onion field sketch, but even more warmed by the full letter which, as ever, roved candidly from the professional to the private, and marked a resumption of the easy, close friendship he and Peter had enjoyed over several years. All the things which had irritated, or distracted, him during Peter's visit, seemed of no consequence when out of sight, and were already fading. The Peter who was on the page and in the heart was wholly admirable. Alden began his reply the same day he received the letter. 'Dear Peter,' he wrote, 'Wonderful to hear from you.'

a kind of living

MICHAEL, RIK AND BUDGIE LIVED IN the back flat of a rambling Topsy house in Sydenham. Over the years one lean-to after another had grown along its sides like fungus on a log, and the back flat was the coldest and oldest. Budgie had crapped out of his varsity courses years before; the other two went working straight from school. Michael had wanted money of his own so that he didn't have to live with his mother and her new partner; Rik thought he could make it as a rugby league player, but so did guys with more talent and determination. The three of them had met as casuals at the woolstores, but more recently seagulled on the Lyttelton wharves. They were pleased how much you could make for doing so little, and none of them had made a good fist of holding down permanent jobs.

Their flat was a cold hole, and all of Sydenham was dingy and moving sluggishly in the Christchurch winter. Fog rolled around the place as if it were a swamp, and Michael and Rik had string up in their bedrooms on which to dry clothes. Budgie didn't bother, and just rested his clothes, which he called airing, between bouts of use. Budgie said the human body was naturally self-cleansing.

In June there was a busy time at Lyttelton and the three made the most of it. Each day they went through the tunnel to the wharves in Budgie's rusted Coke-bottle Cortina, and so in July they had enough money to think of making a break from the Christchurch smog. 'Queenstown,' said Budgie. 'That's where it's at now.'

'I can't ski,' said Rik, and neither could Michael.

'But you can shag and drink, can't you?' sneered Budgie. You bet they could.

They set off on the Friday: early afternoon with the drizzle squeezing out behind them. Budgie's car wasn't much, but he'd spent a packet on an audio system with 6x9 four-way 280-watt speakers, and as they droned south across the plains Budgie sang along to U2 and slapped the steering wheel in time. With his bunched features and small, curved nose he was well named. Budgie lived life for the possibilities of the perishable moment, caring nothing for consequences. 'Queenstown's fucking jumping at this time of year,' he shouted.

They decided to take the Waitaki route on the way there, and come back through the Mackenzie Country. In the four hours or so they took to reach Omarama the drizzle was outrun, and under a chill, blue sky, which was already darkening and threatened frost, they refuelled. Rik said he couldn't find his money, but he'd chip in later. Typical. They bought more beer there, though Budgie said it was okay, he wasn't going to have much while he was driving. 'Pass one over,' he said.

'Just don't become a silly bugger,' said Michael.

'Me! Me!'

'Yeah, don't play the dumb fuck even before we get there,' said Rik.

'Me! Me!' said Budgie joyously. He'd already finished the best part of a can.

Rik gave his giggle. He was half Maori, and though his name was Thompson he said that it was given to the family by the missionaries. When they were in the tussock hills of the Lindis Pass, Rik lit a joint and kept it to himself for few k's until he felt the good weed begin to ease him out, then he passed it among the three of them. No one said anything, and the music was damn loud anyway. The Cortina blatted up the curving slopes, leaving a faint, blue plume behind it. Budgie continued to tap the wheel in time, Michael relaxed more with each lungful of shit, Rik too started to forget all the regrets. Moving along, that was the thing, having somewhere to go to and money to spend when they got there. That was something: better than crouched in the back flat playing poker with increasing irritation, or hanging out at the local pub which never seemed to have any new women, or any increase in the availability of the regular ones.

The winter darkness came early, and Budgie had the lights on well before Cromwell where they stopped for a feed. The cold came swiftly too, once the sun was down. 'Jesus,' said Michael, getting out of the car. They smuggled the takeaways into a pub and kept their backs to the barman. 'We're drinking his fucking beer, aren't we,' growled Budgie. 'What more do they want?' The bar was warm and comfortable; so much better than their flat, or the stinking confines of Budgie's car, so they settled in for a bit.

It was too early for many to be in, but among the few were four women some years older than the guys. There was a younger, plucked-eyebrow girl too, who Rik reckoned was the sister of one of the others. 'She'd do,' he said.

'Any of them would do,' said Budgie.

Michael stopped beside them after going for a leak. 'So are you ladies local?' he said.

'Near enough,' said one. The others continued to talk among themselves.

'Maybe we could come over and buy you a drink,' offered Michael.

'Forget it,' said another, 'but you could send the Maori boy over for Amy here.' The girl with thin, arched eyebrows went red, and yet was flattered by the attention. There was laughter and pushing around the table, and none of the women paid any more attention to Michael, who went off with a silly smile to cover his rebuff.

'No, they're waiting for some guys,' he told his mates, and said nothing about the compliment paid to Rik. 'We might as well be on the bloody road.'

'Fucking out of here. It's a hole anyway,' said Budgie.

'That young one, though,' said Rik. 'I could go her.'

'Yeah, right' said Michael, and 'Sleep well, ladies,' as the three of them went past the women's table.

Rik drove the rest of the way to Queenstown, and Budgie, who always drank more than the others, fell asleep in the back seat, hair spiked up as his head rolled at the corners. Michael took the chance to turn the CD player off. 'Jesus,' he told Rik, 'I dunno how he doesn't go deaf with that bloody din all the time.'

'It keeps him up, doesn't it, and you know Budgie. If he's not up then he's quite likely to be sour.'

They hit Queenstown after ten, and Budgie woke up some minutes before, as if he could smell his destination. There were lots of motels on the main road in, and at the first that showed the vacancy sign, Michael hammered on the office door, but no one came. 'Stupid wankers,' he said. The next had a narrow, steep descent to the parks, but the light was on in a small, glassed room labelled 'Reception'. Michael rang the brass handbell vigorously until a stooping, bald man came through, barely concealing his annoyance.

'Okay, okay,' he said. 'How can I help?'

'The finest unit at the cheapest bloody price,' shouted Budgie, picking an assortment of pamphlets from the display box with the obvious intention of never reading them.

'Set rates,' said the bald man. 'I've a one-bedroom unit left for three nights.' He was the colour of budget supermarket cheese, and wore a cream cardigan with woven leather buttons. 'Plenty of bounce in the beds: now that's essential,' said Budgie.

'There's rules about noise and visitors.' The motelier was of an age to take sexual exuberance as an affront.

'Excellent, my good man, excellent. We certainly don't want to be disturbed in our business talks,' said Budgie.

The proprietor took a small carton of milk from the office fridge and led the way past the parked cars and up external stairs to a concrete block unit with the lake view obscured by a larger building. 'Thank you,' said Rik after the obvious features in the motel had been pointed out, and the bald man was surprised. 'Love the cardigan,' called Budgie to his departing back on the stairs. 'Fucking useless, bald-headed old prick,' he said, only barely less loudly.

Tired though they were, they hadn't come all that way to sleep. There were those girls in the hotels and wine bars, weren't there: girls who at that very time might be considering who to leave with, who to take up on offers made. 'We can unpack stuff later,' said Rik. 'Let's check out the scene.'

'This is where it's at — definitely. I kid you not.' Budgie stopped just long enough to check his face in the mirror, and find it no more compelling than before.

'I'm stiff for it,' said Michael. 'If I can't get any regular pussy this weekend, then I'm going to fucking pay for it. A place like this must be packed with them, and one way or another I'm not missing out.'

'Be positive, bro,' said Rik. 'Aren't we the ones with something special to give away?'

'Fucking right,' said Budgie. He did some energetic pelvic pumps on his way down the outside stairs. 'Have I got plenty to give away.' His car smelled really bad, and as they drove down to the town, Budgie told the others they should clean it up the next day if they wanted women to get in it. 'You guys always booze, chunder and smoke shit in here, but nobody thinks to have a bit of a dung out, do they.'

Downtown was busy, but mostly tourists rather than skiers. The barman told them that there'd been no decent dumps of snow, and the season wouldn't get under way for weeks anyway. It wasn't what they'd expected, but it made no difference. They went into the Huntleigh bar, drank Speight's, and looked around for talent. Budgie always believed that sooner or later his sort of looks would be in demand, Rik knew his were no handicap and Michael had been known to get lucky. Most of the women seemed to have guys with them, but Budgie spied two on stools at the far end of the long room. They both wore quilted jackets, and one had long, dark hair which hung over the shoulder of her jacket as she talked. 'Let's see what they're like,' said Budgie.

'There's only two,' complained Michael.

'Yeah, but they'll have friends, won't they, and two's better than nothing.'

The room narrowed at the end of the bar and Budgie knocked someone's arm as he pushed past, causing a beer spill. 'Hey, watch it, mate.'

'Leave a space then, eh, so's people can get by,' said Budgie.

He would have gone on, but the guy stood up in front of him: tall, rather thin and with a prominent Adam's apple at Budgie's eye level. 'Ever heard of please, or excuse me?' he said.

'Ever heard of fuck off?' replied Budgie.

It became one of those routine confrontations. At first the tall guy had only one supporter, but then two others came back with drinks, and Budgie, Rik and Michael didn't press as hard. The barman said the language wasn't acceptable, and was told to fucking butt out, so he demanded all of them leave, or he'd get the police. The seven of them stood in the street, and because it was very cold and they were pissed off at being ordered out, they mouthed off at each other. The tall guy with the Adam's apple had excellent reach, and without warning caught Budgie in the mouth with a straight jab, just as Budgie finished calling him an ugly streak of whining horse-shit. Budgie would have been into it, but Rik and Michael didn't like the odds, and hauled him off down the street. 'You fuckers are gutless,' said Budgie morosely, and the blood on his teeth glistened in the street lights.

'I'm not scrapping with four guys just 'cause you're a jerkoff,' said Rik, and he kept a hold on Budgie's jacket in case he made a dash back.

'Aw come on,' moaned Michael. 'It's fucking freezing out here. Either we find another pub, or we head back to the motel.'

'Where did we leave the bloody car then?' asked Budgie, and as they headed off to find out he gently pressed his lips with his fingers to test the swelling. 'That skinny arsefucker got in a lucky swipe before I was ready,' he said thickly.

'One to one you would have done him, no doubt about that,' said Michael, and Budgie didn't notice the look between the other two.

A dark, steep slope rose up behind the town, the lake lay like quicksilver below the mountains, and the vibrant stars hung in clusters over it all. But the three guys didn't lift their eyes to any of that.

Budgie insisted on driving back to the motel and was so erratic that the danger kept the others silent, despite being almost drunk themselves. They persuaded Budgie to have the fold-down bed in the main space, and went thankfully to the single beds in the other room. Rik had pyjama bottoms, Michael slept in his underclothes, Budgie took off only his sneakers and windbreaker, and rolled under the covers after smacking the heater about because he couldn't work the thermostat. 'This place is a bloody meat locker,' he complained. 'Jesus, you could freeze to death.' He was asleep in two minutes.

He was still asleep after nine the next morning when Michael and Rik made coffee, blamed each other, then Budgie, for not getting bread, and watched the sleet on the windows of the motel. Budgie's mouth was ludicrously swollen, but without visible cuts. The pillow case beneath his cheek, though, was stained pink with a mixture of blood and spit. 'He'll be in a shit mood when he gets up,' said Rik.

'What the hell can we do in this weather?' said Michael. 'At least the pubs will be open. We can play some snooker maybe.'

Budgie opened his eyes and pulled a face; not a big one because it hurt his lips. He explored his mouth with his tongue, then sat up and scratched himself through his jersey and shirt. 'Have you guys bought any bread or stuff yet?' he said. 'Shit, you're idle bastards. What time is it?'

Michael and Rik sat at the formica table and watched the rain. They'd spent a heap of dough just getting to Queenstown, and it might as well have been a Saturday morning in their own flat. The place was cleaner though, and Budgie was the only disagreeable smell.

'We thought maybe later we'd go down town and check things out,' said Michael.

'Why not. Is my fucking face bad?' asked Budgie.

'A bit puffy, that's all. You're okay,' said Rik.

'Yeah, well you two chickened out on me didn't you.'

'Oh, knock it off.'

They decided to have a late breakfast, early lunch, at McDonald's. Budgie put on his jacket again, but couldn't find the car keys. He roamed the motel swearing for some time, until Michael thought to go out and check the car. The keys were dangling in the driver's door. 'Jesus, you're a dickhead,' said Michael.

'You're lucky the car wasn't nicked,' said Rik.

'How come everything's up to me, eh?' Budgie happily grabbed the keys. 'You buggers are pretty slack yourselves.'

'Anyway,' said Michael, 'no one's going to steal that car for sure. Good thing if they did: maybe you'd do better with the insurance money.'

'What insurance?' said Budgie. 'Big Mac and fries here we come.'

The only park they could find was several blocks from McDonald's, and they had to puddle-jump their way to the diner through wind and rain. Even at eleven o'clock it was almost full, and the three were forced to a table close to the counter. Budgie dried his hair with a paper napkin, and then cleared his nose with it. 'Piss-poor weather, this,' he said to a couple taking their trays past. Two plump girls were at the next table: one wore jeans and a red anorak, the other had a short, thick skirt, and her pale thighs coalesced before reaching the hemline. Both of them had smooth, moon faces, and the one with jeans had large eyes, the dark irises set off by startlingly bright whites.

'I bet you girls are local,' said Rik, casually cutting into their conversation. 'All the best-looking women live in Queenstown.'

They were from Invercargill, but flattered of course, nevertheless. Helen and Alana. Helen was the one with the eyes and anorak: Alana had the better appetite and soft, fair down close to her ears where her hair was drawn back.

'So we're all here for the weekend. What do you know,' said Michael, but he thought they could do better.

Budgie asked them if they'd like to have a drink, maybe play pool somewhere, but they were booked for a lake cruise early in the afternoon. 'Jesus, some day for that,' he said.

'Anyway, give us your number, and maybe we'll give you a call this evening and see how your boat trip went,' said Rik. Alana just giggled, but Helen wrote it out on the back of Rik's hand as a bit of fun before they went. Both women looked bigger when they stood up to leave. 'See you, Alana, see you, Helen,' said Rik. He was always good with names. 'Enjoy the cruise.'

'Yeah, see you,' called Michael.

'What do you reckon?' said Rik when they'd gone.

'Too fat,' said Michael.

'Even fat women fuck,' said Budgie, 'but we'll do a hell of lot better than those two.'

'Yeah, they were fat,' said Rik. 'Good tits though, eh. That's the thing with fat women, and I didn't mind Helen's face.'

'And we need three,' said Budgie, who knew where he'd be in a selection process, but never admitted it.

Michael asked the McDonald's guy if there was a hotel handy with plenty of pool tables, and the three went out and stood in the shelter of the overhang to decide whether to go there. Rik said they could go to the movies, but Budgie said they hadn't come all the way from fucking Christchurch to go to the movies. Rik said maybe they'd come all that fucking way to play pool as they did at their home pub. 'It's different though, isn't it,' said Budgie. 'There's entirely different people here for one thing. What do you reckon, Mike?' If anything, it was raining more than before, and it was cold too. Michael knew that Budgie wanted to play pool because it was one of the things he was good at, and because the movies didn't have booze.

'We can't drink piss at the movies,' he said.

'Fair enough.' Rik was as staunch a drinker as the others, but held it better. It was just that sometimes he liked to forget his life, forget he spent his time with Budgie and Michael, forget that his league trial hadn't worked out — and the movies let him do that.

The pub was a good place to be, though. It was warm and noisy and well lit, and they put three jugs on the window ledge by their pool table, and when they had a refill each of them could stand for a moment, and look out on to the grey, cold street. They still had money left, and it was only Saturday. Budgie was a good deal better than average at the table, and he'd made an effort over several years to memorise a good many jokes about the actress and the bishop, the elephant and the librarian, and other such twosomes. So after a couple of hours he was playing for money with other guys there, and Michael and Rik took it easy on the seats by the window, where they talked about finding better jobs than seagulling on the wharves.

Rik wanted to be a courier driver: an owner-operator so that the harder and better he worked the more he'd make. He said they were always on the run so it would keep his fitness up for league. His fitness was shit over the last year or so, he said. Ten or twelve thousand dollars would be enough for him to get a decent diesel sliding door van, and then he'd be into it. He had an idea that he could approach his amateur club about using team colours for the van, and maybe they'd sponsor him. He already had a track top and so on. It was obvious Rik had been thinking a lot about the scheme, even getting down to the finer points, but there he was blowing hundreds of bucks on the weekend, and the money for the van may as well have been ten times as much.

Michael was impressed by the amount of detail Rik could go into. His own plans were vague, and really just a reaction to the worst features of his present life. 'I'd like to be making progress, you know?' he said. 'A decent set of wheels, maybe a down payment on a place of my own. Nothing shit-hot obviously, but property holds value for you, doesn't it.' A wharfie had said he had a brother who borrowed to buy an old villa and met the payments by having flatmates in four of the rooms. Michael put it to Rik as his own plan, as something he'd been thinking about as keenly as Rik thought about having his own courier business. He reckoned it wouldn't take all that much more than for a van, to have a down payment on a place of his own, and then he'd be a landlord in his own home and the money would come rolling in. 'That's the choice thing,' said Michael. 'You're right on the fucking spot, see, watching your asset and not paying any board, or anything, yourself.'

'Me and Budgie could be your first two flatmates,' said Rik.

'Maybe you,' said Michael, 'but Budgie's not fucking house-trained, is he.'

They had a laugh together, and looked over at Budgie, who was waiting for his opponent to rack up. Budgie saw them look his way and gave the fingers. 'What's that, you buggers? I can hear you,' he shouted, and went on with the game.

Michael told Rik that he'd thought he'd take in mainly women as flatmates, because if they got a bit behind in payments then he could put the hard word on them. 'Now you're talking,' said Rik. 'Ace idea.' Michael began to be enthusiastic about the possibilities himself, and the two of them tried to work out how long it would take to get together twelve or fifteen thousand dollars. The warmth and friendly noise of the pub, the jugs of beer on the window ledge, the thought of having women obliged to them, made it easy to be optimistic.

Budgie eventually met someone better than himself, and lost in half an hour most of the winnings he'd built up over much longer. 'The tin arse got on a roll, that's all,' he said, 'and he hardly had a drink at all. How can you play against a tin-arse wowser fucker,' but Budgie was cunning enough to quit while he was still ahead.

'Having your face rearranged has altered your sighting along the stick, that's what it is,' said Michael. The swelling from the punch the night before hadn't improved Budgie's appearance, or pronunciation. His lips almost met his nose, and the words were lisped. Rik and Michael had a laugh, but Budgie wasn't in a mood to take offence, and smiled as best he could. 'Yeah, yeah,' he said. 'All right for you buggers, isn't it.'

Daylight started to fade early, and the rain didn't let up. The three of them went out to the main door, and talked about having a walk around the streets, but soon decided to stay in the pub. It was cold even under the overhang of the entrance, and they noticed it after the fug of the pool room. The rain slanted in: the low cloud swallowed all but the most immediate buildings. Rik pulled a face. 'This isn't the best bloody weekend to arrive, is it,' he said, and they moved back inside. Michael asked the barman if the place was popular with women in the evenings.

'You'll be mobbed, mate, mobbed.'

'Bring it on,' said Budgie.

They got two plates of chicken wings, two of buffalo chips, half a dozen sausage rolls, and more Speight's. Budgie reckoned that would hold them until later. Rik suggested Budgie shout them from his winnings, but got the predictable answer that he could dream on about that. Michael got a similar answer when he repeated his scheme about buying an old house and paying off the mortgage by having flatmates. So they talked about rugby. Michael thought the ABs were coming right, but Rik and Budgie reckoned they'd get arseholed again by the Aussies. Budgie claimed some expertise, because he always said he'd played halfback for his first fifteen, though he was vague about the school. Michael and Rik had a private joke that it was probably Waikikamukau District High. Rik didn't mind as much as the other two when the All Blacks lost, because league was his real love.

They talked to pass the time, and because it was their customary accompaniment to eating and drinking. Each of them knew the others' opinions almost as well as his own, and the combination of that food and that beer and those opinions was predictable and comforting, though they never thought of it that way. Rather they saw themselves as out there, up for it, whatever it was.

Michael noticed that not many unaccompanied women were coming in, and only one threesome so far, all of whom looked only fifteen or sixteen years old. 'It's this shitty weather,' he complained. 'A lot of talent won't bother going out at all.'

'It's still early, for Christ's sake,' said Budgie. 'They're all still washing their hair and choosing knickers.'

'Yeah, but the thing is that unless we ring Alana and Helen soon then they'll be gone too.' Rik showed the back of his hand to the others, and tapped the smudged telephone number written there in biro by Helen.

'Oh, Jesus, not those fat ones at McDonald's.' Michael was a bit tubby himself, but always critical of women's appearance.

'They were bloody fat,' said Budgie, but from hard experience he'd learnt not to be too choosy. 'I guess we could always dump them if we got onto something better. The real problem is there's only two of them, though the combined fucking weight is enough for all of us, and being up from Invercargill they won't have any girlfriends here.'

Rik said he was going to ring anyway, and all three spent a while guessing the worst of the smudged numbers on the dark back of his hand. 'Ask about a friend anyway,' called Budgie as Rik went off towards the pay phone. 'You never know, and a thin one would bring the average down a bit.' The two at the table watched Rik making his call, and speculated as to the outcome.

'What were their names again?' asked Budgie.

'One was Helen. That's all I remember.'

'Which one was her?'

'She did most of the talking. She had a nice face and good tits, I'd have to say that,' said Michael.

'Amen to all three,' said Budgie, 'and she didn't seem as if her knees were glued together either.'

'They're on,' said Rik when he was back at the table, 'but they don't know anyone else to ask. They're coming here in an hour or so.' This success perked them all up, and they spent some time pooling their recollections of Alana and Helen and exaggerating the best points. Rik went to the lavatory and combed his hair. Michael went later and washed his face. Budgie didn't go, but pushed his hair forward with the flat of his hand, and brushed some chicken scraps from his windbreaker. 'Don't start in with the dirty jokes straight off, you'll frighten them off,' Michael told him.

'Dirty jokes? Me? Where'd you get that idea. Anyway it softens them up.'

'Just take it easy,' said Rik.

'Look, if they take bloody offence then obviously they're not in a shagging mood anyway, and we save ourselves wasting good money on them.' Budgie was pleased with the succinct logic of that. 'Eh? Eh?' he challenged.

'Just take it easy, right,' said Rik.

Alana and Helen were fatter than the guys remembered. Togged up to beat the rain and cold, their bulk was accentuated, and even when they'd taken off a couple of layers there was barely room for five around the table. What smooth, smiling faces and attractive scents, though, and with their coats removed the heavy swell of their breasts shared the table space with the beer jugs and glasses. 'And what would you ladies like to drink?' asked Rik.

'So how was the trip on the steamer?' asked Michael.

'It's fucking fantastic that you've come. We'll have a full-on night, you'll see.' Budgie wasn't going to be left out of making a gallant pitch. He gave his best smile, but because of his swollen mouth it showed the bruised underside of his top lip.

Both women looked their best when sitting, and Alana was more at ease than at McDonald's. A phone call and a second meeting allowed her to feel she wasn't a pick-up. She and Helen gave a lengthy account of the afternoon lake excursion: how cold it was on deck, what a magnificent view of the Remarkables, and how some tall basketball guys from Dunedin tried to hit on them. Rik, Michael and Budgie appeared totally absorbed by the tale, and encouraged it with laughter and rapt attention. 'Hey, don't forget your drinks,' said Budgie. 'You've got some catching up to do.'

'Never trust any prick who plays basketball,' said Rik. 'You did the right thing, absobloodylutely.'

'And you'll have far more fun with us anyway,' said Michael. He was taken again with the sheen on Helen's hair and quick smile.

Alana worked in a plant nursery, and Helen was office manager of a trucking firm. Invercargill was okay, they said: in fact the place was booming again. 'I've always felt Southland was a beaut place,' said Rik, and Michael and Budgie agreed, although they'd never been there.

'Green, shit it's green. Bloody marvellous,' enthused Budgie and he looked complacently at the swell of Alana's jersey brushing the full glasses on the table.

'You can say that again, eh,' said Rik.

The place got very crowded by ten, and rain on the coats of newcomers showed that it hadn't improved outside. The five had a discussion about going somewhere else for a feed, or staying put, having the pub food and making sure they at least kept a good table. 'What do you think, girls?' asked Budgie. 'Your call.' Budgie normally put his own inclinations first, but for the present he was all consideration.

'Money's no worry,' said Michael. 'The night's on us.'

Helen and Alana made a show of indecision, but with the cold and rain outside there was only one answer. Rik went and memorised the blackboard menu, a feat that didn't requre enormous powers of retention. He came back and leant over the women to encourage their choices, and his arm rested easily on Helen's shoulder.

'Those chicken wings are a bit of okay,' he said.

'Really?' Helen glanced at his brown hand with the backpackers' phone number grown fainter.

'Firm but yielding like an old man's dream,' put in Budgie cheerfully.

Drinking and eating together were a form of integration, and their talk and laughter a part of the larger, confused talk and laughter of the whole place. The guys told mutually supporting stories of Christchurch, in which they became stevedores rather than just seagulls, and the women's talk about themselves suggested they were often the focus of male interest, and that they had interesting career options to consider. Budgie got in about his university studies, implying that finally there wasn't enough academic challenge to interest him. All of them agreed that the overseas ski crowd when they came would be a bunch of wankers, though none of the five had any experience of skiers, or skiing. Budgie said it was those bastards who put the price of everything up to buggery.

A band started up at eleven, and the edgy feedback of the electric guitars made shouting necessary. There wasn't room for dancing: even if the guys had been able to, and Helen and Alana not self-conscious about their size. Rik suggested they go back to the motel together, and Budgie gallantly bought cans of some vodka mix because Helen had mentioned she liked it. Rik was going to see him right for part of it later, of course. They burst onto the pavement in a grandiose swirl, but the cold rain and wind soon had their heads down and collars up. 'We'll stay here while you get the car,' Michael suggested.

'Fuck that,' said Budgie. 'All for one and one for all. And you've got as much idea as I have now where we parked the bastard.'

'Once we get back to McDonald's I reckon I'd be right,' said Rik. Helen and Alana kept close together, and the three guys ranged ahead. They talked loudly when under the shop overhangs, and scurried wordlessly across intersections and exposed places, except that Helen swore loudly when she slipped in the wet and nearly fell.

'Shit,' she said, and then a relieved laugh as she recovered her balance. The Cortina, its paintwork falsely bright in the wet, was welcome shelter when they finally reached it, though Alana and Helen were disconcerted by the smell, and rubbed their hands over the back seat surface before sitting down. Rik had adroitly manoeuvred himself there too, and Michael had to sit with Budgie in front.

'My limousine is at your disposal,' intoned Budgie as the car lurched out from the gutter, and they laughed as if he'd said something to deserve it. Budgie was pissed, and it showed in his driving, but the others weren't sober enough themselves to be much bothered.

'If it'd been fine we'd have taken you up on the gondola,' said Michael. 'A fantastic night view up there they say.'

'It's okay,' said Helen. Rik was pressing his leg against her.

Budgie had the bass level of his speakers way up, and the car throbbed its way through the main streets. Most people were in shelter, but Budgie refused to stop for a group on a pedestrian crossing, and gave them the fingers when they shouted at him. 'Dumb fuckers,' he said. He was pleased that he was in his car with mates and two women, and the dumb fuckers were walking late at night in the rain. He was going back to the motel where he'd surely score a shag, and for a while he didn't have to think about working on the Lyttelton wharves. 'Did I tell you the one about the three princesses and the frustrated troll?' he said. And that too got a laugh. Budgie told himself it was going to be an ace night, you could put a ring around that.

None of the three had thought to turn the heaters off when they'd left in the morning, but the motel had been serviced and was very cold. Michael turned each thermostat to high, but at first Alana and Helen kept their coats on. Budgie said once they'd cracked a few more cans they'd never notice the cold anyway. 'And, and,' he said, his impresario voice rising, 'have I got the very thing to cap the bloody night off. Have I fucking ever.' He dug his stash out of his carrybag and rolled a couple of joints. 'If this isn't the best West Coast shit you can get, I don't know fuck,' he said.

'You don't,' said Michael. Budgie didn't know that much about anything, but Alana giggled, and Helen was into it straight away, saying she'd never smoked much dope before. It seemed to warm the room as quickly as the heaters and soon, coats off, three of them were squashed on the sofa, which could unfold for Budgie's bed, and Budgie and Michael sat on cushions in front. All were within arm's reach of each other, easy to pass the joints and cans, and Michael could rest his chin on the denim expanse of Alana's knee, rather wishing she'd still been wearing a skirt.

'Is this the life, or what, eh?' said Rik, and gave Helen a squeeze at her midriff.

'I don't care if it pisses down all weekend,' mumbled Budgie.

He began on his usual litany of stories, but the others didn't bother to listen much. Alana could hold a tune without accompaniment, and she and Michael sang Abba revival numbers and looked at the lines in each other's palms for clues as to the good fortune in wait. Helen and Rik swapped a joint from mouth to mouth and alternated it with kisses. She made a show of smacking his hand when it hefted one of her considerable boobs.

'There are no strangers here, only friends I haven't met,' he said, for a laugh from them all. Budgie's voice became more shrill and insistent as the booze and weed combined. A female shout through the wall told them to keep it down, but they responded with such fierce and redoubled noise that they heard no more from adjoining units. Michael moved just far enough away from Alana so that he could, with drunken deliberation, roll two more joints. 'Hit me again, dealer,' said Rik. His brown face had a sheen of fine sweat, and his lips pouted slightly in relaxation, almost like Budgie's, but in his case not unattractive. His eyes were darker even than Helen's. Budgie drew in from one of the new joints.

'Oh fuck, now you're talking,' he said. 'There was this librarian with only one tit, you see …'

'Rik got up and drew Helen after him from the sofa by gently pulling both her hands. 'We're going to look at the lights from the bedroom for a while,' he said.

'Oh, are we,' she said, giving no resistance.

'You'll like the view,' he said.

'Yeow,' cried Budgie, and waved one hand.

'Oh, will I,' said Helen. She trailed one hand over Alana's shoulder as she was drawn past. 'Help, help,' she said dreamily.

'What do you reckon?' asked Michael.

'What?' Alana was less at ease with Helen vanishing from the room. Budgie sat at her feet with both arms around her legs and his head on her knee. The joint seemed to have gone out in his mouth.

'Just lean back on me,' said Michael, trying to keep the urgency from his voice. She did lean back, but that made his task at the back of her bra more difficult and with the size of her it was no use just trying to push the cups up. Eventually they had her tits out below the undone blouse and rucked jersey, and above a roll of flesh at the belt line. The breasts were smoothly immense and lightly traced with pink indentations from the bra. 'Jesus, look at that,' said Budgie and he edged forward and stretched out a hand which made no contact with Michael's although they ranged the same generous anatomy. Alana was heavy on Michael, and her back made it difficult for him to see what he could feel, but he didn't say anything, or move, in case it put her off. Helen's half muffled giggle went on and on from the other room.

It was a tableau for a time, but Michael could tell from the stiffness of Alana's back against him that neither booze nor marijuana had made her relaxed in the situation, and when Budgie tired of feeling her breasts and began a vigorous effort to undo the belt of her jeans, her reaction was strong and emotional. 'I'm not doing it,' she said loudly and heaved herself up. The round of her left knee, bigger than Budgie's head, caught him in the face, full on the bruises of the night before, and he fell backwards with, 'Jesus, bugger me.'

Alana pulled down her jersey and began to cry. 'You sleazes,' she said. 'I'm not doing it.' She went straight to the bedroom and opened the door. Helen tried to get her jeans back over her large hips. Rik flopped onto his back with the exaggeration of annoyance.

'Jesus, what now,' he said. Alana wept noisily, and her hands were busy under her jersey trying to arrange her bra and blouse. Both women were occupied for a moment, then Alana said through tears that she was going home, that she felt sick, that she wasn't going to be mauled over by those two.

Helen knew her allegiance immediately. 'Two of you on her, you dirty bastards,' she said to Michael and Budgie, as she and Alana put on their coats.

Rik tried to smooth things over, but he and Helen weren't together and happy on the bed any more. He offered to ring a taxi, but Alana seemed to be getting hysterical, and both women were determined to get out straight away.

'Give us the car keys,' Rik said to Budgie.

'No fucking way. Let the silly bitches walk.'

'Give us them,' hissed Rik. 'You want the bloody cops here next?'

Budgie handed them over, and Rik went out, helping the

women down the stairs, talking to Helen as the intermediary to persuade Alana to accept a ride. When hit by the wind and the rain, Helen in particular saw the sense of it, though Alana's sobs and her high, accusing voice were clear to Budgie and Michael at the motel doorway even when she had reached the Cortina.

'Frigid bitch,' said Budgie. 'She got me right in the mouth again, the silly bitch. What's she on about? We never even got into her.'

'Oh, shut up,' said Michael.

'I said all along that it's no good having two women for three of us.'

'Christ, Budgie, you can be a right prick sometimes.'

Budgie sulked after that. He inspected his bruised lips in the bathroom mirror, and swore softly to himself to see fresh blood. When Rik came back, Budgie didn't ask him anything about Helen and Alana, just took his keys, folded down the sofa to make his bed and turned out the light so that only the bedroom cast illumination into the main room. Rik and Michael drifted into the bedroom, recognising that Budgie was shitty. Michael told his mate what had happened with Alana and Budgie, and Rik agreed Budgie was so often a pain in the arse, but both of them were too whacked to talk much, and too disappointed.

'After all that,' said Rik bitterly. 'Another ten minutes is all I needed to make this fucking weekend worthwhile. It pisses me off.'

'Tell me about it,' said Michael.

They fell into a stupor of sleep, in an atmosphere of sweat, booze and the pungency of weed. All of those were habitual, but there was more — the unfamiliar scents of perfume, powder and the women themselves. The rain spat on the windows, the heaters hummed softly at their work, and Budgie laboured for breath through his thick lips and from a pit of oblivion.

None of them got up until mid-morning. Then Rik and Michael went into the main room, ignoring the huddle of blankets that was Budgie. There was again nothing to have for breakfast except coffee: despite their disappointment the morning before, they hadn't remembered to buy anything, or fill in the motel card. 'Shit, I feel rotten,' said Budgie from the blankets, as the others stood with coffee and looked out into the motel carpark. They were all used to the sour drift in the stomach after such a night, but that didn't make them feel any better. The rain had stopped, but the sky was grey, and a cold wind blew from the south-west.

'So what do you reckon then?' said Michael without enthusiasm.

'Well I don't know about you bastards, but I'm out of here smartly and away home,' said Budgie. He sat up and scratched himself under his T-shirt. 'This is a cold, dreary fucker of a place and vastly bloody overrated.'

The others didn't give any argument. They'd half expected Budgie's decision, and because the car was his they had to go with it.

'We may have to pay for the motel for today too,' warned Rik.

'Let the old bastard try to pull that one and he'll see,' said Budgie.

They worked out what two nights would be, and all put in. Rik was short as usual so he had to be the one to go to the office.

'He should pay the lot,' grumbled Budgie as he dressed. 'At least he got a shot away last night, the lucky bastard.'

'You know Rik with money.'

They pulled out at eleven. As they left, Rik reminded the others of his success in getting the proprietor not to charge for the Sunday. The old guy, wearing the same cream cardigan with leather buttons, watched them go from the office doorway. He didn't wave in response to Budgie's bursts on the horn. They had a last glimpse of him setting off across the yard to check the motel.

Budgie set his stereo loose again, but it was more than Michael in the front seat could put up with. 'For Christ's sake,

Budgie, turn that racket off for once,' and he did so himself with a flourish. Budgie took it, said nothing, and drove on mile after mile. They had nothing to say to each other, nothing to share that wasn't accusatory, or representative of failure and lapsed comradeship. Rik slumped against his travel bag and fell asleep.

The normal running noise of the old Cortina was a rattling whine, but among the hills leading up to the Lindis Pass the engine started to miss. Michael didn't want to aggravate Budgie by saying anything about it, and Budgie hunched protectively over the wheel. Maybe the engine could cure itself, maybe it was one of those passing mechanical things, rather than a result of maintenance entirely neglected. Budgie's philosophy was that if the car went, then nothing needed attention. But it went little further, shuddering noticeably on a pull up towards the saddle and then conking out. Budgie pulled into a tussocky flat at the roadside, and still didn't look at Michael. 'What's up?' said Rik from the back, just awake. Budgie tried the starter in sustained bursts, swearing so loudly in between that his feature-crowded face bounced on his shoulders. Soon the engine turned only slowly on the starter motor.

'You're only draining the battery, Budgie, you silly bastard.' Michael couldn't keep quiet any longer.

'Shut your fucking hole. What would you know about it.'

'He's right,' said Rik. 'Have a look under the hood, for Christ's sake.'

Everything under the hood was covered with an accumulation of dust, each layer of which had been gradually and partly absorbed by oil. It appeared as a growth of a greasy, brown fungus, with just a few fossil fingerprints at the dipstick and radiator cap.

'It must be the electrics,' said Michael. ' That's why it was misfiring. Nothing mechanical, I reckon.'

'It's just fucked,' said Budgie with despondent finality.

'Yes, I'd say it's munted,' was Rik's vote.

Budgie went back to the driver's seat, and the starter motor made a last few laboured turns, and then just a soft click when he turned the key. Rik and Michael stayed looking hopelessly at the greasy engine bay. 'It's buggered,' said Rik.

'Thank you, fucking Einstein,' said Budgie. 'You may be shit-hot on fat women, but you know fuck-all about cars.'

Somehow the appearance of Budgie's car hadn't mattered so much when it would go, but broken down in the tussock grass of that high and lonely road, it was all at once overwhelmingly derelict. How had it got so far? The once bright yellow paint was furry with neglect, one wiper was missing, one park light smashed, tyres grey and blandly smooth. At the base of the windscreen panels and the joins of others were casts of rust, as if corrosion were caused by some tiny burrowing animal in the metal. The entire car seemed to droop in an awareness of its own condition.

On either side of the road was a pelt of tawny tussock which tossed and undulated over the treeless hills as the wind swept fierce and unobstructed. It was a landscape that had its own austere beauty, but the three men had no more awareness of it than they had of their own incongruity within it.

They would have to try and hitch a ride to Omarama, and get a towtruck to come back from there. Budgie was going to stay with the car to make sure it wasn't ratted, but the others said it would be okay: who'd want any part of it anyway? Budgie locked his bag in the boot, but Michael and Rik took theirs for safety. There wasn't much traffic on the road at that time of year, and because they were three scruffy guys it took a while before they were able to thumb anything down: a maroon Falcon driven by a rep for one of the liquor chains. He wasn't prepared to tow the Cortina, but was happy to give them a lift to the village. 'Bad luck,' he said complacently when they were all inside and the car surged ahead in a silence that seemed complete after the howl of Budgie's Cortina. Quiet enough that the brief sleet at the top of the pass could be heard striking the windows. 'Not much of a day, eh,' said the rep, and the others agreed.

Not much of a day; not much of weekend either. Jesus.

At the Omarama corner garage the owner said they had a towtruck, but he couldn't leave the pumps and would have to find a driver: might be half an hour or so, he said. The liquor rep was going right through to Christchurch, and gave Rik and Michael the chance to come. They told Budgie in a quick forecourt huddle. 'Otherwise we'll all have to stay the night somewhere, and I'm bloody skint,' said Rik.

'It's not as if I won't chip in for the car repair later,' said Michael. 'It's not as if we can do a bloody thing by staying, can we. You know that.'

'Just fuck off then. See if I care.' Budgie gave a short, hard laugh, then put on the set expression that showed he was absolutely pissed off. Rik and Michael walked together back to the Falcon.

'See you later, Budgie,' called Michael, but Budgie didn't answer and went into the garage shop to wait for a driver.

'Your mate's okay with this?' asked the liquor agent.

'Yeah, it's fine. He's just worried about his car,' said Michael.

'We need to get back to Christchurch anyway,' said Rik.

They didn't feel all that much guilt about Budgie. He'd have done the same as them in their situation. And it was easy and right, wasn't it, to blame him for most of what had cocked up during the weekend. And anyway, shit, they were a long way from home and didn't fancy hanging about for the Cortina to get hauled in and then fixed. Bugger that. Budgie was Budgie, and he'd turn up again soon enough.

'So you guys weren't all that enamoured with Queenstown, then,' said the driver as they set sail into the Mackenzie Country. He thought of some of the weekends he'd had with his mates before he got married.

'Nah, we didn't somehow seem to get it on down there,' said Rik.

'Nah, overrated hole,' said Michael.

poetic licence

TWICE A MONTH THE TE TAREHI Poetry Society met in the small room at the side of the Salvation Army community centre. The Sallies charged only $5 because the poetry chairman at the time of the arrangement was a volunteer helper in the depot's second-hand clothes store. That chairman had resigned as a poet manqué over a year before, but the society had said nothing of that.

Only three poets turned up for the first June meeting, and two of them were lucky that the third was the key-holder, Norman. It was a cold June, and already completely dark though only 6.30. As well as the key, Norman brought a very small heater of his own which he plugged illegally into the Sallies' power. The three of them huddled around it: Norman, Philip and Kap. They held their hands above the heater, and talked mainly of food.

'There's a special on spaghetti with sausages. One dollar a tin for three tins or more. It hasn't sold well like the beans do themselves and they want to move it out,' said Kap, who was part Maori. He wore a leather jacket that had become mottled with age, and although he was thin and undersized, there was a compactness and capability about his body the others lacked.

'I had eggs Benedict,' said Norman. He was a great one for meals that sounded elegant, but were inexpensive.

'I had half a tin of beetroot,' said Philip, and that was borne out by the pinkish tinge around his mouth. 'I thought I had a saveloy, but then remembered it had slid out of the fridge and the dog got to it before me.' Despite the short rations, he was large, and the heavy wool jersey he wore accentuated that. He had the smooth, egg-like face of an indoor man. 'It's not right,' he said, 'the way we have to live to bring our art to the world.'

By ten to seven it was plain that no more poets were coming to the meeting. 'No quorum again,' said Norman, who knew the constitution of any organisation he joined. 'We can't do any business at all, nothing.' He swayed back from the heater briefly in exasperation.

'I could read from my blank verse history of the world,' said Philip.

'No,' said Kap and Norman together.

'I've also got my sonnet sequence, "Omni Scientia"'.

'No,' the others said.

There was silence for a time, and then Norman spoke, 'Something has to be done.'

'Absolutely, but about what?' said Philip.

'About the disregard that we are shown as poets; about the contempt with which we are treated. All of us have published, Kap is a living treasure for his iwi, I have a PhD in linguistics, yet we live on book reviews, school visits, library readings, attending launches for food and wine, and hawking our own work about the city. We have barely a toehold even in Grub Street.' Norman had half risen to his feet, so great was his depth of feeling, and

Philip waited until he had subsided before speaking.

'Poets are always a laughing stock,' he said, 'unless they get on telly. We're the village idiots of today while sensible people get jobs that provide money as a matter of course.'

'I'm going to get money. I realised yesterday that my mortgage is now twice what it was ten years ago,' said Norman. He was the only one of the three who owned a home, and it had always given him a special cachet. 'I wept,' he said simply. 'I wept in the night, and then I decided to do something about it. I asked myself where the source of quick and plentiful money lay, and the answer was — crime.' He had risen in a crouch above the heater to his climax, and the others waited again for him to sit.

Kap showed real interest for the first time, and joined the conversation. 'Poverty is a crime,' he said. 'We're criminals already.' Kap had strong socialist leanings and before becoming a poet had spent time mutton-birding, squid fishing and organising kayaking tours. He'd been a freezing worker too. 'There's crime and crime,' he said, 'if you're talking bloody crime.'

'I am talking crime,' said Norman. 'I'm a desperate man against an uncaring world. I must have security if I'm going to be able to complete my work. What society won't give me as my entitlement I'll wring from it nevertheless. Society thinks poets are ineffectual in every way because they fail to make money, and maybe that mindset is my advantage.'

Norman had never discussed his poverty, or anger, before, although he was a great talker in his rather academic way. Always before he had kept to books, and festivals, his poetry and that of others in the group. The three weren't close friends, in fact, despite the affinity they had as poets. Philip and Kap realised that Norman was at a point of crisis in his life, and both of them had sufficient insight and compassion not to ridicule him.

'Anyway,' said Norman after a short time when neither of the others had made a comment. 'I'm not going to say anything more about it unless you feel the same way.'

'I do feel the same way,' said Philip. 'I'm held back because

I haven't the capital to publish a first collection myself which would give me the exposure to catch a publisher's eye. It's what happens: the pump must be primed. I've cried myself.' He lowered his voice abashedly. 'I've cried sometimes after working for six or seven hours on my stanzas, and not even been able to afford a beer at the end of it, and publishers show not a flicker of interest, not a jot, not a glimmer of hope, or a passing word of encouragement. In all these years of writing I've had seven poems accepted by amateur editors of tin-pot literary mags.'

'The establishment,' said Kap. 'doesn't want the workers to find a voice through poetry. Look what they did to R.A.K. Mason. Crime is a matter of definition, isn't it, eh, and who's bloody doing the defining? The rich bastards at the top, of course. Ripping a million or so off shareholders is an okay thing, isn't it, but lay hold of a bit of cool-store lamb and you're for it.'

All three poets were quiet then, a little surprised perhaps by their immediate agreement that money must be found, and that legitimacy was expendable. They concentrated on Norman's small heater for a time, and the night pressed like a black cat on the one window in the small room. Norman knew as the one who had raised the subject it was up to him to let it lapse, or return to it seriously. He looked at Philip and Kap, so different from each other and from himself. How unlikely a band they made, but Norman remembered the rapidly dwindling equity he retained in his small, brick home and it hardened his resolve. 'Say we were to consider a crime then,' he said. 'What sort would it be?' and before the others could reply he continued, 'Personally I couldn't countenance anything remotely connected with violence, guns, computers or children.'

'Banks are where the money is,' said Philip, 'and in a way it then becomes a victimless crime. I saw this programme where people tunnelled in.'

'Not a rat's arse there,' said Kap. 'They've got far too much security. Get real, Philip.'

'Well, what would be a target for such as us, thinking

hypothetically.' Norman sensed that Kap knew something about crime, but said nothing of that.

'No big outfits or anything. You jokers haven't the knowledge there at all. Neither have I, for that matter. No, it's got to be private, eh — something out there that hasn't been spotted and something that won't hurt working people.'

'I don't quite follow,' said Philip.

'A very rich bastard is what we want,' said Kap. 'A very rich bastard who keeps his head down, and hardly anyone knows about.'

'What would we know of rich people,' said Philip lugubriously. A three-figure sum was a standard of wealth for him.

But Norman felt immediate interest. He'd never much cared for Kap's poetry: ungrammatical, slippage in the rhythms and always a didactic proletarian issue. But Kap's views on crime had clarity and conviction — well, perhaps conviction wasn't the best word, Norman told himself. 'A very rich bastard,' he said, repeating Kap, for he never swore of his own volition.

'Yeah,' said Kap. 'Then we'd be in business.'

'Who would we know?' said Philip. He felt slightly jealous of the attention Norman was paying Kap. There'd never been much between them in the past.

Norman, though, had some standing in the community: certainly not financial, but he tutored at the university occasionally, was a regular on the letters to the editor page, and his grandfather had been a mayoral candidate, missing out by only a handful of votes. But what connection occurred to him in the context of rich people was his membership of Rotary. 'Maybe,' he said, 'I could do a little research and come up with someone.'

'Let's talk about it, just us, after the next meeting,' said Philip, but Norman was uncomfortable about tagging their meeting as prospective criminals on to the regular Poetry Society night. It wasn't guilt so much as a sense of the disparate nature of the two enterprises. So they agreed to a separate meeting in the Sallies room the next Tuesday, and Norman as keyholder practised his new attitude to morality by deciding there was no need to notify the church, or to pay an additional rental.

Norman and Philip felt awkward at that first Tuesday meeting, coming from the shadows into the small room again for such a different purpose. Norman led the way with key and heater, aware of the peculiar juxtaposition of their Salvation Army venue and the purpose of their coming together. Such ironies were lost on the more practical Kap. 'Jesus, it's cold,' he said. 'On with that heater, Norman.'

As the one short bar somewhat reluctantly began to glow, Norman wondered if he should make any formal opening of the meeting, but Kap made it unnecessary. 'So have you found that quiet, rich bastard for us, Norman?'

Norman thought he had. On two occasions at Rotary he had heard members, wealthy by his own standards, talk deferentially about a certain elderly man who made money at will on the share market, yet had virtually no profile at all in the city. And he was said to have a good proportion of his wealth in tangibles of art, gold and antiques. Money wasn't mentioned, but it seemed likely.

'So where does this fat cat live?' said Kap.

'He's not listed in the phone book,' said Norman, 'but I got an address from the electoral roll.'

Philip and Kap were impressed, but didn't say so. They knew that Norman was one of the few members of the Poetry Society who could have succeeded in the world on its own terms; he could have had a comfortable academic career, or used his administrative flair to climb the corporate ladder, but he had followed the muse of poetry.

'So where is it?' said Kap.

'Probably on the nobs' hill in Parkgrove,' began Philip.

'Cut it,' said Kap.

'It's a place up on George Grey Terrace set behind a brick wall that must have cost a fortune itself.'

'I'll do a recce,' said Kap. Once he'd got the address, he

wasn't interested in prolonging the meeting. He said there was nothing else they could do until he had sussed the place, and that it was no use just sitting about talking. Norman could see the sense in that, but felt that so short a meeting was a reflection on his assumed chairmanship, and Philip was dismayed that crime, unlike poetry, didn't necessarily provide him with social companionship for several hours, and that he'd have to return to his unheated flat overlooking the cemetery.

'I wrote a poem on burglary yesterday,' he said hopefully, but Norman pointed out that they had to maintain a distinction between their evenings for poetry and those for planning crime.

Kap did his recce over two nights. On the first he just adroitly scaled the wrought iron gates to the rich bastard's section and padded cautiously around the outside of the house to check for security systems, or dogs. On the second he assessed all the points of possible entry and established that the ground floor at least had a standard alarm system.

'I need to have a chance to check the second-storey windows,' he told the others at the next meeting in the Sallies' room. 'Some excuse to find out if they're wired.' The three leant together over Norman's heater and pondered.

'When Baghdad went missing, I remember I went round every house in the neighbourhood. I saw and heard things that day I'd no knowledge of before, even though I've lived there for years,' said Philip. He was like that: seemingly out of the loop, and then occasionally coming up with something in an artless way which fitted the bill nicely.

'Good one,' said Kap. He and Norman knew of the parrot, and recognised its value immediately, and Philip was so gratified to have made such an effective contribution that he happily left the detailed planning to the others. 'We'll have to plant him somewhere there,' said Kap, 'and it gives us a reason to have a ladder, for Christ's sake.'

'It could just work,' said Norman. 'It has a sort of domestic element which may deflect suspicion. The thing is, though, will we be able to get Baghdad back before the whole thing goes on too long?'

'His wings are clipped now,' Philip said, 'He can't fly far and if I took a chocolate almond he'd come back from the dead.'

So the scheme was for Philip to plant the cockatoo on an upper window ledge while Norman sought permission for recovery at the front door, and Kap waited in the car. There was a tacit understanding that Norman and Philip, with their suburban demeanours, would be the better front men. Kap drew a plan for Philip so that he'd know which window was the target, and Norman rehearsed a little tale for the rich bastard, or whoever came to the door, to explain their presence on the property. Philip said he'd need the others to chip in money for the chocolate almonds.

They went the next Thursday, at four in the afternoon while the light was still good and the gate unlocked. Kap established that nobody was about in the grounds, then Norman with the ladder and Philip with Baghdad in a cage went to the south side of the house away from the living quarters, and screened from the road by the birches and chestnut trees of the generous section. They placed the ladder beneath the window chosen by Kap. Philip climbed tentatively with the cage, urged on by an impatient Norman, and set a surprisingly unruffled Baghdad on the windowsill. While Philip returned the ladder to Kap at the gate, Norman went to the front door and sounded a chime which echoed deep within the house. In response a plump woman in swelling jeans and embroidered black top came to the door. Norman apologised for intruding, and explained that his friend's parrot had escaped captivity and been seen flapping into her property. 'We can see it on one of the windowsills on the south side,' he told her.

'Just a minute,' the woman said. She disappeared for a moment and returned with a pair of sneakers far more disreputable than Norman expected in a rich bastard's house. 'So which window?' she said briskly.

When they reached the south side, Philip was standing gazing at Baghdad above him. In creased grey slacks, Fair Isle jersey and with a cheap haircut above his pale, lower-middle-class face, Philip was a picture of innocence without assuming any pretence, and Baghdad, his sulphur crest resplendent in the soft winter light, was totally convincing also.

'If you wouldn't mind Philip here going inside for a moment, I'm sure the parrot would come quietly,' said Norman. 'He's really very tame, but was frightened by a Doberman pinscher when my friend was grooming him.'

Philip picked up the cage at his feet and smiled. 'I've got chocolate almonds,' he volunteered. 'Baghdad will do anything for chocolate almonds. Perhaps you'd like one yourself.' He proffered the box with his other hand.

'Don't mind if I do,' said the woman in jeans, and she shook a couple out for herself. 'Okay, you'd better come inside then. Leave your shoes at the door so nothing gets trodden in.'

They walked back to the front, and Norman whispered to Philip to remember to feel around the window frame while retrieving the parrot. The woman closed the door on Norman with no apology, and the sound of her conversation with Philip faded as they made their way down the hall. They returned promptly with Baghdad serene on his perch, clasping an almond in one claw and balancing on the other leg despite the gently swaying cage.

'Perhaps you'd like another one yourself?' asked Philip as they were reunited on the expensive tiles of the entrance foyer.

'Don't mind if I do,' she said and shook out three in an accomplished way.

'Thank you so much for your co-operation,' said Norman. 'It's such a relief to have him safe again.'

'Okay then,' she said. 'Just make sure you close the main gate on your way out.' As an afterthought she added, 'He doesn't say much, does he.' Presumably she was referring to Baghdad rather than Philip.

Buoyed up by the success of having got a look at the inside of the rich bastard's house, the three had an impromptu criminal planning session at Norman's heavily-mortgaged house. Kap was looking forward to some of the chocolate almonds he had partly funded, but Philip had got through all that remained. 'The housekeeper or whatever had a good few of them, remember,' he said defensively.

'Can we move to more germane issues,' said Norman. He foresaw a time when the price of a packet of almonds would be irrelevant. 'Tell us about the window and the house.'

Philip did, and the others were impressed that he had noted as instructed that the woman had not switched off any alarm when he went in, that he'd run his fingers around the window frame while retrieving Baghdad and felt no wires, and that the room seemed to be a spare bedroom. 'Bingo,' said Kap. 'That's the way to go for sure. We'll be bloody in there.' Philip could also describe the basic floor plan of that part of the house he'd seen. He was beginning to think he had a natural aptitude for crime, but he said nothing of that to the others. He tried to think of any criminal poet of note and none came to mind. Oscar Wilde was in another category. Surely there was an opportunity in such a situation. Maybe he could expand his poem on burglary into a series of odes, or a blank-verse ballad. Experience beyond the law could perhaps give his poetry a hard, anti-social edge that would appeal to a worldly reading public previously unimpressed with his writing.

Philip hadn't featured in the original plan of the night robbery of the rich bastard, but after his success with the parrot he had the confidence to argue for his inclusion on the basis of inside knowledge. Norman came round to the idea too, more on the grounds that all three of them should share equal responsibility. Kap would have preferred to act alone. He imagined Philip blundering into things in the rich bastard's darkened house, and Norman having an inflexible and complex plan of action. 'Okay, okay,' he said, 'three musketeers it bloody is, but once in I call the tune, eh?' Norman and Philip agreed.

They chose a night with a small moon, and were favoured as well with cloud cover. First they took the aluminium ladder by car, and Philip and Kap squeezed it through the bars of the wrought iron gate, then hid it in the rich bastard's shrubbery, while Norman drove back several streets and parked before joining them on foot. The three of them stood for some minutes out of sight, waiting to see if they had been noticed. The breeze of the winter night was cold and dry, catching in their throats and sinuses. Philip couldn't repress an urge to quote — '"Is there anybody there?" said the traveller, knocking on the moonlit door.'

'Knock it off,' hissed Kap. He wore dark blue overalls, and since entering the rich bastard's grounds had put on a balaclava which gave him a suitably villainous appearance despite his skinny frame and lack of height. In jerseys and sneakers the other two were still innocuous despite unconsciously adopting theatrical crouches and whispers. There was one barking dog, far off towards the main road.

Kap led the way towards the south side of the large house, and Norman and Philip carried the ladder behind him, sinking into a flower bed they had overlooked in the darkness. When the ladder was positioned beneath the window ledge on which Baghdad had perched, Kap climbed up with an almost carefree agility. He took a portion of old tea towel studded with Blu-Tack from inside his shirt and stuck it on the window, then struck it firmly with the back of his hand. They heard a little glass fall inside, but there wasn't much noise, and after shivering silently for a minute or two to make sure the breaking pane occasioned no lights or movement, they decided to go in. Kap carefully folded the towel around what glass adhered to it, and passed it to Norman behind him, then he reached in and unlatched the window. He went through with one sinuous movement and in the light of his small torch cleared shards from the carpet so that Norman and Philip wouldn't tread on them. Both of them had more difficulty clambering through, but eventually all three were standing inside and Kap drew the window frame in. The ladder was enough cause for suspicion without an open window as well.

'See, it's a spare bedroom,' said Philip, as he made a quick inventory with his flashlight, but the others were not as impressed with his local knowledge when they were inside themselves.

'Keep your light pointed down,' Kap said.

It was a large room, soft carpeted and with a matching suite in dark, highly polished wood. There was a silver-backed brush and comb set on the duchess and a Venetian vase without flowers, but no personal items. The bedclothes were half folded back and without sheets. Norman and Philip had concentrated so much on the objective of gaining entry to the rich bastard's house, that they were somewhat nonplussed as to what to do now it was achieved. They waited in the darkness for Kap's leadership. It wasn't cold: the rich bastard obviously had a very efficient heating system which reached even the unused rooms of the house.

'I reckon the rooms below are the most likely,' Kap said, and headed quietly down the passage to the stairs. In the darkness his balaclava head was like the unsharpened end of a giant pencil. Norman and Philip followed, keeping their pin-point lights directed at the carpet apart from brief flashes to get their bearings. Philip enjoyed the wonderful smoothness of the balustrade as he went down the stairs: everything about the home was superbly grand to him. The downstairs passage was even more impressive in the night than he remembered from his day visit with Baghdad, and the leadlight flowers in the front door panels gave just the faintest glows of red, yellow and blue.

By the cautious opening of several doors, Kap soon found which room was which. The formal lounge could have accommodated Philip's entire flat, with rank on rank of shadowy sofas and armchairs. Kap gave a long exhalation of satisfaction when they reached the study. It was a large, book-lined room with a bay window at the far end. The light from Kap's torch flitted over the book spines, the heavy leather chairs, the polished desk and cabinets. He drew the curtains in the bay window, careful not to touch the window or its surrounds, and turned on the brass desk lamp.

The rich bastard may have been elderly, and keen on traditional furnishings, but he was obviously not behind the times in respect of communications. There was a state-of-the-art PC set up on the desk, as well as the most expensive model laptop in an open travelling case of tooled leather. 'My God,' whispered Norman, 'you could crack Pentagon codes with this thing.' Philip, who still wrote longhand in a school exercise book, just gaped at the apparatus as a cannibal would at the whiteman's musket.

'If we can't find anything else, we'll have that laptop,' said Kap.

But what they really wanted of course was a commodity that couldn't be traced — cash best of all. Kap began to go through the desk drawers. Two were locked, but posed little obstacle for Kap, who marred the burr walnut with a little noise and no qualms. The first drawer held personal diaries going back over twenty years, the second had financial records, chequebooks both current and exhausted — and two large, white envelopes with a good deal of money in each. Kap ruffled through, and the only colours that showed were the rust and red of hundred-dollar bills. 'This is the rich bastard's petty cash,' said Kap bitterly. For him, the stunning inequality in respective financial positions justified some redistribution.

For Philip, so much cash could only be explained if the rich bastard were engaged in nefarious activities. Of the three, Norman faced the greatest test of conscience, having by experience and house ownership some sense of property rights. But he steeled himself by the thought of his growing overdraft and the scandalous neglect of his talent. 'Anything else worth taking, do you think?' he asked, pushing himself to total commitment.

There were objects of course, some silver, and paintings that were original, as Norman knew from drawing a finger softly across the surface of a couple to feel the raised pigment. The three poets had talked about art works in their planning sessions, and decided they were not only awkward to get safely through the upper window and away, but difficult to sell without arousing suspicion. While Norman and Kap fossicked in the rich bastard's cabinets, Philip drifted to the bookshelves at the far extent of the light from the desk lamp. He used his torch discreetly. 'There's a lot of poetry here,' he said. 'A good deal of the nineteenth-century romantics, but also more modern stuff — the Black Mountain school and so on.' He carefully took a handful of the slimmer volumes whose titles he couldn't read on their reduced spines, and spread them on the bookcase ledge. 'There's even New Zealand poets,' he said, 'and the better ones at that, except we're not represented of course.'

It was not a welcome discovery to find that the rich bastard was a lover of poetry. They preferred to think they were robbing a philistine whose only interest was money. 'It'll all be just for show,' said Kap. 'Don't you bloody worry about that.'

'There's some wonderful first editions of Georgian poetry,' said Philip as a result of investigating further.

'Investment you see, that's what it's about, rather than any artistic affinity,' put in Norman. He was wondering if his poetic muse would be tainted by the night's activities, but then thought of his swelling mortgage.

'Anyway,' said Kap, 'Let's quit checking the bastard's books and get out of here with what we've got.' Kap realised that the less they got to know about their victim, the easier their consciences would be.

Norman put out the desk lamp and they went back down the wide lower passage and up the stairs. Was there just the slight reverberation of the rich bastard's snores as the three headed for the particular spare bedroom that gave access to the ladder? They went down in ascending order of agility — first Philip, who had difficulty getting through the window, followed by Norman, and then Kap, who took just a moment beforehand to put the silver brush, comb and mirror inside his shirt. The metal ladder was very cold.

The cloud had lifted a little, and in the weak light of the moon their breath made smoky plumes in the cold air. They scuttled awkwardly into the shrubbery with the ladder, and Kap went to bring the car to the gate. The rich bastard lived in an area where people slept soundly and lacked frivolity — perhaps lacked small children as well. There was no traffic and no lights were visible in the large, well-spaced houses. When Kap returned, Philip and Norman tied the ladder to the roof rack and Kap drove them gently away, his hair on end not from guilt, or anxiety, but because he had pulled the balaclava free of his head.

'How much do you think there is?' asked Philip.

Keeping one hand on the wheel, Kap took the two bulky envelopes from his jacket. 'Thousands,' he said. He passed them to Norman beside him, who in turn handed one to Philip in the back seat. 'All in bloody hundreds, you see,' said Kap, 'and for that rich bastard it's so much chicken feed.'

They drove through the winter night with a sense of successful brotherhood. Each of them felt a surprisingly avaricious satisfaction, but also a surge of creativity. Kap revelled in the irony that the rich bastard's money would support him while he wrote his epic verse tribute to the joint colonial contribution of the tangata whenua and the nameless immigrant workers. Norman, his mortgage now safely beaten back for a while, had recovered his self-respect and ached to push on with the winnowing of his poetic oeuvre with a 'best of' collection in mind, while Philip saw the realistic prospect at last of being able to launch his blank verse history of the world into the bookshops and the hearts of readers everywhere. Surely the poetry of all three would in time grace the rich bastard's bookshelves, though he would never realise his role in bringing that about. Time would tell whether their muse could countenance their sins.

a modern story

IF RUTH WAS WORKING LATE, BEFORE a court day, say, or a quarterly review with a corporate client, she would relax for a few minutes every two hours by listening to talkback radio. The mixture of absolute dogmatism and complete ignorance on the part of both callers and host would often set her laughing at midnight. She wept with delight sometimes, and would copy down malapropisms, truisms and fatuous pronouncements to repeat to her colleagues. Talkback gave a voice to a nether world whose denizens seemed to vanish at cock crow and the dawn of reason.

She was listening to Graeme of Putaruru who claimed to be effluent in three languages, when her lover called. 'What are you wearing?' he asked. 'Just kidding. No, the thing is I've got to come up with a fourth panellist for the session on public perception of DOC policy.'

'It's a known fact, isn't it,' said Graeme of Putaruru, 'I mean you can't be rich and honest, eh? Know what I mean?'

'I'm flat out,' Ruth said.

'Love it when you talk dirty, but I'm really pushed here and it would be such a help, it really would.'

'Decent citizens, though,' Graeme of Putaruru was saying, 'decent citizens won't put up with stuff like that. I mean, in a nutshell, think of the kids and that. Money's just money when you come right down to it. You can't take it with you. Stands to reason, really.'

'I haven't time right now,' said Ruth.

'I know, but you'll do it and I adore you,' her lover said before she could put the phone down.

'You're a man after my own heart, Graeme,' said the radio talkback host. 'One of the silent majority not afraid to be heard. Good on you, mate.'

Dr Tom Cleves was her lover. Dr Tom was a great talker and not bad-looking in a gawky sort of way. Dr Tom could talk a cat out of tree, and had long wrists and ankles that protruded from his cuffs. He was a senior lecturer whose speciality was geomorphology, and he was especially sensitive to the disparity between his salary and Ruth's income. Probably in his heart he agreed with Graeme of Putaruru, though he would have expressed it more impressively. Not to Ruth, of course.

Ruth was a few months from forty, and considered first rate at her job in a profession which paid dividends for being so. She wasn't quite such a glib talker as Dr Tom, but she was brighter, better organised and worked harder. Her other advantage was that she was a woman. She looked just fine in a tight winter skirt, and she realised how susceptible to flattery men were: especially about attributes they wished they possessed. Take Judge Sparner, for instance. The judge was a very smart man, but didn't need any affirmation of that. When young, though, he had hankered to be a sportsman, and still laboured through the city streets at dusk to stop himself getting fat. Ruth only needed to see him at it once, pale almost to luminosity in the twilight and with a red reflector strip on his T-shirt. The next time they met socially, she told him casually that he had the figure of an athlete and must have threatened the clock when he was young. Nothing more was needed. Thereafter in Judge Sparner's court she might jut her hip a trifle, but didn't need the obsequiousness shown by most other counsel to get his sympathy.

Even Justice Hawke, who presided in a higher court, was won over without ever realising Ruth's calculation. His wife told her that he had the idiosyncrasy of being an obsessive Janeite, and so when before him she would include subtle allusions to Mrs Bennet, Frank Churchill, Pemberley and Mansfield Park. Justice Hawke would lift his eyes from the boredom of the bench in quizzical appreciation and recognition, and was known to have said in chambers that Ruth was the epitome of sound, modern counsel.

Dr Tom told Ruth more about the DOC panel when they met on Thursday for lunch at the Avanti Café. Their meetings during week days were almost always outside the bedroom, because Ruth worked hard, and being unmarried and well off could restrict sex to a pleasant relaxation at her discretion. Dr Tom's feelings on the issue were not canvassed, despite his fluency of expression. 'We've got the regional head of DOC, the local Greenie candidate, and that Eckhold character who's chairman of the Tourism Operators' Trust,' said Dr Tom, 'We need you when legal issues come up.'

'I don't know anything about DOC and environment legislation.'

'Come on, Ruth. A couple of hours browsing through the DOC establishment document and the conservation acts, and you'll run rings round them.' They both knew it was true. 'It's not rocket science, just a feel good session to show the department is conscious of the need for community outreach, as the dean likes to put it. His own outreach is restricted to women postgrad students.'

When Ruth analysed her relationship with Dr Tom, she came

to the conclusion that his volubility and general knowledge were important to her. She herself tended to a reducing focus on the law, which was mitigated by the broader view of her lover. Dr Tom lacked her cutting edge, but was more interested in the wider world and better informed of it. He read, he listened, he questioned, he assimilated and assessed. And, like all born teachers, he liked to instruct others. For much of the time they were together, Ruth was able to treat him rather as a quality radio programme, taking in a good deal of material when she thought it useful, and tuning him out otherwise. The advantage of his not being a radio was that she could prompt him by her questions. Dr Tom acted as informant and research assistant as well as occasional partner.

So she could hardly refuse to help by being on the panel to discuss the role of DOC. The evening was held in the university's Great Hall, and the panel discussion preceded by twenty minutes of chamber music by the music department's tutors. It was a chill night, and the limited heat from the old radiators drifted upwards towards the lofty ceiling. About one hundred and fifty people sat clustered together in coats, scarves; a few wore beanies. Even the classical music seemed rather pinched and thin, although it carried well in the cold air. Dr Tom had the task of thanking the musicians, and introducing and chairing the panel discussion.

'For God's sake don't take all night getting things under way,' Ruth had told him, but Dr Tom had come across an anecdote concerning Shostakovich which went down rather well, and made a virtuoso display of puffery in his introduction of each panellist in turn. Dr Tom was born and raised in Otago, but bore no resemblance to the stereotype of Southern Man. He was all attenuated sensitivity and ardent communication. He spoke without notes, without a stumble; he raised a laugh or two quite without causing offence, but Ruth was disappointed that he wore a bulky jersey and that the flaps of his jacket were inside the pockets. The dress sense of academics was the butt of some of her most caustic comments in chambers.

The Greenie and Ruth were excellent speakers, the other two only so-so. The Greenie woman and Ruth agreed on quite a few points, including the unspoken one that they disliked each other. Their appearance made the gulf between them obvious. The Greenie had ginger hair, fat cheeks, and a paua medallion the size of a dustbin lid; Ruth was black and white, except for fine, blue stockings on her shapely legs which were at once discreetly erotic and more overtly intellectual. Ruth spoke less than the others on the panel, but received equal applause to the Greenie at the end of the night. Had men been better represented, she would have received more. Without making any claims at all, and having spent only three hours on the legislation beforehand, Ruth made such an impression of specialist expertise that she was within a week approached by two magazines for comment in articles concerned with conservation, and her firm received strong inquiry from possible clients concerned with the same issues. Dr Tom was full of rueful admiration, even though the dean gave him moderate praise and said he'd like the opportunity to see more of Ruth. Quite what impression Ruth had made on another member of the audience in the Great Hall that night wasn't apparent until several days later.

Thursday the 29th in fact: 10.29 p.m. It was a windless, cold night and Ruth was proceeding in an easterly direction from the cafés and wine bars towards her flat, which was part of an inner-city conversion of a former furniture warehouse. A man was following her at film noir distance. He crossed the street several times so as to mix his tracks with other people walking there, and he kept his distance. Ruth had first noticed him an hour or so before, when they had both been in the Pied Piper bar. She had been having a drink with Majorie Mackle, and the man had been sitting two stools down and listening as best he could. He wore a calf-length, black coat and, despite being thin on top, needed a haircut.

When she turned off into Furnell Lane he did too, more obvious and more furtive with fewer people about. When she waited an extra phase at the pedestrian lights, he didn't approach, but instead stepped into the doorway of the reflexology clinic. Ruth's flat was upstairs and reasonably secure. She felt no danger. Since her secondary school days she had been accustomed to the interest men took in her — all sorts of men. She didn't turn the light on inside the flat, but went close to the window so that she could look down into the street. The man stopped for a little outside the locked entrance to the stairs. Ruth was looking almost directly down on him so that his face was barely visible. His balding head showed clearly in the lights, though, and the longish hair over his ears. He walked on with his hands thrust deeply into the pockets of his long coat, and his shoulders slightly hunched against the cold. So, okay, now you know where I live, thought Ruth.

Five days later, when she was appearing for the prosecution in Gudsell v. Crackerjack Spray Irrigation Systems Ltd, thereinafter referred to in court as Crackerjack, Ruth recognised the man in the public seats of the courtroom. He was younger than she had assumed from the first nocturnal glimpses, and his features were regular. He took a considerable interest in the case, especially when Ruth was speaking, and after her cross-examination of the Crackerjack CEO, he clapped loudly and was rebuked by Judge Affenhalfe, known by the legal fraternity as Judge Half and Half because of his rigorous impartiality.

Ruth's next awareness of the stalker came not through a sighting, but the loss of a black bra which she had hung with other clothes on her small balcony to catch the early afternoon sun. The balcony overlooked a private carpark and service area at the back of the building, and was assumed inaccessible from there. In normal circumstances Ruth would have accepted the loss as a freak of the wind, or not noticed it at all, as she had many clothes and was usually too preoccupied to keep track of individual items. On this occasion, however, she made the connection with the man who had been following her. She examined the balcony rail and the supports, and found recent scuffing on both. It was circumstantial, but she had no doubt and took particular care after that to keep the door to the balcony locked.

And two nights later, when she was returning from her pilates class, Ruth saw the guy again. It was only just after six, but already dark, and the tenants' carpark was not well lit. He was standing silently well back by the brick wall with a collection of Otto bins around him, but she recognised the heavy coat and his hair spreading on its collar. Ruth gave no sign of having seen him, and he made no movement, said nothing, as she left the service area to reach her apartment from the street.

'Someone's stalking me,' Ruth told her mother when they talked the next day on the phone.

'He's after your body,' said Hilda matter of factly. 'Men are always after one's body. If only they could show some lust for the mind. Your father was just the same. Utterly repugnant, so I insisted the union not be consummated.'

'Don't be ridiculous, Mother,' said Ruth, 'How do you explain the existence of Anthony and me then?'

'Oh, I can't remember that far back,' said Hilda. 'Did I mention I'm suing your father again?' Ruth was amazed once more how rapidly Hilda was able to bring any conversation back to her own selfish concerns.

'A man is stalking me in the dark, Mother, stealing my underclothes, scaling my balcony.' The fact that Ruth herself wasn't greatly alarmed was surely no excuse for her mother's lack of maternal concern.

'Everyone's being stalked these days,' said Hilda. 'You're not special in that at all. They're pathetic, lost men who watch screen pornography, and then go weeping and creeping into the night. They're as common as lice in the neighbourhood here. Your father would have gone the same way if it wasn't for that hussy who works for the ministry. I believe they've been buying Italian furniture.'

Ruth knew Dr Tom would be more caring, but hesitated to tell him of the stalker lest it strengthen his case for the two of them to live together. On the other hand, her training prompted her to ensure she had some early corroboration in case she needed to resort to the law.

'How absolutely frightful for you,' said Dr Tom, in a post-coital glow the following Sunday. He was referring not to what was post, but Ruth's revelation that she was being followed. 'We'll go to the police tomorrow and have the nasty bastard arrested. It's what I've always said, though, isn't it. A good-looking woman living on her own becomes a target for exploitation in myriad ways: it signals vulnerability. I'm not suggesting any weakness on your part at all, but it's the perceived situation that attracts the con-men and creeps. And you never quite know what lengths these people will go to. Miranda Crowe in media studies let in a salesman to talk about underfloor heating, and three days later found a disembowelled hamster on her doorstep. Definitely the police tomorrow. I've no lecture until eleven.'

'No,' said Ruth. 'I just want you to be watching outside on Wednesday night when I come back from pilates so you can verify that this guy is following me. Don't approach him or anything, though. You got me on that?' She was already almost fully dressed and businesslike.

'As you wish, my darling,' said Dr Tom indulgently. The sight of Ruth dressing was surpassed only by the sight of her undressing, both rare enough. But he knew to say nothing of that.

So on Wednesday Dr Tom waited in the unlit doorway of Dwight & Dysome Real Estate at the start of Furnell Lane. He was thin and cold, and jiggled his shoulders and knees in an effort to warm up. He concentrated on the slight melodrama of his role to pass the time. I'm skulking here, he thought, waiting for my lover to pass with a stalker at her heels: well, perhaps not at her heels, but dogging her footsteps. Will her high heels echo on the night pavement, and the two shadows flicker fitfully over the disparate building fronts? Dr Tom knew well enough that Ruth would not be walking in high heels, but such imagination gave welcome distraction until reality arrived.

A tall male jogger in a hooded sweatsuit came past, his breath whistling through his teeth; two young women in loud conversation who gave Dr Tom a quick glance without ceasing talk; an Alsatian, quite alone, which ignored him and loped from one sniffing point to the next. Then Ruth from her pilates class, punctual as ever, the blue of her jacket catching the street light. And after a time with nothing in Dr Tom's view, yes, the stalker just as Ruth had described him — the long, dark coat and the uncovered long, soft hair. Dr Tom counted to twenty before leaving the doorway and following him down the street. When Ruth went into her entrance, the stalker stood out by the gutter, waiting until the light came on in the upstairs apartment. As Dr Tom drew level the stalker lifted one foot and scrutinised the sole as a reason for loitering. 'Crisp at this time of year,' said Dr Tom, but there was no reply.

Dr Tom did the block, and when he came again to Ruth's apartment no one was outside. He used the buzzer and spoke into the grille. Ruth let him in, and they sat for a while by the heater.

'Definitely the stalker,' Dr Tom said. 'And he's wearing shoes with thick, yellow soles.'

'How old, do you reckon?'

'Hard to say,' said Dr Tom. 'Maybe mid-forties, and he seems a bit beefy, though maybe that's the coat. Anyway, there's no doubt about it and we should go to the police tomorrow.'

But Ruth refused to do that. She had never, in her considerable dealings with the police, been in the role of supplicant, or victim, and didn't feel that way, despite Dr Tom's opinion. There was action that she wanted to take on her own initiative.

Dr Tom found it more difficult not to share the knowledge concerning Ruth's stalker. Over drinks with his colleague Dr Quaill of the psychology department, when their talk had come round to obsessions, Dr Tom came out with it, justifying the revelation by saying that he wanted a professional opinion as to whether Ruth was in significant danger. Dr Quaill reacted with considerable interest. He said that it so happened that he was working at that very time with television producer Ellen McElvie on a fifty-minute documentary on stalkers, and that they were looking for an on-going situation to be the core element of the programme. It would eschew prurient and sensational approaches, and could well become a defining documentary on a growing and little understood phenomenon.

Dr Tom backed off rather, aware that he wasn't authorised to mention the stalker to anyone, and here, almost before he could catch his breath, was talk of television coverage. But Dr Quaill, with his understanding of the subtleties of the mind, was not proposing that he, or Dr Tom, say anything at all to Ruth. 'These things are often best discussed within the sisterhood,' he explained. 'I imagine Ruth and Ellen McElvie to have a good deal in common, and if Ellen makes contact directly, our part in all this will be minimised. Have you noticed that tendency in the gender?'

'I have,' agreed Dr Tom.

Ruth admired Ellen McElvie's work, especially the series on the glass ceiling for professional women, and the persistence of patriarchal attitudes in legal documentation. 'We thought, through your work, you may have experience of the stalker syndrome,' Ellen said during her first phone call, 'maybe even something first hand — you're an attractive woman with a high profile. I've had unwanted attentions of that kind myself, but not lately. The programme will feature both sexes as objects of this sort of dangerous fixation, but overwhelmingly it's women at risk.'

'You understand I have to be very careful about the sort of publicity I receive, because of my work,' Ruth demurred.

'I do,' said Ellen. 'And as I think my record in the industry shows, this won't be at all tacky. We're bringing in Dr Quaill from the university here as a consultant, and a woman superintendent from police headquarters. No pressure, no pressure at all, but if you'd like to come in and talk I'd be delighted. I feel we would work well together. I feel it's an important and topical subject that needs a more rigorous study than it's received hitherto.'

Ruth was both flattered and interested, but she was accustomed to flattery and never let it overcome her perceptive rationality. It was too much of a coincidence that Ellen McElvie approached her about the programme just at the time she was being stalked. Dr Tom must have let something slip, and she saw it as further evidence that he should not have full access to her life.

It's a truism that knowledge is power, but one to which Ruth attached considerable importance. She saw it borne out almost daily in her work, and had no intention of agreeing to be part of the television programme, despite her support of its intentions, until she knew more of the man who was apparently besotted with her. She had no difficulty in obtaining that information. Howard Parsons was a private investigator often employed by Ruth's firm, and something of an acquaintance as well, though not as close as he wished. He and Ruth belonged to the same squash club.

'No contact at all,' Ruth told Howard, after giving him a description and the time she would be leaving her pilates class to walk home. 'Just the address and a name.'

'Maybe we could meet for a coffee when I've got the info?' Howard said.

'Just leave an envelope at the office,' said Ruth. 'I'm absolutely snowed under at the moment.'

'If you need any surveillance of your flat, or anything. These people can be unpredictable, you know.'

'I'm fine, Howard. Just the name and address, and absolute confidentiality. Thanks,' said Ruth. They both knew it was a class thing that stood between them, though this was not acknowledged.

Tony Plax was the stalker's name, and Ruth was easily able to access the further information she wanted. Video and DVD were Plax's livelihood. He was the proprietor of a large rental library in the Anglia Mall, and lived with his mother in the family home by the sea. Ruth could find no record of complaints, convictions or debts. Perhaps the women of his adult videos had palled, and he had switched to Ruth as a breathing fantasy in the real world. Perhaps her combination of looks and ability had a mesmerising effect on a man who existed in a morass of the average, the ordinary.

Certainly to Ruth he seemed little threat, directly or through the television programme that might disclose him. She met with Ellen McElvie, and the two women, at the top of their professions, had an immediate rapport. Ruth agreed as stalkee to be the central figure of the documentary, though she didn't say that she knew the stalker's identity. It wasn't any vulgar publicity that Ruth sought. She thought it important for women that a programme of that sort be made, and well made, and the opportunity to give her views in prime time on several social issues could only assist her career.

However, just when Plax the stalker had become of some use in Ruth's life, he stopped appearing. He was not in court, no more of her clothes went missing from the balcony line, he was not to be seen following at a distance after her pilates class or during café visits. After two weeks, and with filming to begin within a few days, Ruth gave herself twenty-three minutes between clients to think about the situation, and decided with four minutes to spare that she would be pro-active. Later that evening she rang Tony Plax. 'Are you Mr Tony Plax?' she said.

'Yes.'

'Mr Plax, my name is Ruth Doubleday. I'm the woman you have been stalking.'

Tony Plax took a long, audible breath, but said nothing.

'We need to talk,' said Ruth.

'I don't think I know you. I don't recognise the name.'

'Don't bullshit me, Mr Plax, please. Don't force me to take action to your detriment. Just make sure you're at the fern house in the botanical gardens this Sunday at 2 p.m. Two o'clock, Mr Plax.'

Ruth wanted a third party at the fern house meeting, not so

much for her safety as for a witness. She didn't wish Dr Tom to know of her plan, and in any case he had already proved incapable of keeping things to himself. 'Mother,' Ruth said to her on the telephone, 'I'm meeting the stalker in the gardens on Sunday, and I'd like you to be there. Not with me, but at a discreet distance as an observer.'

'It's my bridge on Sunday afternoons,' said Hilda. 'You know I have a regular partner and that it's bridge on Sunday in the winter, and golf from October to April.'

'It's quite important to me.'

'That's just what your father used to say: it's important to me. But is it important to me? I used to reply. I never cease to be amazed at the selfishness of people. He had the nerve to come round, you know, asking for some family photographs.'

'It would only be a few minutes at two o'clock. I've told the stalker to meet me at the fern house.'

'Why can't he come to you?' said Hilda. 'I thought that was the benefit of stalkers, that they always came to you, and now the two of us have to go off to the gardens to meet him. There's nothing in the gardens at this time of year except dead heads and duck droppings.'

'Do you still want those duty-free perfumes when I go to Sydney next week?' said Ruth evenly.

'Just a few minutes then,' said Hilda. 'I'd have to be home by two thirty otherwise we won't get through enough hands to make it worthwhile. I'll make my own way there.'

Sunday had a shroud of diaphanous cloud behind which the winter sun was just a pale glow. The fern house was heated, and Ruth stood just within the doors, brushing the fronds of hare's-foot fern with her coat. She had deployed Hilda deeper within the green aisles, almost out of sight and comfortably out of earshot unless voices were raised. In appearance Hilda was the most innocuous of minders: small and skinny, and with thinning hair despite the time and money she spent on it. Her shoes and handbag were Florentine, her coat English, her perennial expression one of homegrown dissatisfaction. She mouthed at Ruth and tapped her watch impatiently.

It was the cue for Tony Plax to appear at the end of the path between the drab winter beds and approach the fern house. He strolled with a pretence of confidence that wavered when he saw Ruth behind the glass door. At the entrances he stood abashed, not able to reach out and open the door and be face to face with the woman of his fantasies. It was Ruth who opened the door. 'Come inside, Mr Plax. We can't talk in the cold and it's private in here.' How naturally she assumed territorial possession of the fern house although she had no greater share of ownership than Plax.

'I don't quite know . . .' said Tony Plax.

'No,' said Ruth. She was of equal height, had perfectly arched eyebrows and a direct gaze.

'I'm not sure why you wanted to see me. I don't think we, ah, actually know each other.' A bowed frond of elkhorn was undulating in the disturbed air of Plax's peripheral vision and he found it difficult to look directly at Ruth.

Time is money in the professional world, and in the upper echelons of that world time has a scarcity value beyond even money. Ruth was also aware that Hilda's bridge friends would soon be gathering. 'Mr Plax, you've been following me in the night. You've clambered onto my balcony and stolen an item of clothing. You've drawn attention to yourself in court in cases with which I've been involved. You're a stalker, Mr Plax.'

'Maybe we've happened to be in the same place together, or going in the same direction. There's no harm in that. Anyway, not lately I haven't.'

'Enough of this prevarication — I have credible witnesses,' said Ruth. 'You stalked me for several weeks, and then abruptly you stopped. Normally that would be the end of the matter, because I'm not at all interested in your sordid motivations. The fact is, however, that I'm to feature in a television documentary concerning stalkers, and I require you to continue as such until the programme is complete. Apart from that we need have nothing to do with each other.' Ruth could assume her formal and directive manner very easily; Dr Tom considered there was a danger of it becoming her normal voice.

Tony Plax made an effort to assert himself. 'First you accuse me of stalking you, and then complain that I've stopped. What sort of — ah — jiggery pokery is that?' He knew that he had begun quite well, and ended weakly. 'I don't know what you're on about, and don't want anything to do with any TV programme.'

'The bridge people will be at my house,' shrilled Hilda from her half-shrouded position far down the fern house.

'My God, who's that?' said the startled Plax.

'Some mad woman,' said Ruth. 'Nothing to do with us.'

'Anyway, I won't do it,' said Plax.

'Either you agree to do it here and now, or I leave for the police station immediately.'

Mr Plax was fairly caught and he knew it. What had seemed so bright and tantalising, what he had reached out for hesitantly, had become his master. 'Please don't,' he said. 'Okay then, I'll carry on as before just until the TV thing is over.'

'All you have to do is be yourself, be a stalker, for three more weeks. I don't care what you say, or don't say, if you're approached.'

'You seem different to me now,' said Tony Plax sadly. 'It's what I've been feeling, that there's something hard about you outside court as well as in.'

'I can't remain another instant,' called Hilda, bearing down on them in thin animation, so that the ferns bobbed and curtsied and Ruth and Mr Plax had to stand single file to allow her past. She clutched her Italian handbag for security as she went by Tony Plax, left the conservatory door open and headed for the carpark.

The cold air eddied into the fern house. 'One more thing,' said Ruth as she turned her collar up and prepared to go. 'You're to have a haircut and buy a decent pair of shoes. The coat's passable, but I won't be stalked by a man with hair spreading onto his collar and such cheap shoes. I happen to know you're not without means.'

'I'll be glad when it's over,' said Plax with sudden vehemence.

In his humiliation he could think of nothing else to say. Despite knowing he was in the wrong, he felt deeply he was the victim of obscure injustice.

'You have only yourself to blame,' said Ruth as she put on her gloves and left the fern house. 'You're lucky to get off so lightly. Close the door after yourself.' Plax did so with a show of petulance.

'I just wanted to get to know you a bit,' he said, beginning from habit to follow her and then stopping. 'There's no crime in wanting to get to know someone you admire, I reckon.' He fingered the long hair at the side of his face, as if conscious of it for the first time. 'Anyway,' he said, 'You're different than I thought.'

Ruth didn't bother to make any answer. He had taken up as much of her Sunday as she could spare. Hilda was right: the park was all dead heads, duck shit and frost beneath the bushes in winter. There was court work to be prepared, and Dr Tom would have to be put off so that she could get it done.

It was an excellent documentary, a critical and ratings success beyond any other that year, and won two prizes at the annual television awards. Ruth was confidentially invited to consider joining the judiciary, but chose instead to continue a remarkable career in private practice. Occasionally she agreed to appear on the more serious television programmes, and she continued to take a particular pleasure in listening to talkback radio. Dr Tom felt increasingly marginalised in the lofty significance and affluence of her life, and married Miranda Crowe from media studies within eighteen months. Tony Plax, having been given a stern lesson in the workings of the modern world, faded back into the nondescript existence that is the fate of most of us.

family circle

NAYLOR HAD KNOWN SINCE HE WAS FIVE years old that he was adopted. The only mother he knew told him, in the presence of the only father he knew, and because he loved them both it didn't bother him. As far as he could recall, no one during his childhood had accused him of being a bastard on any other grounds than personality, and being adopted was an okay thing. He'd known several kids who were adopted and it was no big deal.

Although older than most, his mother and father seemed much the same as other parents; better than many too. He'd invited mates home feeling quite easy about his position there and his friends' reception. Naylor and his parents ignored his adoption. The three of them were happy with the family the way it was. Naylor didn't spend time in adolescence looking at himself in the mirror and wondering about his genetic inheritance, or whether he was related to someone famous.

He knew he was loved, but even that he thought little about. He just got on with the selfish and absorbing business of growing up — and he was good at it. He did well physically and intellectually. He worked quite hard and got prizes, but not so hard that he isolated himself from his fellows, or aroused animosity. His parents gave support and encouragement without promoting an exaggerated view of him as special. Both of them were achievers, and so achievement was accepted, even expected in a non-demanding way. Opportunity, application, achievement was the natural sequence.

When the crisis came, adoption wasn't the cause, or at the centre of it. His parents, Helen and Greg, became seriously ill together, as they had done most things together and seriously, although their afflictions were different. Helen was diagnosed with leukaemia, and Greg with systemic heart disease two months later.

Naylor received the news of the outcome of his mother's tests while he was at Bristol University doing the postgraduate one-year MSc course in management. 'Your mother's got leukaemia, I'm afraid. We've just come back from the clinic,' said his father, emotion and constraint at odds in his voice. The window of Naylor's second-storey flat faced Wales, he was told, but all he could see was the high façade of a shoe shop with giant advertisements. He watched the colours leach out, the poster expressions become more fatuous as he talked with his father. 'No, we think you should see the year out, Naylor. It's the sensible thing. But your mother looks forward enormously to your return, you know that.' In blatant refutation of Naylor's sense of the world, the early promise of sunlight was on the city.

It was dark, however, and slanting rain glinted multi-tinted in the shifting light of the shoe shop neons, when his mother rang two months later. Naylor stood at the same window to receive the second blow. It occurred to him that was the typical way of it — his father ringing to pass on the bad news about his mother, and then she in turn being emissary for Greg. Both undoubted concern and a desire for control were evident in that, perhaps. Was it easier to question an intermediary rather than the sick person personally? 'They think it's a congenital thing,' she said. 'At least that persistent tiredness is explained now. There's a decision to be made concerning the advisability of surgery. The worrying thing, too, is that he insists on looking after me when he's not up to it.'

Nothing truly awful had happened in their lives before, and now two of them faced imminent death, and the third was on the other side of the world in pyjamas, watching sleet machine gun a street slick and gleaming in the night. 'We want you to stick it out over there and finish the course. Only a few weeks to go really, aren't there, and it doesn't make sense to come back so close to completion. Your father's very keen on you finishing and not worrying too much about us.' The typical rationality of it took him closer to tears than any discussion of symptoms, or prognosis, for it was so much part of their natures, and he had benefited from it so often. In his final weeks at the university he began to have powerfully disturbing dreams of childhood, and his academic work suffered. His world was breaking up.

It was not Bristol's fault, but his year there became almost entirely negative in retrospect: pleasant things were overwhelmed by concern for his father and mother, and guilt for staying on, although that was their wish. The city that he had found unpretentious, yet truly cultural, became just a place of exile, and the university course an unwelcome tie. He took no gifts from England to bring home, and instead bought jade turtles for his parents at Singapore airport on his way back. What he would have liked to unwrap for them was good health, but that was beyond him; beyond him also was an adequate expression of his love and gratitude.

He made the attempt on his first evening home, when he and his father sat by his mother's bed, and Helen and Greg told him of the rather precipitate sale they had made of their joint optometry practice, and their hope that his firm wouldn't shift him away from Wellington now that he was back, so that he could live in their home as he had for so many years. The house had been built by Greg's father and had a clear view over Evans Bay, where the planes would come flying low on their descent to the airport when the wind was southerly.

His mother had a special pillow, rather like a massive and inflated bow tie, which both raised and supported her. She was at a stage of her illness which gave her a passing elegance as she thinned. Only too soon that attrition would become monstrous. 'We've decided not to have treatment,' she said. 'The specialists say medical intervention wouldn't gain a great deal of time.' Naylor's father had told him all that in considerable detail, but he realised his mother gained some comfort by being able to go over it all now that he was home with her again. He held her left hand, which throbbed with a surprisingly strong pulse, and was warm and dry to the touch. 'Your father wants me to be able to stay here as long as possible, and of course I want that, but only if he doesn't insist on trying to do everything himself and jeopardise his own health. I'm going to have someone to help, in addition to the hospital nurse visits. It's expensive, of course, that sort of private care.'

'Naylor doesn't care how much it costs,' remonstrated his father.

'You must have everything that helps,' said Naylor. The term medical intervention still lingered in his mind: one of those expressions that doctors proffer, and patients accept for the small comfort of its precision.

'I'm just being realistic. We have to watch money now that both of us have stopped working, and the clinic's sold,' Helen said.

Both his parents were astute in matters of business, but his mother was the one who had dealt with the financial side of their profession, while his father had concentrated on keeping up to date with advances in optometry. She went over the investment of the sale money with him, and the other main family assets.

Naylor could see what a worthwhile distraction it was for her. She took evident satisfaction in the security she and Greg had built up while still having full lives. Naylor made himself ask questions and keep the topic alive. As the three of them talked, he realised that his mother's concern wasn't entirely that he himself was a beneficiary, but that money was a weapon against her death. Not in any futile effort to defeat that end, or even prolong it, but to preserve dignity and choice; to have the palliatives to avoid some coarse, ignominious farewell. He was ashamed to find he knew virtually nothing of her childhood in which such fear of poverty must have been grounded. 'There'll be money left for you when we're gone,' she told him with evident satisfaction. 'We've always been determined on that.' And Greg nodded, not at all offended by the assumption that his own death was near.

'I don't need any money,' Naylor said. 'I'm fine. My job's fine.' He didn't have any student debt because they had supported him through varsity; he had a good job and even better prospects. 'You and Dad should take every medical advantage, irrespective of cost.'

'Oh, we've paid into insurance for years so at least that's okay,' she said. 'Tell me about your university work. We haven't congratulated you properly about the MSc yet.'

His mother had always had a pale and even complexion, but on her thin face and neck he noticed patches of pink, and the tendons of her neck were evident even though she lay propped and apparently relaxed. She'd had a hairdresser come the day before he arrived home, so that she could look her best.

Naylor told them of his course, his tutors, the New Zealand expat geographer who had befriended him, and whom he'd visited frequently in Bath on a borrowed Vespa scooter, avoiding the motorway. A large plane came up the bay as they talked, and from habit they paused their conversation for the brief time of maximum noise, then resumed quite naturally. His mother had a view across the water towards Miramar and took an interest in yachts and the occasional fuel ship which she'd been too busy to notice before.

'I missed you both a lot,' said Naylor. 'Seeing things over there, the struggle some people have for a decent opportunity, I reckon I've been lucky. You've both made it easy for me.' He had the inclination to say more, but the family wasn't overtly demonstrative, and with both his parents unwell it didn't seem a time to become emotional. He could feel his mother's hand throbbing within the palm of his own. 'By the way,' he said, and stood, held up a finger for patience and mystery, then went to his room to fetch the Singaporean jade turtles. Turtle talk provided a release of sorts, even though death had joined them to make a foursome which wouldn't be broken until Helen left with that new partner.

Naylor worked only mornings for what was left of the year. A nurse visited each day, soon twice each day. Naylor and his father encouraged friends to come in the mornings, because Helen tired quickly. For some time they had a drive in the afternoons to Makara perhaps, or Days Bay and Eastbourne, but that, too, was eventually a labour for her, so the afternoons became a time of rest for both parents: Helen propped in the arms of her encompassing pillow, Greg in his own room with a less exalted view of agapanthus and red hot pokers in the sloping garden. Both of them seemed to sleep more easily in the afternoons with the curtains drawn, than during the nights, when Naylor would hear his father pad clumsily to the lavatory, and not flush it in an unavailing effort to leave others undisturbed. And hear his mother's plaintive, reduced cough, or wake when his own doorway was vaguely illuminated with the last reaches of the light from her room as she sought distraction.

Some of those afternoons he worked in the garden, although it was a task he disliked, because he knew Greg might attempt it himself if the section became unruly. Both his parents loathed neglect and untidiness. Some afternoons he went into the city to a wine bar, whether he had a friend to meet or not. Some afternoons he sat with his mother, who had lost all elegance, except that of her nature.

Several times when she was awake during those afternoons she at last wanted to talk about not being his birth mother, knowing that soon he would be on his own. She said they had hoped having an adopted child would lead to them conceiving one of their own, which happened often, but not in her case. That wasn't the main reason for adopting him, she emphasised. He was wanted very much for himself. 'For years I was afraid of any odd-looking letter which came, in case it was from your mother, or the adoption authorities, and you'd be taken away from us for some reason. I tried not to show that fear, but recently when we were talking about you, Greg said he had exactly the same apprehensions, especially just after the new adoption legislation came into effect in 1986.'

'But I'd be ten then.'

'But we always knew your birth parents would be somewhere, and surely they'd love you.'

'Well, obviously they didn't care enough to make the effort, and it's never really bothered me. You know that.'

That particular afternoon the sky was very blue, and the sea of the bay also. Naylor wore shorts and his Bristol University T-shirt. He sat on one of the wooden kitchen chairs that had become a fixture by his mother's bed. Terminal illness seemed an anomaly on such a day, and his mother, though weak, wanted to talk rather than sleep. 'You know it's all quite straightforward now, finding birth parents. There's a whole website on it. You must have done a search?'

'I haven't,' Naylor said truthfully. 'You and Dad never brought it up, and it never bothered me. What's the point, after all?'

His mother thought there were several points, the most significant that she was dying and that Greg's life was insecure, but she made only oblique reference to what was so self-evident, while the blue sea shimmered, and six or seven small yachts of the same class drew wakes upon it. She told him it could be important some day to have medical knowledge about his parents, and that the longer he put off trying to make contact the more difficult it would be.

'We've got a copy of your birth certificate,' she said. 'We were given it when we adopted you. I don't think many got that.' She took it from a heavy, brown envelope on the bed and passed it to her son. The certificate gave his full name as Naylor Robin Coombes and his mother's as Frances Emily Coombes. There was nothing in the space reserved for the father. 'There'll come a time when you'll want to take it all further,' his mother said. 'I'm sorry now we didn't do something earlier. The more people who love you the better.'

'I don't think I've missed out on anything at all,' Naylor told his mother.

That evening Naylor and his father had a slow walk while the nurse gave Helen a bed wash. An easy walk was good for Greg's heart, the doctors said. Unfortunately Hataitai was mostly up and down and they had only one route that didn't involve exertion. Naylor was tall, but his father was even taller. They had always enjoyed the private joke when people referred to Greg having passed on that gene to his son. Greg had a habit of stooping to other people in conversation which some mistook for condescension, but was consideration. Naylor watched his father's tall, slender body sway as he walked, rather as a giraffe sways front to back, not side to side, so that the high body remains in balance. His father was an abstemious man who didn't smoke, ate sparingly and drank good whisky when he drank at all. It certainly wasn't lifestyle that gave him a dicky heart. Maybe it was the asthma that had troubled him especially when he was younger. Despite himself, Naylor thought of what his mother had said regarding a medical history. He wasn't aware of any particular weaknesses, but who knew what his genes had in store for him.

Naylor kept his pace down, and told his father about the birth certificate and Helen's new-found enthusiasm for him to make some inquiries regarding his birth parents. Greg squeezed his eyes shut momentarily and compressed his lips, as he did when making some concession, some declaration, or coming upon emotion. 'Your birth mother did get in touch,' he said. 'It wasn't long after the new legislation and some counsellor or other approached me with a letter from her. That's the way they do it evidently, or they did then. I accepted the letter, but didn't tell Helen. You know how she feared just that. I accepted it, and replied saying I thought it best that contact wasn't made. You were going off to secondary school and had enough to cope with.'

'What did it say?'

'Just that she didn't want to poke in after all those years, but she'd never forgotten you and would appreciate any information. I told her I didn't think it was the right time, and that was it. There weren't any more letters. I don't know what happened to that one, otherwise I'd give it to you even now.'

They stood on the corner that marked the turning point of their walk. The sun had gone beyond the hill and dusk was blurring the sharper demarcations of the day. A steady breeze came in from the sea, which was hidden from view. 'I had to make a decision, and I hope it was the right one,' his father said. 'I admit it was as much for us as for you, especially Helen.'

'You did it for the best — and it probably was.'

His mother almost stopped eating in the last weeks, and died earlier than the doctors, or her family, expected. She went on a morning she was being visited by a relative she'd never much liked, and while Greg was making coffee. He told Naylor maybe she chose to avoid the visitor in that way. It was a form of humour Helen would have enjoyed. The funeral was non-religious and well-attended, and both husband and son spoke, but Naylor felt a dissociation and lack of grief which arose not from any deficiency of love, but an inability to accept that someone so integral in his life was there no more. No reference was made to Naylor being adopted: most people wouldn't have been aware of that.

Afterwards, though, he found himself thinking about it a

good deal, and talking about it too with his father. It was not at all that he sought replacement for his mother, but for the first time he felt curiosity, which was partly the consequence of his mother's death: a sense of permission when the inquiry she had encouraged could not possibly threaten her.

Greg was encouraging also, perhaps partly as a self-imposed penitence for stifling that approach by letter many years before. And the mystery of it was a mild intrigue. 'Of course your birth mother may be dead, your father too for all we know, but I think you should consider them as well as yourself. Maybe your birth mother is all alone, or unhappy. Maybe she still wants to know about you. And there's no obligation on either side: that's the good thing, as I see it. Definitely no obligation. None at all.'

They were talking in the lounge on the evening of the day spent helping Helen's sister pack up her things. In time, his father said, he'd move back into the main bedroom with its en suite and view over the sea, but not for a while. Helen's presence was still strong there, and neither wished to diminish it. During the nights immediately after the funeral, Naylor had woken sometimes thinking his mother had turned on her light, thinking he heard her muffled cough. There would be nothing, though his father still padded to the lavatory, still left it unflushed — habit, or a transferred consideration, Naylor wondered. His aunt had suggested some of Helen's jewellery be given to her female relations, nieces in particular, though no such bequests were in the will. Naylor was surprised at the vehemence with which his normally placid father refused to consider that. Naylor was to have it all, he said. They'd talked about it, he said, he and Helen, and just because Naylor was male didn't mean the personal stuff shouldn't be his. And just because he wasn't theirs by blood didn't mean that either, though neither Greg nor his sister-in-law spoke of that. 'Give away the clothes and all that spare linen in any way you like,' Greg had said. 'And take what you like of the dinnerware sets. We're indebted to you for your help.'

In the evening, though, he did talk of adoption and Naylor's options. 'It's completely up to you,' he said. 'You've already got the birth certificate. You can look up the surname in the Telecom White Pages: it's not a very common name. If she's married since then you can check the marriage records. It's up to you, though. Maybe something good could come of it for you and her, maybe not.'

Greg clearly saw the likelihood that he might soon follow Helen, and that Naylor would be left only relatives with whom he had legal connection. Although his father rarely talked of love, he was both sensitive and consistent in its application.

It was a distraction as much as anything else at first, the search for Frances Emily Coombes, and it had as well the element of detection. Naylor was surprised, however, by the comparative ease with which he was able to track his mother down. The changes to the law facilitated it, as did access to official records, and he soon knew Frances was still alive, that she had married and taken the surname of Hollister, and that she lived in Sydney by the zoo. The hard part was deciding if he wanted to make contact after leaving it so long. The satisfaction of his only recently aroused curiosity would be little compensation if any reunion turned out badly, and it wasn't as if he felt any driving need to find Frances, even after Helen's death.

It was a dream that made up his mind. Nothing apocalyptic, or even particularly surreal. He dreamt his father died in the same way as his mother and of the same disease, and that at the funeral, which was held in a very open, paddock-like space, a spiky-haired woman wearing an orange skivvy and grubby tracksuit pants stood up unbidden, and said that the loss of parents was sad but natural, while the loss of a child was unnatural and grievous. Naylor didn't at all think the woman represented his birth mother — rather she reminded him of a mature student in his Bristol University study group whom he'd rather disliked — but the idea that his mother might have suffered in some significant way because she was denied knowledge of him, remained strong.

He said nothing to Greg about the dream. His father would

be doubtful of such provenance for any contact with Frances Coombes, or Hollister. Naylor gave instead the rational, commonsense reasons his father had given him, and Greg was satisfied in this way with his own persuasion returned. He agreed, too, with the advice Naylor had been given by the Adult Adoption Central Registry, which was to write to his mother, but have a counsellor in Sydney approach her to see if she wished to receive the letter, and, if so, by what means. Who knew how she might react, or if the husband had been told of Naylor's existence.

The letter said nothing of Helen's death, and not a lot about Naylor and his life: just that he was now independent and wondered if Frances still wanted to make contact. The reply was prompt and came directly from Frances herself. She didn't have any other children, she said, and made no reference to her husband. After such a long time, they should meet as soon as possible. She suggested, in what Naylor took to be a joke, that they toss for which of them should travel to see the other, 'though maybe it would be awkward for your family if I came over. I don't want that. Minimum expectation, no demands, but how I look forward to seeing you.'

Naylor wondered if his father was well enough to be left by himself, but Greg said he would be fine, and promised not to overdo things. 'I think it's better you go there,' he said. 'If it all gets a bit tricky, you can choose when to disengage. Not that there's any particular reason to think it will, but there's the potential for a great deal of emotion, isn't there,' and he squeezed his eyes closed at the thought of the heightened feelings a woman could be capable of in such a situation. 'But she said minimum expectations and no demands, didn't she. Good, good.'

So not long before Christmas, Naylor flew to Sydney, and then took the ferry across the harbour, and a taxi to his mother's house close to Taronga Zoo. The day was overcast and hot, the house was wooden and unexceptional, Naylor's feelings were confused, and for a moment he considered turning back. Instead he looked at attractive treetops in the distance, and guessed they were in the zoo, then he used the wrought iron door knocker that was in the shape of a woodpecker.

What did he expect there in another country and unfamiliar surroundings? How, at twenty-six years of age, was he meant to greet his mother for the first time? At the very second the door opened there came a single, piercing wail from the zoo. 'It's the bloody howler monkeys,' the woman said. 'I'm Frances — give me a hug.' She was short and he was tall, which added to the awkwardness of the brief embrace. 'Come in, come in,' she said in a consciously cheerful voice, and led him inside. 'That too,' she said, when he was about to leave his bag.

They walked right through the house and onto wooden decking at the back which looked out to a square of lawn, four rows of vigorous tomato plants, and neighbouring houses on slightly lower ground. In the centre of the lawn a spray hose attachment rotated with a faint protest, and the water made a soft hiss in the air, and a repetitious patter on the grateful grass. Naylor and Frances sat on wooden patio chairs and took stock of each other as they talked.

'It'll be strange for a while, won't it,' she said. 'I think we should aim to become friends first, and then let things happen naturally. My God but you're tall. I know you're Campbell now, but it means a lot to me that you first name's still Naylor. I chose it because it was my dad's name, and he never completely gave up on me.'

'Mostly I come across it as a surname,' he said.

Had he expected some genetic frisson on meeting his mother, an instinctive bond immediately apparent between them? Well, it didn't happen, but there was pleasure and goodwill, and curiosity too, beneath the wariness which at least Naylor showed. Both of them were aware of the incongruity — a mother and son who were complete strangers to each other, making rather routine conversation in mundane surroundings. The unseen zoo was the only external sign of any peculiarity, and exotic hoots, shrieks and ambiguous cries occasionally punctuated their conversation.

There was so much for each to find out about the other, and such sensitive care not to push interest into interrogation, that peripheral topics took hold. Naylor was told all about the tomatoes in the whispering spray and their importance for Frances's favourite pastas, long before learning that no longer was there a Mr Hollister on the scene, and Frances heard all about Bristol University in the first hour or so, but not that Helen was dead.

And as they talked they studied each other, letting their gaze fall briefly in consideration, rather than embarrassment, when their eyes met too directly. Naylor could see nothing of himself in his mother, unless it was her hair, which was brown, soft and limp like his own. She was perhaps five-foot-five and slightly overweight, but Naylor was surprised how young she looked, and realised he had illogically been expecting her to be Helen's age. Her skin was smooth, her bust unaccentuated, and her hands, spread on the wooden armrest of the chair, were small. She was an unexceptional woman, one you would pass in the supermarket aisle without more than a glance, and Naylor was slightly disconcerted by that. He realised he had subconsciously assumed his mother to be different, to be outstanding to him, because of their relationship. That she wasn't, caused not so much disappointment as a faint bewilderment.

'It's an odd situation, isn't it,' he said, realising she might be feeling much the same.

'Jesus, that's certainly right. But it's special too, don't you think, to meet up like this after years and years.' There came a particularly loud trumpeting from the zoo.

'Must be feeding time,' Naylor said.

'For me it's like living next to the railway tracks, or the ocean: the noise becomes so familiar it hardly registers, unless some new creature starts up.' They both listened for a moment but the zoo didn't proclaim itself further. 'Why don't we ask each other two questions before I get something for us to eat? It might make it easier to relax afterwards,'

'You mean difficult questions?' said Naylor.

'Ones to get out of the way, yes. Short answers now and perhaps the full explanations when we know each other better.'

'Fair enough.'

'You go first then,' she said.

It made a game of the situation, almost, but a game that permitted licence. The zoo was quiet as if even the animals there wished to hear the questions and answers, and the spray from the hose attachment caught the sun briefly in a glitter of rainbow fragments.

'Why did you give me up?' he asked her. 'I'm not at all bitter, though.'

'I was nineteen years old, unmarried, and my mother said it would be best for everybody.'

'Who was my father?'

'I knew that would be the next question. He was a tutor at the polytechnic where I started a journalism course. He was in his early forties and married with three daughters. When I told him I was pregnant he gave me $5,000 and the brush-off. I can give you his name if you want it.'

'I've got a name,' said Naylor. 'Anyway, he's probably dead by now, isn't he.'

'I haven't a clue,' said Frances. 'But it wouldn't be hard to find out. But it's not just him to consider — you know now you have half-sisters?'

Naylor asked her if she had more children of her own, although he knew the answer, and she smiled and shook her head. 'That's another reason why it's so great you've turned up. I did try to get in touch, you know, years ago now, and Mr Campbell was against it.'

'I know,' Naylor said. 'He thought it best for me and Mum — Helen.'

'He wrote a very kind and thoughtful reply. Although I was disappointed at the time, it made me think he must be a very intelligent man, and I was glad to think of him as your father.'

Naylor knew the opportunity was there to talk of his parents, to say that Helen had recently died, but he was surprised by an almost overwhelming gust of grief and couldn't at that moment talk of one mother to the other. 'So it's your turn for two free questions,' he said, and Frances smiled again.

'Did you often wonder who your real parents were?'

Naylor had no more sensitivity than was usual in a young Kiwi guy, but he was aware of the need for tact above honesty in answering that question. 'I did quite often,' he said, 'but Mum and Dad never brought it up and we were happy as we were.' Frances was waiting for more. 'And I suppose because, as far as I knew, you'd made no effort to get in touch, I just put it to the back of my mind.'

'I've never wanted to be one of those mothers who give away a baby to someone else to bring up, then expect to be welcomed back when the hard work's done.'

'Fair enough.'

'Were you happy — are you happy? When I'd think of you that was the thing for me. I'd tell myself, he's happy for sure, with people who love him.'

'Like most kids I had ups and downs,' Naylor said, 'but I was lucky with my family. It was a very secure place for me, whatever else happened.'

'And you've done so well — your degrees and that. Everyone's proud of you, I bet.'

Frances stood up and went down the steps of the deck to turn off the sprinkler. The last of the water fell with a patter on the lawn and tomato plants. In the back yard of the house beyond them a guy had a push bike upended on its seat and handlebars for a mechanical check. 'I've got a green salad and some ham on the bone for us,' she said, 'and some blueberry muffins. Do you drink wine, or beer?'

'Beer usually, but I'm easy.'

'You can sit here and listen to the zoo, or you can come inside while I get it ready and talk.'

'The zoo's pretty quiet now. I'll come in,' said Naylor.

In the small kitchen they continued to talk as Naylor cut ham, and did what else he could to help. He learnt that Frances hadn't gone on with journalism, that she was office manager for a sizable courier firm. She'd had bad luck with men, she said, without giving details. Now she was happy living by herself although she still had friends of both sexes. 'What about yourself?' she asked casually, without glancing up from the salad she was preparing.

There had been no one special since he left for study in Bristol. The subject, though, heightened the peculiarity of the situation. He was standing in the kitchen of a stranger, who happened to be his mother and was asking him about his love life. And the thing was, he found it easy enough to answer, because there was no history of emotional intimacy between them: no premises in their lives which both had tacitly accepted as private after years of discourse.

He spent that night in a small, green room with mismatched furniture. The bed-ends were of natural wood, the chest of drawers painted white with ceramic knobs. He occupied the full length of the bed, and could feel the wood with his feet. Maybe it was a young person's bed. For a long time he didn't sleep. He found himself listening for the noises from the zoo and trying to identify them. Although the species were drawn from all over the world, he imagined that most of the individual animals had lived in zoos all their lives, and unlike himself would feel no sense of displacement at all.

He experienced a mixture of emotions from the day. Chief among them, to his surprise, was a sense of sadness and guilt concerning Helen. Meeting and talking with Frances had strangely unlocked his grief concerning the mother he knew: maybe he must farewell one of them before he could draw close to the other.

'What do you think we should do today?' Frances asked him at breakfast. It was a prelude to her idea of visiting friends later in the morning. He had only that full day before flying back home, and considered it strange that she should want to share much of it with other people. At first he thought the motive was to relieve the pressure of being one on one after all the years apart, but he realised Frances wanted to show him to other people: to have the satisfaction, long delayed, of being a public mother. It was a little embarrassing, but also endearing in a way.

Alistair and Jude Soloman had an expensive home out of earshot of the zoo and with a fine view across the harbour. They had their own computer firm, which specialised in developing stocklist software for retailers. Alistair was large, brown and hairy everywhere except the top of his head. He had the direct joviality typical of success. Jude was smaller, browner, less hairy, but equally friendly. Her husband told Naylor with some pride that she was the one in the firm with the brains.

The four of them sat on black leather sofas close to the large lounge window with its view of the sea. 'We've been trying to get Frances to come and work for us,' said Alistair. We need someone like her to organise us — a sort of practice manager. It's all got too big for Jude and me to handle and still push ahead the creative stuff.'

'I can't think of a quicker way to spoil our friendship,' said Frances. 'You both know that.' She had told Naylor that she had known both of them for years: she had been Alistair's girlfriend and Jude's flatmate.

How much they knew about Naylor, however, he wasn't sure; certainly neither Alistair nor Jude showed any great curiosity about his sudden appearance in Frances's life. Most of the talk was of living in Aussie, and business management. Alistair in particular was interested in Naylor's course at Bristol University and whether theoretical business models had a useful translation to actual firms and specific conditions. Naylor enjoyed the discussion. Alistair and Jude were lively challengers without any antagonism at all, and the observations Frances made were full of common sense.

'Stay for lunch,' said Jude Soloman warmly, when it was already past one, and Alistair gave a bushy eyebrow flash of endorsement, but Frances said they'd better get back. When the two women were talking on the way to the car, Alistair took the opportunity to say something personal for the first time. 'That Bryn Hollister,' he said. 'No good at all. A bugger of a man, in fact. He ripped your mother off financially as well as everything else. She probably wouldn't tell you that. Anyway, good to meet you, good to see you. We think the world of Frances, and she's been so excited since you got in touch.' He put a very clean, very hairy, hand on Naylor's shoulder briefly. 'Hope to see you again,' he said.

'Did you like them?' asked Frances as they were driving home.

'Yeah, I did. Two people pretty much on the ball, and they've obviously done well. I'm not sure, though, why you wanted me to meet them now.'

'I suppose I wanted some of my friends to see you so that I could talk about you with them later and they'd know who you were. And I suppose I wanted you to see that I'm not all by myself. I was thinking last night how I must seem to you, in my mid-forties and my job isn't very glamorous, and I haven't got a flash house, or a flash car. I'm just getting back on my feet after the marriage thing.'

'As long as you're okay, what does it matter if you haven't got a mansion like your friends,' said Naylor.

'I guess the Campbells had the best of everything when you were growing up. Both of them being professional people and self-employed.'

'We don't live extravagantly,' said Naylor.

They had a walk in the afternoon, and went to the zoo. It seemed a waste to Naylor to be so close, to hear the noise of it, but not enter. Frances hadn't been for ages, she said. The places on your doorstep tend to get overlooked, don't they, until someone comes from outside and is interested. They took the funicular, they viewed the open savannah sections, they appreciated the culturally correct elephant premises, but Naylor enjoyed most the big crocodiles. Their sinister weight as if carved in old iron or pewter, yet those bodies so solid on the banks could, when immersed, hang just below the surface of the water.

The zoo gave them immediate and various topics of conversation when their own inventory failed. It was odd that their second day together was more difficult than the first. Not that they had discovered anything in each other which aroused dislike or distrust, just that the first urgency of meeting was waning and to talk of intimate things was no easier. To admire the silken menace of the tigers was a relief from any consideration of the future. To watch the frantic social interaction of monkeys at feeding relieved mother and son for a time from the quandary of their own relationship. The awareness of kinship is not enough in itself to allow access to the heart: Frances and Naylor were well intentioned, but still essentially strangers.

Most of the evening they filled with explanations of what each had been doing in all those years apart, and what ambitions each had for the future. Events and achievements in particular had a protective rationality: they ended with a sort of curriculum vitae knowledge of each other. Later, however, in the small green bedroom, with the bottom of his feet touching the wood, and unable for a second night to sleep much, Naylor heard Frances crying. It wasn't loud, or high-pitched, but in the silence of the night he was sure of the sound. He wanted to ignore it; told himself how intrusive, how awkward, it would be to make any response. But his self answered back and said it was his mother weeping, and that tomorrow they would be separated again as they had been almost all their lives.

To his relief the sobbing stopped, but then he heard Frances walk quietly through to the kitchen, and faint, yellow rods outlined his door, which was ajar. She had turned on the kitchen light. Naylor was reminded of the Helen and nights of her illness. He saw from the bedside digital clock that it was 4.30 in the morning, and he reluctantly got up and went to the kitchen. Just before he entered he found himself squeezing his eyes and mouth closed, a quick expression of unease much in the manner of his father, and his affection and understanding for Greg flicked out strongly for a moment.

Frances wore a blue towelling dressing gown, and her feet were bare. She stood by the sink with a mug in her hands and the window behind her was darkly reflective.

'I didn't mean to wake you,' she said.

'I heard you crying and thought I'd better come out.'

'It's what you were afraid of, I suppose. To come over here and find your mother is a flaky woman who blubs in the night.'

'Actually I thought things were going pretty well for a first meeting. I reckoned that we were okay, though of course we're just starting to get to know each other.'

'I promised myself, and you without you knowing it, that I wasn't going to get all emotional. Young guys hate that, I know. Well, all guys do.' Frances came to the table and sat on one of the chairs. Naylor did the same. He had no dressing gown, and was barefoot as well, but there was warmth in the Australian summer night. He was still pale from his time in England, and his feet were the colour of skim milk. Four thirty in the morning at the kitchen table is a time for straight talking in anyone's understanding of such things. Even the noises of the zoo were temporarily in abeyance.

'You can tell me,' said Naylor.

'There's nothing special,' said Frances. 'The thing is I feel guilty. I've always felt guilty, and it's stopping me saying the things I want to say. It's stopping me reaching out the way I feel I should. After Mr Campbell wrote and said it was best not to make contact with you, I had counselling on and off for quite a while about the whole business. One of the things the psychologist said was that guilt is incapacitating, and Jesus, is that true. Nothing I can say or do really changes the fact that I ditched you, just as your real father ditched me. Nothing from now on can ever change that.'

'No one blames you,' said Naylor.

'I blame myself,' she said. 'Maybe, though, it's not just guilt, but knowing now I'll never bring a child up. I'll never be a mother to you in that way.'

'You're still my mother.'

They came to it at last, sitting tousled before the dawn: what each thought could come of their meeting. Perhaps it would be the closest, most candid time, they would ever have before they drew back to safe ground; perhaps it was the threshold of some growth of intimacy. They made more coffee and talked as the sky gradually lightened outside, and the cries and calls of the zoo were further herald of the day. Naylor felt at last he was able to tell Frances that Helen was dead: to praise her to his living mother without sense of betrayal, or competition. He'd half expected to weep at the disclosure, but instead felt relief and gratitude, and went on to speak of Greg as well. In the past there had never been anyone to whom he felt he could praise his parents as they deserved. It was Frances who cried a little as well as smiling and nodding her head to encourage him. It was Frances who took his hand, with neither feeling awkwardness because of it. 'I'll always envy her, though,' she said.

'I lied as well,' she said then.

'Lied about what?'

'About your real father and me. It wasn't true what I said yesterday about that.'

'So who was he really then?'

'Oh, he was the married journalism tutor and all that,' said Frances. 'True enough about the money too, but what I didn't say was that I loved him, and I think he loved me. Maybe I still love him and that's why I'm alone now. Love can be unbearably painful, can't it. Their garage was on the street and we used to meet there at night — sit in the car and talk, make love in the back seat. In all the times I was in that car the engine never started but Jesus, we went some places. We switched on, Errol and I.

'I'm not just talking about sex. We really talked. Know what I mean? We trusted each other to talk about anything at all: sometimes the first silly things that came into our heads, sometimes the most personal truth we knew. The garage always smelled of fish and macrocarpa, because his fishing gear hung by the door, and one side of the garage was lined with firewood.

'But he wasn't prepared to leave his wife.' Naylor was unsure if he wanted any rehabilitation of his father's reputation. In fact he'd been somewhat relieved to strike him off.

'I was nineteen, he was forty-two and with a family. What future could there be in it? We cried a lot, and although the sex was like a drug there was a sort of desperation about it which we never acknowledged, but which made it sad. Secretly he wanted to be a war correspondent, not a polytechnic tutor. Stuff was going on overseas and he was always talking about it and wishing he was there. He felt his life was on too small a scale, I think: that he could do more if he just got an opportunity.'

'So after the pregnancy and the money you never saw him again?'

'No, but I went to the place one last night without telling him. The garage's back door was always unlocked, and I went in and sat in the car and bawled for a while, with just the smell of fish and macrocarpa to remind me of everything. Then I went home. Put your mistakes behind you: that's what my mother kept telling me. Put your mistakes behind you. Maybe she never was in love. I can't hate him, you know. Even now I don't hate him. I'm not much older now than he was then, and often I'm no more satisfied with my life than he was with his.'

'He'd be an old bugger of seventy now,' said Naylor. 'Have you thought of that? You wouldn't want to run across him now even if he was alive.'

'He was always a good-looking guy.'

'I wondered where I got it from,' Naylor said. He didn't want things to get too heavy. In truth he felt an absence of curiosity regarding this father, rather an increased loyalty to Greg

Campbell, who could also be seen as an old bugger of seventy odd, with heart failure imminent, but whom he loved. The half-sisters were another matter altogether, one too difficult to even consider for the moment — maybe ever.

He would be gone in a few hours. The full sun of the day would come, the zoo would begin its public function, Frances would be cheerfully practical again and he would take the ferry across the harbour and then take to the skies to return home. He would return, having met his birth mother, and with the new knowledge that he had sisters, so rather than things being solved, or finished, they grew more complex and more emotionally demanding. But then that is the nature of a family. In each other they had met something of themselves hitherto missing, and felt strengthened by it, even as they recognised the challenge.

images

THE VIRTUES OF MY FATHER'S CHARACTER, which I recognised as a boy, became obscured by their familiarity and my arrogance as a youth. Now that he has been dead for quite a time, those virtues are clear to me again, and I realise that he was a fine man. Sometimes in the night I see my father in his prime, and what forms most commonly is the image of him standing on the verandah, with the sleeves of his white shirt half rolled up, and that inward smile on his long face.

My father was a policeman — a detective, in fact — in the days when the qualifications for entry were still demanding. He was six-foot-one, and he never went to fat the way a lot of other policemen did. He ran in the evenings long before that became fashionable: he was the instructor at a fitness class set up for the city police force. He took pride in his physical capability and appearance, not from vanity, but self-respect and because in his job he expected a lot from his body.

I can remember when my father was a uniformed policemen, but more typically I recall him in mufti when he'd been promoted to detective. He was detective inspector in the end, but I was long gone by then. Sometimes he wore grey slacks and a Harris tweed sportscoat, sometimes his dark blue suit, but always a white shirt, and a grey hat when he went out. The hat, I think the style was called fedora, had a dark band and a dint in the top, which my father would sometimes correct with a chopping action of his right hand. Most men and women wore hats in those days when going out, of course. In the image that comes at night of my father on the verandah in his prime, the sleeves of his white shirt are always rolled up in a particular way: not twisted tightly right up onto the biceps, but just two or three folds so that the material lay about halfway between wrist and elbow, and the brown skin of his forearms showed, with the thick, black watchstrap on the left one. When we were together, when he was talking with me, he'd often rest his left hand on my shoulder, and his strong forearm and big, plain watch would be close to my face.

My father was a family man. He and my mother were disappointed, I think, that I was their only child, but that gave me an even greater sense of being loved and being secure. My father often worked long hours, and odd hours too. That's the way it is in the police, but Mum and I always knew how important we were. Once, he promised to take us to see my mother's brother who was sick in Auckland. They told me he was sick, but they knew he was dying, I suppose. Just a couple of hours before we were due to go, the station rang and the superintendent wanted my father to come in urgently, and he wouldn't. The telephone was on a table in the hall, with no chair beside it. People used the phone quite differently then. And I heard my father say that he had expressly asked for this day off, and that it was important for his family, and unless he was given a written order he was going to go. And we did go. My mother saw her brother, and he died of some intestinal thing quite soon after.

My father was very strong like that. He formed his own convictions; he trusted his own judgement, not in a dismissive way without paying heed to the views of others, but because that's how he thought a man should be. A man should be able to form a reasoned and fair view of the world and act accordingly, rather than going along in an unexamined fashion.

My father wasn't a great one for books, although he read the newspaper carefully, listened to radio broadcasts of the news and sport, and encouraged me to read. Immediacy was the priority in his job and his life: he was directly involved with the forces that promoted stable societies and those that threatened them. I think he would have been a good reader if he'd had time. He had a very clear mind and reduced things to order, without forgetting that people have emotions, and that not everything is accessible by logic. He would see things in a month, that the dentist, or city councillor, wouldn't see in a lifetime in the same city. Some must have been awful things and they accounted for the few times when I remember him white faced and silent in the house.

Those of us brought up in a secure and loving home have had one of the great advantages of life, and I'll always be thankful to my parents for that, and make certain allowances because of it. Apart from the few times I remember my father showing particularly the stress from something in his job, he was cheerful, and a good talker. And a good listener as well. He was a positive man who knew all about the malice, deceit, hard luck and cruel desperation out there, yet thought the community had benefits which outweighed them. If people just stood firm for their principles and each other then he believed things would be okay. There was little cynicism in my father, despite his profession being one that encouraged it in some.

When I talk of my father being in his prime, I suppose I mean when I was fourteen or so, and the pensioner murders were all the city talked about, and big national news too. Three old ladies all bashed to death in separate incidents in six weeks of summer, and things done to them that the newspaper reports only hinted at. After killing Mrs Donalds the murderer sat down in the same room with her and cooked himself the fish she'd been saving for her tea.

My father wasn't home very often during that time, so much was going on. They brought in extra detectives from other districts, but my father said local knowledge would be the answer. Almost always there's someone besides the perpetrator who knows enough to make the difference, he said.

Russell Roddick and I talked about it a good deal in the second storey of the old woolstore, overlooking the overgrown river path from the reserve. We'd found a squeeze-through entrance on the railway track side, and had a place among the wool bales for our beer, chocolate, magazines and books. Russell reckoned the murderer wasn't after money because pensioners never have much if they're living by themselves, and he must just like kicking and punching old people to death. Russell asked me if my father had said much about it, and I could honestly say he hadn't, because that would have been unprofessional. He did say that anyone who could do a thing like that, and not just once, was far worse than an animal. But then everyone in the city said that.

Russell was a good mate and we remained friends right through secondary school. He became a seismologist, of all things, and the last I heard he was in Turkey with plenty to study there. In the old woolstore hiding place we used to talk a lot of rubbish, but also at times we got on to topics that now surprise me to recall — whether our school went on too much about sport instead of academic subjects, whether we should go overseas after university, or stick to New Zealand. Both of us finally made the same choice.

I think my father knew all along who the guy was. In a place that size the police would have a pretty good list of criminals and odd people of one sort or another, and soon narrow the suspects down. It must have been a matter of getting sufficient evidence to justify an arrest.

There was nothing in the paper, nothing official, but not long after school went back, it became known the police were looking for Gil Dipport, who'd been in prison several times, and had bad blood in him, so Russell's father said. I asked my father about it one evening when he, Mum and I were sitting on the verandah after tea. 'Well, he hasn't been seen around since the attacks,' my father said, 'and we need to talk to everyone with a record. Someone must know something.'

'You've got more on him than that though, surely,' my mother said. She understood the code of understatement that was my father's way.

'Well, yes we have,' my father said, but he wouldn't go any further than that, and I don't think he would have said much more to my mother even if I hadn't been there. My parents were close and loving all their lives, but he tried to leave the police work at the door as much as he could. Some families of policemen suffered, he said, because it got about that they knew a lot of what was going on.

'Anyway,' said my mother, 'he'll be well away by now.'

'Gil's never been more than ten miles from this place in his life,' my father said.

There's only one other thing to tell, because all I remember is quite clear and simple, really, not a long story. Well, it's absolutely clear and unequivocal in my mind's eye, though perhaps not so simple after all. Two evenings later I went down to meet Russell at our hideout. I ran in the drizzle through the shunting yards and metal scrap yard, and squeezed through the secret entrance. I went up to our place on the second storey. Russell hadn't arrived so I smoked a cigarillo very carefully, because we could easily have set the place on fire, and watched through the dirty window the creek and the track from the reserve which was almost hidden by the clumps of fennel and lupin in some parts, and clear on the creekbed in others.

It gave me start to see my father walking slowly from the town side. His white shirt showed clearly and he wore no coat, no grey hat. The fine, drifting rain was just beginning to stick the shirt to his shoulders, so he couldn't have come far. He stepped behind one of those half-fallen willows which still continue to grow, and I thought he was going to take a leak. Then I saw a stooped, bald man coming the other way, from the reserve, in and out of view among the lupins. He carried a axe handle, or something similar, and I knew it was Gil Dipport. Why else would my father be waiting there?

And when my father stepped out, Gil Dipport didn't try to run back the way he'd come. I guess he knew my father's capabilities. He just backed into a clear bit of the creekbed and waited with the axe handle, or pick handle, or whatever.

I noticed my father had slipped off his shoes to give him better grip and balance. Maybe they said things to each other, but I was too far away to hear, and almost at once my father began walking up on Gil. He got hit on the arm and the neck, the bruises were there for weeks, but he soon got the better of Gil and wrenched the wooden handle from him, sending him onto the ground where he sat dazed with his legs out in front as if he was at a picnic.

Then my father took a good grip of the axe handle and hit Gil with it the way you would a dog, all the strength of his arms in the last foot or two of the blow. I've never told anybody before. That's the other image I see sometimes at night, as well as my father on the verandah with us in his white shirt with sleeves rolled up, and smiling.

I think my father was a fine man, an exceptional man, I really do. I can't think of a better family man. He's been gone a good many years, and when in the night I have this unbidden memory of him I tell myself it was too long ago to be sure of things now: too long ago and too close to childhood to bear any scrutiny.

fellow citizens

'THE THING IS,' SAYS BRYCE CRANE, 'that the ERO report strongly favours a senior member of staff attending the residential Barker House Course on Contemporary Student Management.' Bryce looks away, peruses the grey limestone carving beyond his office window, pushes out his bottom lip in the oddly infantile manner that shows he is about to pronounce. 'And I concur,' he says. 'I concur, and what's more, I think you are the ideal person to go.'

I don't want to go. I give plausible explanations for not wanting to go, but in truth I think such courses are a disruption of routine and of little practical benefit. Maybe Bryce thinks so too, but neither of us wants to be on record as being quite so reactionary. The course would look good on my CV, and I would be proved supportive of Bryce's vision for the school. I would pay my dues and be in a stronger position to refuse the next course invitation: something even more fatuous, perhaps, such as professional buddy programmes, or the motivational aspects of sound nutrition.

'I appreciate your willingness to consider it,' he says. 'I know it's time away from all the things you've got going here. I think we need to follow the ERO recommendation on this, however, and I intend to make particular mention of it to the board.' He gives me the sudden, intent smile that is his badge of approval. So I'm committed to a trip to Auckland, and five days' full-frontal exposure to the latest educational theory on mutually beneficial relationships between staff and students.

Barker House is a modest conference centre crowded by mature trees, close to Grafton Gully. It can accommodate twenty-four people in six rooms that resemble dormitories in plainness and uniformity. If indulgent spending occurs within the Ministry of Education, in-service courses show no sign of it. Housekeeping, as course leaders refer to it, is the subject of much puritan instruction and review at each day's session.

After arrival I receive a typed information sheet, which shows I'm assigned to room four, and I choose the bed beside the window. A small window with a view of a full fifty centimetres before a vast, pocked tree bole blocks all. The information sheet lists twenty-one teachers as course members, including three Aucklanders with dispensation to sleep at their own homes. I see on the sheet that I'm to share room four with Branimir, whose surname is a blur of less common consonants, and Quentin Wavell. The room has no evidence of either. I leave my yellow pyjamas on the pillow to assert my claim to the window bed, and my suitcase at the foot. Maybe I should sit and read the course notes, which were posted to me a fortnight ago, but instead I decide I'm entitled to a freedom walk before the official welcome and opening plenary session at eleven. Yes, that's what the sheet says, as if hundreds of us are gathering from across the world, instead of twenty-one New Zealand teachers at Barker House.

I don't wish to get lost and haven't much time. I find a small triangular park, with most of the trees strange to me. All the plants are lushly green, trusting in a regular and generous rain unknown on my own South Island east coast. Even the sun here seems to have a moist lick to it. It's half-past ten and the relieving teacher will have released my Year 12 chemistry class and headed for the staffroom and a cup of tea. I miss the drink, but at least I am spared the staff notices that always accompany it: the deadline for reports, the postponed meeting of the sports committee, a hospital report on an ailing colleague, updates on the proposed new uniform. The Auckland traffic frets at the sides of the small park, but the giant palms with manicured trunks are listless, and on the edges of the curved gravel paths the night's rainwater lies placidly. Reluctantly I head back for the course opening.

We gather in the main conference room: not much more than a large lounge offering stackable chairs with green vinyl seats. The course director is Dr Mike Menzies, dean of humanities at a college of education. He proves by his welcome to have a smattering of well-pronounced Maori, a suave delivery and a sense of humour. I resolve not to be cynical. Theory and practice in any discipline are driven by different priorities, and so the connection between them is often disappointing for those in both areas. Move an individual from one to the other and naturally the priorities change. I tell myself I will measure Dr Menzies on the intellectual appeal of his theories rather than their usefulness to the traditional boys' school in which I work. How long such tolerance can be maintained, who knows?

Most of the other men assembled for the course look as conventional as me. Lesser professionals, we wear dark slacks, cheap shoes and expressions of humorous resignation. The women are less uniform in tribal affiliation; some are quite fashionable. The working wives of lawyers and businessmen with social lives of giddy heights, perhaps. Two or three of the people I recognise from other courses, or sports trips to their schools, but none I know well.

One person stands out. A tall man with longish, grey hair and the face of a Jewish psychiatrist. He has steel-rimmed glasses and hands so heavy that they droop from his wrists as he sits listening to the director. He wears a pale shirt with buttons, but no collar, like the top of long-johns, and light boots with the suede worn from the toes. He asks Mike Menzies a question concerning the trend in American society for same-sex peer groupings to break down at an earlier age, and the repercussions for schools. He is not challenging, or showing off, and the director responds avidly to a significant point. It's not a New Zealand accent that the tall guy has, though his voice is clear. From where I'm sitting I can't see his name tag, but I have a bet with myself that he is Branimir with the surname of consonants, one of my nominated room-mates. It's the way things often are, and the name is suggestive of his appearance.

In the lunch break of this first day I find that he is indeed 'Bran', my room-mate, though there is no sign of Quentin Wavell. He and a certain Adele Seed from a Catholic girls' school are AWOL from the first roll-check. May they be satisfactorily clasped naked together on a motel duvet.

I show Bran our room. He sets down his worn, soft leather carrycase on a bed, and we go for lunch, which is bagged in cellophane through which can be seen a filled roll, an apricot muffin, a banana and a small packet of juice. Bran and I join others who are sitting on wooden forms in the shade of the overbearing trees at the front of Barker House. The topics of conversation don't include anything mentioned in the director's introductory lecture, but rather are of sport, the facilities at Barker House, the latest political ruckus and the petty, persistent grievances of our profession.

Bran stretches his long legs and crosses them at the ankles. He's not wearing socks, and beneath the pale, dry skin of the exposed anklebone is a close congregation of small veins almost the colour of a bruise. He says little, but his posture and expression signal goodwill and at the same time a sense of intrinsic separation. He closes his eyes in the warm shade and rests. The jutting, slightly goatlike profile of his face is accentuated by his greying beard, and the nails of his large hands are very pink and clean. One of the more attractive women tells of being propositioned by the taxi driver on her way in from the airport, and Bran smiles without opening his eyes.

The focus of the first afternoon session is equality in language transactions. The first speaker is from a university department of education, and argues that students should be entitled to use the language that comes naturally to them, rather than one imposed by the school, which puts them at a disadvantage. None of us even bothers to argue with someone so far removed from classroom realities, but the buzz groups that follow entertain themselves with examples of the students' language of choice, and then the conversations drift from the agenda to the little selfish, mundane things that occupy most people most of the time. Bran is not in my group, but I notice him lean forward, forearms on his knees, to tell a story that is rewarded with a burst of laughter.

The speaker who follows afternoon tea discusses written contracts as a disciplinary measure, and displays a variety of formats on PowerPoint. Not much of it is new, but at least he has a few good anecdotes, and a wry acceptance that there is no easy way to curb perversity. I like him for that, and for the large and very human mayonnaise stain on his shirt. In the late-afternoon dreamtime of the second buzz group I manage to avoid becoming the selected team member to report back, and then recount with some success a story of my own about a Maori lad who hid in the detention room cupboard and aped my actions behind my back.

The evening meal at Barker House isn't until six o'clock. The director, with a hopeful enthusiasm, has set an overnight task for each room. Ours is on the value of traditional prefectorial systems compared with more recent means of involving students in institutional leadership and management. Bran and I constitute the team, for Quentin has still not appeared. As I change my shirt in room four, Bran asks me two questions: am

I a wine drinker and do I enjoy reading Oliver Sacks? I answer yes to both, and Bran says he is going to like me, and suggests we walk to the Nexus Wine Bar, which he says isn't far away. 'We must retain a stake in the real world,' he says. Amen to that.

It's still warm, but he puts on a shin-length black leather coat and looks more foreign than ever. 'Maybe it's strange that you have lived in New Zealand all your life and I've been here only ten years, yet I know Auckland better than you,' he says. I don't find it that strange: most people seem to have a better understanding of Auckland than I do.

As we walk down the slope towards the city centre, Bran tells me he is Croatian, from the city of Osijek, and that he migrated because of the wars of nationalism in Yugoslavia. I haven't asked for this information, and it occurs to me that Bran's pre-emptive explanation is a form of limitation. I know almost nothing of the Balkans, and Milosevic is the only name I recall from a flood of media war coverage. I take a punt by mentioning the Dalmatian influence early in our history, but Bran says his people weren't coastal at all.

The Nexus Wine Bar has a narrow entrance in a side street, but goes a long way back, with high seats all the way down. 'It's just as well to get a bottle,' says Bran, and he buys a red. I have a feeling even at this stage that we are not going to make Barker House by six. He undoes the buttons of his long coat, and the dark leather slips to his sides as he makes himself comfortable on the stool. He asks me what I do for exercise, and we talk of sport and gym work. Bran is knowledgeable about fitness, and talks to me about the value of those forms of regular exercise that don't involve impact stress on the joints. 'Swimming is much better than jogging once you're over forty-five,' he says. Putting his two fists together he demonstrates cartilage and ligament wear in a knee joint. 'Extension and repetition are good, but continual abrupt impact's bad,' he says. 'You see these joggers on the concrete with cheap running shoes, and you know they're doing harm to themselves.'

I compliment Bran on his English, and he tells me that he spoke it in Europe long before he came out here: part of his university studies, he says. I imagine him as a runner, cross-country, perhaps. He must be over fifty, but still lean, with long arms and legs. He would be one of those effective, but slightly ungainly stamina runners who lead with the head: sharp features hung in front, and knees and elbows dangerous in a pack.

We have finished the wine, and I buy a bottle of Australian cab sav. We talk for a while about the new chemistry syllabus and the difficulty of interesting kids in any form of science other than special effects for television and computer games. I say it's got worse since the ministry has increasingly opposed any classroom experiments with even the slightest chance of mishap. When I was a fourth-former I remember our science teacher, Jetarse Barnes, throwing a chunk of potassium into the swimming pool and its explosive scamper across the surface.

'You're sick of it, aren't you?' says Bran, and I agree. 'I can imagine teaching becoming very wearisome,' he says. 'That same volatile mixture of energy, apathy and ignorance coming on renewed year after year.'

Without any discussion we accept that we are not going to make the Barker House meal, or the course task for the next day. The next day itself seems a reasonable target. We order a plate of wedges and a cheeseboard as the wine bar fills with people on their way home from work: mainly office guys in short-sleeved shirts and black shoes. Bran still sits in his open leather coat and with just the long-john top beneath. He has a habit of rinsing each mouthful of wine through his teeth before swallowing, and behind the heavy lenses of his glasses his eyes are distorted and loom like fish in a bowl. He hasn't been teaching long and finds a great deal of amusement in it. 'I never realised the lack of dignity that's involved with being with kids. It's what I notice most, and maybe it's a good thing that teachers are not given any respect by their students.'

'What did you do before teaching?' I ask.

'I was a paediatrician in Osijek. I lost everything in the war,' says Bran. 'Yet I was luckier than many, and had the contacts to get out.'

'So why aren't you practising here?'

'Oh, it's the verification of qualifications thing, you know. Procedures drag on, and I seem somehow distanced from that life now. I don't think I want to build it up all over again.' I sense that even with a good deal of wine in him, Bran doesn't want to get into the whole business. It's weariness rather than reserve, I think, and the realisation that my ignorance is too complete an obstacle.

'Would you like to come with me to some people I know in Herne Bay?' Bran says. 'It gets pretty crowded here now.' The noise is making it difficult for us to talk without raising our voices, and elbow room is minimal. Bran finishes the last of the wedges with two quick forays of thumb and fingers, asks for a cork to plug our unfinished bottle of wine, buys another to take with him. As we ease our way through the crowd to leave, some of the people look curiously at him, not so much because of the sweeping leather coat and long-john top, I suspect, as for the bearded face with its goat-like chin and jaw, and the dark eyes blurred beneath his glasses. 'We can get a taxi at the corner,' he says.

The taxi driver is Samoan, and slightly surprised to be subjected to a series of quick-fire questions from Bran on his experience of being a comparative newcomer here. 'The main thing is not to lose your language, otherwise you're cut adrift,' Bran says as we arrive in the dusk at the Herne Bay address. 'Say something to me in your language about your village and your family there,' and the driver does, smiling and obliging, but slightly embarrassed nevertheless by the almost anthropological intensity of Bran's interest in his life. 'Good, excellent,' says Bran, as if satisfactorily concluding an examination at his clinic. 'Language is the body of a culture,' he says as he pays the fare.

The two of us stand in the gathering darkness in front of a two-storeyed wooden house set close to the road. Bran politely gives me a little background on his friends as we climb the steep outside stairs to the upper flat. 'Marek and Ewa Baranowski,' he says, 'and Ewa's sister, Anna. They're not Croats, of course, but Poles. Marek was a financial controller for a large machinery works in Radom, but fell out with local politicians. Here, the only work he could get at first was in an abattoir, and that's where I met him. Now he works for an accountant, but his qualifications are not recognised.'

All three are at home. Marek is tall and heavy-featured, his wife plump and blonde: it appears to be her natural colouring. Anna is younger, perhaps forty, square-shouldered, nimble, and with a serious face. None of them speaks English as well as Bran, though both the women are more assured than Marek. The lounge windows have no curtains, and give a view of a partially lit suburbia, most of the lights static, but the roads marked by a channelled procession of firefly vehicles. The Polish trio don't seem surprised by Bran's arrival, or my own inclusion in the visit. There is a photograph of the Pope in the small hallway leading to the lounge, and I remember reading somewhere that most Croats are Catholic also. Ewa praises the South Island landscape, although she hasn't been there, as a way to make me feel welcome, and Marek thanks us for the wine. Anna slips away briefly to bring glasses for us all.

They are energetic in movement and conversation, these people new to the country, and often seem surprised by the way things are done here. They have many points of reference and comparison from outside New Zealand, and their surprise is sometimes amused incredulity, often admiration and gratitude. Marek is amazed at the ease of access to the countryside for ordinary people; his wife extols the lack of corruption in everyday transactions; Anna praises the conditions of our workplaces; Bran the price of meat. They all say they cannot believe how naïve and amenable to political cajolery we Kiwis are. I've had little contact with such new citizens, and think of the thousands of people from rich cultures who have come here for new opportunity, or to escape all manner of personal and crushing misfortune. We drink and talk, we eat cheese, many European names are used, and I feel that I am in some enclave of our population quite new to me. Bran and Marek have a lengthy discussion that seems to prove that the golden rules of nutrition and financial investment are the same: diversity. Marek's English is difficult for me to follow. Anna sits down on a pillow by Bran's chair and rests an arm on his knee. She is well fleshed but not fat, and her hair shines. I realise she is at least part of the reason for Bran's familiarity with the family.

The street and house lights glitter below, as I am called upon to explain the grip of sport upon the psyche of my country, and though I disclaim any authority — my opinion is no better than anyone else's, I say; how would I know, I say — they call me to account.

'You born here,' says Marek.

'Your people have been here for generations,' says Ewa.

'You know no other home,' says Bran. That is obvious and true, and I've not thought of it before. In this company I must accept the mantle of spokesman for my country.

As the talk and the night move on, I realise that these people are political in a fundamental way strange to me. They are familiar with historical policies of many countries, and have vehement opinions as to the outcomes in Europe and elsewhere. Also they share a cynicism that shows itself by turns as sadness and anger. As we talk of Jews and Palestinians, Bran bursts out against the slanted media coverage. 'Everything is fucking doctored,' he says. 'All of it selected to support some predetermined view. A TV image, like statistics, can be made to prove whatever you want. Maybe truth outside our immediate experience has always been a received commodity, eh?' He leans forward urgently, and his bearded head hangs before us. 'Terrible things can't be explained to those who weren't there. Simplification becomes so easily a lie.' He realises that he has begun on heavy stuff, and I'm a stranger. 'Never mind, never mind, we're happy here,' he says harshly, but gets up and walks about to ease the mood. He takes up some of our coffee mugs as an excuse to go into the kitchen. 'Never mind me,' he says with a wide smile, pausing at the doorway. Anna follows him from the room with a cheese knife that has fallen to the floor.

They leave the kitchen, but don't return to the main room. Marek and Ewa continue to be kind hosts, though I'm finding it increasingly difficult to maintain the concentration necessary to understand his English. If my mind wanders, then I find it difficult to pick up the thread of what he is saying. Ewa is sensitive to this and throws me a line from time to time. She worked part time as a translator before coming to New Zealand. No, not in English, she answers me, but Russian to Polish and back again. Her English isn't exact enough, she says. There's not much call for Russian-Polish translation here, and she fears her skills are slipping. She has German, too, which used to be at least the standard of her English. How rich a linguistic background many Europeans have, and now she is stranded on the single bar of Kiwi idiom. I have the unaccustomed feeling of being under-educated.

I feel able to ask them why they left their country, because we have been drinking together, and because it's unlikely we will see one another again. Ewa glances at her husband, and he gives a nod in deference to her better English. She has large, expressive features: her eyes have dark make-up despite her blonde hair. For the first time I notice she is wearing gold hoop earrings. 'Large-scale industry in our country is very political,' she says. 'You know? Marek supported certain economic reforms and made enemies by doing so. Some way would have been found to make him at fault for financial things going wrong. He was in the financial management of industry important to the government.'

'Governments — they interested in money and employment,' says Marek. 'Here, political influence in industry not largest because this a young country, and corruption is a sort of rot, and much gets worse with time.'

Ewa asks me if I've travelled overseas, and is interested that I've been no further than Australia. It's after one o'clock, though, and no sign of Bran — or Anna. I say I'd better get back to Barker House, and ask if I can ring a taxi. Marek insists that he will drive me there, and I accept. Ewa excuses herself, and I hear her tap on a door past the hall photograph of the Pope. She comes back to tell us that Bran is staying longer. Neither she nor Marek seem at all surprised by this, so why should I be?

'Tell him I'll see him tomorrow,' I say. I may well never see him again.

Ewa stands at the top of the outside stairs as we leave. She looks older outside her rooms. Here in Auckland it's still warm after midnight, and as on all my visits this surprises me. Marek has no garage for his car, and it's parked in the street a little way down: a Nissan about ten years old. He tells me there's no use having a good car if you can't keep it off the street. We have something of a discussion about the whereabouts of Barker House and the best way of getting there. I tell him I don't want to put him to any trouble, that I'm embarrassed Bran and I came without warning, that I can get a taxi. 'I want take you,' says Marek.

As he finds fourth gear on a longish stretch, he asks me how long I've known Bran. 'About fifteen hours,' I reply. I think of my first sight of him at the Barker House opening session, of his easy empathy with others in his group afterwards. I remember his long leather coat unbuttoned in the Nexus bar; I imagine him lying on the compact and shapely body of Anna, and the open and undisguised pleasure he will take in it. Her skin catching what light there is, surely, while his own long torso will be dark with hair. Maybe he will ask her to speak in her own language, and maybe he will understand. 'We met up at this course for the first time. I gather that he was a doctor in Yugoslavia and came out to get away from the ethnic troubles.'

'In Croatia,' says Marek.

'So he had no family?'

'A wife, two old sons. One son died by the Serbs in Slavonia.'

'Can't he get permission for them to come out?'

'He doesn't wish his wife come. He fifty-six, maybe fifty-eight, and say he wants woman who choice say yes, not say no.' Marek laughs and gives a shrug. 'That so I drive you home.'

'Right.'

'No, no. You must find more difficult than I say it. Bran had the true, important life in his own place. Now that passed away — ruined, yes? ruined? — here is where he finish his time.' I wonder if Marek is giving an explanation for his own life as well as Bran's. Not in what he says about women, but about people who lose so much of their life that they haven't the heart, or the time, to attempt a full rebuilding, and settle for a more immediate, ad hoc and temporary existence. Maybe that's what it's like to be dispossessed of your country and your career, to lose your position in your own community and find yourself undervalued in a new one. Unlike Marek and Ewa, maybe Bran and his wife suffered too much together for them to be able to go on in partnership, and they seek out new friends who don't carry the same burden.

Marek tells me of working with Bran in the abattoir when they were both new arrivals: how Bran quickly became skilled with the knife, especially jointing, although surgery wasn't his thing. And he used to sing in his own language to pass the time, and sometimes encourage Marek to sing also, and the Maori and Islanders there liked to sing, so that often in the midst of the swaying carcasses, the sluicing of blood clots from the concrete floor, the languages would be Polynesian, Polish and Croatian, not English at all.

'I had the fortune Bran didn't get,' Marek says. 'I and Ewa will be happy. Bran, he leave too much of himself in Croatia.'

Barker House is in darkness when we arrive. Marek lowers his head and stares through the car window at the massed darkness of the trees that crowd around it. 'The food good?' he says.

It's after 2 a.m. and I hope I haven't been locked out.

The place seems strange to me. I have trouble recalling where the main entrance is. I set out hours ago with Branimir the Croatian, and now I am returned by Marek the Pole. Things have assumed a shifting uncertainty, and 'Contemporary Student Management' seems irrelevant.

'How old was Bran's son?' I ask just before getting out.

'He was full grown up,' says Marek.

I shake hands with him through the car window, and then he drives away, the only car on the street except for a single taxi.

buster

My criminal apprenticeship was served with Buster Marrot, and though I never achieved even journeyman status later in life, and the skills decayed, two trade attitudes have remained strong with me: a proprietorial view of the possessions of others, and a disregard for authority.

Buster was fourteen, and not at all fat despite his nickname. He was dark, smiling and cat-like in movement and essential independence. Buster came about the middle of a large Catholic family which lived three houses from us by the bridge on the main road out of town. The Marrots had a gaunt, two-storeyed house all of weatherboard, and fitted in two lodgers as well as seven children. One boarder was always out when I was there; the other was a man called Stokes who had been an alcoholic shearing contractor, but was just an alcoholic by the time he boarded at Buster's. He had so little, and was so easily deceived, that Buster hardly bothered to steal from him. Stokes finally drowned by accident, or design, in the river close by, but that was years after I'd moved, and my recollection is of a quiet, smiling man with washed out eyes, who would stand with Mrs Marrot in the kitchen and peel vegetables for her. Buster's dad was a casual slaughterman at the works: something of the executioner's presence hung about him, and I always felt my breath constricted when I saw his narrow, sharpened knives laid out on oilcloth on the workshop bench. Buster said his dad could kill easily with just his hands, but still had to slit throats to bleed the sheep.

Buster went to the Catholic school, and was a year older than me. A year is nothing between adults, but it's a clear distinction at fourteen. I don't think Buster would have bothered with me if he'd had any of his school friends living close, and in the weekends I didn't see much of him. Without any discussion between us it was understood it was a don't call me, I'll call you situation. Yet Buster never put me down when we were together, although he was the leader by seniority and nefarious vision. 'You're a bloody quick runner, all right,' he'd say after we'd scarpered from some difficult situation. 'You've got a good head on you sometimes,' he said when I suggested selling the eggs we'd stolen from Mrs Philips to the Egg Floor. Mostly I remember him calling in the evenings of summer week days, our crimes played out in warm twilights, but there were earnest winter sorties as well.

I never saw any viciousness in Buster, but all his energy went to extort benefit from the world. He was unashamedly amoral and the risk of getting caught was the only consideration and deterrence in any of his plans. He seemed to have bypassed the interests which preoccupied other early teens — Scouts, balsa wood aeroplanes with real engines, rugby — but not yet moved on to sex. Buster was a materialist. Money and possessions were his goals, and he knew them interchangeable. Stolen money bought him what he wanted, and stolen items he didn't want he could flog off for money. He never passed a shop, or a works yard, without casing it for advantage, and he had several regular places that he milked, rather than making just one big hit, which would be noticed.

Borrell's Light Engineering and Metal Scrap in Cook Street was one of them. Borrell's had heaps of roughly sorted iron rusting in their back yard — old stoves, dismembered farm implements, girders, railway tracks — and a wooden barn which had lead and copper piping, brass and bronze fittings, stainless steel taps and basins, laundry coppers, stacks of ornamental wrought iron like that which decorated the Marrots' verandah and ours. Buster knew how to get into the barn through a high window and unbolt the side door. We'd come into the yard from the rough section at the back which had piles of power poles amid the long grass and lupins where we hid Buster's cart. In the dying light we'd sneak out some of the more expensive metals, but nothing that was distinctive enough to be remembered. Copper piping and lead sheet flashings were two of Buster's favourites. Some bits we sold back to Borrell's several times over. I admired Buster's restraint. He knew just how much and how often the trick could be pulled without arousing suspicion. The yard man once said that he liked our enterprise in fossicking stuff out and earning a bit for ourselves. He didn't realise the extent to which his company supported that initiative.

Buster was a bit of an artist in his felonies. He cut a rectangular hole in the pages of the library copy of The Hunchback of Notre Dame into which he could slip a packet of Pall Mall, or a chocolate slab, and close the cover. He had a bull-dog clip on his shoulder blades held by a string around his neck, and it was my job in the stationer's to attach a Wheels mag or Batman issue beneath his jersey, and he'd saunter out, often stopping to talk to the sales girl just for the hell of it.

Sometimes he organised a big heist, like the three yellow railway tarpaulins he stole right off some wagons loaded with boxes of vegetables in the sidings. He sandpapered off the logos, and sold the tarps for over a hundred dollars to the owner of a crayfish boat. No wonder Buster always had money in his pocket and rode a bike with blue metallic paint and gears. I wasn't there when he got down on the tarpaulins, but I was when he burgled Acme, and the outcome is clear in my mind.

Acme Warehouse stored a lot of the bulk supplies for grocery shops and dairies in town. It was a long concrete and corrugated iron building between the RSA and a yard of yellow and red agricultural machinery. Acme were in a different league to Borrell's in terms of both opportunity and security, and Buster was determined to find a way of getting regular access to so much good stuff. We sat in his father's workshop while he made a list of the most desirable and easily disposed of items. The workshop was our usual den, because Buster shared a bedroom with two brothers.

Buster was especially interested in cigarettes. He hoped to be able to take a couple of cartons every fortnight or so without them being missed. That was Buster's calculating and far-seeing nature, even as a fourteen-year-old. At the time I didn't realise his vision of criminal possibility was precocious. Tinned goods were high on Buster's list also: baked beans, pineapple slices, asparagus tips, salmon, tongue. Buster had placement sorted out for them all, and the juvenile anticipation I felt at the chance of gutsing barely registered with him.

The modern Acme building was a considerable challenge to Buster, and he worked on it. He spent a good deal of time in unobtrusive observation, and even went in and spoke to one of the storemen on the pretext that he thought he was able to buy things in bulk for a Christmas Sunday school party. The warehouse had an alarm system on the main doors, Buster said, and no windows. There was a large extractor fan high on the side away from the road, and for a time Buster wondered if we could find a way of removing the fan at will. We did a recce in the early darkness of a July night, carrying a plank surreptitiously through the back streets and then leaning it against the warehouse. I held it while Buster monkeyed up and checked the fan mounts with a torch and crescent. He decided it was too big a job, and besides, there would be too much risk coming and going with goods through such a visible and difficult route.

Buster switched his interest to the dwarfed, glass-fronted office annex to one side of the main doors. It had its own access to the store, and Buster reckoned that, as an add-on, it didn't share the concrete pan underlying the warehouse. We had several sessions sitting around his father's neatly laid out and whetted knives in the workshop, during which we drew in Buster's maths book possible tunnels from the RSA shrubbery and the machinery yard. Reluctantly we decided the plan was too risky and too slow. I suggested somehow getting an imprint of the key on a piece of soap, a comic book fantasy which Buster put aside without ridicule. In fact he said it reminded him that the office had a Yale lock with an inside snib, and this gave him the idea of hiding in the office until after closing time.

We began close planning by taking my father's binoculars down to the RSA shrubbery after school, and lying concealed there on damp, cold ground to spy on the dark-haired office woman. We learnt she spent a good deal of time doing her fingernails, and more time on the phone. She liked to eat white chocolate and take her shoes off when the sun was bright through the armour glass. There were no cash transactions that we observed, although lots of lists from the storemen and delivery drivers. Buster said there would have been lots of cheques in the morning mail which we never saw, and that they'd be in the squat iron safe, the key of which she kept in her purse. We also discovered that the key to the door from the office to the main store was kept beneath a potted cactus on the filing cabinet. The first time Buster saw her through the binoculars take the key from its hiding place to lock up, he gave a long, low whistle. I knew then he'd seen something important. It meant we could move on to the next stage of the plan.

The thing was that the office had only one possible hiding

place, and Buster was too big for it. The annex was very small with just the dark-haired woman's desk, two high filing cabinets, the safe in a wooden cupboard, and the shelf with pot plants, vacation postcards and the electric jug. One of the filing cabinets was angled in a corner so that the woman could reach it from her desk, and in the recess of that angle Buster reckoned I could squeeze and hide. I had misgivings, but these were balanced by the pride I felt in being necessary for success, able at last to perform something that was beyond Buster himself.

Buster went to the office and asked if Acme might have a job for him after school. The woman didn't bother to consult anyone and said no, but Buster confirmed that the office door had a Yale snib lock, no alarm that he could see and that the gap behind the filing cabinet should be big enough for me. That's how I ended up late on a blustery afternoon waiting around the side of the Acme building for Buster to signal from the RSA bushes that the office woman had gone through to the warehouse. It was in some ways the most tricky stage of the whole thing, even though Buster said that most of her absences he'd watched had given enough time for me to get in. Buster told me to pretend I was having a fit if she did come back before I was out of sight. I thought a fit might come quite naturally in those circumstances.

Buster gave the thumbs up from an RSA bush, and I was round the corner to the office without any conscious decision. I stepped onto the desk and then the filing cabinet, for a moment thought the space between it and the wall was insufficient, but then with the energy of fear wedged myself out of sight, my shoulders and head hard in the corner, my knees splayed for room.

On the small patch of blue carpet between my legs was a thin scurf of dust, debris and dead insects, including a bumble bee almost as large as a ping pong ball, dried flower petals, a brass drawing pin, a used tissue. I tried to relax and breathe with my mouth open to make less noise. There was no way I could know if the woman had returned, until I heard her cough at the desk and then take a call from a shopkeeper impatient to receive an order of cereals. To pass the fifteen minutes or so before closing time I imagined the most attractive tinned foods piled high in the warehouse: stacks of fruit salad, corned beef and sweetened condensed milk. And I thought of Buster's praise for my part in the carefully planned operation. I hoped I wouldn't need to sneeze, or fart, and tried not to think of the consequences. The dark woman's perfume was heavy in the confined office.

I heard one of the storemen say he was on his way, and soon after there were the sounds of the office woman preparing to go home: the key turning in the door to the warehouse, its scrabble under the cactus pot, the clicking catch of a handbag, and finally the light turned off, the surprisingly loud slam of the office entrance door and a rattle as she checked it was secure. I relaxed mentally, but was so physically constricted that little movement was possible. I decided to count to three hundred before puting my head up. It was almost black behind the filing cabinet once the light was off, and I knew that even outside a winter night would be coming fast.

After three hundred I gave an awkward push upwards, but nothing happened. Maybe I would be stuck there all night and die, while Buster looked through the window without being able to help. A desperate struggle, and I got my top half out and was able to lift myself over the steel cabinet, and drop beside the desk where I was shielded from the full-length glassed side of the office looking out to an asphalt park and then the road. The RSA bushes were an indistinct wind-blown shadow, and I knew the interior of the office would be even darker to anyone outside, yet I hesitated to move about openly. I counted another hundred for good measure, in case the second storeman was slow to leave. I went to the outside door and released the Yale lock so that the door was pushed back strangely on my hands by the invisible wind. I put my left hand out and gave the thumbs up for Buster, not knowing if he'd see in the dusk.

Buster was there almost immediately, breathing heavily, not from nervousness but the sprint across the parking area. 'Bloody great. Well done,' he said, and closed the door behind him. I told him how much of a squeeze it had been. 'I knew you could do it. Shit hot,' he said, and put the binoculars carefully by the door. 'We've got to remember these.'

He took the key from under the cactus, opened the door leading to the warehouse and we went through. Just enough light spilled in from the unlit office to show the outline of two forklifts and the monolithic racks beyond. With a small plastic torch, Buster led the way down the first of the alleys between the store racks. The place was Aladdin's Cave. In the blade of Buster's torch mountains of wealth rose up disguised in sombre cartons and pallets. The racks had printed tags to identify the stores — sanitary products, petfoods, beverages, tinned soups, spices and essences. You could have spent a whole life in there and not wanted for much, I reckoned.

As we came round a corner from brown and icing sugar there was a sound in the dark like a mallet on a wooden peg, and Buster went down in front of me with a hissing cry, the torch skittering away on the bare, concrete floor. 'Shit, shit,' he said in a suppressed, angry voice. 'Just grab the torch,' he said when I knelt down by him, and when I brought it back he snatched it and shone it on his feet. His left foot was in a gin trap which was chained to the rack. The serrated jaws were sunk into Buster's ankle just above his sneakers. It was an old trap, heavily corroded although it had been given a recent oil rub all over.

Buster told me to kneel down close to his foot and take hold of one side of the jaws. He took the other. 'Try not to touch my foot,' he said, 'and pull slowly when I say.' We did it carefully, because I could tell what Buster feared was that one of us would lose grip before there was space for him to get his foot out, and he'd get another dose. When the foot was free, Buster moved it cautiously, saying, 'Shit, shit, shit,' because of the pain. 'I don't think anything's broken,' he said. The sock had soaked up what blood there was, though there was the pearly glint of Buster's round ankle bone. He sat with his back against the rack and rested for a while. I was horrified that the storemen would lay man-traps, but Buster said the gin trap would be for rats he reckoned, big bastards after all the food. I was all for getting out straight away, but with Buster's pain and anger welled up obstinacy as well. 'Take the torch and nick a couple of cartons of cigarettes,' he said. 'I'm sure as fuck not leaving with bloody nothing at all.'

So finally we were back in the little office and with the key replaced beneath the cactus pot. We let ourselves out into the dark, with a cold wind whistling at the warehouse corners. I carried the binoculars and one carton of cigarettes; Buster leant on me and tried to keep pressure off his left foot. There was nobody around in the night, and we went slowly into the RSA grounds and cut across to the river path which would take us home. Buster kept swearing when his foot got a special jolt, but he said that the warehouse people wouldn't have any idea what had sprung the trap, and we could get back in the same way anytime we damn well liked.

We never did, though, for a variety of reasons that are lost to me now, and neither do I remember seeing much of Buster after that night. When we parted close to his place, he said I could have one of the cartons, but a couple of packets was all I wanted. Buster gave me an odd, rueful grin before he limped off into the windy darkness, as if to remind me that you have to expect such things when you go up against the world.

minding lear

MONEY WAS SCARCE AT THE END of the university year. Well, it was always scarce, but then it was just that twitchy time between the end of lectures and the start of exams. My landlady said a friend of hers was wanting someone to look after her old dad for a few days while she and her husband had a break. Fifty dollars a day with food and accommodation, and I could spend most of the time swotting, my landlady said, because no doubt the old guy would mainly be sleeping. Maybe Mrs Lills was keen on me taking it because she'd be sure of her last few weeks' rent. Maybe her motives were altruistic and she wanted to help both me and her friend.

Mrs Lills was a tall woman with skin like a trout's belly, and everything she cooked was stringy like herself, but she set very few rules in her house and didn't interfere in my life. Mr Lills was a diesel mechanic and away most of the time on offshore fishing boats. Occasionally when I came in for a meal he'd be there, his nails ringed with grease, and he never recognised my presence, never spoke a word, as if we were on separate planes of existence, although sharing the same time and space. I wondered sometimes if we would be able to walk through each other with just the whisper of images passing.

Angeline Moffit was the friend's name, and she said if I was interested in the terms, I could come over the next morning, or the one after, to meet her dad, but no later because she had to get someone sorted as soon as possible. Angeline and her husband were going to Nelson for several days. She said the doctor told her it was imperative she have a break, absolutely imperative. I could tell from her voice that she was gratified to be the recipient of such an impressive word. My landlady said that wasn't the all of it: their marriage had been drifting, and Nelson was a second-chance honeymoon.

I went over on the morning after. The Moffits lived in Rosedown, close to the golf course, and seemed to be better off than my landlady. They had ranchslider doors that opened onto a broad concrete patio on which old man Ladd sat in a substantial chair amongst lesser, white plastic ones.

'Dad,' said Angeline Moffit, 'this is Brian who's going to keep you company when we're away.'

'Away?' said Dad.

'To Nelson and Blenheim. We talked about it, and Brian's going to make sure you're okay.'

'Brian?' said Dad. Later I was to realise that Dad was at his best in the mornings, and that's why Angeline Moffit had asked me to call round then.

Mr Ladd was eighty-eight, and suffering some sort of painless physical implosion: a big man, collapsing in on himself so that his shoulders were no longer at right angles to his spine and his head hung like a pendulum in front of his concave chest. His daughter told me he'd been the manager of an engineering firm with two hundred and seventy people, and five branches in the

North Island, but what had once been robust and secular appeared to me at first sight mournful, pious and ecclesiastic. His hands were steepled in supplication, his large eyes upturned in abandoned sockets and shadowed by thickets of grey eyebrows.

'Brian's coming back on Sunday, Dad,' Angeline Moffit said, 'and he'll be company for you when we're away.'

Dad didn't say anything, but his eyes rolled at me for a moment, and the bones of his chin worked loosely, like a hand beneath a sheet.

On Sunday after lunch I put a few clothes, my books and swot notes, in my squash bag and went out to Rosedown on my Suzuki. Angeline and her husband were keen to get on their way, enjoy the imperative break from work stress, and achieve the equally imperative repair in their marriage perhaps. She said she'd written everything down on a pad by the phone, but she went over it quickly nevertheless. The first commandment, and underlined, said Dad must never be left alone. So much for squash, I thought. 'Dad's doctor is Dr Morley Smith,' said Angeline. 'I've got the number there, except he's away at present and someone's standing in.' They drove away in a white Corona and, after a quick wave to me, I could see them shrug off care and begin a relaxed conversation.

Dad and I had a little more difficulty gaining rapport. He was convinced I was a spray man come to moss-proof the rooftiles, and didn't see why he should have to pay me to watch television with him. 'It's too windy to spray right now,' I told him, and although there wasn't a breath outside, he was mollified. I cottoned on early that it was more productive to debate with Dad on his own terms than appeal to reality.

Women's beach volleyball was the TV programme, and Dad and I sat in the creaking Sunday afternoon and let time pass. The women were powerful, yet shapely, and Dad nodded and blinked, sometimes scratching the top of one hand with the fingers of the other. There are some big dogs which are very lugubrious, ears, lower eyelids and the gleaming sides of their mouths all drawn down. Dad was a bit like that, but his skin in parts was scaled like a dragon's. When the volleyball women had stopped flopping onto their backs in the silky sand, Dad forgot the television and told me it was time for wine and cheese.

I wondered if he was having me on, but the checklist by the phone had no prohibition on wine and cheese. There was one of those round, soft bries in the fridge, and cans of local beer. Dad was interested in the cheese, but waved the beer aside. 'Wine, Mr Mildew, wine,' he said in a tone that implied he was humouring me rather than the other way around. The effort of getting out of the lounge chair gave him hiccups, and when I followed him through the house, rather than discovering wine, we ended in the sunroom, where Dad stood behind the warm glass and looked over the golf course. I discovered a rack of bottles in the cupboard under the stairs, and took a pinot noir back to the sunroom as an incentive for Dad to return to the lounge. His eyes hardly left the bottle, and he stopped only twice for a hiccup session. 'Now you're talking,' he said. 'Who did you say you were again?'

'Brian.'

'And what do you do in the firm?' he said.

'I'm just here to keep you company till your daughter's back.'

Dad gave a shuddering yawn which ended in hiccups, and after shuffling into a calculated position with his bum towards the big chair, let himself fall back into it. Wine cured his hiccups and took the place of conversation. I watched some European soccer, and soon Dad was dozing with a piece of cheese, like a nub of chalk, in the hand resting on his lap. Awake, or asleep, he breathed always through his mouth, and his lips had an absolute demarcation between the dry, faded outer rind and the gleaming red swell within.

Angeline hadn't left a great deal of prepared food — perhaps she thought I had to earn my money somehow — but there was a large packet of savouries in the deep freeze, and I took some of those for our tea. I wanted to make a good start on my exam revision in the evening. Dad wasn't good at the end of the day, however: that was something I had to learn. He woke up when the sausage rolls and potato-topped miniature mince pies were heating, and bowled the pinot noir bottle with a random sweep of his arm. While I tried to get the stain out of the carpet before it set, Dad began with anxious interrogation. What time was it? Where was his family? Who was I? Who was he? Why hadn't he been asked to sign off the general accounts? When was his left leg to be amputated?

'I didn't know you're going to have a leg off,' I said.

'Who in their right mind would put up with it twitching all the time? The doctor said better to do it at home so that the Inland Revenue and the benefit people don't know. They reduce superannuation payment limb by limb, the bastards.'

'Okay.'

I put the plate of savouries between us to cool, but Dad had lost awareness of such mundane things, and bit into a very hot roll, spat it out and cried out in anger and pain. It was an oddly childish error and childish reaction.

'I'm sorry,' I said.

'You're stupid,' he said. 'Who are you anyway? I thought you were going to spray the roof and then piss off. Why don't you go now.' With tears still shining in the nooks and folds of his old face, he began to finger other savouries with a fearful interest. 'What's in these, anyway?'

'Sausage, egg and bacon, mince — things like that.'

'That's all right then,' Dad said. 'You need something to put lead in your pencil, not all lettuce leaves and bloody bran. You can't do a day's work on rabbit food.'

'Eat these up then,' I said, and he did, enjoying the flavour once they'd cooled a bit.

But after tea it was still broad daylight at that time of year, and how could you expect a grown man to go to bed. Dad couldn't concentrate on the television, yet was absorbed for almost an hour arranging the loose armrest covers on his armchair. 'Where did you say we are?' he asked finally when he'd lost both sleeves down the squab sides.

'At your place.'

'This rat hole doesn't ring a bell with me,' he said in a voice worn with age, a husky echo like a mournful wind in lakeside reeds.

'Well, it's your daughter's place, then, and she looks after you here. It's good to have family for support, don't you reckon.'

Dad drooped his lower lip in silent derision, almost fell asleep, then looked across at me for a time. 'Where do you fit in again?'

'I'm a sort of cousin, on the other side of the family,' I told him.

'I thought you said you're going to spray something.'

'Yeah, that too,' I said.

'Most things could do with a good spray.'

In the summer twilight, almost nine o'clock, I guided Dad to his bedroom, and left the curtains open so that he could see over the golf course. There were just three boys feeling with their feet for balls in the pond, and the blue-grey dusk softened their distant outlines. I put Dad's pyjamas beside him on the bed and gave him privacy so that he could undress, but when I went back, he was still sitting there and had taken off just one shoe, which he was holding to his nose like a wine glass. 'These aren't my shoes,' he whispered. 'Not by a long bloody chalk they're not, and I'm hungry. I haven't had anything to eat. If you don't eat you don't shit and if you don't shit you die.'

'What about all the savouries and cheese? What about the wine before you clobbered the bottle?'

'What do you mean?'

'I mean you've had your tea.'

'I'm hungry,' he said.

I got Dad a piece of white bread and honey, and gradually got his clothes off as he passed it from hand to hand. He had a jersey, shirt and singlet on despite summer, and his bones were the only strong lines on his white body. 'There'll be someone in the house tonight, won't there?' he said.

The whole business of getting him off to bed took much longer than I'd thought, and I didn't try to get any swot done after all. I told myself that I'd have a routine for the three days. After watching triceratops and brachiosaurus shaking the earth for half an hour, I switched off the TV and went to the bedroom Angeline had assigned me, which doubled as her husband's study. The bed was more a settee, and little further than nose distance from the grunty desktop PC and inkjet colour printer. Most of the books were about structural engineering: titles like *Ferro Concrete and Earth Tremors*, *Stress Coefficients in Angular Steel* and *The Place of Design in Practical Construction*. There were a few rugby books, with the photograph pages sticking out slightly from the remainder of the text.

I fell asleep with my face in the eerie green glow of a digital clock, close enough to swallow. A dream of monsters possessed me utterly until a utahraptor reared up and cried, 'I need to shit. Why has this bloody place no lavatory? Rats, rats everywhere, but no lavatory.' The incongruity, and perhaps the scale of consequence, woke me suddenly, and the kiwifruit clock numerals showed almost 3 a.m. Old Mr Ladd swayed in the doorway, half hobbled by his falling pyjama trousers. 'Too late, too late,' he mourned in his stage whisper, and sobbed as he let loose on the floor.

For just a moment I imagined that if I closed my eyes I could return to the lesser terrors of giant carnivores, but the reek of reality was too strong for that. Whatever Angeline was paying me it wasn't enough. I tried to persuade Dad to stay put in the doorway so at least there would be only one clean-up site, but he wandered, desolate and tearful, soiling all as he went. Corralled in the bathroom at last, he reluctantly stepped into the shower, but there somewhat recovered his spirits in warmth and steam.

'Who are you again?' he asked.

'I'm your man Friday,' I said. 'I'm your minder while Angeline's away.'

'She was a wonderful kid, so affectionate. She and my wife were like sisters, and often when I came home from work I'd hear them laughing even as I got out of the car.'

I was almost in the shower with him, reaching through the doorway to make sure he was cleaned up. A situation of intense physical familiarity and yet we were complete strangers. It was easier, though, because I knew that soon he would have quite forgotten his recent humiliation, while his daughter's affection endured in his memory. And she would be a wonderful kid, a glowing and retrospective emblem, no matter how cursory her later regard had become.

In new pyjamas, Dad went obediently to bed, but not to silence. As I cleaned up in the hall and bathroom, he talked on and on about his life in a time before I was born. Awareness of a listener, rather than a partner in conversation, seemed to be his need. 'Are you there?', he'd call from time to time, and a word in reply, or a bang on the plastic bucket, was enough for him to continue. He told me that Angeline had always made his birthday cake after she was eight, that his son Theo could have been a world beater in gymnastics if he'd stuck at it.

'Good, was he?' I said, after partly opening the bathroom window and coming to his doorway. 'Where is he now?' It was out before I remembered my landlady telling me that Angeline's brother had died overseas.

Dad didn't reply for a time. His head and shoulders were darker shadows against the bed-end. Then, 'You'll be old yourself in time,' he said. 'See how you like it when your turn comes I say. How would you like to go without food for days?'

'We've had plenty to eat, though.'

'Useless prick,' Dad said emphatically.

Half an hour later he was snoring and the smell of shit was growing fainter throughout the house. I weighed up whether I should ring the stand-in doctor the next day and say there was no way I could cope with the old guy. In the few hours' sleep that followed, I had another dream: not about dinosaurs, but gymnasts. A whole flock of them performing at once very high on wires, bars and trapeze. All men with cut-away singlets, and superb musculature. All wheeling and spinning and leaping without effort, and all with a Dad's head on their young bodies like a lugubrious mask. I could hear the smack of taut equipment, and see the faint drift of chalk from their palms as they prepared for each exercise. Maybe that's how Theo passed the time since his death.

No wonder I slept in. Dad was humming ballads as I made sense of my surroundings. 'Hang Down Your Head, Tom Dooley' was the only one I recognised. My own father sang it sometimes.

'Who are you again?' Dad asked me when I was helping him with his underpants. He was at his best in the mornings.

'I'm your helper.'

'Helper?'

'And maybe I'll spray the roof,' I said.

Dad seemed pleased with something familiar in that. 'Just so,' he said with hollow, echoing satisfaction.

After the grotesque pantomime of the night, the sunlit Canterbury morning promised a conventional sanity. Dad ate toast with ginger marmalade and discoursed on factory management, taking me for a member of his team. 'You see,' he said, 'it's not important now whether I know anything about engineering at all. It's leadership and man-management skills that are important to run a company. It's a truth that seems to have to be discovered over and over again. People think the best chemist should run the pharmaceutical company, and the top academic head the university. In fact it's all about motivation and team building.'

'Isn't that American touchy-feely bullshit?' I said. If Dad Ladd was up to coherent discussion in the mornings then why not have intellectual stringency.

'I thought so myself at first, but it's their palaver that's false, not the premise. Take this deal at the moment with the stainless steel casings for Hentlings.' But Dad's voice then lost resolve, as he realised there was some discontinuity between the Hentlings contract and his Monday morning breakfast with a stranger. Bewildered pride stopped him saying more, and he concentrated on his coffee, his head cantilevered far over the table. In the afternoons and evenings when Dad was well away I played anarchic fool to his Lear without scruple, but in the mornings, when he regained something of his original self, I was just an imposter and voyeur, and a sad discomfort was often the tone.

Dad then gazed out across the golf course, his great, loose eyes sliding glances at me when he thought he was unobserved. Defensiveness is a ploy of age, as the mind itself proves unreliable. 'I'm here to keep you company while your daughter's away for a few days,' I said, to spare him the indignity of yet another inquiry as to where he was in the world and with whom.

He nodded firmly, as if he'd been sure of that all along. 'It's good weather here at this time of year,' he said.

I hung out Dad's pyjamas bottoms on the line, aware that more articles would have disguised his little accident, but then realised that he had no recollection of such recent things. Some afflictions ameliorate their own effects. A whole day with Dad stretched ahead. For a time I encouraged him to talk more of his management practices and attitudes, but he grew impatient with the lack of sophistication in my questions, and after explaining the professional development system he'd instituted to identify management potential, he fell silent and ignored further promptings.

There was no way I could stand being housebound for three days, and I decided if Dad couldn't be left alone, then he'd have to come with me. I asked him if he played squash and although his answer was noncommittal, I told him that he was bound to enjoy watching anyway. 'We can get a break out of the house,' I said cheerfully, in that positive, sweepalong way that works sometimes with kids. Dad gave a lopsided grin. I rang Martin and told him to meet me there.

I wasn't entirely irresponsible. I put the one helmet on Dad, and even though the sun glittered in the blue, summer sky and the breeze across the golf course was warm to the touch, I buttoned him into his ankle-length, dark, Jack the Ripper coat, and encouraged him to climb onto the Suzuki behind me. The squash bag I held between my thighs and rested on the handlebars. 'Hang on tight, and lean in when I do,' I told him. He did hold on, and as the little bike screamed its way to the squash club, I was aware of Dad's long face at my left shoulder. Did he wonder how it had come to this? A man who had been general manager of an engineering firm employing two hundred and seventy people, trapped on the back of a 125cc Suzuki driven by a stranger who had come perhaps to spray the roof for mildew.

'Sit here,' I told him at the club, and folded his coat to pad the wood of the tiered seating looking down on the court. As Martin and I played, I checked every now and again that Dad was still there. 'Are you okay, Mr Ladd?' and at least once he nodded. A mishit sent the ball into the seating, and despite there being nowhere for it to be lost we couldn't find it anywhere. I shook Dad's greatcoat and felt the pockets several times, I even patted him down like a policeman searching for weapons. He took it all with equanimity.

'Weird,' said Martin. 'Maybe he's swallowed it.' I wished he hadn't said that, for a squash ball is pretty small, but Dad seemed to be breathing okay and in no discomfort.

'It's not warm here at all, is it,' he said. 'I was wondering if there might be a nice piece of pork for lunch.'

Martin and I played two more games, then I took Dad to the lavatory and togged him up for the trip home. 'Been nice to meet you,' said Martin, whose mother had lots of visitors to the house and was up on manners. I expected Dad to ask who he was again, but he wasn't always predictable and it was still morning. 'Likewise,' he said and compressed his bushy eyebrows in a smile.

Little conversation is possible on a motorbike, unless you shout, but when I stopped at the Ilam Road lights I could just hear in my left ear Dad humming one of his ballads. It reassured me that riding as pillion passenger had no terrors for him, and that a squash ball wasn't lodged in his windpipe. He was no quick mover any more, but once he got a grip such as that around my waist he held on well.

Dad didn't get any pork for lunch, but I did some cheese on toast, and we sat on the patio. Despite the heat he kept his long coat on, and it didn't worry me. I wanted to insist on having my own way only in issues that mattered. Why shouldn't he sit with a winter coat in the summer sun if he enjoyed it? 'It's a class coat, that,' I said.

'I had one like it in the battalion.'

'You were in the war, then,' I said.

'Everyone was in the war,' said Dad in the voice Brando used for *The Godfather*. It was something else I saw no reason to contradict him on. There's all sorts of war, after all. He fell asleep suddenly quite soon afterwards. One moment he was puckering his lips and running a finger on his unshaven neck, the next his head was back on the chair and his nose was casting a shadow like a sundial marker.

For an hour and a half I was able to concentrate on the constitutional effects of the American Civil War. No question came up on that, of course. I had a beer on the quiet too. It seemed to me that I was entitled to keep a little ahead of Dad in regard to alcohol.

Mid-afternoon Dad woke. I looked up from my books to see that he was observing me quizzically. His mouth had fallen open and the sun caught the white stubble on his neck. I knew what he was thinking. 'Who am I again?' I said. 'I'm Brian who's looking after you. Okay?' He nodded with a certain nonchalance to suggest he knew that, then he worked hard at generating a cough strong enough to shift the phlegm accumulated during his sleep. 'Did you enjoy it at the squash courts this morning?'

'Squash?'

'This morning we went down on the bike to the squash courts. Remember?'

'Ah,' said Dad in a guarded and equivocal way. I thought that as he'd forgotten it already I could take him there each morning and it would be a fresh experience each time.

We had a mug of tea, and then I found his triple-head shaver at the bottom of his wardrobe and gave him a shave. He quite enjoyed it, moving his head about to tauten the skin at my direction and closing his eyes in the direct sunlight. It had been some time since anyone had taken any care in giving Dad a shave. Long hairs, missed day after day, lay in fold lines of his skin and his upper lip had been neglected. 'I use a cut-throat most times,' said Dad, but that must have been years ago, for there plenty of moles and blemishes which would have come to a bloody end. I noticed that the skin over his collarbone was very pale, and the fine creases formed small diamond patterns. The tip of his left ear was eaten away slightly by a scaly skin cancer. His cheekbones were pronounced rims beneath his eyes. It was a ravaged face, but strong nevertheless. Dad ran his hand over his features with satisfaction, and two white butterflies tumbled in a courtship dance through the warm air inches from his head.

'You look a new man,' I said.

'I've got very stiff, you know.' He tested his arms by stretching them out, then lifting them above his head slowly. 'You do get stiff with age,' he said. 'Nothing to be done about that. I suppose I'd better be heading home soon.'

'No hurry while it's so warm,' I said. 'Enjoy watching the golfers for a while, then we'll think about things again.'

I did a bit more on the Civil War, but just being aware that Dad was awake made it difficult to concentrate. Even sitting and at rest, the business of living necessitated a range of noises: exhalation was accompanied by a small wheeze, he smacked his lips from time to time, and gave the occasional shuddering and dolorous sigh. And every now and again one of his slightly curled hands flipped suddenly and was still again.

As the sun slipped and the shadows grew from the golf course pines, I began to wonder about Dad and me in the coming night. Maybe the motorbike ride would help him sleep; maybe more physical exertion would help as well. 'How about a walk before tea, Mr Ladd?'

'Eh?'

'We could stretch our legs before tea.'

'Stretch your own legs. Who are you again?'

But with the false, importunate bonhomie that comes so naturally to a carer, I hauled Dad up, gave him his stick and encouraged him off the patio and down the drive. His resistance was expressed by turning a little away from me as we walked, and stopping often to explore with his stick any plants to the side.

We began the small, seemingly never-ending block, and I disliked myself for the hope I had that no acquaintance would see me out walking with the old guy, yet maintained that hope just the same. It wasn't a trendy way to spend time on a summer afternoon, especially as he still wore his heavy coat in the last glare of the sun. Dad would stop from time to time to have a good cough, or peer into people's properties if he noticed movement. Self-consciousness is lost with the passing of years. A woman was kneeling on a groundsheet near her letter box to do some weeding, and after watching with interest for some time, Dad turned away, saying in his hollow but penetrating way, 'Women get big arses later in their life, don't you think, Warren?'

'Who's Warren?' I said, urging him roughly on down the street, but without the courage to turn round.

'What's that?'

'Who's Warren?' But Dad just gave his slow, soft smile. Whoever Warren was, and what brief neurological flash had linked him to our day together, was gone for the moment.

When we'd done the circuit and arrived home again, Dad was down to a shuffle. He was interested and somewhat sceptical to be told that was the house he lived in. He had entered that late afternoon free-fall from connectedness which I came to know well. And the fall was into the whirling chaos of each night. 'I'd never buy a house like this,' he said derisively. He was a little ahead of me, and he looked back with his head hung low and the whites of his eyes showing, the way a horse sometimes looks back around its flank.

'It's Angeline's house, and you live with her.' Even in late afternoon his daughter's name struck a chord somewhere, and he didn't contradict me, but came with some reluctance towards the front door.

'And you are again?'

'I'm Warren.' I admit my intention was investigative, a hope that in denial he might reveal this Warren, but Dad's malady was too subtle for my amateur psychology. 'You still haven't sprayed for mildew,' was all he said.

I closed the big glass doors to the patio, but pushed Dad's padded lounge chair close to them so that he was full on to the setting sun. Such comfort activated his appetites. 'Wine and cheese would be very acceptable,' he stage whispered. So I took another red from the cupboard beneath the stairs, but, learning from experience, used a mug for Dad, and kept the bottle well away.

Dad sank so far back into the easy chair that it looked as if some sort of suction was at work, and the sun through the glass on his gunslinger coat must have put his temperature well up, but his face remained pale and he gargled happily in his mug. 'I thought I might cook bangers and mash for tea,' I said. In my second year, when I'd been flatting, it had been my stand-by when rostered for a meal. For visitors my variation was to make a packet gravy and have peas as well. I'd received compliments, not all sarcastic.

'The Germans make a good sausage,' said Dad. 'Here the sausage is a poor man's food, but in Europe they know how to make a sausage, and how to treat it.'

'I thought you hated the Germans. The war and all that.'

'The war. I'm not talking about the war. Who said anything about the war? I thought you said something about sausage.'

'You're right,' I said.

'In the war the food was bloody awful.'

'Mine will be better,' I said.

'War is never better,' said Dad huskily. He looked at me rather belligerently from the depths of the chair, but when I topped up his wine mug his expression softened.

I moved to another topic. 'I wonder how Angeline is enjoying her holiday.'

'She always keeps in touch, always has. Not like some,' said Dad. 'We hardly hear from Theo. What sort of job does she do now?'

'I don't know.'

'It's something to do with work. Some sort of work, I know that.'

'Right.'

I made a good fist of dinner, though I couldn't find any packet gravy. However Dad sank into one of his repetitive spells, and after asking me over and over who I was again, he began complaining that rats were gnawing at him during the nights. 'I don't want to sleep in the rat room again tonight,' he said.

'I don't think there are any rats here,' I said.

'No one can sleep with rats at you all night. The buggers come out of the wardrobe, I reckon.'

'Let's close the wardrobe door then tonight.'

'Oh, they bite to buggery, those buggers.' Dad pushed the coat sleeve up a bit and displayed his pale, waxy skin. 'What's that, then,' he said. 'Scotch mist?' There were no bites that I could see, but that didn't mean Dad hadn't suffered: pain can be the consequence of belief.

'No one likes a rat,' I agreed.

'I don't want to sleep in the rat room tonight.'

'No one likes a rat.' Dementia's repetition is so easy to fall into.

I did the dishes while Dad in the lounge railed against the rats, and then I watched a Mafia movie on television with the sound well up. It was hopeless to try and swot while Dad went on. He had dried up by the time the film was over, just nodding to himself and giving the occasional knowing chuckle, which fluttered in his open mouth. There is a cocoon of self-absorption that surrounds the very old and the very young.

For this second night I was determined to be better prepared, and I cajoled Dad into a lavatory visit before he went to bed. Getting the big coat off him was a bit of a test: his affection for it had increased during the day. 'But I'd better have it ready for when I go,' he said testily.

'Where are you going?'

'Back to my own place.'

'Where's that?'

'Same place it's always been.'

'But you won't be leaving during the night.'

'What would you know,' said Dad. I reminded him to wipe himself and flush the bowl, then showed him the way to his bedroom.

'Why are these rooms always in different places?' he said.

'All part of the grand puzzle of life,' I told him.

'I think you're going mad,' he whispered.

Once Dad was tucked up I tried to do more swot, but after the night before I was apprehensive of interruption later in the night, so went to bed at eleven myself. So as not to face the vivid envy of the digital clock face, I lay on my back. Technology was at first a distraction there as well, for on the ceiling was a smoke alarm like a pig's snout, and it cheeped softly to warn that the battery was low. The regular, subdued insistence became finally a lullaby and I fell into a routine anxiety dream of academic failure.

Dad's cries of despair woke me. Piercing, vehement cries, utterly distinct from the echo chamber hoarseness of his everyday voice. 'The rats are here again, the buggers, ' he called, and when I went in and put on the light, he was sitting forlornly on his bed with his big hands clasped. He must have been out earlier in the night because he had piled some books against the wardrobe door, and had a maroon blazer on, but no pyjama top. 'Rats are king here,' he said accusingly. Tears glittered on his face. 'Where are my wife and family? Where is my life?'

'Where are the rats?' I asked to appease him. His other questions were too tough for me, and called for a divine answer. 'They've all buggered off,' I said. I pushed books away from the wardrobe and opened the door. 'See. Nothing to worry about.'

Dad didn't answer, but his expression showed he thought my display was mere naivety, and that he and the rats knew a thing or two.

'What is this place?' he said finally.

'It's your daughter's place. You live here.'

'How can it be Angeline's place when she lives with us? She's still at school, so how can she have a place? Why doesn't anyone tell the truth any more? The world's full of liars now. I tell my staff that deceit is the worst failing, and self-deceit the worst of all.'

I thought Dad was bound to query my appearance in his life, but in that night no doubt I was just one more enigma in a pageant of glaring inconsistency. He sat morosely for a time, breathing heavily, as if defeated in one round and having little hope of the next. He looked at the skirting board in front of him with a dull obstinacy. 'I'll get back to my home and family,' he said, 'rats or no rats. You don't know as much as you think you do.'

'You're right there,' I said, with exams in mind.

I got him to lie down again, and didn't bother hassling him about the blazer, or the reason for his wish to leave the light on. I'm sure Dad was a believer in priorities when he was a captain of industry. For me it seemed the way to go in aged care. Food, booze, warmth, light and rats were all important things; what you wore in bed, or said to passing acquaintances, was of little account.

'Leave the light on for the migration of the monarchs,' he said with some dignity. I thought he meant butterflies rather than crowned heads, but the connection to either was obscure.

'Where are they headed?'

'Rings of Saturn,' said Dad with soft assurance.

'Of course.'

I stood on the patio for a while, which was dimly illuminated by the light through Dad's curtains. I could hear him humming to himself in an almost cheerful way, and the golf course across the road was a dark gap bounded by lights of streets and houses. I wondered by what random happenstance old Mr Ladd and I should end up there together, and what small connection it might be with future oddity in which both of us were absent. Maybe his long, dark coat would clothe a jazz musician of the house in time; maybe he'd written a sonnet of censure in regard to rats and folded it in some crevice of the wardrobe from which a buck-toothed child of immigrants would draw it out. Perhaps our tangential conversations would lodge in the Pink Batts, and flap down again decades after into some other verbal banquet of senility.

Dad was asleep when I went back in. The blazer was open and the hair of his chest thick, but almost colourless. I pulled up the sheet, turned out the light, and shook a fist at the wardrobe as a warning to the rats not to start anything. Groggy with bewilderment and fatigue, I lay down on my own bed, pulled my scrotum free from my thighs, and was comfortable. To green numerals and a chirping smoke alarm I was oblivious. Sleep closed on me like the grave.

When I opened my eyes next morning, the clock at the end of my nose showed well after eight o'clock. I spent several minutes working out what was the day of the week, and was amazed that it was only Tuesday. Surely I had been responsible for Dad a week or more. I wondered whether in extreme old age time itself slowed, along with the other functions of life, and if that perception was contagious. To what extent could time drag its feet before halting altogether?

Metaphysics gave place to action when I heard Dad wandering the rooms in search of the lavatory. It lay, of course, behind the one door he hadn't thought to try. 'Hard luck,' I said.

'Bloody place.' He still wore the sports blazer, and his pyjamas trousers were wet, but nothing worse had happened. There'd be sheets to wash as well, I reminded myself. He voided with sound like a dredge emptying, and the smell billowed through the house in almost visual intensity. Dad gave a long sigh of relief. It wasn't a bad start to the day. 'Who are you again?' he asked as I helped him dress.

'I am the Panjanmandarin of the Empire of the Rats.'

'No need to get shirty,' said Dad.

'Remember the rats from last night?'

'What rats?' he said, scornful in the comparative logic of morning.

'Anyway,' I said, 'let's have breakfast.'

'What's the chance of an egg?' he asked.

After breakfast Dad started to get ready for work, but I told him that he'd retired years ago, and he agreed and went out to his favourite place on the patio in the morning sun. I took my notes on the poetry of Herrick and joined him. Already there was a ladies' foursome on the fairway closest to us. Their laughter just carried the distance.

'Do you like women?' asked Dad in his soughing voice, and his lantern face hung in their direction.

I said that as a generalisation I was in agreement.

'There weren't many women in the war.'

'No.'

'Women underestimate their anatomical measurements and men exaggerate theirs. That's something I've noticed is a difference.'

I was surprised by Dad's perception, even though it was morning. Every now and again the clouds cleared and the original sharp landscape of Dad's mind was revealed.

'What else do you reckon about women?'

'They're much more reliable as workers,' he said. 'It was my policy to hire women if the jobs were suitable.' Dad enjoyed the sun: kept his face to it even as its summer intensity grew. He had an almost reptilian instinct for heat. Two or three minutes later what he took as a new thought occurred to him. 'There weren't many women in the war,' he said.

'So you said.'

'Did I?'

Throughout the morning I got a little revision done. The high points of our interaction were a couple of trips to the toilet and a shave. The lavatory visits were as laborious as ever, but the shave took a good deal less time than the day before, because we'd done such a good job then. Dad did have another intellectual crescendo, about cars, when we were having a cup of coffee. 'What sort of car do you drive, Warren?' he said. So Warren was with us briefly again.

'I've got a motorbike.'

'One thing that I allow myself in business is a decent car. It gives clients confidence in the firm, but also there's pleasure in the possession of it. Not something posey — no turbo nonsense, or fruit salad colours. A quality six-cylinder three-litre saloon, say, and I prefer manuals. I've never taken to automatics the same.'

'What have you got now?' I asked, knowing he hadn't driven for years.

'A Saab, but I'm not sure where it's kept. Since I've been staying with you here, I'm not sure where it's kept. If you could find out we could take a spin to Feilding, or Taupo. I used to have to drive a fair bit on business and enjoyed it. A long trip on a good road without much traffic, and everything in the car ticking over nicely and the world slipping by without being able to get a grip on you.' Dad's voice was quiet and he was restful in the sun. I imagined him as a busy manager, having a few hours to himself in his company car as he went from one city to another. And not knowing in those rather pleasant interludes that a time would come without any pressure of work at all, without a car, sometimes without a memory.

'Which was the best car you ever had?' I asked him, as a test.

'I had a V8 Customline which was a damn good car.'

'What were Customlines?'

'The big Fords,' said Dad. 'I bought it new and she did over a hundred and fifty thousand miles without missing a beat.' I could see that the recollection of that car was of considerable satisfaction to him: his wrecked face had a half-smile and his hands were at ease in his lap. Maybe he was thinking of the sheen on the Customline when he'd just polished it, the burble of the V8 when he fed it the fat, times on holiday with Viv, Angeline and Theo all close to him. Maybe he was rather caught by some glimpse of himself, lithe and on his way up in business.

I opened a tin of sheep's tongues and we had sandwiches for lunch. It was the sort of meat that Dad managed well and it suited summer. I brought out a few lettuce leaves too, but neither of us were great on salad. Small tasks require a good deal of application at Dad's age. Just to get the sandwich to his mouth without losing the tongue filling was for him a task requiring not just tactical hand movements, but a full strategy.

'Would you like to go down to the squash courts again this afternoon?' I asked, but of course yesterday was further from Dad's recall than the Ford Customline of history, even at midday.

'Eh?'

'You could watch me play squash, Mr Ladd.'

'Could I,' he said, amiable and uncomprehending.

Martin was keen enough to have a break from study, so I dressed Dad in his full-length Wichita coat again, and left him standing dark and incongruous in the bright sun while I brought round the Suzuki. 'Is it time to go?' he asked as I put his helmet on.

'Into the sunset, pilgrim.'

'It's not sunset yet,' said Dad as, twisting round, I helped him find first the left footrest, then the right. Through the summer streets we went, and the guilt I felt was not for any danger that the old guy faced, but for history and literature neglected.

Despite his visit on the day before, Dad saw everything at the courts afresh: the glass court back and the upper seating, the changing rooms with coffin lockers. He was introduced anew to Martin and found inaugural pleasure in it all. 'You didn't hide the ball yesterday, or swallow it?' asked Martin, but Dad just gave his most quizzical smile to disguise incomprehension. He sat on the top seating for a while, and I forgot him in the concentration on the game, until after losing a close set I looked up and realised he had gone. He wasn't anywhere I looked inside the building, but when I went from the main doors into the carpark, he was sitting on the small concrete wall, his eyes closed in the sun, singing softly to himself. 'I wondered where you'd got to,' I said.

Dad opened his eyes and fell silent. He squinted at me without giving anything away. 'I'm waiting for my wife to pick me up,' he said formally.

'I'm taking you home.'

'Who are you again?'

'Brian. I'm looking after you while Angeline's away.'

'Angeline's away? No one told me that.'

'I'll just get my gear and we'll be off,' I told him. Martin was a bit disappointed we didn't get another few games, but was okay about it. He knew it was a job for me, and thought looking after a very old guy was easy money. I'd started with that idea myself.

On the way back Dad didn't seem so good on the pillion as on the way down, or during the rides the day before. He wasn't hanging on as well, and didn't lean in on the corners. I cut down the speed, and shouted to him to keep a good grip. How would I explain to Angeline if he fell off, or had a seizure of some sort. I made a small, one-sided contract with God that if we got home safely I wouldn't take Dad on the bike again. His left foot did come off the rest and drag on the road, but by then I was down to jogging pace and able to stop before Dad was swung off. He didn't complain, but his increasing bewilderment made me feel all the more guilty, and I was again surprised at how quickly he could change from competence to ineptitude. I apologised to him when we were home, but he had lost the sequence of cause and consequence.

He wouldn't take the coat off, and sat on the patio rubbing his left leg. I gave him a mug of sweet tea, and started on some notes about the Wakefield influence on New Zealand settlement. I hoped the heat of the late afternoon sun, redoubled by the greatcoat, would lull him to sleep for a few hours, but he showed increasing bad humour and fearfulness. He complained about his sore leg, though unable to remember the cause. He complained about being left with a stranger in a house he didn't much like. 'I won't have to spend the night here, will I?' or 'I'm not going to be here when it gets dark am I?' he asked a hundred times, but paid no attention to any of the placating replies I made. I ignored him in the end. Angeline said he'd been a top administrator, but in the bad times all that was left of that serene and calculating efficiency was a querulous anxiety. 'It's a very cold house at night, this,' he said morosely. 'Who are you again?'

'An academic failure in Gotham City,' I said.

'You talk nonsense,' said Dad. His low-slung face turned away from me and he continued the conversation with himself. 'I'm certain we said there was to be underfloor heating right through the living area and the bedrooms. It'll be the rats, the buggers, that have chewed all the wiring. It happens all over the world at night. After the war there was nothing to stop rats spreading at all. In the desert I could always hear them breeding in the night.' Dad peered into the bright sun as if it were blackness over the shifting sand, and cracked his knuckles. The hollow whisper of his voice seemed to be coming from a barren place deep inside.

It was going to be a bad evening. With the exams looming I was desperate to get a decent night's work done. When Dad came out with the predictable request for wine and cheese, I took it as a sign and decided to let him drink enough to enter some Valhalla to which war and rats could not accompany him. For the first time I made a serious inventory of the grog cupboard and found, behind a carton, a bottle of Napoleon brandy which I'm sure Angeline and her husband had forgotten. I brought out also a bottle of shiraz to soften Dad up and provide a glass or two for me. We started on the patio and when the sun had gone down moved into the lounge. We had a mince pie each before I introduced Dad to the brandy. 'Are the others going to have a glass?' he said, all good humour by that time.

'The world has our invitation,' I said.

'Include the orchestra in that.'

'Even the celestial choirs,' I said.

'We'll all be at the start line by 0500 hours,' said Dad.

'Amen to that,' I said.

'Amen.'

For a couple of hours the wine and brandy loosened Dad's tongue and he hummed tunes and talked of his family as if his son and daughter were still children, as if his wife were still alive. Perhaps those years had been the uplands of his life. But then he sagged in his chair, steadily sipped brandy and made small noises with his loose lips. Twice I stopped studying to take him for a leak, and he went meekly, allowing me for the first time to get possession of the gunslinger's coat, and lifting his arms without expressing indignity when I worked his zip. I think he would have kept drinking brandy as long as I continued to pour it, but when the bottle was almost empty and the time was after eleven, I put his arm over my shoulder and helped him into his bedroom. It's not easy undressing a very old, drunk man. Dad was all inconvenient elbows, and limp yet recalcitrant feet and hands like dying flatfish. When he was sitting on the bed and I was tugging his pyjama jacket on, he came out with a whispered echo of a conversation long gone. 'There weren't many women in the war.'

'Not many here either,' I said.

'There was one nurse.' Dad's voice had almost disappeared.

'Good on you,' I said.

'Very few women in the war, in fact,' and as if this was her cue, Angeline rang from Nelson.

'So how's Dad?' she asked. I told her that he was fine and that he'd just gone off to bed. 'Everything okay then?' Everything was fine I said, and mentioned that he seemed brighter and more active in the mornings. 'Yes, that's the way of it,' she said. 'You're not leaving him alone at all, are you?' I could reply quite truthfully on that, but not to the next rapid interrogation. 'You're making sure he's taking both sets of tablets, green and pink?' I told her there were no problems there, and made a mental note to find the pill bottles and chuck out the number Dad should have taken. I riposted with a question of my own about the undoubted pleasure of her holiday. 'Yes, it's been quite nice, thank you, but I'm sure we haven't had a chance to unwind properly yet.' There was something in her tone which made me think she thought my inquiry overfamiliar. 'Well, anyway,' she said, 'do your best until the day after tomorrow and I'll see you then. Don't take too much notice of stuff Dad says at nights. He gets a bit wandery when he's tired.' I told her I thought he'd sleep pretty soundly.

He certainly did that. I checked on him a couple of times before going to bed myself. He could have been dead except for the snoring, and hadn't moved an inch since I put the blankets over him. The snoring was reassuring because at the back of my mind was a fear that he might die in the night, and the post mortem show an exceedingly high blood alcohol level. I took the brandy bottle across the road and flung it into the soft darkness of the golf course, and then, in the exaggerated anxiety that comes late at night, worried about the fingerprints that would be clear upon it. The guilt I felt in drugging the old guy in that way more than undid the scholastic peace that had been my motivation, and eventually I went to sleep with my mind wiped of any revision, and a decision that for the rest of my wardenship I would allow Dad the natural expression of his age, his condition and his metamorphosis of character. At least alcohol had dealt to the rats of dementia, and a deep barking dog was the one animal to inhabit the night.

The only obvious consequence of the binge in the morning was a monumentally soiled bed — a soon forgotten indignity for Dad, and a rightful punishment for me. 'Why is there always a terrible pong in this house?' Dad asked when I had finished getting the worst off the sheets in the tub and then put them in the machine. He showed no signs of a hangover and waited with some impatience for his breakfast.

'I'm going to give the place an airing today,' I said humbly. He was alive and I was so thankful: my vision of the night which saw him stretched out dead drunk in the most literal way was still fresh. 'Tomorrow Angeline comes home and everything needs to be in order. Where are these pills you should be taking anyway?'

'You don't get rid of a stink like this with pills,' said Dad scathingly.

For the first time since I'd been looking after Dad, there wasn't a clear sky. It was still warm, but a high sheet of pale cloud hid the sun. The patio wasn't as attractive without the direct strike of the sun, and after breakfast we stayed in the lounge. Dad was quiet as I shaved him, tilting his head on command and enjoying the busy feel of the electric razor on his skin, but when that was done he wanted to talk about going back to his own home and family. 'I could rent this place out,' he said. 'Investment properties like this can be good little earners if you're not facing on-going maintenance.'

'Angeline's living here though.'

There was a pause. In the mornings Dad had the ability to process some of the things he heard and to notice inconsistencies with his own sense of earlier life. 'How old's Angeline now?' he said cautiously.

'In her forties,' I said, with greater conviction than I felt.

'So she lives here all the time?'

'With you.' I avoided the complication of her husband. Dad nodded, as if he'd known these things all along, his head swaying like that of a Chinese processional dragon. He made a steeple of his big, wrinkled hands, a typical gesture, and his eyes slid behind their sagging lower lids. He was doing his best with some question to himself, but couldn't make anything of it. 'And you are again?' he enquired, almost apologetically.

While I read through my notes on a revisionist history of the New Zealand wars of the nineteenth century, Dad was content to hum and sing to himself while playing with a thread from the band of his thick, blue jersey, but after I went out to collect the mail I found that he had a box of documents on his knee, and he became intent on a scrutiny of them. I tried to concentrate on my work, but after an hour or so I found the obvious repetition of his actions distracting. He would take each envelope, or paper, from the box, manoeuvre it before his face for a time then place it on the coffee table beside him. When all were accounted for, he would replace them in the box and begin all over again, giving just as much concentration to a document on its third or fourth appearance as on its first.

'What have you got there, Mr Ladd?' I said finally, from comradeship rather than curiosity.

'I need everything in order before I go back to my wife and family,' he said.

'Well, that makes sense.'

'I don't seem to be quite on top of things the way I used to be.' His voice was quiet, more self-aware than usual. The limited admission had greater poignancy than his more flamboyant claims. I left the Maori and the colonial militia, and gave Dad the attention he deserved when at his best.

'You're eighty-eight,' I said, 'and I suppose everybody's memory is slipping a bit by then. You're still pretty good on all the early stuff.'

'Things seem different somehow. Why is it that I have to

spend so much time by myself these days?'

I had no easy answer to that. In Dad's whirling times I could play a sort Mad Hatter counterpoint of non sequiturs without belittling him, but when he was in the same world deference to that realisation was due. 'Your wife passed on some years ago and now you live here with your daughter. She's on holiday this week and I'm keeping you company. My name's Brian.'

So much contemporary truth was a shock for Dad. He relaxed back in the chair and his face assumed an added mournfulness. He rubbed the back of each hand in turn and eventually gave a small, wry smile. And was there in his eyes for a moment an ineffable realisation of his own condition? 'That's right. Of course, of course,' he affirmed to himself, 'Viv had a heart attack and she's buried at Padleigh. Yes, of course. And this is Angeline's house.'

But he didn't show any interest in his daughter's home. His voice faded, and he looked out to the uniform pale cloud high in the summer sky. The revelations of comprehension were of no more joy to him than the perils of senility. Maybe as a natural means of escaping both, he fell asleep soon afterwards, and I worked on through the skirmishes of the 1860s. Dad's mouth hung open and his theatrical, fly-away eyebrows were ludicrously luxuriant. Maybe the wine and brandy from the night before still had some claim on him; might lead him gentle into some good night.

At midday I slipped out of the lounge and assessed Angeline's pantry with lunch in mind. On the one hand was my wish for ease of preparation, on the other the mercenary consideration that food was a part of my conditions of service. Maybe simplicity at noon and indulgence at the end of the day I decided. Baked beans on toast topped with two poached eggs apiece was the outcome. I was pleased all of the yolks were intact, but when I woke Dad he had no flattering comments. 'I suppose there's worse things than beans,' was all he said. 'People don't eat them the same now, though, do they. Something to do with roughage, or saturated fats.'

'You don't have to force it down,' I said. I was surprised by the resentment I felt at his criticism. My response gave me an understanding of the greater scale of fury a committed chef would feel if Provençal Braised Pork with Saffron and Truffle Stuffing were disparaged.

'No, no, it's okay.' Dad trailed his knife through the egg yolks. 'I can get through it.'

Dad was not a malicious person. He said he'd help with the washing up, and managed to find a second tea towel and dry one flat plate before I finished everything else. A long afternoon stretched before us and I wanted to move out of the lounge to give some sense of progression to the day, and also get Dad away from his box of documents. The patio was warm and pleasant though the high cloud still reduced the sun to a general and suffusing glow. A small girl on a small trike did endless, intent circles on the neighbour's drive, and on the smooth expanse of the golf course people towed their trundlers and had time for unhurried talk. Dad seemed restless until I remembered his long coat and helped him put it on. Incongruity is of no concern in old age: the weight and texture of the coat must have been pleasing to him and he loved the heat.

'I played a bit of golf myself,' said Dad. 'It wasn't my sport of choice, but in business it's useful to be able to play golf without making a goat of yourself. Especially in Asian countries, you develop a sense of business opportunity and personal trust by playing together.'

'So deals are made on the course.'

'Not so much that, but Japanese and Singaporean businessmen like to get a sense of your personality that way.'

'Were you any good?'

'Not really,' said Dad, 'but it got me to the table without too much embarrassment and I had good products to sell. Do you know know anything about mechanical engineering?'

'No.' I thought that was the end of the conversation, because Dad said nothing for a long while and hummed quietly.

'What is it you do know about?' he asked finally, and I almost congratulated him on holding onto one line of thought for so long.

'I'm still at varsity, studying English and history.'

'You do the roof spraying as a part-time thing then?'

'That's it,' I said. Life was too short to tease out absolutely fact and fiction. The end justifies the means when you're talking to someone like Dad, and the thing was to keep him as happy as possible it seemed to me. 'What would you do if you could have your time over again?' I asked him.

'Over again?'

'Would you live your life differently if you had a choice — a different job, different country, stuff like that.'

'I was always a good organiser.' Dad seemed quite interested in the self-analysis. 'My mother and father were muddlers and I reacted against that, I suppose. Logic, systems, the application of reason — that's what I brought to business. People sneer at administrators because they don't understand the skills involved.'

'You did okay, though.'

'People think it's paper shuffling, not real work,' said Dad. He seemed about to say more, but then closed his eyes briefly so I prompted him while he still had a chain of thought.

'So what is important for a manager?'

'People not policy. The best systems in the world are useless if you don't carry your staff. People skills make the difference from the factory floor to the boardroom, that's what I say.' And Dad said it with surprising coherence. It was surely the best I saw him in all the time I was there and gave me a glimpse of the person he had once been. It was perhaps achieved with some effort, however, for afterwards he concentrated on rubbing his hands, and making sly sheep's eyes at me. 'So are you in some sort of business?' he said finally.

'I'm keeping you company.'

'Ah, yes, that's right.' Dad's voice had the pretence of

assurance, but his soft expression was one of increasing bewilderment as his mind moved from the steady recollection of the far past to the morass of the present. 'Yes, of course, that's right, yes,' he said to comfort himself, looking over to the abandoned trike in the neighbouring section. The child had vanished without us noticing.

Dad leant back and closed his eyes; I returned to my swot notes. No way was I going to risk another squash trip with him on the pillion seat, although I felt stale from lack of physical activity. I was envious of the happy gaggles of golfers who straggled over the well-kept course, and whose laughter carried quite clearly to me. I wondered if any player there ever glanced across at Dad on his patio and had some premonition of their future.

Dad snored for an hour and a half beneath the luminous warm cloud of the summer, and then woke with a good deal of lip smacking and fidgeting. For another half an hour he hummed and half sang snatches of songs from the forties and fifties, some of which had become popular again. He wasn't conscious of me during this time and I carried on working while the opportunity was there. Finally his awareness circled out and he became quieter, coughed softly in a slightly self-conscious way and regarded me from beneath the thatch of his eyebrows. I said nothing. I wanted the mood and relationship to be of his making, rather than always imposing reality as I saw it on Dad's variable world. I made coffee for us both, and settled in my patio chair again, still without a word. It wasn't a ploy for my entertainment: let Dad kick off, and I'd just run with the ball. Dad began in his own good time.

'Tell me about your time in Ecuador, Warren,' said Dad in his reed-bed whisper. So the sun was over the yard arm, or some such thing.

'It's mostly forest in Ecuador and very hot. They have a lot of insects and bats, but a very shaky economy.'

'Any rats?' asked Dad.

'No rats. It's an odd thing, there's an indigenous tropical lily there and its pollen inhibits the breeding of rats. Ecuador is the only country in the world completely free of rats. They have monkeys with coloured bums, though, and those fish that reduce horses to skeletons in no time at all.'

'But no rats, eh,' said Dad.

'Absolutely not, Mr Ladd. You say that you don't give a rat's arse there, and the locals have no idea what you're talking about. On the other hand there's scorpions as big as saucers and beetles bigger than tortoises to do the scavenging.'

'And are the tortoises any threat?'

'Only to the babies,' I reassured him. 'In Ecuador babies are always left in hammocks, never on the ground where the tortoises can get at them. Even so, you notice that a lot of children there have a toe or two missing.'

'How long did you have to stay there, in Whatsit?'

'Oh, I was in Honduras for a couple of years. I had to oversee the establishment of professional development best practice guidelines for the drug cartels.'

'But no rats at all, you say?'

'I brought one of the Venezuelan lilies back, and I'll put it in your room. No rat will come near the place, believe me. The pollen may make you sneeze a bit, but as for the rats it's adios amigo.'

'And the turtles?'

'It's too dry for them here, and MAF won't let you bring them in because of the possible diseases,' I said. 'You should have a really good sleep tonight.'

'Well, the nights seem to be getting longer.' Dad's tone was glum. 'I can't seem to get my joints comfortable for any length of time.'

'Maybe we can suss out where those pills are.'

'I suppose it's always warm in Guatemala?' said Dad.

'But in the rainy season,' I said, 'the water comes so high beneath the pole houses that you can hear the alligators scraping their tails against the piles, and the giant toads cluster on the windows until the light is blocked out.'

'Rats are mighty swimmers, the buggers,' said Dad.

At some stage the little girl next door had reclaimed her trike and was again circling intently: I think the three of us were slightly dizzy. Dad gave a yawn which displayed a lower lip like that of an elephant, and massaged his face. I wondered if Angeline would notice if I took an inch or two off his eyebrows, but then reminded myself that neither he nor I would feel any better as a result. Boredom is not often a productive motivation. I wondered also about the mutual effects of our time together, whether the consequence of the meeting of my youth and his extreme old age would be a more intermediate and beneficial setting for us both: a median view of life.

That day's evening meal was the last I needed to consider, for Angeline and her husband, marriage restored if all went well, were to be back next morning. A sense of closure gave significance to the occasion, and I went out to Angeline's deep-freeze and found a heavy pack of pork slices. A few games of squash and I would burn off the fat from the desirable crackling; in Dad's case surely he didn't have enough time left for cumulative diet-related diseases to be a threat. 'I thought we'd treat ourselves to pork, Mr Ladd,' I said, and got together carrots, potatoes and peas as a counter to that indulgence.

'Ah,' said Dad, 'I could do with a drink.'

'Okay, but we're not having as much as last night.'

'Eh?'

'Nothing. You're just not going to rip into it the way you did last night, though it was my fault.'

'What happened last night?' said Dad.

'Nothing,' I said. 'You slept like a dead man because of the booze.'

'Who's the dead man?' asked Dad.

'We'll have one bottle of red with the pork,' I said, and Dad nodded.

I moved Dad into the lounge, and put a tray on his lap as preparation. There was something on the television about rearing livestock in barns in the American Mid-West — all very American Gothic, and Dad had difficulty in getting a handle on it. I tried to keep his interest up as I cooked dinner. I didn't want him getting his papers out again and recycling them endlessly. 'Looks like a pretty big operation they've got going on those farms,' I said, coming in to give him a very moderate top-up.

'What's that? Dad was gazing at the screen as if it were a box of snakes.

'All those cattle indoors for months, aren't they?'

'Cattle — is that what they are?'

'Aren't they?'

'Look sort of funny,' he said. 'It's dark, isn't it. I reckon there's something wrong with the picture.'

'It's just being inside, I suppose.'

'Who wants to watch cattle inside all the time? What the hell is this all about I want to know,' said Dad. He had a good point arrived at in a roundabout sort of way.

Dad enjoyed his pork. He did take eternity cutting it up, but I resisted the urge to do it for him. Many of the peas escaped him and lay on the tray, his lap, or the carpet around him like green beads. We had a packet of shortbread biscuits for afters, and a cup of coffee.

'Is Viv coming in?' Dad asked. He always spoke fondly of his dead wife.

'No.'

'What about the children?'

'Angeline comes back tomorrow.'

'Tomorrow,' said Dad with surprise and emphasis, as if he had been convinced her return was to be the present day, or any day other than tomorrow. He steepled his hands and worked his long, loose face like a pantomime actor. 'And you are again?' he said.

It was the one day we hadn't had an outing, and so without bothering about any confusing preamble of intent or agreement

I stood Dad up in a scatter of peas and we went out into the warm decay of the summer day. The golf course was all vague nature in the twilight. Houses we passed were at their best, blemishes hidden, and weeds not readily distinguished from their invited cousins. It was a slow outing. Dad's walking stick was varnished, and had a rubber stopper on the end, and he lingered as ever to poke at things: unusual letter boxes, shrubs intruding across the footpath, a dog turd. 'How long have I lived here?' he asked. Death can be a sudden fall of the curtain, the cataclysmic closure; it can also be a gradual deprivation of those aspects of consciousness we need to remain in touch with the world. Dad at times seemed in a dinghy drifting further and further out from the rest of us on the shore. 'I'll need to get back to work tomorrow,' he said.

'What's so important?'

'My son, Theo, is joining the board. It's what I've always wanted.'

'That's really great,' I said. 'I bet he'll give you a lot of support.' My landlady said Theo had drowned in Nepal, and hadn't liked his father anyway, so in regard to his son at least, Dad's loss of short-term memory was a blessing for him. 'Well, you haven't got the skills to make a contribution at that level, have you,' he said candidly. 'And no degree.'

'You're right.' I didn't need reminding about such things.

It took us a while to complete the small suburban block and the dusk was more pervasive by the time we reached home again. Dad would have walked right past the gate and begun another slow circuit, but I directed him up the path from which he swung at a few parched flowers with his stick.

'So who are we visiting here?' he asked.

'We live here,' I said.

'Like hell we do,' but nevertheless Dad was willing to come inside and be surprised by every room all over again. 'We've had our dinner, have we?' he wanted to know, and, with rather more diffidence, 'Are you staying the night?'

'I'm Brian, here to keep you company.'

'You'll have to excuse me if I don't entertain you. I've a good deal of work on. Business, you know.'

'That's fine.'

After sundown the bad times came for Dad — well, other world times at least. It showed in his increasing uneasiness and fidgeting. As well as all the stuff with his hands, he pulled strange faces, puckering his lips, or stretching them in an exaggerated and mirthless grin, shooting his bushy eyebrows aloft, and clamping his lower jaw out. All a quite unconscious exhibition of gurning. I wondered if it was a sign of lesser, gremlin personality traits normally suppressed by the deliberate imposition of an integrated character; a sort of geriatric possession having nothing to do with right or wrong. We began the laborious process of getting him ready for bed.

And it was marked not just by mutual effort, but mutual indignity. He wasn't sufficiently supple, or balanced, to soap himself in the shower: arthritis made it difficult for him to raise his arms above his shoulders, or to touch his own feet. I stood in the doorway of the shower to help, lathered his wobbly head, watched the shampoo suds slide over the corrugations of his collapsed chest. Dad gasped happily in the hot jet and the swirling steam, and would have fallen several times had I not gripped his elbow. He was all bone and tendon, and the nails on his big toes were thick, opaque and yellow. As we stood together afterwards in the bathroom and I dried his bum and cock with a lush, blue towel, the incongruity of it all gave me a brief laugh, and Dad chuckled just to follow suit. Two strangers — Dad couldn't even remember my name — so intimate, so innocent, together. 'Is it morning, or night?' he whispered. His hair stood up damply and his eyes roamed in their deep sockets.

'Night,' I said. 'It's night now.'

'Will the rats come for the pomegranate seeds?'

'Not a chance now we've got the Ecuadorian lily,' I said.

'Of course. Of course, and what a relief for all,' he said.

'There weren't many women in the war, you know, but I saw a falcon high up above the desert before the tank attack.'

As I swotted in the lounge, I could hear Dad singing to himself in bed. There were some words, some humming, and a good deal of pom pom and pum pum as he entertained himself. He talked to himself too, posing such questions as why the sheet had got caught up, where the wardrobe door led to, and when he'd need to get up to leave in time for the meeting. And he answered each question with interest and patience as one might to a friend. In a moment of wishful thinking I imagined the night was to be peaceful and mercifully swift.

I went to bed with a head full of the battle of Gettysburg: Cashtown Inn, Willoughby's Run and McPherson's Barn, and photographers with the armies for the first time. But barely had the smoke cleared when I was woken by the noise made by Dad barging about in the dark hallway. The slick, green numerals told me it was 3:36 a.m. and Dad was weeping loudly. I went out and lit up the hallway. Dad had taken off his pyjamas and wore dark suit trousers and his beloved long coat. 'Where am I?' he implored brokenly. 'And who the hell are you?'

'I'm Brian.'

'Who?'

'I'm keeping you company,' I said.

'Where's Viv and the kids?'

I began an explanation to bridge some thirty or forty years, but Dad turned away with a hollow moan and wandered back into his bedroom. Nothing related to the present was any consolation to him. There seemed no option but to follow him through the looking glass. I persuaded him to exchange suit trousers for pyjama ones by pointing out he had no underpants, but agreed that the coat of the high plains drifter was useful in protecting him in case he was visited by the rats from the other side. Dad went reluctantly back into bed, and to settle him I sat under the covers beside him, for at four o'clock it was cool enough wandering in my boxers. 'Angeline's coming tomorrow,' I said. 'You'll like that.'

Dad nodded, his lined face glinting with tears. 'What about Viv and Theo?'

'Yep, the whole family.' So could I assume power of life and death, and summon back his wife and the watery Theo? Anything to keep his mind off the rats; anything to help us drift through the darkness without despair.

'Things haven't always been easy, you know, Warren,' Dad admonished me. 'We had a truckload of trouble with Theo. For a while there he just seemed to go from one scrape to another and we were at our wits' end.'

'I suppose most young guys go through a time when they're fooling with drugs and stuff.'

'You don't know the half of it,' said Dad. 'You know he was still stealing money from us when he was nearly thirty years old. He had a baby with a girl in Sydney and he abandoned them both and went trekking in Nepal.' Dad stopped and listened for a time. 'It's very windy outside,' he said, yet everything was still.

'A real southerly buster,' I said.

'Anyway, things haven't always been easy. But they were both great kids and Angeline was never any trouble at all. You worry more about your kids than your own life, do you know that?'

'Absolutely.'

Dad was quiet for a time, but his hands and face twitched and shimmied as the outward show of some inner agitation, a string of Tom Thumb crackers somewhere along his nervous system. I thought maybe a song or two would calm him, and allow me to go back to my own bed. I was tired, and worried about Dad's condition.

'Let's sing a bit,' I said.

'Eh?'

'Sing a bit. You like that.'

'What time is it?' said Dad.

'Time to sing,' I said, but then couldn't think of anything that both Dad and I would know well. I finally came up with 'Waltzing Matilda', and then 'Lili Marlene'. Dad enjoyed that especially, and the singing was more successful than I'd hoped. Only once he stopped singing and put a hand to my mouth, then said, 'Listen to that storm outside.' There was no wind at all, or maybe winds cracked their cheeks for Dad that I was too young and temporal to hear.

'Maybe it's inside,' I said. 'Let's drown it out.'

We sang 'How Much is that Doggie in the Window', and 'Some Enchanted Evening'. Songs are sung by people and in places never contemplated by their composers, and for reasons quite inexplicable in normal times, and we must have been as odd a juxtaposition as any. Eighty-eight-year-old Mr Ladd and twenty-year-old me, strangers in bed together well before the dawn. When we had sung ourselves out, I told Dad I was going to my own room. 'Do you want the light left on?' I asked him.

'Better had,' he said. 'Maybe it's the swordfish making all that noise outside.'

'They're not doing any harm,' I said.

'Things haven't always been easy, you know, Warren.'

'So you said.'

'Why have I got this coat on in bed?'

'You might have to get up for a piss.'

'Nothing's like it was before,' said Dad and he lay back on the pillows. 'Someone keeps coming in and watching me when I'm asleep,' he whispered.

'How do you know?'

'I can hear them breathing,' Dad said.

I stopped in the doorway for a last check. There he lay with the top of his black coat poking out from the bedclothes and his caricature of a face on the pillow. He was looking back at me, and I bet he was wondering who I was again.

'It'll be morning soon,' I said.

I dropped into my bed as if pole-axed, and into a pit of sleep too deep even for dreams. I awoke to full daylight and the noise made by Dad as he tried to manage himself in the lavatory. I hoped to God he'd taken off the coat, and found my appeal divinely answered. The other things could be washed easily.

'Did you have a good night?' I asked him, wondering what he remembered of the swordfish, the southerly and the songs.

'An okay night, I suppose,' said Dad vaguely. 'It's not as comfortable as my own bed, somehow.'

We had our last breakfast together, and Dad was too polite to ask who I was, so I told him anyway. He perked up when I said that Angeline was returning before lunch, and gave me a history of her school achievements, which included awards for physics and impromptu speaking. In the fifth form she gave a reading from the Book of Job at the school prizegiving. 'Theo didn't do himself justice at school,' Dad said.

There was a full, gleaming summer sun for my last morning with Dad. He sat on the patio again in his black coat and seemed to gradually expand in the heat. I had found his best shoes for him to wear in honour of his daughter's homecoming, and their domed, black toes shone at the end of his grey trousers. While I had a clean-up inside the house I could hear Dad talking to himself from time to time, but there was no anxiety in his tone. He seemed to be scrutinising and rearranging bits of his life from long ago. I took particular care to hide the last empty wine bottles well down in the rubbish bag. I packed my gear ready to leave and put it by the Suzuki. 'Are you getting ready to go somewhere?' asked Dad as I came back to the patio with mugs of tea.

'I've got exams in a few days,' I said, and he gave a little chortle as though pleased to be missing out on such things himself. I wanted to wish him well, but wasn't sure how I could do that with sincerity when I knew what was happening to him: the inevitable path before him. 'You look after yourself and don't worry about things,' I said. How could I thank him for not dying on me during my time of supervision.

'Thank you. Thank you,' he replied huskily. 'The nights get longer, don't you think? I suppose I'm not doing much during the day to tire me out.'

Dad was having a snooze when Angeline and her husband

returned, but he woke up and knew her immediately, though I thought perhaps he was for a moment surprised to find her so grown up. What a hug they had and then a flurry of questions and answers about their trip and our stay, which bewildered him, and after a minute or two he turned to Angeline's husband and politely asked him who he was again. Welcome to the club. 'Goodness, Dad, you're wearing that greatcoat on a scorcher of a day,' said Angeline and she raised her eyebrows at me.

'He feels good with it on,' I said. 'He likes the heat, doesn't he.'

Angeline called me into the lounge to give me my money in a manila envelope. 'Was everything all right?' she asked, looking at me keenly. She and I knew there was a rich history to my stay, that there had been wild moments on the heath, but that nothing would be served by the rendition of it blow by blow. To talk about it, to admit to such things as we knew, would give them substance and power.

'He wasn't so good at night, but otherwise things were okay.'

'That's the pattern of his dementia,' she said.

It wasn't easy to say goodbye to Dad, for in some ways I never really got to say hello. I wished him well and took his big, loose hand in mine, and he said thank you and that it was a pleasure. But when I was on the motorbike, about to start, with my squash bag balanced on the tank and handle bars, he stood up from his patio chair and called out, 'Warren, Warren.'

'What is it?' I said.

He gaped at me for a moment, gave a rueful smile. 'It doesn't matter,' he said in his hollow voice. 'I'll tell you next time.'

Angeline smiled as apology for her father's confusion, her husband raised a bland hand. As I rode down the drive I had a last view of Dad standing in the hot sun in his black, gunslinger's greatcoat. In all that mundane suburban scene he was the innocent and hapless harbinger of howling winds, swordfish, lilies and rats, womenless wars, and the high cliff before the chasm.

margaret's view

Yes, Daryll had his name on the door. Well, not his name actually, but his title, his institutional position — it amounted to the same thing. Personnel and Publicity Manager, in black lettering on a grey strip which could well have been the off-cut of a formica benchtop. The opposite office had an identical strip that said Maintenance and Resource Manager — which was Eddie Fairbrother — and in the alcove between them the desk of the secretary they shared. Margaret Benn, an intelligent, older woman with long service in the company, had been the CEO's personal secretary, but, unable to cope with the new on-line computer system, she had been demoted, and felt it keenly.

Eddie gave her his monthly maintenance report to type, and they both made the usual pretence that something apart from the summary would be read by those to whom it was supplied, and then he carried on into Daryll's office. As always he walked past the desk and took his place before the window. Daryll's room had a better view than his. From Eddie's window there was only the precipitous side of the canning block and a small part of the staff carpark; the personnel manager's window had a view of the firm's main entrance and the long, straight road that was the escape from it. There were the phoenix palms that the founder had brought back from America fifty years before, and the ample lawn with no seats on it whatsoever.

Eddie drew his lips back from his teeth mirthlessly and sucked in his breath to show his annoyance. 'They're thinking of moving the drinks machine to our end of the corridor,' he said.

Daryll surprised himself with the flush of anger that he felt: anger at the news, anger at the means of its arrival, anger at the extent to which he was aroused by such a petty part of the scheme of things.

'Bosworth told me that he'd been asked to make some measurements to see if the thing could be accommodated at this end,' said Eddie. As maintenance manager he had recently become aware of the real flow of information — from Bosworth, the plant carpenter, to himself, not the reverse.

They both knew, these men of middle management, the consequences of having the drinks machine placed next to them. Stains on the carpet, the constant interruption of their secretary's work: idle, noisy, sexually interrogative people standing around exchanging idle, noisy, sexually interrogative banter, and spilling into the two offices if they had a chance — just to use the phone a tick if that's okay, or borrowing a seat for Celia who's feeling a bit crook, or assuming that proximity carries responsibility, and making complaint that the Coke font has taken three dollars, but delivered nothing in return.

All this the two of them were willing to discuss, but they also had to admit the real significance — that the drinks machine would be a mark of Cain at the place of least importance on their floor, and that all the staff in administration would recognise it as precisely that.

'This place is just a rat-house since Fastieur was brought in,' said Eddie, and he glanced quickly back from the window to see Daryll's face as he made the criticism. Eddie had begun in the firm with the previous CEO, who had been able to see his conventional directness and doggedness at first hand, and give them moderate reward in due course. Eddie wore a dark suit and a red and black striped tie. He had once been muscular and was still solid rather than fat, although his neck sat on his collar, and his belt had a forty-five-degree angle. The previous CEO had come up the hard way, as had Eddie, whereas Fastieur had a degree in economics from Auckland and a PhD in business management from Chicago. His front teeth were capped, his memory retentive, his arguments in a realm of theory which inhibited practical men such as Daryll and Eddie.

'We're going to be done like a dinner by this guy,' said Eddie. 'We're going to be arseholed out and our feet won't even touch the ground. He's one smooth bastard, you've got to say that.'

He was right. Daryll had noticed at recent meetings signs that others of the management team were on more confidential terms with Fastieur, hints there had been earlier discussion which excluded him, occasional in-jokes that passed him by. A far more overt signal had been the CEO's decision that the advertising agency was free to contact him directly instead of necessarily going through Daryll. 'I won't have efficiency threatened by ossified channels of communication,' Fastieur had replied when Daryll complained. Ossified was the sort of word that Fastieur could produce quite readily in conversation.

'Arseholed out. That's what'll happen to us all right, Daryll. And no golden handshake either. Before I go I might just haul off and king-hit the bugger.' Eddie went back to the door of Daryll's office, feeling a bit better for his directness. He paused there for one more delivery. 'If we don't come up with something soon,' he said, 'we're gone-burgers, dog-tucker, dead meat. No use us pretending anything else. That drinks machine, you see, that's the kiss of death for sure,' and he crossed the alcove to his own office, almost brushing the elderly secretary who must have heard all that was said, leaving Daryll's door ajar.

Daryll had photocopied a cartoon from the Industrial Gazette. He was going to pin it up in the outer office. It showed two eggs and one was saying 'I just want to get laid one more time'. Daryll had thought it funny, but after Eddie's visit he screwed it up and threw it at the cane basket in the corner. Eddie was right, Eddie was on the button: the two of them had been targeted by Fastieur and the board. He'd seen it happen. First you get cut out of the loop of top information which you need to compete, then your most influential functions are devolved to others, then you're ripe for the chop, disguised as restructuring. Daryll felt seedy and second rate, and for a moment helplessly abject. His shoes were scuffed, and his suit coat on the hanger behind the door was of everyday material and heavily creased. Eddie was on the button all right: the drinks machine was as good as a loaded gun.

Daryll worried at it all weekend, but he didn't say anything to his wife. Over many years he had attempted to keep his work separate from his personal life. His own childhood had been afflicted with a father whose moods and viciousness in the house reflected his bitter incompetence as a store manager. Daryll's own children knew little of his work, and by the time they were grown up such stoicism had become a habit. So he dug out the compost as a preparation for winter, he watched a television movie about a sensitive man dying of Aids, and on Sunday evening he and his wife went to dinner with the Bruckners, where the talk was of the excessive leniency shown by judges in sentencing, and the need for greater regulation of the sharemarket. And during all of that weekend he had a growing apprehension that he was to lose his job, and find himself, at fifty-seven and with cap in hand, door-knocking for another. On Sunday night he dreamt that he went to Warren Bruckner's office asking for a job, and Bruckner criticised his scuffed shoes and said there were several ex-judges better qualified for the job. The conversation was nonsense, but the embarrassment of being a supplicant before his friend was so real that Daryll woke with a low, sustained groan. The fear of failure is deep-seated and remorseless.

'No, nothing. Nothing's wrong,' he told his wife.

'Maybe just the beef Wellington,' she said. 'Emma's great with it, but it just sits, don't you think?'

Mid-morning Monday he took his coffee into Eddie's office, and closed the door behind him. 'You're right,' he said. 'Odds on, we're the next to go. I had a memo today that the board was to look at management restructuring, and asking me to give a full job description.'

'Me too.' Eddie wore a new, blue shirt with his best suit. It seemed a sign that he wasn't going down without a fight. Daryll glanced at the high polish he'd put on his own shoes before leaving for work. Neither of them would just roll over. 'We're the bunnies in the sights all right,' said Eddie. 'We're to get the bum's rush. We're the chickens for the chop. Our use-by date is up.' Both of them were conscious of a strong will to resist.

They talked about their situation without holding back. They had different personalities and backgrounds, yet had always got on well, and a common threat made an additional bond between them. Daryll said he'd spent time in the weekend deciding who in the company might be counted on for support, and how influential those people were. He ran them past Eddie and it wasn't a reassuring list, yet there was just a touch of satisfaction in Eddie's face at the end. 'And?' he said.

'You tell me,' said Daryll.

Eddie levelled a finger at the closed door which separated them from the secretarial alcove. 'Margaret,' he said.

'Margaret?'

'Margaret,' Eddie said.

Daryll didn't see at first how Margaret could figure in things, an elderly secretary without influence, but Eddie pointed out that she'd been close to Fastieur for six months, and then dumped for a younger woman who understood software and took the title personal assistant. Eddie said they had to get an angle, any angle, not just wait to get the bum's rush when Fastieur was ready. 'You know how professional Margaret is,' said Daryll. 'You won't get her telling any tales even if she doesn't like him.'

'There might be something, though. We're talking survival here, and Margaret knows stuff, and he demoted her. She doesn't like the bastard and neither do we.'

'Well, maybe you should have a talk with her then.'

'No,' said Eddie, 'you should have a talk with her. You have the right way with women in the office — you've got the words for it. I somehow seem to get on their wick, up their noses, offside. I've never had a comfortable language for women, and I've stopped trying. I always feel as if my bloody fly buttons are undone.'

It was true. There was a crudeness in Eddie's language from which women pulled back, even the younger ones. Nothing of sexual threat, nothing of superiority, just a sort of provincial male directness which they had taken pains to get beyond in their own relationships and careers. Eddie was intelligent, but not sensitive: his unvarnished language showed too much of the true timber. 'Anyway,' he said, 'if Margaret has something on Fastieur, and she's willing to tell us, you're better at knowing if it's useful. Worth a try. Maybe he's getting a leg over one of the women in the office. We need something. We're dead meat right now. He's got us by the balls, over a barrel, by the short and curlies.'

So Daryll asked Margaret to come through to his office, and put the one other chair he had — tubular and with a red vinyl seat — closer to his desk than usual. The threat to his job and self-esteem made him in some ways less preoccupied than before, and he found that surprising. He had never discussed with Margaret the way in which she had become secretary to Eddie and him; her failure to excel with computers despite all her ability and experience. He had extended no sympathy to her in her humiliation, just taken advantage of her skills, and she had sought nothing but the pleasant, professional relationship he offered. And now he and Eddie asked for her help. Had he even looked closely at her before? Had he looked at her as he might look at a mother, a sister, a wife, a neighbour, a woman who grappled with the same vicissitudes in the same world? What description could he have given of her, he thought, as he regarded her with new interest. Wasn't it likely that he must go through something of her experience after all? Or worse perhaps — arseholed out of the company entirely, as Eddie would say, given the chop without a pay-off. And he observed her even as he talked of the fears he and Eddie had, their knowledge that Fastieur and the board considered both Personnel and Publicity, and Maintenance and Resources, were management portfolios that could be more efficiently integrated into the overall structure.

Margaret was externally a soft woman, marginally overflowing in middle age the physical contours of her youth. Her face and neck had a quilted effect, creases and a slight engorgement, often tinged with a pink flush, especially on her neck. Her clothes, too, were soft, and enveloping, so that seldom was more than her face and hands on view. But she was neither a self-effacing woman, nor a strident one. Calm, efficient and reliable, she went about her business, and kept out of the business of others. Daryll knew her husband had left her years before, but imagined she had a small, active dog to keep her company. She would walk it on a long, red lead and she would have trained it not to bark at night.

'Do you have a dog, Margaret?' he asked her.

'No.'

'No pets at all?'

'I share a tabby cat with my neighbour,' said Margaret. 'It stays with him during the day, and comes over to me in the evenings.'

'Well, anyway . . . You can see why Eddie and I are worried, and I guess it could mean another upheaval for you too. You know they're thinking of plonking the drinks machine down here?'

'Neil Bosworth came and did some measuring. He said they wanted to get it away from reprographics because people were complaining about access to the copiers there.'

'And Eddie and I have been asked to submit job descriptions for the coming restructuring,' said Daryll.

Margaret nodded, but didn't say anything. Daryll had a feeling that she knew the whole nature of the conversation, but was patiently allowing it to progress all the same. He was sitting behind his desk and Margaret was on the vinyl chair. A familiar situation, but this time it was not professional: he had to ask her for help and advice, and he'd never thought to offer her either in the past.

'Eddie and I wondered if you had any ideas about what we should do,' said Daryll. 'Whether we should threaten a personal grievance case, or go directly to some of the board members.'

'I've got no influence, Daryll. I'll write in support of you both if you like, but what good will that do? If the two of you go, what chance is there for my job anyway?' Margaret didn't often use his name, and it marked somehow the unusual equality and frankness they had embarked on.

'You were Fastieur's secretary for over six months, though,' said Daryll. 'We don't expect you to do anything you're uncomfortable with, spill anything confidential. It's just that you know the guy: how he thinks and that. I find him difficult to read, and Eddie says he's a slick wanker.' Daryll would never have used the word wanker in his own conversation with Margaret, but by placing it as Eddie's language it caused a greater informality in their own, and Margaret smiled. 'He is a slick guy, isn't he,' said Daryll. 'Always working the room and aware of his impact on others. Always in business mode.'

'And always willing to learn, always well prepared, and not

easily deflected from his goals.'

'Yes,' said Daryll. All those things had to be admitted, and more. Before coming to them, Fastieur had been head of NatuFood in Melbourne and turned the company around in three years, increasing profit by sixty-eight per cent and market share by seven. 'But Eddie and I don't see why we should make it easy for him.'

Margaret's hair was completely grey, but she neither dyed it nor wore it in the frizzy curls Daryll had noticed were often the fashion with older women. Her hair wasn't long, but still had some weight and natural fall. She was plump, but without the fussy activity that often accompanied female plumpness. Daryll recalled that quite late in life she had completed a degree in zoology, or biology, something like that, and nothing to do with her everyday work.

'What do you think we should do?' he asked her, and she told him she didn't see confrontation as the best response, not in the long term, because Fastieur and the board would win anyway. Better to put aside pride and anger, she said, and look at the situation in a businesslike way. That's what Fastieur was doing. There was nothing personal in his wish to get rid of them, unless you thought his conviction that the company was better off without them was personal.

'And we're not indispensable, are we,' Margaret said. She suggested they put a redundancy and prompt resignation proposition to the CEO which he and the board might consider rather than face a protracted disputes procedure. No threats, just a practical approach to secure an outcome all could agree to.

It wasn't what Eddie and Daryll had wished for from Margaret. Eddie in particular had hoped maybe there was something she knew that would enable them to twist Fastieur's tail: a secret of sex, or double dealing, like those disclosures in the movies of corporate greed which enabled the little guys to show the ugly face of capitalism. 'It's gutless, isn't it,' he said when Daryll passed on Margaret's advice. 'It makes it so easy for the bugger if we go cap in hand.'

'That's the point,' said Daryll. 'The easier it is, the better deal we're likely to get.'

'I'd rather take him on, stir up as much shit as possible, do as much damage as I can before going down.'

'Now you would,' said Daryll, having worked through similar feelings himself. '*Now* you would, but after a few months you'd kick yourself for a mug. And anyway, as Margaret says, if Fastieur doesn't want it the easy way then the hard way follows.'

Eddie was a touchy guy, but he wasn't a fool. They were standing in the carpark and he looked away from Daryll and took a deep breath. He looked past the staff cars to where the line of company trucks began, each with the bold, new logo Fastieur had introduced: a golden sheaf of wheat on a circular green background. He gave himself time to think, and he accepted the sense of what was being said. Instinctively he wanted to have a go at Fastieur one way or another, but he knew Margaret was right. 'I couldn't deal with him personally on it. I'd be into a row within minutes and probably plant the bastard. You and Margaret would have to front up initially. I couldn't do it.'

'If that's what you want,' said Daryll.

'That new friggin' logo,' said Eddie, looking at the trucks. 'We don't even process any wheat, for Christ's sake.'

'Fastieur says it's generic — a universal symbol of agriculture.'

So the three of them talked to a lawyer, then met at Daryll's house on the Saturday before Easter, and his wife provided pineapple muffins and plunger coffee before leaving them to it. A package deal is what they decided on. All for one and one for all, said Eddie. Ten thousand for each year Eddie and Daryll had been with the company, and half that for Margaret. Amicable resignation within one month and non-disclosure of agreement if that's what the board wished: a CEO's testimonial letter for each. Eddie wanted reference to personal grievance cases if agreement wasn't reached, but Margaret and Daryll talked him out of it. 'Everyone knows the score,' said Daryll. Eddie stood to gain $140,000 and the others somewhat less. They weren't huge sums, but then Eddie, Daryll and Margaret weren't high flyers working for a corporate giant.

'We still get arseholed out though, don't we,' said Eddie. 'We get the boot and down the road. Shafted in a big way.'

'We make the most of the situation,' said Margaret. 'As a threesome we become part of the process to our own advantage.'

It was a decent handshake, realistic for both sides: and, as Margaret said, Fastieur was a businessman. Daryll and the lawyer had one meeting in the CEO's office, which was furnished more like a lounge. Fastieur was polite, reasonable, and made concessions on small points. 'I'm really happy that we can resolve the situation in an amicable way,' he said. He recommended it to his board as a clean, quick, three-in-one redundancy package, and it went through. Eddie even bit his tongue at the official farewell and accepted a set of golf clubs, though afterwards he said to Daryll he'd like to ram them up Fastieur's arse. From what they saw happening subsequently in the industry, all three considered they'd done all right. Fastieur praised their work ethic and loyalty to the company.

After seven months Eddie landed a job managing a fish processing plant at Lyttelton. Daryll became Advocacy and Information manager at the polytechnic, and Margaret didn't look for full-time work, but became the editor of the *New Zealand Science Gazette*. Their new jobs divided the three, as their old jobs, and the threat to them, had brought them together.

One year after the redundancy Daryll asked his wife if they should invite Margaret for dinner but, when he rang, Margaret said perhaps not because she'd been diagnosed with a form of sugar diabetes and eating was a bit of a business. 'I wanted to thank you for the redundancy last year,' Daryll said. More and more I realise we did the smart thing, and it was your idea.'

'We didn't let feelings get in the way,' said Margaret. Her voice was quiet on the phone. What would she be — almost sixty? Daryll visualised her plump, slightly quilted body and thick hair. Maybe the neighbour's tabby cat had become a permanent resident now she no longer went to work.

'How's Eddie?' she asked.

'He's manager for Ocean Products in Lyttelton.'

'Oh, that's good news.'

Most likely Daryll wouldn't talk to Margaret again; their lives were very different. Maybe he'd bump into Eddie only once or twice more. That's the way it is: circumstances bring people together in alliance, and for a while they confide in each other, rely on each other, confront threat with their unity. Then circumstances change and people go their own way again. Daryll wanted to say something of that, but couldn't phrase it.

'Anyway,' he said, 'Diabetes can be a beggar, I hear, but they've got so many great drugs these days, haven't they.'

'Oh, it will settle down all right,' said Margaret. 'I can do most of the work for the Gazette at home.' Her voice was positive and clear.

'You look after yourself then, Margaret,' Daryll said. 'And we'll keep in touch.'

Already he was running out of things to say. He was keenly aware of being a fortunate person with a job, financial security, a partner and okay health for his age. The feeling passed over him like the aromatic puff of a summer breeze, and left him briefly thankful.

arnal retent and a place in history

ARNAL RETENT CONCENTRATED ON GETTING HIS legs to move safely beneath him and avoid the grey ice of the puddles. He had slept on the concrete floor of the lavatory cubicles in the trailer park, and the cold was in his bones despite the roll of sacking which he kept stored behind the door. He was off to the Redeemed People of Jesus Mission to cadge a cup of oxtail soup in return for a ten-second spot on RPJM radio expressing his gratitude to Jesus for salvation. That oxtail soup with the heat pulsing through the cardboard cup, some traces of a cut herb swirling on its rich surface.

The stretch limo slowed quickly as it reached Arnal, but even so its black, burnished length seemed to keep passing like a passenger train. Arnal took no notice at first; what possible connection had he with a world of stretch limos. When the car stopped, he did glance at it in case it threatened random violence, but the one-way glass of the windows was almost as dark as the limo itself. Then the back door nearest to him opened of its own accord, and from the far side of an expanse of opulent leather, a man in a suit beckoned to him and spoke.

'Mr Retent, I'd like to talk to you for a moment about matters to your advantage.' Arnal could feel warmth escaping from the interior and that was enough to draw him in: that and the polite use of his surname, and the knowledge that anything which happened to him was likely to be an improvement on his present life. The door closed behind him automatically. The limo accelerated smoothly away with only an adder's hiss. 'Mr McKnife,' said the man, and he reached a long way with his hand to shake Arnal's as a reinforcement of the introduction. 'Would you like some oxtail soup as we talk, Mr Retent?' and from one of the cabinets below the glass partition which separated back and front seats, Mr McKnife took a spun-chrome thermos and poured soup into its cup top.

Mr McKnife's hand was dry and strong, his shirt cuff a pale blue held with a silver link. He had a square, articulated chin like that of a ventriloquist's dummy. 'I'll call you Arnal,' he said, and it was a decision not a request.

'Sure,' said Arnal.

'You see, Arnal, you've been chosen, and this time by someone who can do more for you than the Jesus Mission.'

'It's some television thing, is it?' said Arnal. Sometimes when he was allowed to watch television at the caretaker's house, he saw programmes in which ordinary people down on their luck got to have one incredible chance to turn their life around.

'Better than television. You get the opportunity to take a place in history. Hell now, isn't that something.'

'I don't understand,' said Arnal.

'You have the chance to do one big thing, and go down in history for it.'

So Mr McKnife told Arnal how bad a job the president had

been making of leading the country recently, the disturbing economic and social consequences, and about those prominent, concerned citizens who had courageously banded together to find a way to rid the country of someone who was so blatantly debasing patriotic values of right-thinking people.

'What's that to do with me?' asked Arnal. He took no notice of politics; barely knew to which party the president belonged. He was so far to the edge of his community that even the power of the centre was muted.

'The man who stops the president will be famous,' said Mr McKnife.

'So?' The limo had halted at downtown lights, and Arnal sat in the luxury of the back seat, looking out at the cold people scurrying to work. Their faces were pinched in the chill and their ears, if visible, seemed to stick out pinkly into the frosty air. Arnal was only a couple of metres away, yet was warm, seated comfortably, sipping soup. And private — able to see, while not being seen himself. All his life he had been on the outside, and he had a sudden glimpse of life on the inside.

'So where do I fit in?' he asked. He still thought that maybe it was some sort of TV thing.

'Have you ever wondered what it is that gives someone a place in history?' said Mr McKnife, and carried on without waiting for an answer. 'Action which alters the course of significant events, that's what,' he said. 'Most people give a lifetime's devotion and it's still not enough, and just a few people find a short cut. You ever heard of Bob Ford, or James Earl Ray, or Gavrilo Princip?'

'Princip seems familiar, I reckon.'

'Well, you were a bright enough kid at school, weren't you, but I guess you don't read much these days. Let me assure you that those names are in the best history books, and they'll still be remembered in a hundred years. Bob Ford was a hick nobody who shot Jesse James in the back for the reward, Ray shot Martin Luther King Jr, and Princip assassinated Archduke Ferdinand

and pretty much kicked off the First World War. And think of Lee Harvey Oswald? Such names are imperishable, Arnal.'

The limo had reached the central city, and continued to glide from block to block among the high-rises. It drew glances even from the blasé office commuters because of its size. 'More oxtail soup?' asked Mr McKnife. Arnal's sneakers were like rotting fish on the soft, grey carpet of the limo's interior, but he'd long ago stopped feeling embarrassed about his appearance. He had no substantial emotional connection with other people.

'You want me to shoot the president?' he said.

'Fat chance,' said Mr McKnife. 'She's better protected than an eastern potentate, or a soccer star. But there's maybe a window of opportunity, see. Two things fortuitously have come together. A special function at which the president will enhance her popularity by briefly meeting a cross-section of citizens. We can get you in at the bottom of that representative cross-section, Arnal.'

'And the other thing?'

'We have an organic explosive. The very latest thing, and maybe a month or two before the president's people get onto it. We take out your guts, see, Arnal, and replace them with organic explosive shaped like intestines. No X-ray or ultrasound screening will pick up a thing, and then as you meet the president you just punch your own stomach, and there's your country redeemed and your place in history.'

Arnal had never been to a flash do, where everybody was dressed up and you needed to show an invitation at the door. He imagined, too, that you'd get a fair bit for blowing up a president. 'There'd be a lot of money and stuff in it, right?' he said.

'Arnal, Arnal,' said Mr McKnife patiently. 'Absolutely nothing can change in your life beforehand. You can guess the scrutiny you'll come under once you're suggested as a member of the group to meet the president. It's afterwards you get your reward, Arnal, in history, and also knowing that you've done a grand thing for your country.'

'I don't think I could go through with it,' said Arnal frankly. He'd never been a brave man, and life had ground him down all the more.

'But the beauty is that once your insides are out, then you're going to die anyway, so the shrinks tell us you don't worry at all about setting off the stuff. Heroic fatalism they call it, Arnal, and evidently you go out on a hell of a high.'

Both of them were quiet for a while; both of them sat back in the warm comfort of the limo, and watched the morning traffic building in the city. Arnal recognised some frontages that they had already passed once before.

Finally Mr McKnife spoke again, almost diffidently. 'It's a matter of the quid pro quo, Arnal, isn't it. Let's face it, people with a good life wouldn't touch the offer. I wouldn't myself, for Christ's sake: I've got career prospects beyond your comprehension, and kids to see through university. But your life is shit, always has been. We know how you live, Arnal. You clean the lavatories for the trailer park, and you've a key to lock them at 10 p.m. Unknown to the caretaker, when you lock them you stay inside, and sleep there in one of the cubicles on sacking which you roll up in the mornings. There's something gone wrong with your stomach, isn't there, Arnal, and you spew a lot in the mornings. Even the street kids make fun of you. Sometimes you try to piss, and nothing comes for a long time'

'I need better food,' said Arnal.

'No family that we can find: no friends that matter,' said Mr McKnife.

'I got cousins somewhere.'

'You ever had a sexual experience apart from self-abuse?' asked Mr McKnife, glancing sympathetically from the window at the office girls.

Arnal didn't answer. The dark, long-wheelbase car dipped and hissed among the traffic.

'It's completely up to you,' said Mr McKnife. 'But what we're offering is a place in history, an absolute immortality in the sense that your name will live while those around you will be forgotten. Noteworthy, yes, that's what you become. At a stroke you jump ahead of millions of people who gave you no recognition at all. It's completely up to you. I reckon, though, it's a quid pro quo well worth considering, Arnal.'

And Arnal was considering it, for he knew the state of his own life, and what was being offered. He imagined himself meeting the president and having that moment absolutely in his command. One punch and he could vault the wretched insignificance of his whole life, and have a place in history. Arnal Retent, the man who assassinated the third President of Australasia. Yeah, it had something of a ring to it.

journey's end

SOLITUDE AND MOONLIGHT ARE FLATTERING TO a body, and in the night it hung at equilibrium there in the water. The head was bowed, the arms relaxed, and the smooth curve of the back was nudging the surface. The only agitation was the brief flurry of moths as they flew in from the playing fields and ended in the pool. A faint wind moved in the silver birch trees by the enclosure: the cool, dry air of the summer night. A hedgehog was surprisingly loud in the flaxes, and the moonlight cast shadows from the low, wooden school buildings, and made silhouettes of the stock trucks parked in Hammond Transport next door.

The body was naked, but not especially pale, and presented a serene, smooth back to the world above, keeping any expression to itself. The left arm was bent naturally from the torso as if raised in a casual farewell. Night and nature are quite accepting of circumstances that constitute an affront to the conventions of day.

Hamish and Shaun Simpson were often the first to the school grounds on a Saturday. In such a small, country town no distinction was made between community and school facilities. The area school had the only pool, the only tennis courts, the single gym and the better hall of two in the town. Hamish preferred not to play with Shaun, who was two years younger and didn't give enough opposition in tennis, but his mother said he wasn't to go bothering people early in the day. Hamish, at fourteen, had a blond and lanky athleticism. 'Just one set,' he said, 'and a swim, and then I'm going round to Martin's and you have to bugger off.'

'Okay,' said Shaun. He could have said that he had friends of his own to catch up with later in the morning.

'And we're just going to use the old balls too.'

'Okay.'

Nine-thirty in the morning and it was already hot. The grounds around the four asphalt courts were burnt brown, and by the time the boys finished playing there was already a shimmer at surface level. Hamish won six–two, and neither brother realised that the challenge inherent in the age gap was the main reason Shaun would eventually turn out the better sportsman. As they wandered towards the pool, Hamish complained again about the confusing number of court markings they had to put up with. 'Jesus, the girls' netball courts should be separate, or something. Wouldn't it be great to have some decent courts? Those nets are stuffed.'

They intended as usual to take off their underpants and swim in their shorts. As they neared the baths enclosure they saw Susan Bevan and Janie McIlwray coming across the playing field. Had Hamish been with friends of his own age he would have said something about Janie McIlwray's increasingly good tits, but he just thought about them, and being preoccupied with that didn't notice the body in the pool.

So Shaun was the first one. He knew immediately what it was, but his words were as if to ward off recognition. 'Jesus, what's that?' He was just through the wire netting gate, and he stepped back a bit. The body didn't look good in the full light of day. The bum seemed exposed in a more ignominious way, and the shoulders and neck seemed puffed up. Neither Shaun nor Hamish thought to stop the girls walking up behind them, and so Susan and Janie saw too, and began to cry. Janie's mother thought the consequent trauma was the reason for a whole bunch of things that went wrong for Janie in the rest of her life. Hamish told them not to go any closer, and he ran past the school buildings, through the main gates, and across to the Wilton house, and that's how it became official. Because Hamish was the oldest of the four at the pool and raised the alarm, people got used to saying that he found the body, but his brother Shaun was the first to see it; after the murderer of course.

An ambulance and a police car came from Ashburton. The constable hung coloured tape right around the pool enclosure to keep the locals away from the scene, but the ambulance people didn't disturb the body: they knew a corpse well enough when they saw one. Over eight hundred people lived in Writhford, and by the time Detective Senior Sergeant Bell arrived from Christchurch after lunch most of them knew there was a dead woman in the school swimming pool. The McIlwrays, Bevans and Simpsons were the initial family sources, but then the news centres became, as always, Ron Tepple's garage, the Melbourne pub and the minimarket. Some young people hung around in the school grounds, half-hearted in their games and more interested in anything that went on at the baths. Adults came also, disguising their interest by seeming to be just passing by, but gawking nevertheless. Paul Secker, the school principal, stood with great seriousness beside the Ashburton constable long after they had discussed those matters that fell within his responsibility. Paul was reluctant to leave before he'd had an opportunity to repeat to the Christchurch police all he'd told the constable about the pool's compliance with the relevant regulations, and he wondered if perhaps a television crew might arrive and want a statement from him. As the body wasn't that of any of his students, there was, perhaps, opportunity rather than responsibility.

Detective Wynne Bell had been a city cop for twenty years — Wellington, Hamilton, then Christchurch — and his parents were both radiographers, but his mother's people were farmers and he'd spent a good deal of time working on farms as a young man. As he drove across the plains towards Writhford he noted the grip drought had on the properties he passed: the crops undersized, the pasture burnt off except where the irrigation devices moved slowly over the paddocks like giant stick insects, spraying water in sweeps and undulations, sometimes splashing it on the sealed road. Spend money to make money was a new farming creed, and very different from the conservatism of the older farmers he'd known.

Had the body been of some local kid in the baths, Wynne wouldn't have come out; or if it had been a clothed and identified adult, at least initially. But a naked, long-haired young woman when no local was missing, now that was different.

He wanted the body out as soon as he had made a note of its posture in the water. Paul Secker was willing to be a helper, but Wynne thanked him and asked him to leave the enclosure. The ambulance men held a blue plastic sheet up in a clumsy attempt to stop people seeing as the two policemen lifted the body out. They took off nothing but their shoes and socks, knowing that their trousers would soon dry. The woman's body was put on a low trolley stretcher and that went entire into the ambulance. The body, not tall, was of an olive-skinned, almost chunky young woman with a gold chain necklace. Wynne noticed two scratches on the left side of her neck. The armpits were unshaven, and he wondered if that was a sign of European nationality, or maybe an expression of feminism. The hands were small, almost childlike, and aroused in him a sadness and pity which his professional calm couldn't completely contain. When the body was covered, except for the face, Wynne asked

Paul Secker to come and see if he recognised her. 'I'm pretty sure it's no one from round here,' said the principal.

Once the ambulance was gone, quietly, without siren, the school grounds seemed mundane again, despite the police and their cars, and the bright plastic incident tape. The concrete pool with its clumsily painted blue lane lines on the bottom, and thistledown, leaves and drowned moths eddied into the corners, was an unlikely place of death, or drama. The heat and bright light seemed to exclude the chance of dark subtleties, or threat. Wynne and the Ashburton constable began a search of the baths enclosure, and then the brown grass beyond the pipe and netting gates. Some of the Writhford watchers were stirred to imitation for a while, fanning out around the grounds and buildings in the hope of finding some intriguing evidence, but it was too hot to keep up that enthusiasm for long, and most drifted away in the mid-afternoon shimmer.

'What do you reckon?' said the Ashburton constable, after they found nothing of interest on that part of the field where it was most likely a vehicle would have pulled up. 'I didn't see major injuries, but she sure as hell didn't get in there by herself. It's sex, I suppose. The gold chain's still on her.'

'Maybe.' Wynne had dealt with several drowning cases, but he knew the circumstances of this one had just the sensational elements the media looked for in a crime. There would be all sorts of pressures to get a result: all sorts of scrutiny. He went with his colleague back to his car and they sat in the front seats, each with a door open to catch any breeze and dissipate the unbearable heat within the vehicle. 'I'd better start with the kids who found her,' he said. He thought of taking off his police trousers to help them dry, but decided it might cause comment.

'Two of them,' said the constable. He opened his notebook. 'Two brothers, Hamish and Shaun Simpson — they came over for a swim after playing tennis.'

'I'll start with them. It's too hot here now anyway. I'll ask the teacher guy if he's got a room here we can use to co-ordinate things. Who's the nearest uniform who'd normally deal with things here?'

'Ennis Tregonning at Penthurst, I suppose.'

'Get on to him, would you. We'll want him on the team for sure.' Wynne wasn't excited by what had happened: he wasn't daunted either. He knew behind that quietly floating body must lie a history of pain and desperation, and that there'd be more of both to come. The public's expectation was that his quarry would be a monster of wickedness, but his own experience led him to believe he was looking for a person who had made one more bad decision than the fates allowed.

Lucca Gasparini was hot also, in the Mediterranean winter. Early in the afternoon he sat in his singlet on his small balcony and read the letter from his daughter. She wrote that it was fantastic in Australia, that she had work on a Langhorne Creek vineyard with other young people, mostly casuals like herself, people backpacking, or on vacation. She said there was one other Italian — a guy from Brindisi. 'What a rathole,' muttered Lucca, for he knew Brindisi, a dirty port city where he'd been unhappy for two years. She wrote that everybody ate too much bad food in Australia, and that on Wednesday she was to fly from Sydney to Christchurch: to New Zealand, which people kept telling her about. She was okay for money, she said, despite the airfare.

'She's going to New Zealand. She's okay for money,' Lucca shouted over his shoulder, but if his wife heard she said nothing. Lucca had never been outside Europe and his geography was weak. 'Where is New Zealand?' he called. He looked up to the old part of the city, and then out over the sea. Sometimes a mirage of Corsica appeared there, some freakish effect of temperature inversion, but not that day. Lucca wished that his daughter was at home. He missed her a great deal though he never thought to tell her that, or his wife. He missed her strength, energy and intelligence. He missed her love. A family should be together as the natural way.

Ventimiglia is the first Italian town after you cross the border from France, geographically nothing distinguishes it from its near neighbours of the Côte d'Azur — Menton, Cap Martin, Monaco — but the difference is plain in other ways. Ventimiglia is unpretentious, less tarted up for the tourists, less expensive. The French drive across the border to the markets there, and buy cheap liquor. The place and the people don't put themselves on show in the way of the French Côte d'Azur. From his balcony Lucca could see the market space by the rivermouth and stony beach, though the stalls were there only once a week. Across the river was the steep hill with the old yellow village halfway up, and some market gardens. He never went there. He didn't find the residue of his country's history interesting at all. Lucca Gasparini was a practical man who had studied civil engineering in Genoa, and worked for the municipality of Ventimiglia. He reserved his emotional responses for his family, for food, and for soccer.

'She's in Sydney,' he said loudly. His wife didn't reply, but his son Salvatore came out and stood beside his father in response. Salvatore should have been at school, but he had an ear infection and was pleased to be still in official convalescence and have his father's company until he went back to the office. 'Your clever sister's in Australia.' Salvatore was eight years younger than his sister and the gap was sufficient to ensure that he didn't feel diminished by her achievements.

'I'll go to Australia too one day,' he said.

'A lot of Italian people have gone there and stayed.'

'Kangaroos live in Australia,' said the boy.

Lucca Gasparini read the last of his daughter's letter again, and felt once more how much he missed her. In Writhford so far away it was hotter than Ventimiglia, but he knew nothing of that. His daughter's letter told them that the next day she was to fly to Christchurch: to the New Zealand everyone kept telling her about. What a beautiful country, they said, such a beautiful country. By the time Lucca had her letter, of course, she had already made that journey.

Ollie McDonald finished baling hay in the culvert paddock by 4.30 in the afternoon. He was one of a dwindling number of farmers who hadn't gone over to the large round bales, and he left the paddock scattered with the smaller rectangular bales of lucerne as he drove the baler back to the farm sheds. Ollie's farm was flat and largely bare, and from habit he looked at the pasture and crops in each paddock he passed through, kicked at the ground as he opened one gate after another for himself. His father would have been amazed at the massive automatic irrigation machine that Ollie could set up, but everything came at a cost, and Ollie watered a paddock only after careful consideration of its use and a check of soil moisture levels. Farming was a business, wasn't it, as Ollie was so often told.

Until the last couple of years Ollie would have done another job after putting the baler away, and not gone into the house until six, or half past, but when his wife was ill with cancer he had routinely knocked off earlier. In the house he'd talk to her loudly as he got a simple meal — he in the kitchen and with his voice travelling through to the bedroom. He'd grown accustomed to getting little reply because of her weakness.

Christine had died over a year ago, but Ollie still went into the house at five, prepared some vegetables to have with his cold, pink mutton, and talked loudly to the tabby about the same things to which he'd received no answer when his wife was alive. About the local fight for resource consents for more irrigation, the thistles in his neighbour's property, a word with the beekeeper who had hives on his property, an unfamiliar blue Lancer parked by the creek, and recent local land sales. What they had never talked about, and was never imparted to the cat when Christine was gone, was the disappointment that there were no children and no grandchildren: no sense of continuity for farm and family, no boisterous innocence, no loving demands that would distract Ollie from self-absorption.

The sun was still shining close to the hills when Ollie finished his meal, but he went outside only to feed the dogs, and the chooks straggling across the yard. Then he closed the Venetian blinds in the lounge and opened the bottom cupboard where, below his box of current farm accounts, he kept four videos of people having sex. Ollie knew each one by heart. Often, immediately after watching his videos, Ollie told himself he wouldn't bother again, that it was shaming and of no use, and he would push them to the very back of the bottom cupboard. But always, days, maybe weeks later, they were taken out again.

He decided on Rich Bitches Get It *and fast forwarded to the pool orgy. Ollie sat in the shadowy lounge in his work clothes and with his shoes off, his hands relaxed yet still in the half clutch of a working man, and he watched beautiful women apparently getting a great deal of pleasure from vigorous sex. They were like no women he knew; like no women he had ever known. They were a different race of women with smooth, undulating bodies, no practical opinions, and a constant need to touch and be touched.*

Ollie told himself that in real life people didn't have sex which was so prolonged, adventuresome and spectacularly enjoyable — certainly he never had — yet there it all was before him. His own life was drained, colourless, and he was drawn to a world that offered dramatic satisfactions without consequences, or responsibilities. The nor'wester blew baubles of thistledown in the blue sky outside, the sheep trooped to the troughs, the dusty baler cooled gradually in the shed, but fifty-six-year-old Ollie sat in his farmhouse and watched the women of a different race.

The Melbourne was the single pub in Writhford, and locals said it was named after a nineteenth-century British prime minister, not the city in Australia. It was the only building in the town which had any claim to architectural, or historical, significance. It was all weatherboard and had open, matching verandahs both upstairs and down. Behind it was a derelict sod hut which had been the original accommodation house when Writhford was a changing post on the coach road. Paul Secker said they should raise money to reroof it before it collapsed, but none of that got past the talk stage.

Ron and Liz Ormond owned the Melbourne. Usually the five guest rooms were unoccupied, but the bar trade was good and the meals popular. Rebecca Ormond boarded at a girls' private school in Christchurch, which was another reason for Paul Secker's opinion that the Ormonds didn't give the lead they should in Writhford. Dylan Ormond had been at the district high, but only because even his mother and father knew that the expense of a city education would have been wasted on him.

Procreation is a gamble: spin the genes and see what life-long significance the outcome may have. It was clear that Rebecca would never be a beauty. She had the heavy build of her father made more pronounced by the female propensity to width of hip and thigh, and the receding chin of her mother, which would turkey gobble in time. At least she was given the pick of mental inheritance from both parents, and topped her class in algebra and chemistry.

The best Dylan got was physical, and maybe his shallow selfishness was the effect of indulgence rather than the disposition of either parent, who were hard-working and fair in their own way. He had broad shoulders, and a broad forehead with blond, crimped Romney hair. His eyes were blue and glancing, his mood variable: he had a ready snigger, and beneath it all hid his realisation that he had proved mediocre in every endeavour he had made.

He was close to a snigger because of some outrageous talkback on the car radio as he called into the Wrightson's office. Maybe there'd be fax, or email, messages at the office, and he wanted to pick up drench for Ash Prentice. The branch office was combined with a small store that stocked farm goods and a bit of ski and tramping equipment. The window display was rarely changed, and the blue tartan Swanndri on the one mannequin was bleached lighter on the street side. Mrs Poole came in every weekday between two and five, but in the mornings the premises were closed unless Dylan was there. His office was a desk and chair behind the counter, and the computer and fax-phone took a good deal of his desk space; an overflowing wire tray most of the rest. Book work had never been Dylan's strength. It didn't improve his temper to find another reprimand from his superiors in Christchurch. While other rural branches were holding on well, Writhford was slipping. 'Get knotted,' said Dylan loudly, and deleted the message.

He needed a drink. Stubbies of lager from the bottom drawer of his desk filled his need for the time. Work could wait, the world could wait, ineptitude and boredom could be forgotten for a time. There was savagery almost in his drinking, and habit and release.

Dylan wasn't all that interested in being an agent anyway: he'd rather spend time at his parents' pub, or fishing, or skiing. He had a job because he had to do something, and Wrightson's gave him a decent six-cylinder company car. What he often talked about was setting up as a personal fishing guide for rich overseas tourists. He knew of people who were doing it around Queenstown in the south, and Taupo in the north. He thought about that again as he lugged two plastic containers of drench out to his car, and forgot to enter them for Mrs Poole's records. He'd toss the agent's job in before they got round to firing him, and set up on his own. What he'd have to do, though, was persuade his parents to come up with a loan for a decent off-roader: another debt to add to those he still hadn't repaid.

Dylan didn't much enjoy his calls at the Prentice farm. The year before, he'd made a botch-up in getting Ash's first draft of lambs away, and he wasn't allowed to forget it. As he drove through the pinus radiata plantation to the west of Writhford, Dylan imagined how much more pleasant it would be to deal with overseas tourists rather than the narrow-minded local cockies. Almost everything in Writhford depended on the farmers, but though Dylan had lived there all his life, he didn't much care for animals, or crops. Even before the morning's email had given him further evidence of how little he was valued in the firm, Dylan had felt out of sorts. Alice Drumm, the kitchen hand at the Melbourne, was leaving the town and going to a polytechnic catering course in Christchurch. She would no longer come quietly up to his room two or three times a week after her evening shift and lie with him on his single bed. No longer would he feel her warmth while disregarding both her complaints about the cook, and his view of the night sky.

Maybe he should follow her to Christchurch. The one thing that had kept him in Writhford was that he could live free at the Melbourne, eat there and drink what he wanted, all for the odd stint as barman some evenings, carrying in crates, standing in for his mum and dad when they needed to go to a function together. He looked at the reduced, familiar landscape of the plains as he drove to Ash Prentice's, and was bored with it all over again. What he needed for sure was a big offroader to set himself up as a fishing guide. A talk to his mother, then his father, to bring them round was what he planned, and before things became too tricky with his present job.

Dylan came out on to the scenic road to the mountains and passed two hitchhikers without heeding their raised thumbs. A man and woman both with the same flags sewn onto the flaps of their packs. He didn't recognise the flag, but supposed from their height and hair colour they were German. Had both been girls he would have stopped and offered a ride. He liked the boldness of women hitchhikers, and there was always the chance of hitting it off with them. It had happened for him once before, and he'd installed a Dutch girl at the Melbourne for nearly a week without his parents realising the set-up. It was the sort of experience he'd go to some length to repeat.

There was one A-frame chalet house in Writhford, quite out of place even after sixteen years among the rectangular, tin-roofed scatter of other homes. And instead of a proper garden of roses and azaleas, which may have mitigated against oddity, it had an assortment of grasses and tussocks, amid boulders chosen for quartz lines and colours that looked their best in the occasional rains. The chalet had been built as a ski base for a Christchurch man who owned a plant nursery, but he had divorced soon afterwards and found other recreations closer to home.

Merry Saunders rented the chalet, and gave it the care a series of transient tenants had ignored. She liked to sit on the decking beneath the overhang and look over the tousled grasses of the garden towards the mountains. That way she could see across the edge of the school grounds to part of the main road west.

Merry had lived two years in Writhford, but that was well short of a qualification to be considered a local. There wasn't any particular discrimination because of that, or because she was fat. Merry found most Writhford people friendly enough. Once they got past the misunderstanding that her name was Mary, they were okay. Merry had invitations to barbecues, indoor bowls and group trips to the city to see a touring Irish band, or a movie nominated for the Oscars, but on such occasions she was aware of still being by her fat self, and mostly she preferred to spend time on her computer. She spent hours in chat rooms dedicated to large women, astrology, aromatherapy and sexual mysticism. She bared her considerable soul to a sisterhood most of whom didn't even know where New Zealand was on the globe.

At this time, however, it was something natural and organic that occupied her, as she leant her forearms on the broad sill of the bedroom window, and Bernard attempted to clamp himself on the great, curving bun of her arse. 'There now. There now,' he said emphatically, but she said nothing: she never spoke at all during lovemaking despite his entreaties to be loud. She looked from the darkened room of the chalet, though, and with widened eyes observed the urchin heads of her grasses ruffled in the breeze of a moonlit night. Bern was a dentist in Christchurch who often paid Merry's chalet rent, and came out sometimes when his wife had hospital stays for kidney treatment. Merry's physical abundance, the healthy sheen of her surfaces, were a reassurance to him. 'There now,' he said, pulling back on Merry's shoulders.

Afterwards they lay on the stark bed, the sheets and blankets indistinctly pale and twisted on the floor. Merry's self-image was always bolstered by the delight Bern took in her body, but she never had the light on when she was naked. Bern was aware that he also needed the flattery of incomplete disclosure. He had a hairy, rib-striped torso, and thin legs with the toes turned in. Merry wasn't censorious, and valued his kindness and knowledge.

'Do you know any woman who'd like to make a threesome?' said Bern. He was still breathing heavily and he laid one hand on his thin, hairy chest to calm himself. 'Have you got a local chum who's up for it, do you think?'

'I don't think so.' Merry never heard anyone but Bern talk of

chums. It reminded her of wholesome English comics.

'I've always had this fantasy of being pressed between two women: the superabundance of possibility.'

'It flatters your vanity, perhaps,' said Merry. Several times Bern had shown an interest in ménage à trois, but Merry was not attracted by the idea, and she didn't have that sort of familiarity with any of the Writhford women. Bern got up and fumbled in his jacket pocket for a handkerchief with which to wipe sweat from his face. He came back to the bed and patted Merry's head.

'Just what I needed,' he said. 'Marvellous,' he said. 'I'll go and get a couple of stubbies.' Merry could hear his light, pigeon-toed gait down the stairs to the kitchen and then back again: he was nimble for a tall man. 'Jesus, those grasses have grown well, haven't they,' he said. 'From the window down there it looks like real tussock country.' They sat with their backs to the rimu bed-end and drank beer from the bottles. 'I remember when we went into Penthurst and bought most of them,' Bern said.

'I have to water them, but otherwise they're away,' she said.

'You can say that again.'

'How's your wife?' asked Merry without any malice at all, and Bern talked at length about her health, their almost decision to sell the house because of the demands of the large garden. 'I mean, when I finish at the surgery I'm whacked, absolutely done. I said we could afford to have someone do the garden, and some housework too, but she still wants to do it all herself, even though she can't really manage it.' This was how it always was between them: one bout of fierce lovemaking, and then their calmer selves emerged again and they talked of families, Buddhism, his patients, films and politics. Merry was a supporter of the Greens, and Bern endorsed some of their policies, but said they were too impractical ever to be in government.

'How are you off for money?' Bern said. 'Maybe something for the garden, or clothes?' On visits he offered money, and never in an offensive way. He was generous. Sometimes she accepted.

'I'm fine just now. I'm okay.' She watched him, dim in the unlit bedroom, get out of the bed briefly and retrieve a sheet to put over their

lower halves. Even in the summer night they were cooling after their sexual exertions.

'It would be fun though, don't you think? You and I with a friend of yours in bed together. Jesus, the thought of it brings me on.' Bern imagined four large breasts and the intertwining of six arms and legs. He wondered what expression one woman's face would have as she watched him making love to the other. He calculated what combination of positions would form a circle.

'I don't think I know anybody well enough,' said Merry. 'It's not so much doing it, but asking someone, don't you think?' She thought he might dump her if she wasn't able to indulge his fantasy, and she had no one else who cared at all about her: no one at all.

The Simpsons' house was built in green, summerhill block and had large ranchslider doors opening onto the concrete patio where Wynne Bell talked to the family. His stated reason for coming was to ask the boys again about finding the body in the pool, but he was more interested in quizzing the parents about their fellow citizens. The person who finds a body always has a profile in the case, but rarely provides the means to solve it. So Wynne listened to the boys — Hamish did most of the talking — then moved the conversation easily to more general considerations. 'It's not the sort of thing you'd expect in a friendly little place like this, is it?' he said. 'I don't suppose you've had anything similar before at all?'

'Years ago there was a shooting at Kuri Creek,' said Frieda Simpson, 'and a farmer was killed.'

'Yeah, that was the end of a long-standing row over duck-shooting ponds, though,' said her husband. 'Two neighbours at each other for years.'

It was that sort of local knowledge which the detective valued in the Simpsons, and he began casually to draw them out about Writhford and its people. Both of them were local, had lived most their lives there. Frieda's parents had been farmers, her husband's had owned the garage before the Tepples. The policeman let the talk find its own directions. Everything about the township seemed of interest to him: the most ordinary of people had his full attention. He showed no impatience with references that seemed quite unconnected with the case. Experience had made him aware that the thing which doesn't fit often turns out to be the key.

Wynne felt the time well spent with the Simpson family, and not just because of their connection with the case and their value as a source of local knowledge. He felt at ease with them as they were at ease with themselves. Much of his life was spent with people who were maintaining subterfuge of one sort or another, who were unhappily defiant, dysfunctional, or suffering guilt or remorse. Frieda and Ivan and their boys were happy reminders of the majority of people with whom he had less professional contact. Even Ivan Simpson's wary co-operation was natural. Already he was keen to be off, having stayed behind to hear the boys tell their story to the police, mainly because Frieda thought he ought.

'Any oddbods, or weirdos, in the district do you think?' asked Wynne. 'Anyone that comes to mind as maybe having something to do with all this?'

'Can't think of anyone as being dangerous at all,' said Ivan. He was a little surprised at his own unwillingness to be a source of information for the police, when he absolutely wanted the person who had killed the girl to be caught. Ivan had nothing of value to contribute, nothing to hide, yet he felt wary of the unforced questions and unwilling to pronounce on his acquaintances. 'I'd better go,' he said. 'We're harvesting at Spencers' today.'

'Thanks for your help,' said Wynne Bell.

Frieda and the sergeant were left on the patio to talk as first Ivan, and then Hamish and Shaun left. The boys were disappointed the policeman had nothing gory to tell them, or had decided not to share what might have been of interest — the results of the post-mortem, or any suspects he might already have.

'We don't know yet if she was sexually assaulted or not. Being in the water didn't help.' Wynne had waited until the boys were gone. 'We've got no idea who she is, even. No clothes or possessions have turned up, except the gold necklace she wore. We're assuming it's some local guy who got carried away: someone who knew about the school pool and that.'

Frieda wondered about Bruce Donald who owned the minimarket, and who once told her at a New Year's party that if she ever fancied some horizontal dancing then he was up to it. And she knew that Ivan's own brother had a reputation among the younger women. None of that made you kill someone though, did it. She knew just about everyone in the town and there was no one who would go out to kill a girl. She was sure of that. 'I can't imagine anyone here who could possibly think of doing a thing like that,' she said.

The sergeant could have told her that's not often the way of it: that such things start much further back with more acceptable and explicable expectations, then in a rush take the direction of torment and disaster.

Everywhere is the potential for wonder and delight, and everywhere, too, the dark side waits.

Ollie McDonald talked with the apiarist at Bridge Corner about the poor year it was for everybody because of the drought. The beekeeper's truck idled on and Ollie's dogs lay in the shade of the gorse hedge and tongued. 'There's no guts in the pasture at all,' he said.

'You're right,' said the apiarist. 'I've noticed the clover hasn't been anything like as good.'

'The stock just go back before your eyes.'

'It's a bugger all right.'

'Irrigation water's not the same, and anyway the rates these days are killing.'

'It's the pressure from these dairy boys, though. You can put a ring around that.'

'I reckon maybe it's time to put the place on the market while the

going's good and then you've got no more hassles.'

'Could do worse. Could do worse Ollie, and it's worth thinking about, that's for sure, I'd say. Plenty round here have done just that recently.'

Both of them could talk this way for half an hour and not remember a word of it, not meet each other's eyes, give no challenges and no concessions, nothing of their real selves, carry on with their own thoughts. The apiarist was thinking that he'd take his hives off Ollie's property next year; the guy didn't farm in a way that suited bees any longer. Ollie was remembering the apiarist's father who'd got shot by a neighbour years before in an argument over maimai possies.

Ollie was very lonely, despite having lived in the district all his life and knowing many of the people there since they had all gone to primary school together. He missed his wife, but there was a deeper isolation that he had begun to see had always been part of him, even during those years he had played sport with his fellows, joined in community service activities, had people into his home, and gone with Christine into the homes of others.

After the apiarist was gone, Ollie took his dogs with him as he checked the ewes. He'd never had any great liking for sheep: he could take them or leave them. They fulfilled their stereotype of being stupid animals, but they required less hard slog than cropping, and so he had drifted into having more of the farm in grass.

As he worked his way back towards the farmhouse, Ollie thought of the video in which the Eurasian woman came uninvited into the businessman's hotel room. How she could smile so warmly and take off her clothes for a stranger. Ollie was a stranger and wanted to be loved like that.

A dance hall has a musk fragrance all of its own: part of it is sweat and powder and perfumes, deodorants and warm breath; part of it is an emanation of the sheer exuberance of life. There were voices and music, too, which filled the hall and spilled through the main doors, carrying the fragrance out and up until all was dissipated in the warm depths of the summer sky. The louder, brighter and more fragrant the hall became, the more the surrounding buildings were subdued until the hall was the pulsing heart of that part of town, and the surrounding buildings nondescript and reduced in the darkness.

Dylan Ormond stood inside the doorway of the hall in Penthurst. He wasn't consciously aware of the atmosphere, yet was still affected by it. He wasn't good at dancing, and took little enjoyment in it. He was at the Penthurst dance because his Writhford mates were there, and because he wanted to meet girls. He watched them, all the women, hundreds of them, so that you thought with such numbers who could miss out, yet he knew that such a multitude was no target, that you could be like the inexperienced hunter who fires into a flock of birds sure of hitting something, but has nothing fall because he has failed to select a specific target.

People danced in all sorts of ways; anything went. Some gyrated by themselves, but Dylan still wouldn't ask for a dance until sufficient people were on the floor to make him inconspicuous there. He was more comfortable with a girl at a table with drinks, or in his firm's car, or idling at the dance hall door and talking. He would talk about his parents owning the Melbourne hotel in Writhford, about his knowledge of farming, lie about being a personal fishing guide to wealthy overseas visitors. He could bluff a little concerning the latest music. Dylan wasn't bad at talk: maybe it was the one thing at which he was better than average. All the things he talked about concerned himself, though, and he rarely asked a partner about her own life, or referred to her in more than self-serving and obvious flatteries.

'I'd say you've done a lot of dancing — been taught, even,' he told the short girl with the crimson streaks in her hair.

'You don't get taught this stuff,' she said.

'This band really goes for it, eh?'

'Sweet as,' she said.

'Would you like to take a break later and have a drink at Asteroid?'

'Maybe,' she said. He was quite neat-looking in his own hefty way. She could do worse for the night. Being short herself, she quite liked bigger guys, and his teeth were good — white against the tan of his face.

She'd have a fair enough night and not end up on her back. She'd see Dylan several times again, and then cut out smartly after the first time Dylan got drunk while with her. That would be some eye-opener. You wouldn't want too much of Dylan when he was off his face. No flatteries then, no talk much at all, but a lot of physical insistence. She wasn't going to take any more of that.

Merry Saunders was a bit down when she came back from the clothing and ski shop where she worked. The day had been okay until she had overheard a customer remark to her boss that she was some big heifer all right. Merry had always been fat. Right from childhood she'd been fat, and no number of diets, fitness regimes or understand your body books made any difference. She had lived with being fat for over forty years, but a chance remark could still ruin her day.

She wished she could ring Bern and have him talk her into a good mood again, but it always had to be Bern who rang her. Bern loved every inch of her, every kilo, he often said. Merry decided against a blueberry muffin before tea, and went straight to her computer. She went to her web favourites list and opened the Weighty Matters chat room. She had friends there who knew what it was like to be a big woman in a world that feared and hated fat; among a population who saw the inability to keep to medium clothes sizes as a failure of will.

With Donna from Atlanta, Cheryl-Anne from Washington and Nadine from Cincinnati, with Blodwyn, Trisha and ambiguous Evelyn from London, Angela and Rose from Sydney, and Karalyn close in Christchurch, although never met, Merry was with friends. She sat with her shoes off in the only chalet house in Writhford and enjoyed the sisterhood of fat women. It was for most of the time just as good as a drive with Bern, or a strenuous session with him on the upstairs bed. Although the chat-room friends identified themselves in terms of their size, and discussed at times the physical and social consequences of that, they enjoyed in cyberspace a release into weightlessness, a wonderful sense of unity and communion with no crowding together of massive physical presences.

Cincinnati Nadine could talk of her love of dance, and Blodwyn share her fascination with the life of ski instructors. Angela was *completing a thesis on Aboriginal art, and Merry could raise the issue of a threesome. 'My significant other wants me to find a girlfriend to join in with us for sex,' she typed in. She never used Bern's name, though she had told the chat room members that he was a professional man with his own surgery. Merry's topic aroused more interest than dance, ski instructors and Aboriginal art. She was able to forget she was a big heifer, and debate with a sympathetic sisterhood the merits of Bern's request. The chat-room participants were comfortable with such an intimate subject because of the way in which they communicated: able to be most daring and candid, yet too removed to have anything physical asked of them.*

'Dump the weirdo, Merry,' replied Donna. 'The guy's on the slippery path to perdition and hellfire. Damned for sure, and you got to get out of there, baby.'

'There was this article in this magazine I remember which said experiment and openness keeps a relationship alive,' said Angela. 'Don't be closed to new things with your man. You should feel chuffed that he shares fantasies with you, and you know how guys bottle stuff up.'

'Oh, my Rick and I do it all the time. Threesomes, foursomes, absolutely,' said Cincinnati Nadine, who wasn't going to be overawed by some woman at the ends of the earth. 'Nothing new in that, Merry.'

It was the liveliest the Weighty Matters chat room had been for days. Amanda from Durban was stimulated to come on-line for the first time because of it, and was a supporter of Donna's perdition and hellfire position. Merry didn't mention it in the chat room, but the things which concerned her most about Bern's fantasy was whether he saw the other woman as fat, and if he was going to stop coming to see her if she wasn't keen. She'd have nobody then.

Hamish and Shaun Simpson were watching television together in the lounge. They had an end of the sofa each, but their legs mingled carelessly. The parents, unnoticed, observed from the doorway of the kitchen. 'Do they seem okay to you?' Frieda said.

'Seem fine to me.' Ivan put his hand on his wife's shoulder. Since the dead girl was discovered in the school pool there was a mood of anxiety in the town. People wondered how such a thing could happen, and were shaken by the proof that sometimes weakness, indulgence and alienation had terrible consequences. Not everything blows over: sometimes the storm breaks overhead.

'They wouldn't say, though, would they. Maybe they need counselling of some kind. An experience like that could do emotional damage in ways we wouldn't understand. Jill McIlwray says Janie's been badly affected, and she's had her to a psychologist in Christchurch.'

'The boys seem fine. They know they can talk it out with us. We've been over it all once. I think going on about it only keeps it fresh in their minds.'

'You don't think we need to do anything else?'

'I'm no expert on trauma and so on, but hell, the boys know bad things happen and they know they can come to us any time about stuff that bothers them.'

'Think about that poor girl's family, wherever they are,' said Frieda. 'How could anyone recover from it. How could a family bear that much suffering.' Her boys were snorting happily at some inanity on the screen, and their enjoyment was a reassurance. She put her arms around Ivan, who was reluctant to think of the dead girl's family.

'Every now and again a terrible thing happens,' he said helplessly, 'even in places like this. The sooner we all put it behind us and forget it the better.'

But how did you put the murder of a young person like that behind you? How did your sons forget the vision of a body floating in the school pool and the imagined events of the night which had led to such a sight? How did any of them forget that in their own community was a person who had done something so wrong, and yet bought bread like the rest of them and rested in the same sun: a person who might reach out to shake your hand at the bring and buy sale, or come into your home and replace a tap. How did you forget that life itself, which seemed so prescribed for happiness, was always on the knife-edge of tragedy. You couldn't forget any of those things.

That Thursday Ollie woke with stomach pain again. The bedroom curtains had a grey translucence because of the dawn light behind them, and Ollie could hear the birds in their perpetually renewed optimism. He began to leave his bed to check the next room, but then remembered Christine was dead and no longer needed his care. He opened his mouth very wide and kept it so: not so much a yawn, as a desperation that something might leave him, or something be received. The farm had been his father's and his grandfather's. All his life Ollie had felt encompassed by it, part of its pulse and organic wholeness, although he never attempted to analyse, or express, the bond. But now he felt just a husk on the land's surface which would be swept away, quite gone, by the next nor'wester. A farm was just dirt, after all, wasn't it, and it was sentimental rubbish to think that anything you did, any amount of care, meant anything to dirt.

Ollie wondered if he had an ulcer; maybe he wasn't cooking well enough for himself. 'I need to get off the bloody place more,' he said, though the cat wasn't in the room to hear. What he didn't say, didn't admit to himself, was that he wanted the love of the women of a different race, and didn't know how to achieve it. What he didn't say, because he didn't know it, was that loneliness was his ulcer and it was making him sick. He wouldn't work in the afternoon. He'd take the ute and go fishing up at the gorge as he used to do before Christine got sick. Even early, even with the curtains still across, Ollie could tell it was going to be a still, hot day. He'd lived all his life in Canterbury weather and had cause to attend to its nature. From the temperature and humidity within the house, from the nature of the light through the curtains, from the sound of the birds and the lack of electricity in the air, from signs ineffable and instinctive responses — from all these things Ollie knew it would be a blue sky afternoon on the Gorge Road.

That Thursday Dylan was drinking dark ale in his room in the Melbourne. His father had asked him to wash the large windows of the main bar which faced the road, but he was in no mood to be a dutiful son. He was aggrieved that Alice Drumm had moved to Christchurch, and angry when she responded to a phone call with news that she had a steady boyfriend who played for Canterbury B. 'Canterbury B — hey, no shit!' said Dylan, but his derision was hollow. Despite his apparent athleticism he wasn't good at sport.

He'd lose his stock agent's job soon, wouldn't he, and establish himself more clearly as a non-achiever. He'd be stuck at the Melbourne, a country pub, for years as odd job boy for his parents. When he'd asked them for deposit money on a Landcruiser to set up as a fishing guide, even his mother wouldn't consider it. His father left the room without a word and came back with a lined pad page on which he'd been keeping a record for several years of the money lent to his son. He was like that. He held it up in front of Dylan and ran his finger down the column until he came to the total. It was a lot more than Dylan recalled: he'd never bothered with any sort of bookkeeping regarding his debts. Probably his father included interest. 'We just can't go on handing money over,' his mother had said. 'Not at your age if you're going to develop a sense of responsibility. It's not as if you haven't got a job either.' His father had said nothing.

He'd be fired soon, though. Dylan thought of that as he drank bottled beer and looked from his upstairs window to the yard behind the hotel: the gravel turning circle, the tin fences, the crumbling sod hut in which he and his sister had played years before. He'd be fired soon, he knew, because he'd had a second written warning from the Christchurch manager, and he hadn't gone fawning and apologetic to see him. Dylan had very nearly sent a reply telling the manager to shove his job up his arse. He'd be sacked soon and wouldn't even have a decent car. He'd have to ask his mother for her little Mazda whenever he wanted to go somewhere.

He missed Alice Drumm and wished he'd asked her to marry him. He dreaded losing his job even though he disliked it and wasn't prepared to work to retain it. He didn't want to admit that finally his mother had lost faith in him. So Dylan stood looking into the hotel yard, but seeing the future rather than the present and past already there. He was sick of himself, sick of the smell of himself in the room, sick of the opinion of himself he knew others had. He drank in a hurried, urgent way, waiting for the release to kick in. 'Shit,' he said. 'Shit, shit, shit.'

He'd take the firm's car and use the firm's petrol for a long drive, he decided. He'd stoke it along the Gorge Road in the bright sun and let no one at all overtake him. It was a good feeling, that — a few beers in him, a long straight on which he could wind up the Commodore, and the doors shut on all the whole damn, shithouse outside world.

That Thursday Bern hadn't arranged to come out to Merry's, but he rang mid-morning to say he could. 'Jesus, have you been on the net again all the morning? I've tried umpteen times.'

'Sorry,' said Merry, 'but you didn't say anything about ringing or coming today.'

'I can never get through to say anything, can I?'

'Sorry,' said Merry, though she didn't think she needed to be. She'd been checking out a new website called FatChat. Ambiguous Evelyn had passed the info onto her and she'd made contact already with three new people, one of whom was almost exactly Merry's weight and had the same star sign.

'Anyway, a friend's taken her for lunch, then a visit to some display of modern kitchens and dinner. Dozens of these show kitchens evidently, all set up in this wopping warehouse. I might as well come out,' said Bern.

'Okay.' 'I might as well come out' wasn't a romantic line, but she knew Bern didn't mean to be hurtful. Sometimes he brought flowers. No one else ever bothered to visit her, and the FatChat website would always be there.

'Have you had any bright ideas about what we discussed?' said Bern.

'What was that?'

'About you getting a girlfriend around and the three of us having an adventure.'

'I don't know anyone that well,' said Merry. How often did she

have to tell him? Were there people who knew others that well? Merry found it hard to imagine a natural and easy situation in which one woman asked another to come along for a casual threesome sometime, but her social experience was limited. Because of sensitivity her fat world was not a large one. 'Anyway I'd find it embarrassing to ask,' she said.

'Okay, forget it,' said Bern and he kept any irritation, or disappointment, from his voice. Years of living with a very sick woman had given him the dangerous habit of suppressing much of what he felt. 'Look, I'll come out and bring a chardonnay, and maybe in the afternoon we'll take a drive and see what the open-air life has to offer. Like the sound of that?'

Merry did like the sound of it. Almost all of her life was spent alone. That had been the way of it for years. Others had grown used to Merry Saunders being alone, her large figure unaccompanied, but Merry had never grown used to it, as you never do. To stand and talk with the grocer a while, to be accompanied down the theatre aisle for a few seconds by an attentive young usher, to assist in the cake stall of the Writhford School gala and have another woman helper committed to standing beside her — these were things significant in Merry's life, quite inconsequential to most people.

All of that was reason to be thankful for Bern, who never criticised her size, but said he loved all of her body, who talked a lot on the occasions he came out, even if it was of himself; who gave her money and flowers and was only rough when he lost it sometimes during sex and got a bit scary. A run in Bern's Audi down the Gorge Road would be fine. She'd sit there with him and not be by herself, and people could see them together. She'd be with someone for the afternoon even if she was fat.

So now you see her at the end as she was in the beginning. Tullia Gasparini. Not tall, but sturdy and standing to her full height. The dark hair of her race and the olive skin that drew admiration everywhere. What lovely skin, other women said. Oh, you're so lucky. Who cared if she didn't have million-dollar legs. And when she glanced at you the whites of her eyes flashed as they do in the young. She wore a green T-shirt with ITALIA in white letters and a gold chain necklace out of sight.

That Thursday she left Christchurch to hitch through the scenic route to Lake Tekapo. She had planned the trip with two Irish girls she'd met while at the backpackers in the city, but they felt too hung-over after a beach party at Sumner and pulled out. Tullia had been at the party too, but she didn't allow herself to get drunk at such times and felt okay in the morning. She wanted to get on: as the time neared for her to return home she felt a growing restlessness, part enthusiasm to squeeze as much as possible of the country into the last days, part an attempt to speed up time itself so that she would be back with family at last.

She had no difficulty getting a ride: she rarely did. A woman vet took her to the Connick turn off, and she hadn't walked far after that when a stock truck stopped, and the driver offered her a lift down the Gorge Road. He dropped her at the entrance to a farmhouse and yards set back on a shingly terrace where he was to pick up a load of steers. When the noise of the truck had almost died away, and the dust from its passage up the track had drifted like smoke up and away, fading into the blue, Tullia was left with her pack on the side of the road. The sealed road shimmered, a bird sang high above the adjacent paddock, and as the quietness settled she became aware of a high-pitched hum from power lines strung alongside the road. It was all a long way from Italy, Ventimiglia, and the constant presence of people to which she was accustomed: all a long way from a culture that was expressive and boisterous. The vacancy and indifference of the landscape daunted her for a moment despite the birds and despite the bright sun, but then she thought of the kindness she had received from people everywhere, and the exciting experiences in this country and Australia. And she thought of travelling home in eight days to share all those experiences with her family and friends; she thought of what awaited her in a final year at the University of Genoa: she thought of a whole life of which this was only a prologue. And she felt her customary cheerfulness and appetite for new things. She never wanted to be afraid of life; she believed in the goodness of things.

There was something coming from behind down the Gorge Road. Tullia put her pack close to the side of the tarmac and waited to see if she could thumb the vehicle down. The glare of the sun made it difficult to see what was approaching, but she turned the pack so that the stitched flag of her country was clearly in view, and waited. It was a beautiful, unspoiled country, wasn't it? On one side of the road was a line of tall poplars and their leaves were almost on the turn and glinted in the sun, the dry paddocks were a restful sweep towards the distant willows of the creek. Yes, something was coming down the Gorge Road. She stepped closer to the seal so the opportunity would not pass her by.

voices with a common theme

MY MUM HAS THIS DUMB-ARSE NIGHT job at the bakery: mainly buns and muffins to be ready fresh for the morning. Trays and trays of them not sold retail, but for the trade people who call round in rooted vans with racks built in. From my window I can see her walking home from the bus stop, the wooden fences, wet from overnight rain, smoking in the early morning sun. She always tells me not to cheapen myself with boys. Her hair is long and grey, loose on her shoulders as a release from the cotton cap she must wear in the bakery. Part of her blue work smock is poking up from the flat-weave basket she carries. Sao wants to bang me from behind and see her coming closer at the same time. He's excited by the urgent risk of it. He can do it all right and be out of the back door as Mum's in the front. I ask him if he loves me, and he says he's giving me the hard evidence, isn't he? Yeah, right, tell me about it.

This is a voice I want to avoid. It has a spurious adolescent candidness that lends itself to titillation. In fact the relationship between mother and daughter has an intellectual footing, and they have four degrees between them, one a doctorate. My own mother is a performance auditor for the State Services Commission and a very attractive woman to men. She has moved up from one marriage and two long-term partnerships, and now lives with a very wealthy and powerful man whose name would surprise you. She has been headhunted both in her private and professional life. Maintaining equality in any relationship is very important, she tells me, and thinks I take my beauty too much for granted. Squandering is perhaps the greatest sin in her lexicon. Make the most of yourself, she says: keep on the up. She could succeed in so many fields. The economics department at Vic have twice offered her a senior lectureship, and for a while she wrote a wry and witty column giving her take on contemporary gender relationships. One was on judging men by their footwear. But she was too shrewd and too accustomed to flattery to think that either academia, or journalism, offered the sort of life she wanted.

The Asmat live on 10,000 square miles of mud and mangroves on the isolated southern coast of Irian Jaya. Their staple food is sago. Headhunting and cannibalism were customary until the 1960s and sporadically reported even today. Hunting and killing a wild boar is dangerous and confers honour on the successful man. A pair of tusks worn around the arm has a status equivalent to a human skull. In the past, Asmat men used to wear large white shells shaped like tusks through their noses. In 1961 Michael Rockefeller disappeared in Asmat territory while collecting art for New York Museum of Primitive Art. It is a mystery never solved and some blame crocodiles. The Asmat produce splendidly bold woodcarving, but have no tradition of pottery. They consider that the souls of those who suffer an untimely death are prevented from entering the spirit world and roam in limbo. The spirits of women who die in childbirth are considered especially dangerous and powerful. Much of what is essential to their communal culture is passed down from mother to daughter, and among women special words are used which are kept from the understanding of men. The wild pig of Irian Jaya is black.

My own mother was a sloven who used the arguments of feminism as an excuse to escape housework and maternal responsibility. My sister Irene, who is something of a superwoman in both marriage and the workplace, recently described our mother as Dirty Flash: unkind, but totally appropriate. She vacuumed only immediately before any periodic entertaining, biennially painted over the fly spots of the kitchen ceiling, would clean nothing that she could put a lid on, or close a door to, including lavatory and oven. She had several colourful and exotically patterned throws from Uzbekistan, and she would drape them over the most disconcerting of the furniture disfigurements and stains before her friends came for bridge. The cosmetic drawer of her en suite was a glittering midden of glassy prisms, small shiny tubes become snails, and multicoloured fluids both contained and spilt. It reminded me of the clay cliff at Rarangi down which a mat of ice plant cascaded. Such a junk plant, but once each year it flowered in close packed vividness that so threw back the bright sun that you couldn't look directly at the colours. Once, as we sat at the base of the clay cliff with the glaring colour safely behind us, my mother told us to remember that a man's first judgement of a woman was always a sexual appraisal. Irene blew out her cheeks and sighed impatiently. She must have been eighteen or so, but I was three years younger and thought Mum was on to something quite interesting and profound. As we drove home from the beach later, we passed Janine Brocklehunt and her mother shouting at each other in the doorway of the Lund Street minimarket. One of them had probably been caught shoplifting again: maybe both. 'Oh, please,' said Irene wearily.

Janine Brocklehunt's latest psychological assessment was included in my June quarter report — client file 775122JABsubadults2004 — but as with past assessments I don't think much weight can be given to it. Janine has been in and out of the system now for seven years and as an intelligent and unscrupulous young woman she has learnt how to manipulate her interviews and assessments. She is again claiming that she can't remember any of the episodes from which the four present charges arise, and that she has been experiencing blackouts and periods of intense depression as a result of the succession of temporary partners her mother has had in the house. In mid-July she abruptly left her job with the Fernbank branch of Sooper Doop Supermarkets after being questioned regarding toiletry and confectionery stock deficiencies, and has since applied for ACC support as a consequence of alleged back strain suffered while she was stacking wire containers of red drumhead cabbages. The claim is in dispute. Certainly, as I have several times documented — 770422JABsub-adults2004; 769322JABsub-adults2003; 765522JABsub-adults2003 — the core issue is Janine's relationship with her mother and the unhealthy and unnatural competition that has developed between them regarding male companionship. Neither, of course, will admit this as the underlying origin of difficulty, but addressing it is, in my opinion, the only way to move forward.

In J.H. Williams's *Elephant Bill*, he records movingly a singular story of maternal devotion in the animal kingdom. One evening when the Upper Taungdwin River of Burma was in heavy spate, Ma Shwe with her three-month-old female calf was trapped in the fast-moving current. 'There was a life and death struggle going on. Her calf was screaming with terror and was afloat like a cork. Ma Shwe was as near to the far bank as she could get, holding her whole body against the raging and increasing torrent, and keeping the calf pressed against her massive body. Every now and then the swirling water would sweep the calf away; then, with terrific strength, she would encircle it with her trunk and pull it upstream to rest against her body again.' (*Elephant Bill* by Lt.-Col. J.H. Williams O.B.E., Rupert Hart-Davis, London, with a foreword by Field-Marshal Sir William Slim G.B.E., K.C.B, D.S.O., M.C., tenth impression, 1954, pages 90–91.) A sudden rise in the water washed the calf away and Ma Shwe plunged downstream after it, caught it, and with one last gigantic effort reared up and placed the calf on a narrow, high ledge before being swept away herself, fighting for her life. Ma Shwe escaped death in the gorge and returned along the bank to watch over her stranded child until the water receded sufficiently for her to go back into the river and rescue the calf. The calf was later christened Ma Yay Yee — Miss Laughing Water.

Your own mother I know was an immense influence on your life. You talked about her increasingly when we travelled together in Crete and Turkey. I recall sitting in a cave chapel in the underground complex near Konya in central Turkey, almost alone because most of the tour had diarrhoea, and you told me about your mother's habit of giving her family the best of everything she could produce, and being last in line herself: having the burnt piece of toast, the snout end of Belgium, the lopsided cupcake without icing, or nothing at all if there wasn't enough to go round. Everything was given in an urgency of love, you said, even her memory was sacrificed in the end and you would sit with her in the secure unit and retell her own personal history, her own generosity and record of love, and she would exclaim, 'No! Did I do that? Did we go there that year? Was Ronnie really that fond of me? How wonderful that you remember so many things: what a happy life I must have had.'

Your memory had become the single life record for you both. You told me, there in the underground chapel in Cappadocia with guide Rashid's voice reverberating some caves away, and the stone shelf cool on my bum, that when you got married your mother told you that with children would come the greatest joys of your life, and so it was. There had been warnings that the cogs were slipping, you said. She used to place things oddly as memory aids — a bottle of maple syrup balanced upside down on the car bonnet to remind her to shop for groceries;

knickers over the bedside lamp because the council was turning the water off between 2 and 4 p.m.; an old charity envelope wedged into the kettle spout the day before you were to visit. The trouble was that increasingly she forgot what such errant things signified, and increasingly her outward space mirrored the strange confusion of her mind. You laughed as you told me of your mother, but your voice was suffused with love and loss, and I remember the pale ochre figures painted rather crudely on the sloping uneven walls of the underground chapel, and the darker patch by the entrance step where many thousands of people over hundreds of years had steadied themselves as they came in.

'I hate you, you dumb-arse cow,' Janine said to her mother. It was enough that her mum had told her to put the cigarettes down her tits, and that the fucking Bollywood man had caught them, without seeing that snoot Irene going past in a car.

'Oh, just shut the fuck up,' said her mother.

'Tampon-sucking bitch,' said Janine, and she walked away, though the Bollywood man shouted and said he knew who she was all right, and the police were on their way. Maybe they would provide the hard evidence.

'They're welcome to her,' called her mother, and, 'Don't you bloody well walk away on me, young missie. Don't you think you can talk to me like bloody that.'

'Blow it out your arse,' said Janine. She had a crap life, didn't she, so why should she care about sucking up to anybody. Look after yourself is the only thing, the rest to bugger.

Fay Weldon remembers with admiration her mother turning cartwheels on the lawn, short skirt whirling. Nelly Ternan was entirely dependent on her strong and enterprising actress mother even before the death of her father on 17 October 1846 in the Bethnal Green Insane Asylum. Jacqueline Kennedy preferred her philandering father to her mother, who had a quick and violent temper. Elinor Canargue looked after her invalid mother for fourteen years and refused more marriage proposals than that, including one from a genuine tycoon. Barbra Streisand's mother,

Diana, was the daughter of a skilled New York garment cutter who was also a cantor at the local synagogue. There were issues between Barbra and her mother. Boadicea warred with Rome itself to avenge the rape of her daughters. Delia Smith inherited her love of food from her Welsh mother, and the fruitcake made famous in Delia's cooking books is her mother's recipe. Yoko Ono said that she had often wished her mother dead so that she could get people's sympathy, and that once when she ran crying to her mother as a child she was kept at arm's length in case the tears marked her mother's mink coat. The legend of Yauk Thwa tells how a daughter saved her mother from the army of Burmese King Bo-Daw-Pa-Ya who annexed the Kabaw valley in 1812.

A corollary of twentieth-century Western feminism has been an upsurge in academic and clinical examination of the relationship between mother and daughter. Both positive and negative attitudes and trends have been identified, with the preponderance of the former, especially in American academic discourse, surprising some in the field.

Recent Penn State research, for example, indicates that despite instances of conflicts and complicated emotions, the tie between mothers and daughters is of such significance that 80 to 90 per cent of women at mid-life say they have a good relationship with their mother. Behavioural specialist Dr Karen Fingerman, assistant professor of human development and family studies, worked closely with forty-eight pairs of elderly mothers and their mid-life daughters and expressed her findings in her book, *Ageing Mothers and Their Adult Daughters: A Study in Mixed Emotions*. Problems and ambivalence between parent and child are inevitable throughout the continuity of the relationship, not just during the terrible twos, or difficult teenage years, because parents and children are always at two different points in the life cycle. But Dr Fingerman says the relationship between mothers and their adult daughters is one in which the participants handle being upset with one another better than any other.

Diana Mosley appreciated her dear mother patiently and sleepily parked on the chaperones' bench at myriad London balls. Linda McCartney's mother, Louise, died in a plane crash in 1962. Linda said she cared for people, was charming and that everybody loved her. Muriel Spark's mother was full of superstitions and presentiments. She wouldn't wear green, had a terror of thunder and lightning, and thought shoes on the table, or crossed cutlery, bad luck. She turned over the money in her purse when she saw the new moon and bowed three times to it. Muriel adopted the same ritual. So one woman's life merges into that of another: so advice is given and valued — or ignored, or repudiated. Haven't we all been astonished by Jung Chang's three daughters of China?

'People like us must have the religion of despair. One must be equal to one's destiny, that is to say impassable like it. By dint of saying "That is so! that is so!" and of gazing down into the black pit at one's feet, one reaches calm.' (Gustave Flaubert to Ernest Feydeau, quoted in Enid Starkie's *Flaubert The Master*, page 303.)

Sharon Asberger, the greatest Jewish-American thinker of the twentieth century, was asked on the *South Bank Show* who was winning in the battle between good and evil. She replied by asking her interviewer if he had ever considered that the battle had been lost absolutely, and what we endure now is just the murderous dispute among rival candidates to be the Prince of Darkness. It was Asberger, too, who said, 'Language is the moving light on the water of our experience.' That hasn't much to do with our subject, perhaps, but it illustrates the power of the woman's mind. Asberger's daughter, Ruth, is reputed to have the seventh-highest IQ ever recorded.

We expelled Hettie Ransumeen finally. Her mother came puffing straight round to see the principal, of course, and I took her into my office and sat behind my desk. The size and formality of the office have value on such occasions, but Mrs Ransumeen was oblivious to her surroundings. She was wearing a floral frock with shoulder straps, completely unsuitable for her size, and black, scuffed slip-ons from which her ankles bulged. Star-bursts of capillaries beneath the pale skin of the inside of her knees were a haze of red, blue and purple, like the faint wings of butterflies imprisoned there. Her straight hair shook with determination, and she held up truculently the letter of expulsion from the school board. 'You needn't think I'm gunna stand for this here,' she said. Not the odds rightly stacked against her, not her inferiority in so many ways, not even the convinced opinion of every one of Hettie's teachers that she was a manipulative, vindictive little shit, caused her mother to waver in the slightest. I tried hard to dislike her, for her daughter's sake, but could not prevent a growing and grudging admiration. Here was a sort of genetic patriotism — my family right or wrong. Here was the instinct that prompted the plover to drag a wing on the ground in a desperate ploy to distract the fox from the nest. Viewed with reason Mrs Ransumeen was all prejudice and selfish ignorance; seen as another mother she was all guts, coming in against the big battalions to defend her own.

What you have told me about your mother, her support and commitment, has got me thinking. My own mother was very ethereal, very remote. She disliked the grossly corporeal nature of everyday life and could barely bring herself to eat because it was part of an organic process. She was a noted watercolourist and had a fine arts diploma. She would weep for a frosted magnolia bloom, but once bludgeoned to death an old cat that sprayed on the rimu frame of her patio door. Stinking animals were everywhere a dire threat, she said. When I left for university she gave me a letter quoting Greer, Asberger and Kant, and in it told me I should expect nothing in life except essential loneliness and spiritual isolation.

Heather's mother was gleeful, strong and good-looking. In the slanted, golden sun of afternoon she liked to have her inside work finished so that she and Heather could sit on the verandah and wait for Andrew to finish farmwork for the day. They could see past the yards to the productive paddocks on the downs. If there was a spring breeze, single petals of pink and white fruit-tree blossom would swirl up, and then do a drifting, confetti dance in descent before them: if it was autumn the thistledown would float as light grey punctuation on the blue parchment sky.

Heather and her mother would hear the barking border collies and the uniform grind of the ute, or the sound of the Yamaha farm bike, which was a rich, bronchial cough. There would be the savoury fragrances of meat, vegetables and apricot pie from the kitchen, and Heather would feel her mother's arm around her give a little squeeze as they waited, and the sense of loving closeness never entirely left her.

My own mother was very different from yours, but she had her reasons. Your own mother was, I suspect, very different also, but had her reasons. Perhaps in a conclusion there is a need to pull back somewhat from the anecdotal, establish some psychic distance, strive for a reflective and authorial tone. So, let me say, there is no usefulness in the old giving advice to the young, for although both are part of the same ocean, like the outgoing and incoming tides they move in different directions.

celeine and the pygmalion theatre

THE PYGMALION THEATRE WAS IN OUR suburb. We lived next door, in fact, and I remember when that double-storeyed, corner brick building was shared by a butcher and a cycle repair shop, both with flats above them. When I was in the sixth form the amateur repertory society ran a successful fund-raising drive to buy the property and convert it into a one hundred and forty-five seat theatre. The mayoress was a keen Thespian, and the other driving force was pet store owner Trevor Halleck, who wrote three-act farces, and had appeared on television in *Mastermind*, with English vaudeville his chosen topic. I imagine it was his idea to use the name Pygmalion: the butchery had excelled in pork products, and on the brick side-wall the large faded lettering remained — Pork Delicacies and Specialities. The front, though, was repainted in mauve, had royal blue canvas awnings erected over the windows and entrance, and a bas relief of Pygmalion's inanimate lady love. The combination was typical of the divisions within the repertory society: the artistic aspirations suggested by the connection with the Greek myth, but also the provincial humour provided by the pig pun. The mayoress and the farcical Halleck were an uneasy alliance within the organisation at the best of times.

You expect plenty of artistic temperament and egotism in a repertory society, and ours had its moments. Yet the Pygmalion Theatre was a success despite the large initial debt incurred, and a good mix of plays was put on each year, from Shakespeare to Roger Hall, and less well-supported drama in between. Risks were taken, local talent was given opportunity. The Alliance Française presented an evening of historical tableaux; the Society of University Women put on Anouilh's *The Orchestra*. Only the pet shop playwright's broad, three-act innuendoes encountered sustained artistic resistance and were never staged.

I had my first acting experience when the combined drama society of the High Schools did a version of *New Peter Pan*. I remember our excitement at performing in the new theatre: the aisles were not then carpeted, and the society hadn't been able to afford full lighting. Initially my motivation was the opportunity to meet girls, but living next door to the theatre, and seeing something of the comings and goings, I was always likely to become involved. I displayed no talent, then or subsequently, but when I left school and began doing morning shifts at the stock-feed mill, I joined the repertory. I helped backstage and front of house, and was sometimes prompt. I had a variety of bit parts, the success of which were never crucial to the overall performance.

In the end of the Pygmalion closest to my own window, the props and costumes were stored. These built up considerably, and after a while the society hit on the idea of making money by hiring them out. On three afternoons a week, between two and five o'clock, the costume room was open, and proved surprisingly popular and remunerative. Not only was it patronised by groups and institutions wanting to outfit their own occasional theatricals, but it was the port of call for those going to costume balls and theme parties. I grew accustomed to the sight of people lugging out hoplite armour and helmets, witches' hats, scarlet coats with epaulettes, green silk knee breeches, halberds, flounced petticoats and bowler hats.

The financial success of the costume hire depended upon the sacrifice of the society's volunteers. That's the way the amateur arts survive within the community. Middle-aged women generally, who were rostered to give up afternoons for the sake of the Pygmalion Theatre. Many of them had no direct connection with the dramatic productions, but showed goodwill because of some neighbour, niece or daughter involved, or from a vague, genteel impulse that the arts should be fostered in the city. From my window I saw them dishing the stuff out, some with a careless liberality, others worriedly checking their simple accounting by means of a school exercise book and metal cash box.

After I had been working for several years, Celeine Dwyer came to the city, and almost immediately was a force within the repertory society to rival the mayoress and the writer of farces. The paper ran a story with a photograph about Celeine's acting career in South Africa and France, about the drama academy she founded in Birmingham, and relinquished only because of the debilitating effects of diabetes. She had trod the boards with Dawn French and Barbara Knox, it was said, and hearsay at the repertory parties gave her something of a career in operetta as well.

Celeine took acting classes in her own home; teenage girls saw these as a through the looking glass entry to unbridled glamour and fame. The first play she produced at the Pygmalion was *Murder in the Cathedral*, and I was a knight. She was a forceful, loose-limbed woman with dark hair, and no trace of the exotic accent I expected from an actor who had spent so much time overseas. She favoured flamboyant interpretations of character, and indulged traditional theatre's love of pomp and circumstance. 'Emote! Emote!' she would cry from the front seats at rehearsal, and, 'Dominate the stage with physical presence'. The text was always secondary for her, and she hated Beckett, Brecht and Pinter as whining intellectuals.

She took no notice of me, until she discovered I lived next door to the theatre and was sometimes able to be called upon for donkey work. More and more it was Celeine who looked after the costume-hire room on the three afternoons a week, and after a while I noticed that she had students come to her there for lessons, rather than to her home. It was an economical use of time, and in the winter I imagine it meant she could save on heating costs for her own place. Often, in the late afternoon, when I'd come home and had a shower to wash off the stock-feed dust, I would watch a while through the slatted Venetians of my upstairs window, and see Celeine giving instruction in the costume room. Sometimes a girl standing and reading a part while Celeine watched and interrupted, then took the text impatiently and played the part herself with much gesticulation and élan. Sometimes Celeine demonstrating how to walk and turn and pause before delivering the lines, and then a girl attempting to capture the movement of such a mature figure, the conscious stillness to gather in the attention of an audience. Sometimes a girl abashed in mid-routine as Celeine switched her attention to a member of the public who wanted a sorcerer's cape with golden stars and crescents, or the two ends of a stage horse.

One Thursday a delivery truck brought back the complete props and costumes for *James and the Giant Peach*, which had been hired by another society, and Celeine rang to ask if I was at home, and could I come to help. My mother shouted the request through the bathroom door, and took my assent back down stairs. When I went to the Pygmalion, Celeine and two of her pupils had already begun on the costumes, and they were being helped by a Mr Loyall, who had dropped by to hire a musketeer's outfit for a friend's party. Mr Loyall and I carried in the heavy items, and then Celeine gave him his fancy dress at no reduction, and let him go. 'You'll help us with the costumes won't you, Todd,' she said, and pressed the flat of her fingers on my arm as if to test how substantial I was.

The schoolgirls giggled as they hung the garments up. One of them had good legs. Celeine said I'd done more than my share, and we sat down by the desk with the hire book and money tin. She began talking about what parts would suit me in forthcoming productions. Close to her, rather than looking down unseen from my window, I realised what a saturated place it was. All those packed clothes of tawdry opulence — sweat-stained blue silks, faded bodices, grimy open-lace cuffs, suede pantaloons — and a drifting musk of powder, perfume and flesh. Celeine herself was wearing a highly patterned dress with puffed sleeves which, even to me, seemed to have come from stock.

'What do you think of my two helpers?' she asked me abruptly. When I said they were okay, she insisted I was more specific. 'Their bodies, Todd. Have they the bodily presence to hold a male audience?' I said that one of them had attractive legs. 'Susan, Susan,' called Celeine, knowing which one I meant, 'come out here,' and when Susan did come from the racks and stand self-consciously before us, Celeine told her to hitch up her skirt and walk up and down. 'We want to see if you've got the legs for the stage,' she said. Susan walked up and down showing her legs, holding her skirt above her knees. She was both embarrassed and determined. She didn't look at us, but kept glancing defiantly at the clothing racks where the other girl was sniggering in deprecating envy.

Susan's legs were sexy, right enough, but what I felt was awkwardness, and anger of a sort. Neither Susan nor I had come naturally to the situation, and were being manipulated by Celeine for some purpose of her own. I said I thought Susan would make an okay actor, and that I had to go. Celeine laughed and said, 'You men. You men burn, but you're never honest, are you.'

When Celeine was producer, as happened often, she always found some place for me — an understudy role, a secondary part, sets — and always with the promise of greater things as my experience grew. And as I lived next door she expected me to stay after shows and rehearsals to help with the numerous tasks before the lights could be put out in the Pygmalion, and the door locked. Often we ended with a cup of coffee in the little make-up room where there was a Zip water heater over a stainless steel sink, and a few orphan mugs. In that time of relaxation, with the reading, rehearsal or performance over, she would talk frankly to me about other people, and sometimes herself. She had married very early, she said, but her husband, who manufactured bedroom furniture, had no understanding of the arts. She had a son who had gone into his father's business, but she hadn't seen either of them for years, and they wouldn't lend her money. She told me she was a devotee of the theatre, and made sacrifices so she could express her talent. On winter nights sometimes she would hitch close to the one-bar heater as she talked, pull the hem of her dress onto her thighs, and massage her pale, firm knees. Celeine had a hard face, but her upper legs, so less often exposed, were womanly and fresh.

She was a bird of passage, she said, and would rest only a while at the Pygmalion before flying high in the Thespian world once more. She was scandalously derisive of our society, from the mayoress down, but kind towards me, in my presence at least. When I told her that sometimes when I worked in the stock-feed mill, I used it in my mind as the setting for a play, and devised incident, dialogue and stage business in my head, she was supportive. She looked me full in the face, and touched her mug to mine. 'Bravo, Todd, the raw material of great art is everywhere,' she said. 'Imaginative power transforms the most ordinary stuff of life. Think of Dickens in the blacking factory and Baudelaire's domestics.'

Celeine was a power in the drama community, but there's some law of physics, isn't there, about every force creating a counterforce. After the initial rush and novelty of her exotic personality and background in theatre, something of a reaction set in: grumblings about favouritism, her overwhelming confidence, and impatience with those she considered of lesser talent and experience. Gossip began that her Birmingham drama academy was merely a department of one of the city's comprehensive schools, and that her sole contact with Dawn French and Barbara Knox had been as make-up artist. Two mothers complained to the mayoress that Celeine got their daughters to do housework during their tuition hours under the guise of role-play. I came to understand that, in the world of theatre, reputation is a precarious crown.

Celeine still had her supporters, and I had ample proof that Trevor Halleck qualified as one of those. He often left the somnolent goldfish, white mice, terrapins, pure-bred kittens, puppies and Mexican axolotls of his main street shop, to visit her in the costume room of the Pygmalion. As his attentions increased so Celeine scheduled less tuition there. From my Venetians I saw fewer teenage girls, and more of Trevor, leaning towards her in animated conversation, or listening with rapt attention. Once, late in a afternoon of easterly drizzle, I saw him jump up and stand behind her, plunge his hands down the front of her Andalusian drawstring blouse and bury his face in her hair. She resisted him just long enough to lock the door, then swept a rack of dresses onto the floor and was laid upon them. Her pale knees each side of Trevor Halleck's thin and quivering buttocks were almost luminous, and the scene had an odd quality of mime, because distance and two glassed windows quite removed the natural, urgent noises. In the heightened pitch of my fascinated voyeurism, I seemed to see the girls of tuition times there still, practising their turns and elocution unconcerned, acting out assumed roles in a dream of adolescence, stepping over the pet shop ankles, and taking deferential note of Celeine's criticism of their performance, while not commenting on her own. They were ghostly sprites conflated with the adult business in which Celeine and Trevor were caught up. It's never soothing as a young man to watch the sexual satisfaction of others, but I was sufficiently impartial to think Trevor and Celeine Dwyer had the best occupation in the world for a dreary afternoon.

I rarely looked down into the costume room after that, especially if I could see that the pet shop proprietor was there. It was a convenient trysting place, I suppose, though interruption was always likely even when Celeine took to snibbing the door. And she needed me less before lock-up time at the Pygmalion, for Trevor was willing to be her helper no matter how long he had to stay. No doubt they had coffee together from the orphan mugs in the untidy make-up room where she had sometimes made fun of him and other committee members. No doubt she told him of the imminent resurrection of her international career, as she had told me. Perhaps she leant her deep bosom forward, massaged her legs and said bravo to Trevor as she had to me; encouraged him in the dreams he had to become a playwright.

A couple of times I went into the Hallecks' shop because I was curious to see how love had affected him, but there was no discernible change. He was still thin and impatient, restlessly checking the oxygenation of the aquariums, and keeping the sliding trays beneath the rabbit cages clear of dung. The second time, his wife was there too, commenting on the litter of corgi pups. She was taller and more relaxed than Trevor. She never came to anything at the Pygmalion, but had her own interest as a top breeder of Siamese and Burmese cats. Behind the counter were a shelf and display board with the sashes, rosettes, cups and plaques she'd won with one pure-bred cat after another, all with unpronounceable Asian names and impressive pedigrees. It was said that Mrs Halleck had the business head, and that she made a small fortune from the sale of her kittens. Evidently there was a better market for exotic cats than for theatrical farces.

It was a farce, though, that brought an end to the love affair between Celeine and Trevor. One of his own, entitled *Bare Bones*

Jones, which was about the antics of an alcoholic Anglican vicar. I had the part of verger Hayhoe, but wasn't responsible for the weakness of the play. It was very bad: a pale reflection of dated British television programmes, but without the support of canned laughter, or an audience which had any interest in the tradition — as agonising as a fourth form concert. How deadening the thought that Trevor had a whole drawer of such things at home; how pitiful that he considered them his life's work.

Celeine, Trevor and their supporters on the repertory committee had managed to ambush the mayoress at the selection meeting for the year's productions, but surely Celeine had never read the piece at the time, rather supporting her lover on emotional grounds. The history of the theatre has many instances of such origins for careers and plays of outstanding merit, but *Bare Bones Jones* wasn't one. When Celeine held the first reading I could see she was appalled by the text, and when we had the first plain-clothes rehearsal the abject triteness of Trevor Halleck's play was painfully evident. She didn't even have the society's best actors who might carry off a failure with some sense of style, for they had shrewdly made their own assessments of the play's merits, and also saw long-term advantage in keeping in with the mayoress.

Celeine made a desperate rewrite of the play before the second rehearsal, and that caused a shouting match between Trevor and her, in front of all of us. Trevor's fury and indignation were an entertainment immeasurably better than anything in *Bare Bones Jones*. 'I will not countenance any change whatsoever,' he cried several times, with the defensive vehemence of a weak man. A strange, formal expression, and I wondered if he had created it for another of his farces and found, suddenly, some use for it in real life. His temper didn't cower Celeine, however: how easily her background enabled her to rise to the dramas of real life. Her hooting sarcasm and dominating physical presence drove Trevor further and further towards the door, and clustered the cast at the other side of the room for mutual support.

'I won't be associated with a piece of theatre in this form — nothing can be done with it. It's hopelessly derivative, stale, and lacks any comprehension of stagecraft.'

'I will not countenance any change,' repeated Trevor. He was wearing thin nylon slacks, and I could see his legs shaking beneath the material. Maybe I was the only spectator of the dispute who realised that they were lovers, and I was surprised to feel pity for his public indignity: the best effort of his creativity trashed by someone with whom he'd been so trusting.

'I blame myself only for not making the decision earlier,' said Celeine emphatically. 'But there's no way this play is fit to stage.' She folded her arms in a gesture of finality and lifted her face to us in conscious profile.

'Give me back my copies, then,' said Trevor, finding that his only affirmative action. He came to us one by one and took possession of the photocopied sheets, and none of us resisted, or spoke anything of comfort to him, and he went out hurriedly at last in solitary bitterness. Celeine thanked us for the time we had given up, and said she would be casting a new play within a week.

'Would you help me lock up, Todd?' she asked, as the others left, puffed with the news of real-life drama to tell their family and friends. Trevor had gone, shaking and distraught, but Celeine seemed quite over the violent emotion of the quarrel, almost as if it had been a professional scene and she was moving to the next. 'We'll have a cup of coffee once you've checked the place,' she said. 'Make sure the heater's off by the prompt chair.' She was wearing a heavy brocade dress, still with a soiled splendour, which I thought I recognised from *A Midsummer Night's Dream*. At first I had shared the derision of some other society members that Celeine wore stuff from the costume room, but then, in a way, I had come to admire her for it. How fully her life was integrated with her craft, and to her the costumes were perfectly a part of everyday existence. Even the layered feminine smells and mixed perfumes the dresses retained, suggested the chameleon roles available to her.

We sat on the two painted stools in the make-up room and had our coffee. Celeine glanced at herself in the mirror as she talked, flexing her face quite unself-consciously to check the play of light over wrinkles and tendons. 'Do you think I was too hard on Trevor?' she asked me, putting a light choke grip on her neck to firm the jaw line in the mirror.

'I don't think *Bare Bones Jones* is funny.'

'It's a stinker,' she said, 'and I had to kill it as abruptly as I did for everybody's sake. I should have looked at it more carefully beforehand, but I was too busy.'

'Maybe he'll get over it,' I said. I meant, of course, more than just his authorial disappointment.

'Once you let your standards slip you've had it,' she said. 'Once you make the first excuse for mediocrity, or compromise, everything unwinds. Even here at the Pygmalion, the line must be held.' She turned her eyes from the mirror to me. 'Standards of excellence must be maintained,' she said. 'Trevor will come to see the truth of that. I'd love to do Shaffer's *Equus*: my God, there's a play. I'd love to introduce something by Mario Fratti, Brigid Brophy, or Maplin, but our audience here is so uneducated, Todd.' Celeine wasn't daunted, however. She became animated in telling me about a modern-dress version of *Richard III*: how she could produce it in her sleep and have it ready for the time that had been allocated for *Bare Bones Jones*.

Later, as I left through the main door of the Pygmalion Theatre, Celeine stood just inside, waiting to turn out the foyer light. I wondered if the incident that night was cause, or consequence: whether Celeine had to fall out of love before she was able to make her appraisal of the text, or if indeed her devotion to her art was the real thing, and to stand up for her art meant she couldn't lie down with Trevor Halleck. I rather think she meant what she said, and felt a certain admiration that she should uphold so proudly the reputation of theatre, when the profession had granted her so little in return.

Trevor Halleck resigned from the repertory, and I never saw him at the Pygmalion again, as player, or member of the audience, and not as lover for Celeine amidst the colourful yet tawdry treasures of the costume room. No more in the rictus of passion would the gleaming helmet of Achilles pulse before him, no more the cottons, silks and satins rustle beneath his lady's considerable hull. He retreated to the pet shop and the sustainable rewards of animal pedigree, and gave frogs rather than kisses, rolled up his sleeves to clean the aquariums rather than plunging his hands into Celeine Dwyer's bosom, or slapping her white thighs. Maybe he still wrote his unbearable farces in private to vent his creative urges; maybe the humiliation of his one attempted production expunged his obsession entirely.

In the costume room the student girls returned to take their tuition with Celeine, and I felt able to watch again sometimes from my room: Susan with the shapely legs, and all the others, preparing for their wonderful careers upon a broader stage. And Celeine seemed just as peremptory and inspired as ever, conjuring the great world of theatre which is part sweat and muscle, and part the lustre of fond imagination. She held onto both for dear life. And as the instruction went on, in these later times it was slender Trevor who was the phantom, sitting as a shade to listen to Celeine's opinions, or a miasmic holograph attempting to take her in his arms, even as she gestured to the students in elucidation, and they walked through his ghost, quite uncaring of the past.

hodge

I LEFT UNIVERSITY WITH A GOOD degree, but at a time of mild economic recession. I found a job as vegetable packer at Foley's market, and a south-facing room in a back street boarding house in Sydenham. This might seem an introduction to a period of angst and sordid experience, but two things prevented such an outcome. The first was the spontaneous optimism of youth itself, the second was a fellow boarder called Hodge.

Hodge must have been middle-aged, but seemed old to me. He had the room at the end of the hall, and was a run-of-the-mill failure, exceptional only in his infallible bad luck. Hodge was a sort of lightning rod that deflected misfortune from the rest of us. Who knows what it is that makes a man lucky, or the reverse, or why such illogicality exists in a world of just deserts. Maybe it is a proof of karma, and we experience reward for past lives, or must live out expiation. Hodge was a tall man, though incomplete. He had lost his hair naturally, his right big toe in a wood-chopping accident at the Te Awamutu A & P show, and an ear was bitten off some years later by an alpaca that had been eating fermented plums in a paddock next to the Rai Valley store where Hodge stopped to ask directions to some second cousins on his mother's side. His hearing suffered a good deal, and his head tilted towards his remaining ear as if his equilibrium was affected by the loss.

Hodge was surprisingly popular with all of us at the boarding house, for the same reason perhaps that average-looking girls often have a plain friend. No matter how badly things went with us, Hodge was always a consoling comparison. I remember a spring day smoking tinnies among the marram dunes at New Brighton when he was shat on twice by seagulls: now what must be the chances of that, I ask you.

Hodge received only one letter that I know of, a jury summons, and he was delighted at the prospect of being paid to sit in a warm place for several days with free meals, and just send someone to jail. At the selection session, however, not only was Hodge eliminated by challenge of counsel, but a woman present recognised him as the person who came to her neighbourhood the afternoon before the official Salvation Army donation day and collected many of the envelopes.

Even Mrs Thrall, the landlady, took satisfaction in pointing him out as an example of how the male sex ended up. 'There's your own future for you,' she'd say triumphantly to me, or Helmut, or Dylan. 'God won't be mocked, you know.'

Sometimes on a sunny afternoon, when I wasn't at Foley's, Hodge and I would take pillows on to the fire-escape and have a beer and a yarn there. Once his false teeth fell and smashed on the concrete step; another time his heel got wedged between the bars, and Mrs Thrall had to use cooking oil and a mallet to free it. But we had some good hours in the sun. Hodge realised he was sport for the gods, but said that he wasn't as unlucky as most of his family. He told me that his father went right through the war as an infantryman with only shrapnel wounds, shingles and lower rib damage from an encounter with an Italian woman in Tagliacozzo, but then when the returning troopship was in sight of Wellington Harbour, he choked to death on a small bat (*Batis glottum batis*), which escaped from its container and flew into his mouth when he was about to have a beer.

Hodge said his elder brother had seemed the lucky one of the family: a handsome man of prodigious sexual prowess who finally married a stylish Bulgarian woman with substantial investments in natural gas, truffles and Egyptian third dynasty funerary curios. Unfortunately there was a freakish and random accident in which the Bulgarian wife happened to lose control of her Audi, and smash through the side of a suburban house to reveal her husband in bed with a Samoan meter maid. The wife ditched him without a cent, and two of the meter maid's uncles hunted him down to a DOC mangrove swamp reserve in the Hokianga, and castrated him with a boning knife.

Hodge's other brother went to Australia looking for a more propitious citizenship, but after twenty-seven years of unavailing struggle against drought on his outback property he had to sell it for peanuts, and when leaving the station for the last time was drowned in a flash flood that overturned his Holden ute in the boundary creek. They found him entangled with his faithful kelpie dogs, which had prevented him from opening the door and swimming out. When they buried him on the property, the grave diggers discovered a vein of opal that made the new owners one of the richest families in Australia.

There was one sister in the family. Her name was Prudence, but Hodge said she was always called Guppy. She got all the brains evidently, and was awarded a PhD in computer science by the time she was twenty-two. Unfortunately on the morning of her graduation, while shaving her legs in the bath, she dropped the electric razor in and stopped her heart. The Peeping Tom from next door broke down the door in time to give her the kiss of life, and she was rushed towards the hospital, but the ambulance was hijacked by a stoned whitebaiter from the Coast while slowing at the Colombo Street lights. The whitebaiter — who years later won a category award in the Gore Country Music Festival — left the vehicle outside a cactus and succulent nursery on the outskirts of the city, and Guppy was recovered no worse than before and taken to hospital. She made a complete recovery from electrocution except for a forked scar on her hip, but the Peeping Tom carried a mutated lowland gorilla virus picked up when he was helping tribespeople in Zaïre with livestock breeding advice, and he passed it on to Guppy while saving her life. She lost the motor sensory control of all her limbs and spends her time bedridden, constructing highly successful virtual reality games by blowing into a tube connected to computers. 'She's worth buckets of dough, lucky Guppy,' said Hodge, 'but she doesn't want to have anything to do with me because I'd never give her the top bunk in our bedroom when we were kids.'

Mrs Thrall had a cancer scare the last year I boarded there. She never let on to us just what part of her was under threat, but when the day came for the final outcome of the tests to be announced, she wanted me to persuade Hodge to go with her as a talisman. She promised that she'd cook a big dish of toad-in-the-hole for the night meal if we'd agree. I remember the three of us driving into the city on a summer afternoon. As we left the parking lot, Hodge was nearly run over by a pimpled hoon in a rusted-out Falcon coming at him on his alpaca side, and so it was almost inaudible. Hodge stumbled back to safety, but did receive a nasty ankle gash from a skateboarder careering past at the time.

The specialist had the best of news for Mrs Thrall, and as far as I know she's still running that two-storeyed boarding house, happily bitching about the male race and fining guys for taking the house pillows out onto the fire-escape, or leaving syringes in the hydrangeas. It was Hodge, of course, who found it a bad day. When reading an old newspaper in the waiting room he discovered that his ninety-three-year-old mum, the last of his relatives, had been par-boiled and sucked under terra firma by a geyser in Rotorua that opened up without warning beneath an inaugural group waiting for the unveiling of a kinetic sculpture in brass, ceramic and poly resin, to represent the benevolence of the universal life force.

Hodge told me that after this news he was particularly looking forward to his evening toad-in-the-hole as some sort of counterbalance for the vicissitudes of the day, but it wasn't to be. As we passed the last tall building before the carpark, an eighteen-stone woman cast herself from the window of the Weight No Longer Clinic. She had failed to meet her monthly loss target, but she was spot on as far as Hodge was concerned. The autopsy showed eighty-nine per cent of his bones shattered, but the eighteen-stone woman had a miraculous escape, became a born-again Christian trauma consultant, and is now a much-loved panellist on early evening television. Sometimes in my dreams I have this one freeze-frame with Hodge giving a rare smile as he anticipates his toad dinner, and just above his head this vast, pink mass descending.

I miss Hodge, most of all because now he's gone there is nothing to deflect malicious fortune from the rest of us.

watch of gryphons

His apartment was on the Corso Cavour, on the south-east side of the old city. He was quite close to the archaeological museum and the garden of the San Pietro church, from which pale Assisi could be seen on the flank of hills across the broad valley. The view from the upstairs apartment, though, was of the street, and the noises were of the street and kept him awake at night until he became accustomed to them.

Dr Luca Matteotti had met him at the station and taken him to the offices of the department responsible for water and power in Perugia. Rather than any personal welcome at the station, Matteotti outlined the hierarchy within the reservoir project organisation and stressed his own overall supervision and responsibility. The director's manner was distant, but on that first day Paul thought it just the effect of formal English as a second language.

Both the station and the offices were in the new part of the city, and nondescript in a way that made them interchangeable with the station and offices of a hundred other cities. But after the coffee and fruit, the introductions to strangers who would become familiar enough, the director drove him up the hill to the old city with its great walls and serenity. 'The gryphon is the symbol of Perugia,' he said, as they passed through one of the gates with that strange hybrid carved above it. Paul was to see stone gryphons many times again. They were on the main buildings of the square, but also reduced and more roughly carved, sometimes mutilated, above low doors in narrow streets and on some of the oldest tombs. They carried, despite absurdity, vestiges of ancient and superstitious power.

'This was an Etruscan city,' said Matteotti, and Paul didn't reply because he knew nothing of the Etruscans except that they were superseded by the Romans. 'There is a great well beneath the city that is nearly two and half thousand years old. Hydrologists are not new in Perugia, Mr Saville.' The director was smiling, but obviously enjoyed the put-down.

'That's interesting,' Paul said.

It was several days before he first saw the woman from apartment four. As he came up the stairs he heard the loud noise of one of the double-turn locks on the apartment doors, and she passed him with a slight smile as a reply to his greeting at the bend in the stairs. Light brown hair she had and a pale skin. '*Buongiorno*,' he'd said, and she had smiled and glanced at him without much interest. She'd be nearly forty, he thought, and that was all that occurred to him. Three mornings later he saw her in the bread shop when he was earlier than usual for his breakfast panini. She was supple in movement and spoke quietly to the shopkeeper. '*Buongiorno*,' Paul said, and she gave him the same impersonal glance, as if she had never seen him before.

She lived in the apartment one down from him, and always, when he saw, or heard, she went in and out alone. Perhaps because there were boisterous families in the other sets of rooms on that floor, and he and the woman lived alone, he wondered about her sometimes.

In the early weeks, though, he was preoccupied with work. Luca Matteotti proved to be an unpleasant and difficult man who saw no reason for Paul and Jeremy to be on the project team for the new reservoir, and accepted them as consultants only because the joint venture British company insisted. Within the first few days he had queried the need for a full series of bore samples to determine if material to be excavated from the site could be used as fill in the earth dam. 'What else would we do with it,' he exclaimed. He had the habit of looking out of the window of his office as he talked, as if Paul's face was repugnant to him, and he accepted outside calls during their discussions, and kept Paul waiting while he did so.

'He hates us both,' said Jeremy.

'Yes, but you he hates just because you're English. Me, he hates personally.'

'He hates us both because we know our job and we're here,' said Jeremy. Yet Paul knew Matteotti disliked him not just on the grounds of profession, or nationality, but because their personalities repelled each other. Nothing would alter that; nothing would mitigate it. There was some incompatibility which crackled like electricity between them whenever they were together, and which sometimes surprised the two themselves with its nakedness. Some atavistic emotions were at stake which careful formality could not completely cover. Paul disliked the habitual hauteur of the director's expression, his considered and false laugh, refined dress sense, assumption of cultural superiority, laziness, and his habit of observing the outside world instead of looking at the person he was addressing. He was something of a prick, Paul decided.

Jeremy he liked a lot, but the Englishman had his family with him and, although they were hospitable, Paul didn't want to push that hospitality too far and he spent most nights working in his apartment, or in the many restaurants of the old city, sometimes with Italian members of the project team. He enjoyed their company, but his lack of Italian made it difficult for him to develop such friendships.

As he spent much time in the apartment, Paul took an interest in people coming and going around him. The Arcottis and Sarzanos were families who seemed similar in their noisy and happy concentration on children, yet they had little to do with each other. They had no time, perhaps, for anyone beyond the breathless confusion of their own lives. The woman from number four was apart from all that, as Paul was himself. She seemed to have only a fleeting engagement with the world, though outside the apartments must have lain a more substantial life. He grew to know her balanced step in the hall when he was in his own room, and to recognise her from a distance outside by her walk, the cut of her hair and its light brown lustre.

In his mind she was alone always, because he'd never seen her with others, and in that unquestioned, almost unacknowledged, male way he saw little distinction between being alone and being available. So he was surprised, disappointed even, when he came past her door one evening and heard the laughter of a man and a woman in her room. The woman's laughter was quick and unrestrained, at variance with the demeanour he'd witnessed in public; the male laugh was relaxed. Though Paul hadn't paused in the hallway, he felt a moment of aural voyeurism and quickened his pace to his own apartment. Once afterwards he heard the two voices, but never in laughter again, and he never saw anyone coming or going there except the woman. Maybe it was just a visitor, a married lover, or a brother from the other side of the city. A woman like that should have more than a brother's company; should have someone close in the long evenings when Paul himself sat on his balcony, which was little more than a window ledge, and looked over the jumble of orange tiled roofs. They were the gutter-shaped tiles, alternately convex, concave, which Paul was told were originally made by women moulding the clay over their thighs. He had his plans and memos, but often instead of working he would observe the street beneath him, the local people cheerfully walking out to the restaurants, the lift of their voices louder and less guarded than the conversation of New Zealanders. Sometimes he would take the short walk to the high garden of San Pietro church and watch pale Assisi gradually fade behind the dusk that filled the valley. The great stone wall of old Perugia bounded the formal garden, and below it the cars and scooters contested the steep road, becoming visible when night fell only as white and yellow firefly lights although the noise remained the same.

By the second month, the feasibility study involved over twenty men at the reservoir site, and Paul worked among them in jeans and an open-necked shirt. Only one or two had any English, but he joked with them using his few words of Italian, mime and laughter. The Italians loved laughter. He wasn't their immediate superior so he relaxed with them. Sometimes, instead of using his cellphone to call for a car, he would ride back to the city with the men in a van. Matteotti was against such blurring of status. He told Paul that he should have a jacket and tie when on site, and that by fraternising with the men he made it more difficult for the overseer.

Matteotti gave him a ticking off about these things during a routine meeting with Jeremy and several other planners. It was such bad management etiquette that Paul went to his office afterwards and complained. 'You could have asked me to come in and raised these things personally,' he said. 'That's the way it should be in the first instance anyway, not an official blast. I don't appreciate being criticised in front of my colleagues, and in any case all that stuff about clothes and status is incidental to what we're trying to achieve here.'

'It is incidental in your opinion, but not in mine,' said Matteotti. 'On-site relationships have a performance outcome sooner or later.' He was looking at Paul, which was surprising in itself.

'I've no argument with that. It's the nature of the relationship we seem to disagree about. '

'And I told you at the meeting what I expected. That's the whole point, so there will be no further misunderstanding,' said the director. He drew papers towards him as a sign he considered the conversation over. Paul thought it likely that he felt satisfaction in such disagreement, that he saw himself as the bulwark against foreign technocrats who would usurp a legitimate Italian endeavour and encourage a vulgar popularism. Paul looked at the smooth, dark head of the director bent over his papers, and was tempted to say something about their antagonism, and how they might deal with that in the time they would work together, but he knew that Matteotti would see such openness as an attack, and went out without saying more.

Paul had half agreed to meet a group in the evening at a family restaurant near the Etruscan gate, but after the row he didn't feel like company. He sat on his ledge with a bottle of Trasimeno wine and took less pleasure than usual in the Italians passing beneath him. Because of his own mood, the happiness and laughter of others seemed vacuous and banal, and he wondered why he'd come to work among people so different from his own.

His isolation was broken by knocking on his door, and he went inside and opened it. The woman from number four was there. '*Mi può aiutare, per favore?*' she said. '*Ho bisogno d'aiuto.*' Paul didn't understand. 'Help,' she said in English, and beckoned with her hand palm uppermost.

'What's wrong?' he asked.

'Help,' she said again, and went down the hall to her own door, pausing there to gesture to him. When he went in he recognised that the floor plan of her apartment was the same as his, but congested with an abnormal mode of living. The first room had sofas and chairs, but also wood and aluminium contraptions that reminded him of a gymnasium, and a bedroom into which the woman quickly led him had a pipe frame over the special bed, with suspended handgrip and dangling straps.

On the floor was the reason his assistance was needed, and the explanation for his never having heard any man entering, or leaving, the apartment: a naked man of two halves in a twisted sheet. His upper body was well developed in a fleshy way, and his lower half pitifully wasted. 'Did he fall out?' asked Paul, surprised into such an obvious remark.

'Maria doesn't have any English,' the man said. His pronunciation was good, his voice calm. Lying naked and deformed before a stranger, he retained a curious dignity and self-respect. 'Maria was giving me a bed bath and we turned suddenly,' he said.

Even with two of them to lift, it was difficult to get him back onto the bed, and when he was there Paul noticed the sweat on his face and surmised that he must have felt some pain in the fall, or in being lifted, despite the paralysis. Paul had regained enough composure to address him directly, rather than Maria, when he spoke next. 'Can I do anything else?'

'I'll be fine now. I'm all right in the bed, or my chair, but if I ever get stranded, as I did now, I'm too heavy for Maria. Pacciale Sarzano would help, but the family is not there tonight.'

They both looked at Maria, and she smiled, hearing her name and seeing them turn to her. For the first time she met Paul's eyes directly.

'My name's Giancarlo,' the man said, and Paul turned and took his outstretched hand while Maria quickly laid the sheet over her partner's hips to cover his cock in its thicket of dark hair.

Giancarlo's clasp was quite strong, and Paul could feel calluses on the underside of the fingers from the handgrip suspended above the bed. The folded sheet emphasised the physical dichotomy: the heavy, white upper body, and the emaciated legs, the shin bones without flesh so that the flat surfaces showed, and the feet permanently curled in and with contorted toes. Maybe Maria shaved his torso, for it was almost hairless, yet on his wasted legs the hair was darkly vigorous as if it benefited from nourishment there which was useful in no other way.

'What is your name?' asked Giancarlo. He had an intelligent, handsome face, though slightly puffy and with unusual creases at the jawline because of his posture. 'We've been meaning to make contact as good neighbours, and now our laziness has found us out, and we've had to ask your help before introducing ourselves.'

Maria brought another chair through from the other room, and Paul accepted Giancarlo's invitation to have red wine. She helped her partner put on a loose top and covered his legs with a yellow blanket. She took away the large plastic bowl that she'd been using for his bed bath. With her foot she pushed the clean bedpan out of sight. Paul expected her to sit down once she felt the room and Giancarlo were ready for a visitor, but after bringing wine and glasses, she left the room.

'What work are you doing here?' asked the Italian. He seemed eager to hear of anything happening outside the apartment, and yet was to prove well informed also. 'I read everything,' he said,' but see very little. It's so difficult for me to go outside.'

Of course it was: an apartment on the second floor, for God's sake, when he was wheelchair-bound. It seemed an absurd situation to Paul, but he was a stranger and didn't like to ask why they weren't somewhere more convenient. Giancarlo knew about the reservoir project from the papers, and encouraged Paul to talk about it. When Paul complimented him on his English, he said he'd taken it as a subject for his degree, and he'd taught economics at the university where English was used a lot. He said he still did assignment marking, and Paul was again puzzled for there seemed no reason why he couldn't continue to give lectures. There were vans with devices to load wheelchairs, and there was Maria to wheel him about campus. And this time Paul did ask. 'It's difficult for us as a couple,' said Giancarlo a little vaguely. 'That outside world's not for us.'

Paul didn't stay long, despite Giancarlo's friendly interest. He'd entered their apartment as a stranger appealed to in emergency, rather than someone whose company had been sought by choice. Giancarlo thanked him, and called out in Italian to Maria, who came from one of the other rooms to take Paul to the door.

'*Grazie*,' she said, and held out a box of the local chocolates, which Paul refused to take. They had been closer when lifting the naked Giancarlo onto the bed, but there at the door they were two, not three. She didn't smile: she seemed to look for something in his face, and Paul found in hers sadness, apprehension even, rather than gratitude, or interest. The box sank with her hand; she held it as if she was holding the neck of a goose. '*Grazie*,' she said again. As she closed the door he saw Giancarlo's wheelchair at the far end of the room, and the equipment that had surprised him. He supposed Giancarlo worked on it to keep upper-body strength. He remembered the one time he had heard them laughing. How wrong he'd been in his interpretation of it.

Four days later there was a note from Giancarlo under his door when he came back in the evening. He was invited for a meal on the next Friday. Although he spent many nights alone, Paul at first thought he wouldn't go. The reaction was more clear-cut than any reasons he could give for it. Maybe it was because he knew Maria had a partner, maybe it was Giancarlo's disability and the packed paraphernalia that bore witness to it, maybe it was just the possibility that the invitation came only because he had been of use to them. But he went. He went because he was personally unhappy at his work and had not much to do with his nights; he went because Giancarlo was intelligent and spoke good English; he went because there was something about Maria that drew him.

They ate in the small room opening to the balcony. Paul hadn't seen it on his first visit. It was familiar, however, in being structurally exactly the same as the balcony room in his own apartment — and surprising in its décor. In that room there was nothing at all to hint at Giancarlo's condition except the wheelchair he sat in. The floor had light blue tiles, and one wall was crowded with spread book covers. They were not highly pictorial, and all Paul could make out of the titles was that they were scientific.

'It's Maria's job,' said Giancarlo. 'She's a book designer for the university publishers. That's where I met her. It's good because she can work from home most of the time. She uses this table,' and he tapped on the white tablecloth in which fold creases were sharp. He wore a blue shirt not much darker than the tiles, and he gesticulated with his strong, pale hands when he talked. Above the table he was powerful and handsome, and it was easy to forget those useless, clenched, hidden legs.

Giancarlo was a skilful conversationalist. He talked engagingly about himself and his country, but also drew Paul out with genuine warmth and curiosity. Every now and then he'd break off to give Maria a rapid resumé in Italian of what was being said, and she would smile at them both, and make quick comments of which Giancarlo approved. Sometimes she would cheerfully interrupt to offer more food, or wine, then listen again. Late in the evening, when Paul had been enjoying himself by exaggerating Dr Matteotti's faults, and paused to join in laughter with Giancarlo, he realised that he had been talking for a long time and that nothing he had been saying was intelligible to Maria.

'I'm sorry,' he said. 'It's very rude of me to be going on in English all night.'

Giancarlo translated and Maria held up her hands, shrugged.

'She's glad there's someone for me to talk to,' said Giancarlo. 'She grows tired of all my stories over and over.'

'I'm embarrassed that I don't know Italian,' Paul said. 'I should be going to classes, or at least listening to the tapes the company gave me, but all I know are the names of the things I like most in the restaurants, and enough words to buy a ticket.'

'Well, your firm could send you to Turkey next, and you would be back where you started without the local language again. Italy can be breathed, tasted, heard, seen and caressed without an understanding of the language. Maybe, however, I'll teach you just a few special insults to use for your Director Matteotti when next you're in argument.'

The balcony wasn't big enough for Giancarlo's wheelchair, but after the meal Maria and Paul sat close together there, and Giancarlo ran his chair half through the balcony door and was almost with them. While the conversation continued between the two men, and Paul enjoyed it, he was conscious too of Maria's physical presence although she said little. The light from the blue-tiled room behind Giancarlo caught the line of her bare shoulder, lit one cheek and made the red wine in her drooping glass glow softly. People were coming past on their way home from the restaurants. As always, they didn't think to look up, and so were unaware of being overlooked and overheard. They talked loudly and candidly. Paul thought of the many nights he had sat on his own balcony in such a way while, unknown to him, Maria would have been on theirs, and Giancarlo as far into the night as his wheelchair would allow.

'People are happy now that they've forgotten work and had good food and wine,' Giancarlo said. 'After the patrons there's a lull and then the restaurant workers come past too: the waiters, cashiers and cooks. They come quietly, singly, because they're tired and it's just been work for them.'

Paul hadn't seen them, and realised that Giancarlo, maybe Maria too, stayed up much later than he did. What did they talk about, he wondered, when even the night workers were going home to bed?

'And I must be on my way, or I'll still be here when they come past tonight,' he said.

Giancarlo wanted him to stay longer, but Paul asked him to thank Maria for more than his '*Grazie, grazie*' could convey, and she went with Paul to see him out. Giancarlo had wheeled back to allow them from the balcony, but he didn't follow from the blue-tiled room with book covers and white tablecloth. 'We want you to come again,' he called. Paul and Maria went through the room with Giancarlo's equipment, and Paul thought of all the drudgery associated with that and the specially adapted bed he had seen on his first visit. How often did she have to leave her own room to tend Giancarlo; wash him, prise those twining legs apart, turn and toilet him, dress the pressure points, help him grapple with the exercise machinery they were passing. As he thanked her at the hall door, she looked down so that he saw the sweep of her smooth hair rather than her expression. What sort of a life for her, but then Giancarlo seemed a man worth devotion.

Giancarlo and Luca Matteotti — what poles they represented in the reaches of the Italian character, and increasingly Paul sought the company of the former as a compensation for the perpetual guerilla warfare of his job. Matteotti instigated an audit of Paul's expenses. He held a party, at his house in the countryside outside the city walls, to which Paul was expressly not invited, and then spent much of the project managers' meeting talking about it. He sent criticism of the consultants to their London office. None of that seriously threatened Paul's position in the firm, especially as Jeremy and even some Italian scientists were supportive, but it diminished the satisfaction the job otherwise gave him. If you reacted to the director's animosity as a victim you were increasingly treated like one. Paul didn't have a victim mentality: he could cope with Matteotti's dislike as long as he was left alone to do his work.

'Threaten to pack it in,' said Jeremy, who'd talked of doing it himself, even though he was less in the firing line. 'That might smarten him up. Consultants are part of the deal and he can't get the work approved without us.'

'Maybe, but I'm thinking that a crude Kiwi response might be more effective. Something that affects his pride and shows him up in front of others. That's what would hurt him most and make him think twice about knocking me all the time.'

'What, a truckload of sheep shit delivered to his door?'

'Not quite that crude,' said Paul.

'You know, I like to watch his face at meetings,' Jeremy said. 'Each expression is so calculated I think he must practise before a mirror. Don't you think?'

'I bet he does, yes.'

He was in Jeremy's office, where they had been assessing computer-generated graphics of water pressure distortion on various natural fills. The view from Jeremy's window was of new Perugia on the flat. It was much the same view as Paul had from his own office, and always if he looked out he thought of the old part on the hill where he had his apartment: the massive gates and walls that had been fortifications in ancient times, the nonsensical alleys, the whisper of the past, and the pigeons resting in the niches of decaying plaster, lizards basking in the morning sun on perpendicular surfaces. The stepped streets which in an afternoon might be crowded with temporary market stalls, and at night cleared again, with just the scents of vegetables, cheeses and cured meats in the warm, lingering air, and leaves and torn ribbon on the cobbles. The orange tiles once moulded on the thighs of women, perhaps, and the beaked stone gryphons both worn and fierce. And often he thought of Maria and Giancarlo, citizens of the old city yet rarely venturing into it, the only Italian people whose real life was gradually opening to him.

He invited them for drinks and they accepted. On that Sunday he set out fruit and three cheeses with the wine, all spread on a white tablecloth not unlike Maria's, which he had sought out in the shops — and in the duplicate balcony room too, although there were no lovely blue tiles, just floorboards, and no design work on the walls, just one speckled print of Venice. The difference between an apartment owned and one of casual, transient occupation.

An hour or so before they were to come, Paul found a note pushed under the door. Giancarlo wrote that they were very sorry, but illness prevented their coming, and he hoped Paul would forgive the late notice. Paul noted the wording, which gave no indication which of them was unwell. He surprised himself with the disappointment he felt. He ate the cheeses by himself over a week of evenings, but it was only the Tuesday when Giancarlo came to his door. Paul hadn't seen him out of his own rooms before. He wore a red top promoting the Perugian soccer team. It was close fitting and accentuated the purposeful development of his upper body; his legs were covered by a pale blanket tucked at his waist. The chair seemed all stainless steel and plastic handles; very modern, but without a motor.

'We're embarrassed about Sunday,' he said. 'It was something we looked forward to, but health is a fragile thing in our home.'

'That's okay. We'll arrange it again sometime soon.'

'Maria and I want you to come to dinner again.'

'It's my turn.'

'It was your turn and we let you down, so now it's our turn again. Maria likes me to have company. The only thing is, we hope you won't mind if she works after the meal while we talk. I don't know why she hasn't picked up more English, but she's selective that way.'

'So am I,' said Paul.

He went at least once a week after that. He got used to postponements, assuming Giancarlo had some complication that made it difficult for him, maybe some procedure that depended on the irregular visits of a nurse. Giancarlo liked being seated in the blue-tiled room with the book covers on the wall and the door to the balcony open to the warm, slow-moving air. After the meal Maria would often clear the table and work there, while Paul sat on the balcony and his friend ran his wheelchair into the opening, or less often both of them would go into the room Paul didn't like, the one with the special equipment, and he would help Giancarlo into a chest rest with his legs in a sling so that pressure points were relieved.

And always they would talk: about their countries and their lives, about food and wine, about their work and the things they would rather do. They would talk about things quite commonplace to one, but strange to the other. In their conversation they became not only friends, but equals. Paul hardly noticed the wheelchair any more, and was accustomed to Giancarlo suspended in the other room to free him from sitting, the stalks of his legs in loose trousers swaying a little. Sometimes he would do arm and shoulder exercises as they spoke, flexing and swaying while discussing the prevalence of cheating at the university, or asking Paul about time spent in New Mexico and Australia. Often, before he left, Paul would help his friend into his bed, because Maria found the task difficult. Giancarlo would grip the stirrup hanging above his bed and heave himself up, the muscles flexing on arm and shoulder, but someone was needed to assist and guide his useless legs.

Giancarlo had come from a poor family in Rimini. Hardship had sapped the love the family members had for each other, and had driven them apart. Although he had won through to a university education by talent and application, the early days had scarred him. 'Most people are comfortable to live with comparative failure,' he said, 'but for people like me there is the spectre of absolute failure, dying alone in a dilapidated rat hole behind the shunting sheds.' Because he came from a fortunate country and along an easy path to a professional career, Paul found such a fear hard to imagine. 'My worst dreams are of poverty,' said Giancarlo, 'not my legs.'

'You don't walk in your dreams?' asked Paul.

'Everybody walks in their dreams, or flies. And I'm this way because of an accident, not from birth.'

'What was the accident?' Paul felt able to ask when he'd become a friend, but Giancarlo was vague.

'I was hit by a car,' he said, 'and have little recollection of it.'

Maria was more difficult to get close to. It wasn't just their inability to talk the same language, or that after the meal she often worked at her book design. Usually she seemed glad to see him, and welcoming in her own way. She would laugh when they laughed, and listen when Paul spoke, with a smile on her face, eagerly take the translation from Giancarlo and quickly make some reply for him to pass on. They were the best times, and Giancarlo was never more relaxed and witty than those evenings when the three of them were on song together.

But occasionally there were evenings in which Maria was different, when Paul observed without her being aware of it the blank sadness of her expression, and sometimes there was unaccountably an absence in her manner which subtlely rebuffed him.

Only once did Paul and Maria go out into the city together. He had developed nagging toothache, and needed to see a dentist. Giancarlo arranged an appointment with their own dentist who spoke no English, and Maria walked with Paul up the steep, cobbled walkway from Corso Cavour to Corso Vannucci and the cathedral of San Lorenzo. It was mid-morning, warm and still. Perugia was not a prime tourist target, and was large enough to absorb those that came without any threat to its identity. Local people maintained their ascendency and their ways without self-conscious display. Paul enjoyed that. He enjoyed, too, walking with Maria in the streets where he was usually alone, and never before with a woman. Despite the ache in his jaw he was conscious of her attractiveness, and the subtle alteration in the way he himself was regarded as a consequence of assumed partnership: such is the Italian way. He allowed himself to imagine that they were going to a café lunch with wine and confidential conversation, rather than he as patient and she as guide, heading to an appointment with the dentist.

The surgery rooms were not far beyond the square, towards the university buildings on the slope, above a chocolate shop in a narrow, uneven street. Atop the entrance were carved crossed keys, an elephant with an improbably long trunk, and a gryphon — all with the detail worn away by the centuries. The waiting room was small, and most of the close-set chairs already occupied.

Paul and Maria sat side by side without being able to carry on a conversation. She read a magazine, and he leant his head back to relax in the heat, conscious of the throbbing of his lower jaw and the flow of Italian from both a mother and son whose knees were close to his own. Any language incomprehensible to him always seemed to be spoken with excessive rapidity.

When it was his turn for treatment, he and Maria went down a long bare hallway and into a surgery, the one window of which looked into a shadowed and confined courtyard packed with dustbins and motor scooters. Above them, household washing hung absolutely without movement. The dentist was a young man who listened as Maria passed on to him, in turn, the description of Paul's toothache which Giancarlo had given her after he had received it from Paul himself. The young dentist and Maria talked a lot as he worked on Paul's tooth, and nothing was asked of Paul except to open his mouth, or rinse. The dentist mimed each of these actions when required, and showed his enjoyment of the little drama by exaggerating the actions, and laughing after each rendition.

On their walk home, Maria took a slightly different route when they were near the square, pointing and saying, '*Il Pozzo Etrusco.*' It was the well Luca Matteotti had talked about on the day of Paul's arrival in Perugia. In Maria's company it had much greater attraction for him. The well was hidden in the depths of a building old in itself, yet much younger than the well. Maria and Paul went carefully down the spiral steps until they stood to look down into the ancient pit. Electric bulbs above them cast enough light to show gleaming moss on the curving and chinked brick sides, and scores of coins that had stuck there freakishly, representative of thousands more tossed by tourists, and lost far below in the unseen water. The air was cool: Paul could feel it on his teeth made more sensitive by the recent treatment. The place was a testimony to continuity, and Paul imagined the Etruscan women hauling up their buckets there hundreds of years before Christ. And he was struck with the notion that Maria, whose family had been in Umbria as long as they could trace, may well be related to those women.

'*Bellissimo*,' he said inadequately, but couldn't understand Maria's reply. They were standing close together on the little platform, and he took her hand as an attempt to thank her for bringing him. Her hand was cool and passive, but she smiled at him, realising he liked the place. There was nothing flirtatious in her smile or manner, yet Paul had to resist a wish to put his arms around her shoulders. More than at any time before, he wished he had some command of her language. He felt then no physical encounter was possible without some expression of its origins in talk between them. The moment passed without awkwardness, and Maria and Paul climbed back to the modern level of the city, out into the warm sun, and returned to the apartments.

He continued to feel attracted to Maria, but because of the language thing, her sometimes diffident manner and his deepening friendship with Giancarlo, he only once gave any unequivocal physical signal. And even that was on an impulse more of emotional concern. It happened during one of his many evenings in their apartment. He had left Giancarlo to get more wine, and passing through the short passage to the blue room found Maria's bedroom open to him for the first time. It was a strict little room barely lit by the hall light from behind him, and Maria wasn't there. The white cover on the single bed was tight and bare. As he paused and glanced in, he heard Giancarlo still talking from the equipment room, and he turned his head into the light of the hall and made a flippant reply, but he found the sight of that narrow bed, and the thought of Maria nightly there without a husband, powerfully erotic.

Maria was at the table with no work spread out before her.

Her back was towards him and he saw the sheen on her brown hair. She had been withdrawn during the meal, and almost without thinking he put his hand on her shoulder and let it slide a little. 'Are you okay?' he said, yet knowing she wouldn't understand. She gave no reaction to his touch, and then she turned and looked at him briefly with an utter lack of interest; not as any sort of message, but as if he were a stranger a long way off.

Giancarlo was still talking, raising his voice a little to carry down the hall into the balcony room. Paul took away his hand. He went back to the other room, and closed the door of Maria's bedroom as he passed.

'I said you should ask for a car to be assigned to you, so you can drive to places in the weekends. I could make a list of places you would enjoy,' Giancarlo was saying.

'Is Maria all right?' Paul said. 'She's just sitting there at the table without doing anything.'

'She gets over-tired sometimes and emotionally not good. Is she crying? If you help me back into the chair, I'll go through to her.'

'Then I'll push off,' said Paul.

'Push off?'

'I'll go, and let you see to Maria,' Paul said. He wondered if it was his fault, if loneliness in Perugia was making him a nuisance to these neighbours, and he wished he hadn't seen into Maria's room; regretted touching her as he had.

Matteotti became attracted by the idea of an economic overview of the project, convinced that politicians and business people weren't able to understand the mass of statistical and scientific information that Paul, Jeremy and the others produced, and therefore there was a place for a more general document in plain language. 'A project manifesto is what we need,' he told them. 'Something soundly reasoned, but not technical, and with artist's impressions showing what the reservoir would look like when completed. People like a picture.' He had a sample at the first meeting on the manifesto, and he brought it up on his PowerPoint screen — the storage lake sparkling, but inaccurately drawn, and attractive parkland developed on the valley sides. Matteotti was enthusiastic, perhaps partly because it was an enterprise in which he would be largely free of the narrow technical dominance exercised by the practical engineers. He sat by the screen and pointed out obvious things to the others. How well he chooses and wears a suit, Paul thought with grudging admiration, and the director's dark shoes shone like obsidian. He was a man of surfaces, and even his considerable intelligence was so often devoted to image and appearance of one sort or another.

The booklet was a surprisingly big-budget item, and the contract for it went to a firm in which the director's brother-in-law was a partner, though nothing was said of that. When it was completed, the project managers were given preliminary copies. Paul regarded it as a glossy public relations product and only glanced through it, but Giancarlo noticed it on the table when he and Maria came for drinks. 'Oh, take it away if you like,' said Paul. 'The economic guff in it should make good reading for you.' Giancarlo did take it away and read it with interest, criticising the economic sections with growing delight at their inadequacy. He chronicled the most glaring inconsistencies and falsehoods, and found on the internet original data that had been quite wrongly used in the manifesto.

He knew of the firm to which Matteotti's brother-in-law belonged, he said, and their research and findings were not respected at the university. It was an opportunity to ambush the director in a way to which he might find official retaliation difficult. Giancarlo schooled Paul carefully in each area of weakness in the report and provided him with sources and reasoning. He made a game of the preparation: pretending to be Matteotti, or the representative of the brother-in-law's firm, and making Paul respond to their counter-arguments. In the week before the presentation of the manifesto, Giancarlo had the flu, but his mischievous enthusiasm continued, and Paul sat by his bed for several evenings while his friend went over it all again, twisting his hand in the overhead grip as he damned the most telling examples of confusion of actual with projected figures, or glib assumptions not economically sound. He passed on, also, criticisms of the booklet's design, which were Maria's contribution to the analysis.

How Giancarlo would have enjoyed that meeting. The director's pride in his initiative encouraged him to invite several journalists and councillors to the function, foreseeing no criticism. He grandly introduced the manifesto and praised its colour illustrations and bullet-point summaries. He was unprepared for Paul's deceptively casual but informed criticism. At first he tried to bluff his way out, but when he realised the accuracy of Paul's points, and that he was insufficiently prepared to cope with them, he turned the questions to the representative of the public relations firm and said little. It all had a calm professionalism about it, and the PR rep thanked Paul for his comments, saying they would be helpful in the revision of what all of them realised was still a draft document. Yet Luca Matteotti's face had a rigidity of anger and affront, which Paul allowed himself to savour as some recompense for the many times the man had given him a hard time. For the remaining weeks they had together on the project, the director continued his animosity, but considerably tempered by his realisation that Paul was capable of striking back. He had no inkling of what part Giancarlo had played in it all.

Paul wanted to thank his friend for that help, and remembered his idle comment about a car for weekends: he would offer to take Maria and Giancarlo away for a day. The outside world's not for us, Giancarlo had said at their first meeting, but Paul thought they were cooped up in the upstairs apartment too much. Perhaps that was a reason for Maria's mood swings.

Paul went to their door and proposed the trip. 'I'm going to take you both up to the reservoir site, and you can see where the lake will be,' he said. 'All the times I've been going on about my work and the place, and you've no idea of it. We'll take lunch and find a spot somewhere with a good view.'

'I don't know about the chair. The stairs, then getting it in the car,' said Giancarlo, then quickly spoke to Maria in Italian.

'I'll get one of the vans,' said Paul. He didn't care if the trip provided an opportunity for Matteotti to criticise him.

'These stairs aren't easy,' said Giancarlo.

'You'd like to see the site, though?'

'I would like that.'

'Why are you living on the second floor with a wheelchair anyway?' Paul knew him better now.

'We own the apartment. We've been here a long time, since before the accident. And there's no balcony on any of the lower apartments. Maria must have a balcony.' Paul could understand that: how many times she must have finished tending to Giancarlo, even with the best will in the world, and then had time on the balcony to which his wheelchair denied him access. No doubt she and Paul often sat out of sight of each other on separate balconies and watched the roof tiles lose their colour, the locals drift into the street, and the pigeons crouch in nooks in the stone or plaster walls like blue-grey apostrophes.

On the Friday evening before the planned trip to the project site, Paul went to the vehicle yard and signed out a modern van with both a sliding side door and a back hatch, so that Giancarlo's chair would be bound to fit in one way or another. He drove very little while in Italy, because he had a fear that in emergency he might instinctively pull over to the wrong side of the road. Once clear of the city, however, he knew there would be little traffic on the way to the reservoir valley, and he wanted his friends for one day at least to be freed from the apartment and be in the sun, in fresh moving air, and among trees and grasses and gardens, and the hills beyond Assisi. It was something he could do before leaving: a token repayment for the many nights of hospitality in the room of blue tiles, and the talk and comradeship.

The weather was promising that Saturday morning, but when Paul went to Giancarlo's apartment, his friend seemed slightly apprehensive. He opened the door himself, which was in itself unusual. 'We had a bad night. Sometimes I get stomach problems and it means a difficult night for us both,' he said. 'She's resting now.'

'Maybe we should call it off?' said Paul.

'Could we just leave it for another hour and see how she feels? Both of us have been looking forward to it.' Giancarlo hadn't shaved, although it was the time at which they'd agreed to leave. Paul had never before seen him in the morning, or unshaven, and his large, handsome face seemed raffish, but older.

Giancarlo was clean-shaven an hour later, and wore a leather jacket of quality and appeal. Paul wondered for a moment what other things he would discover about his friends merely by moving with them beyond the rooms of his apartment, or theirs. Maria was ready to leave too, although the fatigue of the night showed in the passivity Paul had noticed at other times. She made an effort, however, to match Giancarlo's deliberately upbeat tone, and replied to Paul's greeting. They had a small ritual which mocked their mutual language deficiency. Paul would wish her good morning and ask about her work, in Italian, always with the words by rote, and she would reply equally briefly in English with the same inquiry. Giancarlo had almost given up the struggle to interest them in acquiring each other's language.

Giancarlo had predicted difficulty in getting him down the stairs to street level. Paul found he was right. His friend was heavy, the chair awkward and the stairs steep and cramped. Paul placed himself below, and Maria was behind to control the descent. Giancarlo had his own powerful hands on the wheels, yet Paul at times had almost the full weight of both man and wheelchair, and he was relieved when they reached the lower hallway. 'There, nothing to it,' he said reassuringly, and tried to keep his breathing steady. The next challenge was to get Giancarlo from the chair to a seat in the van. They chose the front passenger seat for him: although access was more difficult, the seat gave him more support and he could see ahead clearly. As Paul closed the door and stepped back, he thought how handsome Giancarlo was framed in the van window. His longish, black hair was combed straight back in the Italian way, the leather jacket emphasised the bulk of his powerful shoulders, and his face had a calm intelligence. No one would know that he was physically half a man, that he was so dependent on Maria.

They drove through the narrow streets, past the civic buildings with their guardian gryphons — those winged lions with fierce heads of eagles. Paul remarked on them again, and Giancarlo said they were one of the most ancient of all the monsters of antiquity, even appearing on the frescos of Knossos. 'A combination of the greatest power and pride in nature,' he said, 'but even the gryphons couldn't save Perugia from the Romans in the end.' Giancarlo, the underprivileged boy from Rimini, had developed a great sympathy for his adopted city. He said again proudly that Maria came of an old family in Perugia with so long a history that she might well have Etruscan blood.

He loved the fertile countryside of Umbria too, pointing out the various crops to Paul, the maize, beans, tomatoes, gourds and vines, and tilting his head often to say something to Maria, who said little in reply. There were the old rural homes, a few quite grand, most functional and undecorated, with no gardens. There were new homes too, testimony to the growing prosperity of Euro-currency Italy. The new homes were not farmhouses, nor were they gracious mansions. They drew attention to themselves with a spurious exaggeration of the traditional architecture. 'No doubt your favourite, Dr Matteotti, lives in one of those,' said Giancarlo. He had accepted Paul's enemy without question as his own, as friends do. Paul knew, though, that Matteotti, with all his faults, had a genuine sense of his own culture.

As they drew out of the broad valley and into the hills, there were more vineyards and then olives. The olive groves were grey-green, in some lights almost pewter, and the catching nets were spread beneath many of the trees. Some of the ancient stone walls of the terraces had broken down. In small gullies that had no evidence of water flow, grasses and lavenders grew. In one, resting pigs were roughly fenced.

A bluff overlooked the narrow valley in which the reservoir was to be built. Paul had been there often with members of his team, with visiting politicians, or dignitaries, to point out what was proposed for the scheme. From a coarsely grassed parking place a track of fifty or so metres, which Giancarlo's chair should cope with, led upwards. Paul and Maria pushed him, and he kept talking about the fragrances in the country air which had become strange to him because he spent all his time in the apartment. From the lookout Paul could show them where the earth dam would be built, where the lake level would rise to along the hillsides, and where there was an especially porous stratum that was a worry to him.

'What gets flooded?' asked Giancarlo.

'Mainly farmland that has already been bought and the houses removed, but at the top end of the valley are olives that will be cut down after this last harvest, and other full-grown trees around what used to be a small monastery. That was the big argument, really. It's the only building of any historical importance. In the end, though, it was realised that if the lake level were to be kept below the monastery then the whole project wasn't worthwhile.'

They made an odd group there on the bluff. Paul keen to have his friends understand the work he did; Giancarlo responsive not just to the explanation, but to the rare experience of being on a hill in the open air; Maria standing back a pace or two and working with her fingers at the fabric of a small bag she carried, rather than interacting with the other two. Giancarlo relayed to her much of what Paul said, and she nodded almost as a child nods in expected obedience to adults. Paul asked him if she was feeling unwell, and Giancarlo said it was just tiredness and not having the language to join in their conversation. Normally Maria moved gracefully and held herself well, but she stood there a little hunched and downcast, seeming reduced, almost cowed by the reaching country, the drop to the valley floor and the exposed expanse of the sky, hazy at its extremes. When Paul tried his talisman Italian in an attempt at contact, she replied with her rote English and a forced smile.

The two of them guided the wheelchair back down the dirt track. Paul opened the hatch and set out their picnic there on the carpeted floor of the van — bread with salami and tomatoes, cheeses and olives, individual fruit tarts of different flavours, wine in plastic tumblers. The stainless steel surfaces of Giancarlo's chair flashed in the sun, high in the blue sky lengthened the vapour plumes of invisible planes. The moderate wind brought summer scents and summer insects, but no noise from the small valley where the farms had all been sold. The two men began to talk of Matteotti, with Paul telling of the latest test of wills, and Giancarlo offering the most preposterous solutions to the feud.

Neither of them noticed that Maria had left the picnic and wandered away, until Giancarlo suddenly stopped laughing, and looked urgently around for her. She wasn't at the van, and they saw her at the lookout, close to the wooden rail that guarded the edge. She was in an odd pose — almost, Paul thought, like some *Titanic* movie burlesque, and he started to laugh. But Giancarlo gave a gasp as if struck heavily, and lifted his body from the wheelchair by his arms, in sudden, futile urgency. He then fell back. 'Quickly, quickly,' he implored, and without a word Paul took off up the track.

Maria had climbed beyond the rail when Paul reached the lookout. He stopped running, and moved tentatively towards her. 'Hey, Maria, it's me,' he said. 'Don't go any further out there.' Surely the urgency of the situation would enable her to understand English just this once.

She stood on the lip of the bluff, and as Paul stepped over the rail and edged towards her, he was aware that there was an odd wind coming straight up the cliff which held the long grass of the edge in a fluttering free fall. Maria seemed to lean into it, to be held up on its steady insistent breath. 'No, no, Maria,' he said, and he took her left upper arm in his hand and steadied them both on the fluttering edge in the whine of upward wind. He could see her face, and it was the face she had shown him on the night he had passed her open bedroom. It was a face of absence and desolation, of some deep separation from the world. 'Hey, careful now,' he said. As she leant forward, he leant back, neither of them in any struggle, but rather a momentary ballet. Paul's greater weight and strength began to tell and he drew her back from the edge until he could feel the rail behind them. Maria gave a little sigh, and said something in Italian in a low voice. She allowed herself to be drawn back onto the path, and to walk down to the van, with Paul holding her arm as if nothing had occurred.

Giancarlo hugged her waist and talked in Italian soothingly, but she said little. 'We shouldn't have come,' he said. 'I knew she wasn't well and we shouldn't have come.'

'What is it that she suffers from?' asked Paul. He had for the first time some understanding of the true relationship and dependence the two of them had — the complexity of it, the fragility and the fearful possibility. His friend looked up at him from the wheelchair, his face close to Maria's side. He was about to speak when his large eyes brimmed with tears, and he looked wordlessly at Paul for a few seconds and then said, 'I can't talk about it. I cannot manage to talk about it now.'

What had begun that morning, at least on the part of the two men, with pleasurable anticipation, ended as a grim ride back to Perugia, though the sun still shone. Giancarlo was strapped in the back so he could hold Maria, who leant on him with a sort of dull fatigue, and said nothing of what had happened at the lookout. Had life become for her a grey monotony, or worse, and a descent against the wind of no more significance than the trailing threads she picked at on her bag?

She was little help back at the apartments in getting Giancarlo up the stairs and, try as he might, Paul was unable to do it safely himself. He went to door of the Arcottis, and because Signor Arcotti was away, his wife and a woman visitor from Rome came somewhat apprehensively to help. With that assistance the three finally made the upstairs hall — powerful Giancarlo distraught by his concern for his partner and unable to take command, Paul without the language and afraid worse things might yet happen, Maria listless and sad, seeming always half turned away.

They went through to the blue-tiled room, dim because the shutter doors to the balcony were closed, and Maria sat by the table spread with her work, while Giancarlo first gave her two white pills with water, then made coffee.

'I shouldn't have suggested the trip,' said Paul. 'I didn't realise it might be too much for her.'

'No, no. It's a cyclic thing,' said Giancarlo, 'but irregular, and I should have seen the signs, but it seemed a chance for once to be back in the world.' He expertly manoeuvred the chair to put himself as close to her as possible, and put his strong, large hand quite over both of hers on the table. 'She'll be all right. It's part of our life together,' he said simply. He spoke to her in their language, but she made no reply, just put a weary shoulder against his.

'Is there anything I can do?' asked Paul.

'Yes, what we'd like is for you not to be afraid of what happened; not to be afraid of any of this; to come and see us again just as before.'

They sat in an easing silence for a time while Paul and Giancarlo drank coffee, while Maria had her head half bowed and rested on her partner, and the afternoon light bloomed softly through the full-length shutter doors of the balcony. As Paul rose to leave, Giancarlo lifted his hand with one of Maria's within it and touched his friend's arm briefly. 'I'm glad I saw the site before it was flooded for the reservoir,' he said. 'Something will be gained and something gone forever, perhaps.'

'I hope Maria feels okay soon.'

Giancarlo spoke to her, and she made the effort to glance up at Paul and spoke in reply. Giancarlo nodded vigorously and clasped her around the shoulder. 'She said not to blame yourself. She will feel better again and again, and worse not so often,' he said.

On the way back to his own apartment, Paul stopped at the Arcottis' door to thank Signora Arcotti. She came out a little warily, but relaxed when she saw he was alone. Her English was adequate to say she was happy to help, but that Giancarlo never went out and perhaps it was better that way. 'She sick,' said Signora Arcotti shaking her head and switching the subject to Maria. 'She run across him in a car, you know that? Yes so. The big, handsome man and she run across him.'

'I didn't know.' Yet somehow it was news of a kind he felt he had been awaiting from one source or another. Signora Arcotti clasped her hands to her breast, gave a shrug and held the pose quite unself-consciously to express her pity, and the powerlessness of us all, then she went back inside to her visitor from Rome.

During the final weeks of his stay, Paul went often to his friends' apartment in the evenings, and there were no more postponements, or misunderstandings on his part of how it was between the couple. When Maria was feeling well, he would stay later, there would be more wine and laughter, and he would often put Giancarlo to bed before leaving. On the bad days he would drop in a paper, talk briefly with Giancarlo over strong coffee while Maria sat lost within herself, and then go.

She was well on the day he left, and kissed him for the first and last time as she and Giancarlo farewelled him at their door. '*Buongiorno Maria, il lavoro, come va?*' he said, playing their game to the last, and she replied with her English. He thought of her on the cliff above the reservoir site, and how she had begun to lean into the rising wind. He wondered what terrible world she had to journey through, and how fortunate Giancarlo and she were to have each other, how connected they had become through affliction. 'I'll miss you both,' he said. 'Let's hope we'll all be happy.'

'Happiness is the absence of pain,' replied Giancarlo, and his strong hand tightened on Paul's.

'*In bocca al lupo*,' said Maria. Paul asked Giancarlo what that meant.

'It's a good luck wish between friends,' he said. 'Being in the mouth of the wolf, and yet unharmed.'

There had been wind and rain in the night. When the taxi paused by the old wall, Paul saw liquidambar leaves stuck to the pavement, their stalks insolently up, small scarlet swans on the dark road. The taxi wound down the hill from the old city, past the gryphons of stone who had witnessed so much pain and so much happiness. Luca Matteotti had first mentioned the gryphons but he was nothing to Paul, who remembered, rather, Giancarlo telling him of those fabulous, threatening creatures that had never existed, yet had been powerful in the human imagination for thousands of years. We all have things we cannot do, and sometimes life makes us do them, his friend had said. Maybe in Maria's Etruscan dreams the gryphons still take protective flight against her demons.